MISSION BEYOND THE ICE CAVE
Atlantis-Mexico-Zotola

**BOOK II of the
GALACTIC SALESMAN TRILOGY**

I0680856

written by
Robert S. Sanders, Jr.

illustrations by
David DuBois

color cover drawing by
David DuBois

proofread and edited by
Paul Wulfsberg

Spanish proofread and edited by
Rudy A. Zapata-Rdz.
and also by
Hilda Gonzalez-Elizondo

illustrations by
David DuBois

color cover drawing by
David DuBois

cover design, typography and text production:
Parris Graphics & Printing
Murfreesboro, TN

Library of Congress Catalog Card Number: **99-94892**

ISBN: 1-928798-00-4

type: young adult, science fiction adventure

Armstrong Valley Publishing Company
P.O. Box 1275
Murfreesboro, TN 37133-1275
Phone: 1-615-895-5445
Fax: 1-615-893-2688

Table of Contents

This novel is dedicated to Chispo, Rinto and Fraxino from Zotola on the planet around the star Al Nitak in the Orion star system. For their existence in their reality, I write this story for them. I wish I knew them in real life.

The Flowering Sun Tree

(Liriodendron chinense, Liriodendron tulipfera)

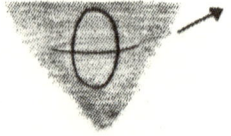

Each flower holds a sunshine in its cup
The yellow sun gives forth
Through its orange flames
To the green of life . . . the **forest**
A sacred story this was
To early modern humans.

They brought with them from Lyra
That piece of heritage, that knowledge
So sacred to their race
When they colonized Earth
1.6 million years ago.

A reminder of their home world
A tree of great size
Of superior characteristics
Fast growing and long lived
Its leaf growth pattern so unique
There is no comparison.

The sacred Flowering Sun Tree
Of Lyran origin it came
For a new beginning
For a new life
To a new world . . . **Earth**.

Introduction and Character Sketch

This novel, MISSION BEYOND THE ICE CAVE: Atlantis-Mexico-Zotola, takes place in the summer of 1985 and is the continuation of MISSION OF THE GALACTIC SALESMAN. The same teenagers have been enjoying their summer travels, and as this sequel opens, they are called to visit Antarctica, the frozen former homeland of what used to be Atlantis. They transport there and by chance meet up with two fellows, Rinto and Fraxino Zapatero, who suddenly arrive in their vehicle-craft from the star Al Nitak in the Orion Belt. They have come to do some research of their Atlantean heritage, and they explore an ice cave together. Venture with them as they discover what the cave walls contain.

Six of the eight characters go home with them to the land of Zotola, home to many of the descendants of Atlantis. They live in a city called Zantaayer, a beautiful, clean city nestled within the Ciruclar Mountains and situated on the northern coast of Zotola. Their society is on the same level of technological advancement as their cousins on Earth. However, the air is crisp and clear because there are no fossil fuels used, since they never had a coal age.

Two more characters go home early in the story, leaving Andrew, Chris, Robert, and Steven to enjoy the fun and adventures with their new friends.

With Rinto and Fraxino Zapatero, they become very good friends. They are wizards to say the least, and they have an uncanny ability to interpret crystals, grow them, and harness their knowledge and intelligence to operate their vehicle-craft (a Zotolan Velosa cruiser craft), their computer system, and ultimely to fulfill a mission in Mexico. Rinto is more into mechanics and personally modified their vehicle-craft so they could use it to teleport to other worlds. Fraxino, with his interest and enthusiasm for rocks and minerals, has his input with creating the on-board main controls crystal.

Chispo Colancha is a lively character, always full of spark and enthusiasm. He is Rinto and Fraxino's nearby neighbor and good friend, and he quickly joins the others in all of their activities. His ability to interpret and perceive messages stored within crystals and holographic materials is well above the norm, nearly as fine tuned as Rinto and Fraxino's abilities. He and Robert Joslin quickly become close friends and are astounded at the synchronicities by which they meet. Chispo also helps Robert discover the mysterious origin of the Liriodendrons, the Tulip Poplars.

With Chispo's suggestion, they travel to an ancient galactic dump site in a desert valley south of Zantaayer, where they uncover a large crate of holographic metal plates evidently brought in by the Atlanteans when they came to their new world 12,500 years ago. Find out what they contain when Rinto, Fraxino, and Chispo later examine them on their crystal base computer system.

Tom, the galactic salesman, comes forth with another mission. He wants to establish telephone communication with Al Nitak, but he discovers an obstacle. Communication with the Orion Belt is blocked. He offers them a hefty reward. Can they, with the help of Rinto, Fraxino, and Chispo, succeed in pinpointing and eliminating the problem to clear the mysterious block?

Venture with them as they travel to the mountains of southern Zotola and meet an ancient endemic race of green humans. Find out what their culture has to offer and how they are linked both to Atlantis and to Mexico.

Follow them as they travel to northern Mexico where they make new friends and have numerous adventures, like analyzing some ancient paintings, discovering more coincidences, experiencing some danger and conficts, and exploring and searching the slopes of Mexico's mountains.

CHAPTER 1

MESSAGE FROM ANTARCTICA

June 28, 1985, 5 PM

"Well, we still have two entire months left," Robert brought up. "Do we want to return to Aleyone or do something else?"

"Let's return to Aleyone," said James.

"Yeah, of course *you* do, James," Chris teased. "I know why *you* want to return."

"Chris, you'll never live that down, will you!" James remarked.

Suddenly, Morris detected a slight ringing in his ears. "Hey, everyone! Quiet!" he called out. "I'm hearing some sort of message."

Everyone became silent.

"It's strange," Morris continued, "but I think it's something to do with that exotic crystal, where it came from. Yes, I'm hearing it! Antarctica! Something about . . ." The message faded.

"Well, what Morris? What is it?" Robert asked.

"Be patient, Robert," he answered. "Give me a chance." He paused a moment. "Here we go. I've got it. I'm hearing it again. Something about the civilization that used to live in Antarctica before it became flooded and frozen."

"Flooded and frozen?!" Paul remarked.

"Quiet, Paul!" Morris directed. "Let me listen. There's more." He paused a few seconds. "That Antarctic civilization flourished until the exotic crystal was stolen, after which everything went downhill. The Earth slid. The seas rose. Everything flooded and then froze. All was lost. It's fading now." Morris heard no more. "That's it, I believe."

"Huh!" Steven declared. "What was that all about?"

"You got me," James admitted.

"Where do you think that message came from?" Paul asked.

"From the exotic crystal, no doubt," Morris answered.

"I say let's go up on the ledge to the crystal and see if we can get the rest of the message," William suggested.

"Good thinking, William," said Robert. "Come on. Let's go right now."

Everyone agreed to it, and all eight of them transported to the ledge way up high on the cliff situated on the eastern face of Mt. Timpanogos in Utah, where they had placed the exotic crystal earlier that day. They materialized at different places along the narrow ledge, and they gathered around the crystal and the Archaeopteris seedlings that they had planted around it.

"Okay, everyone," said Morris. "Let me concentrate, and with some luck, I'll hopefully figure this message out." Morris placed his hands on the crystal, hoping to receive a visual image and more of the strange message. The crystal started glowing with various colors of forest green. Everyone stood quiet and still as they watched Morris.

"I'm getting something. Yes! A visual image. I see a white landscape with mountains in the distance, and it's twilight. It's telling me about the remains, hidden underneath. Something about a few of them that never left . . ." Morris paused. "That's odd! What's it giving me that for?"

"What, Morris?" Robert asked with curiosity.

"It's a number," he answered. "It's saying, '60375 . . .Go meet him.'"

The others looked at Morris with understandable curiosity, except for Robert, who had a look of surprise on his face.

"Morris, what was that number you said?" Robert asked with enthusiasm. "Say it again."

"60375," he repeated.

"That's what I thought I heard you say," said Robert. "Huh! That's just like it was in the dream! I can't believe . . . Morris, I've got something to tell you."

"What is it, Robert?" Morris asked in a calm manner.

"I didn't tell you this, but you know the second night we all camped in the Eucalyptus forest on Vega a week and a half ago?"

"Yes, of course," Morris recalled.

"Well, I had a fairly clear dream that night that I was talking to you on the phone, and we hung up. I decided to call back, and when I went to dial your number, there were a bunch of cut cable ends stacked around the dial of my phone, and instead of dialling your number which is 896-0278, I dialled 896-0375. That number the crystal told you matches the last five digits of the number I dialled in that dream."

"Hmm . . .You're right! It does! Who did you reach?" Morris asked.

"No one," Robert answered. "I got a strange slow busy signal."

"That's weird," Morris remarked.

"Whose number is 896-0375?" William asked.

"I have no idea," said Robert, "and I have no idea why I dialled a different number when I dreamed I called Morris."

"Why didn't you tell me about this sooner?" Morris wanted to know.

"I didn't think it was worth mentioning," Robert replied. "It seemed insignificant in comparison to that dream you had of talking to that Eucalyptus tree the night before."

"Yeah, that's true," Morris agreed. "Fair enough."

"I don't know about you all," said Chris, "but it seems *very* significant now."

"Yeah, I'll say," Paul remarked. "Let's get to the bottom of this."

"But how?" Robert wanted to know. "And what did it mean by, 'Go meet him.'?"

"Well, it must be referring to someone else," said William.

"In Antarctica?" Robert asked. "With a phone number?"

"Don't worry about that right now, Robert," said Paul. "What about the cut cables you said were stacked around the dial when you dialled this other number?"

"Oh, yeah . . ." Robert began.

"Robert, I believe I can answer that," Morris offered. "I didn't tell you all this, but my parents are about to lose phone service. We got a high phone bill last month. Mom's aunt in Kentucky is really sick, and she's been on the phone a lot about that recently."

"Sorry to hear that," said Robert. "You don't think you'll really lose phone service, do you?"

"Probably will," said Morris.

"Do you think you'll get service back again?"

"Oh yes, one day," he answered, "but it will be a few months before we can pay off the bill."

"All right, that answers the reason for the cut cables," Paul pointed out, "but what about that different number? Will that different number be your next phone number, Morris?"

"I don't know. Could be."

"Morris, I know I didn't tell you about that dream before," Robert stated. "What a coincidence that the crystal would tell you the last five digits of a number I dialled in a dream!"

"All I can determine, Robert, is that you were meant to have that dream," said Morris.

"I guess so," he admitted.

"Maybe the *crystal* put that number in your head when you had that *dream*," Chris speculated.

"No, I don't think so," said Robert.

"We'll wait and see what comes of that," said Morris.

"Well, let's go ahead and have the visual image, Morris," William requested, "so we can all go to Antarctica."

Morris looked at everyone and said, "Right, everyone, here it is." He transmitted the cold white scene with mountains in the distance which reflected the sun's low rays at twilight. The others commented on how cold and desolate it looked. With that done, they transported back to the stone hut where they had their backpacks. They had a lot to ponder before deciding what to do next.

They entered the hut and prepared and ate supper. While they were doing so, they discussed more about what the message from the crystal meant.

"Morris, what do you think the message meant by the Earth sliding, seas rising, and everything becoming flooded and frozen?" Robert wanted to know.

"I don't know if you realize it, but the continent of Antarctica used to be 2,000 miles further north than it is now."

"Does that mean it used to not be at the South Pole?" Andrew asked.

"That's right," he answered. "See, in addition to Earth's plates moving a few inches a year, there is a phenomenon called Earth crust displacement in which the whole shell of the Earth literally moves around 2,000 miles and relocates itself with a new position."

"Aw come on!" Andrew remarked. "You know that's not possible."

"Why not?" said Morris. "Keep in mind that Earth's mantle is basically smooth, and why couldn't the Earth's crust move over it?"

"But how?" Andrew wanted to know.

"Centrifugal force," he answered. "You know the Earth spins on its axis every day."

"Yeah, I know that, but we don't just go sliding around on the Earth's mantle every day," Andrew pointed out.

"Yeah really, of course not," James agreed.

"Wait!" Steven called out. "I think I've got it. It seems possible to me that the polar ice caps build up disproportionately and that with an imbalance of glacial ice weight at the poles, the centrifugal force of the spinning Earth would literally cause the ice to slide toward the equator, pulling the whole of Earth's crust along with it."

"Bingo!" Morris declared.

"And the ice," Steven continued, "now displaced and nearer the equator would melt, and the seas would rise as a result."

"Can you imagine the tidal waves that would result from such a displacement?" William pointed out.

"Yeah, it must have been awful, to say the least," Paul agreed.

"So, let's see . . ." Robert began. "Antarctica, which used to be in the temperate zone, must have been sent into the South Pole and therefore froze."

"Exactly," Morris verified.

"So, how long do you think one of these displacements would take?" Chris asked.

"My best guess is that it took only a few days," Morris replied.

"A few days!?" Chris remarked. "Is that all?"

"Oh yes," Morris insisted. "It's a surprisingly violent occurrence. After all, there are plenty of frozen mammoths in Siberia and Alaska, and they are all bunched together with broken trees and other brush, like a huge tidal wave swept in there and threw them all together."

"Morris, I say you're just making all that up," Andrew commented.

"No, I'm not. There is plenty of documentation to back me up. People have been mining the frozen remains of mammoths for most of this century, especially for their ivory tusks. You can believe me. It's true."

"Oh, yeah," William recalled. "I've actually heard that there are restaurants around Fairbanks that serve mammoth steaks."

"Really?" said Steven. "How is that possible? That was thousands of years ago when they were wiped out. How could their meat be any good now?"

"Up there in the arctic tundra," Morris pointed out, "the ice preserves them very well. In many of the mammoths, there is still undigested grass in their stomachs. Before the Earth's crust suddenly slid, Siberia and Alaska used to be in the temperate zone."

"Hmm . . . Yeah, that does make sense," Steven admitted.

"See, the occurrence took place so fast that the mammoths were almost instantly frozen," Morris explained, "and there was not time for decomposition to take place."

"Oh, I see," Steven realized.

"That is strange," Chris remarked.

"How many thousands of years ago was it?" Paul asked.

"It was around 12,500 years ago," Morris answered.

"Okay, so what do we want to do next?" Robert asked everyone, changing the subject. "Do we want to go to Aleyone, Antarctica, or somewhere else next?"

"Let's go to Antarctica," Paul suggested.

"Yeah, let's go there," Andrew agreed. "I'm for the adventure."

"Yeah, me too," Steven added.

"Boy, we're going to need some warm clothing if we go there," William reminded everyone. "It's the middle of winter down there."

"That's true," said Robert.

"Not only that," Morris added, "the wind really howls down there too."

"How are we going to transport home to get warm clothing without our parents seeing us?" Steven asked everyone. "They think we're on a road trip in Robert's car. We can't just all show up at our homes to get more clothes."

"That's true," Robert admitted. "Wait, I know! William, why don't you and I transport to our homes and get some warm clothes for all of us. Between your family and mine, I know we have enough snowsuits and winter clothing for the eight of us."

"Yeah, that'll work," said William. "After all, your parents and my parents know the truth. What do you say, everyone?"

"Go for it," said Andrew.

"We'll be waiting here," said Morris.

"Okay, we'll be back in a couple of hours," said Robert.

Robert and William walked out of the hut and transported to their homes in Tennessee. Morris and the others continued talking about Antarctica.

"Morris, did you say this crustal displacement took place 12,500 years ago?" Andrew asked.

"That's right."

"Wasn't that about the time Atlantis sank?" Andrew further asked.

"It was," Morris calmly replied.

"Huh! Do you think that Atlantis was actually Antarctica?" Chris asked everyone.

"I haven't said anything about it before," Morris told them, "but I suspect that could be the case. After all, Atlantis is referred to as being in the middle of the ocean, and Antarctica meets that requirement very well."

"Hmm . . . You might be right, Morris," said Steven, "but what about what Tom said. He told us that it was where the Bermuda Triangle now is."

"That's likely misinformation," Morris explained. "Tom isn't from Earth, as you all know, and he could easily have been misinformed."

"Maybe that area was an outpost or a colony of Atlantis before it sank," Paul speculated.

"That was probably what it actually was," Morris agreed. "Atlantis likely had several of these outposts, like where the great pyramids of Egypt now are."

"Do you think the Atlanteans built the pyramids?" Andrew asked.

"Could be," said Morris. "See, there are actually some very old maps of the world in existence that were actually drawn by the Atlanteans, even though our present day society won't admit it. Their reference point is from Antarctica, and it is shown as ice free on these maps."

"Huh! That's strange," Chris remarked.

"There are a lot of things we still don't know," Morris admitted.

"That's true," said Paul.

"Actually, "Steven brought up, "I have heard that the first sea travellers several hundred years ago used Atlantean maps for their navigation, and I believe I remember seeing that Antarctica appeared ice free."

"Yes, that's true," Morris agreed. "They used Atlantean maps. Think about it. Where else would our early explorers have gotten world maps?"

"Yeah, that's true," said Paul. "Good point."

"Speaking of Antarctica being ice free in the past," James brought up, "I'm sure it was because there are Southern Beech trees in South America, and Antarctica was what connected Australia to South America in the past."

"That's true," Morris agreed, "but that was the distant past. There is fossil evidence that Southern Beeches grew in Antarctica millions of years ago. In fact, there is a 16 million-year-old fossil forest at Admiralty Bay. There were Southern Beeches, trees like the Norfolk Island Pine, ferns, and other unnamed flowering trees."

"Oh yeah, I've heard about that," said James.

"What about the Eucalyptus trees?" Chris asked. "Aren't there any of them in South America, and were there any in Antarctica?"

"No, there aren't," James answered. "As you know, the Eucalyptus trees showed up suddenly around 35 million years ago, and it was 5 million years prior to that time that Australia broke away from Antarctica."

"Oh, yeah. That's right," Chris recalled. "Morris' dream."

"That seems amazing that the Eucalyptus trees are of extraterrestrial origin," Steven remarked, "but what you just said, James, seems to lend evidence that they are."

"That's right," said James. "They certainly didn't show up in Antarctica."

They continued discussing Antarctica. Robert and William later returned after dark with plenty of warm clothing, and they decided to camp in the hut overnight.

The next morning was clear and cold. Frost was all over the ground, and all of them got up soon after sunrise and had breakfast.

Afterwards, they put on all of the warm clothing including snowsuits, hats, gloves, and warm socks in preparation for going to Antarctica.

"Boy, we sure are bundled up!" Paul remarked.

"I'll say," William agreed, "but we'll need it for down there."

"That's for sure," said Chris.

"I don't know about you," James brought up, "but I'm not so sure I want to go down there after all. It's just that it's so cold."

"What, are you thinking about Aleyone instead?" Robert asked.

"Right."

"Well, why don't you come with us anyway," Robert suggested, "see if you like it, and if you don't, then transport to Aleyone."

"Yeah, okay. Fair enough," said James.

"Are we all ready?" Morris asked.

Everyone answered yes.

"Does everyone remember the visual scene?" Robert asked.

They answered yes, walked out of the hut, and transported away to Antarctica.

CHAPTER 2

THE ICE CAVE IN ANTARCTICA

They arrived to a cold scene and found themselves standing on a sheet of ice and windswept snow. Mountains could be seen in the distance, and their sides were bathed in twilight. The wind blew fiercely and made it seem most inhospitable. For some, it was a struggle to stand up. With difficulty, they began walking toward the distant mountains.

"Man, this is impossible!" Paul struggled to say.

"I know," Chris agreed.

"Let's see if we can just transport ourselves over to those mountains..." Andrew suggested.

"...and take shelter from this awful cold!" William finished for him.

"Good point," said Robert.

At this point in time, suddenly a group of Emperor penguins passed in front of them and somewhat startled them. They were sliding on their bodies and were using their flippers to cause themselves to slide.

"Oh, wow!" Steven exclaimed. "Look at that!"

"They're Emperor penguins," Morris said. "They're the largest type of penguin in the world."

"Really?" Robert responded.

"And they're very smart too," he continued. "They're different from the other species as well, because they come here in the dead of winter while all other penguins go north to warmer climates."

"That's strange," Robert commented.

"Why would they do that?" Chris wanted to know.

"I believe their purpose is to serve as a guardian through winter," Morris explained, "and for that reason alone, they act in a manner opposite to that of other penguins."

"Interesting point," said Steven. "I hadn't thought of that."

"Do you think the Atlanteans may have had something to do with that?" Andrew brought up.

"Could be," Morris admitted. "You may have something there."

"Maybe like they're mascots or leftovers from the days of Atlantis," Paul added.

"Here, let's get over to those mountains and take shelter from this cold," William requested.

"Yeah, really!" Robert agreed. "This wind must be blowing 100 miles per hour!"

They transported themselves to the foot of the distant mountains, and much to their relief, the wind hardly blew at all. The steep slopes of the mountain now towered above them, most of them being covered with snow, ice, and glaciers. Further up, there were areas of exposed rocks and cliffs, and large sections of ice and packed snow hung over the edges of those cliffs. They decided to start climbing to get a better view.

"Where do you think we are, Morris?" Paul asked.

"Antarctica, no doubt," he answered.

"Oh, I *know* that," Paul continued, "but what part of Antarctica?"

"I'm not sure, really, but I lean toward the possibility that we are in the area where the main center of Atlantis used to be."

"You mean it could be under all of this ice?" Robert asked.

"Could be, or very close," Morris concluded.

"Actually," said Steven, "I've heard theories that Atlantis could have been in the Queen Maud Land area of Antarctica."

"Oh, really?" Chris responded. "That could be where we are, then."

"Hey everyone," Andrew called out. "Is that a cave way up there?" He pointed up the mountain slope.

The others looked up the mountain in that direction, and William commented, "Well, maybe it is."

"Let's go on up there," James suggested.

They agreed and began the climb up the slope. The going was difficult in the snow. At times, they slipped and fell, but the soft snow kept them from being injured. They would have simply transported to the cave, but out of pride they felt the need for a challenge and adventure, so they chose to walk and climb instead.

Suddenly, only a few minutes after they began their climb, they heard a strange humming noise behind them. Steven looked around first. "Oh, wow! I'm not believing this!" he exclaimed.

"You're not kidding," Paul agreed.

There on the icy plains, only a few hundred meters away from the foot of the mountain, sat what looked like some sort of a craft. It was mostly green in color with a tinge of yellow and brown, and it's headlights and tail lights were on. It appeared to have wheels on which it sat and looked not too different from some futuristic car or van.

"Here, let's transport ourselves over to it right now," Robert eagerly suggested.

"Wait," Morris cautiously warned them. "We don't know who or what it or they may be. I'd advise everyone to wait here until something or someone emerges from the craft."

"Yeah, you're right," Robert admitted. "Good point."

They watched the craft from where they stood on the mountain slope. After a minute, a door opened and two beings appearing very human emerged, and they closed the door. They began walking toward them.

"Oh my goodness!" Steven exclaimed.

"What do we do now?" Andrew wanted to know.

"Just stay calm, everyone," Morris directed. "They're walking right toward us. They'll likely see us soon enough."

"What about calling out to them?" Chris asked.

"Let them find us first," said Morris.

"Huh! They look like humans sure enough!" Chris declared.

"Who could they be?" James wanted to know.

Suddenly, one of them looked up and spotted them and stopped walking. The other one then also noticed them and also stopped. They appeared surprised. Robert, afraid they might turn and run, decided to call out to them. "Hey, how's it going?"

"Shhhh . . . Quiet, Robert!" Chris ordered.

"Pretty good. How about you?" one of them answered.

"What do you know!" William declared to the others. "They speak English."

"Man, what are you dudes doing way up there on that hillside in all of this cold?" the other one called out to them.

"Dudes?" Robert quietly said to the others. "They sound like two young guys, like we are."

"Yeah, but we don't say 'dudes', even though a lot of others say that," Morris pointed out.

"We're just down here exploring around, *dudes*," William called out, answering his question.

"Cool, dudes!" the same one replied, and both of them started up the slope.

"They sound friendly enough," said Robert. "Let's go back down the slope and meet them."

"Yeah, okay," Paul agreed, and the eight of them began descending. In minutes, they met up with them.

"Well, I will say!" Andrew commented first. "The two of you are human beings, just like we are."

"True indeed," one of them replied.

"Where are you all from?" Robert asked them.

"We're from what you call the Orion system, from the star called Al Nitak," the same one replied. "My name's Rinto Zapatero, and this is my brother Fraxino."

"Nice to meet you. I'm Robert Joslin, and these are my friends. We all live in Tennessee." All of them introduced themselves.

"You live in another star system?" Chris asked.

"Right you are," Fraxino answered.

"But you know English. How?" Chris wanted to know.

"Oh, we've visited Earth several times," Rinto answered. "As a matter of fact, we've spent time in Tennessee."

"Oh, really?" Chris responded, no doubt surprised.

"That's right, man," said Rinto. "Our next door neighbor has spent more time in Tennessee than we have."

"You even talk like Americans," said Morris.

"That's where we went to learn English," Rinto explained. "See, our ancestors used to live on Earth until around 12,000 years ago when they fled from Earth and arrived on our planet Artenia, the third planet out from our star, Al Nitak. We've come here to research our roots."

"You mean from the days of Atlantis?" Morris asked.

"Right," Rinto replied. "We've determined that Atlantis was in the region which is now under all of this ice."

"That's the same conclusion we've come to," Morris commented.

"Oh really? Cool!" Rinto declared.

"So, dudes," Fraxino asked. "What brings you way down here to research Atlantis?"

"Well, it's a long story," Robert began. "The eight of us here got involved with a galactic salesman named Tom from the Sirius B star system. Morris here met him in a dream, and this galactic salesman had us build him a galactic communications device to link Earth's telephone network with his star system and with others as well."

"Cool!" said Fraxino.

"That's right," Robert continued, "and we, with the help of William's father, gathered some phone equipment and helped Tom build the device a few months ago. Tom gave us the gift of transporting ourselves by thought, and the eight of us here have been taking adventures ever since."

"Oh really? Where have you guys been?" Rinto wanted to know.

"We've been to Tasmania, England, Sirius B, Vega, the Pleiades, and to Utah in the western United States."

"We've got at least two months left before school begins again," Steven added. "So, we're going to pack in as much as possible."

"Cool!" Fraxino commented again.

"Anyway," Robert went on, "Tom sent us on a search on planet Aleyone in the Pleiades to find a large, egg-shaped, green Fluorite crystal which was stolen from Atlantis over 15,000 years ago and deposited way up high in the mountains on one of Aleyone's large islands in its southern hemisphere. By our instincts, we actually found the exotic crystal and brought it back to Earth and placed it on a cliff high up in the mountains in Utah because that's where it telepathically requested that it be put."

"Soon after placing it there," Morris now explained, "it started telling about Antarctica. So, we've decided to come here to research Atlantis. It said something about a few of them that never left."

"Cool!" said Rinto. "Well, what do you say we begin looking?"

"Sounds good," said Andrew. "Just before you two arrived, I had noticed a cave way up the slope at the base of that cliff." He pointed toward it. "We were just starting to walk up there."

"Wow, dudes!" Fraxino exclaimed. "Let's go up there and explore it."

All ten of them began the climb which took an hour.

"So, tell us," Paul brought up, "What's it like on your home world?"

"Actually, our planet Artenia is very much like Earth," Rinto explained. "The Atlanteans brought a lot of things with them when they fled from Earth. They decided to settle Artenia because it was most like Earth, and they already knew that because of the galactic trade that was in existence then."

"We live on the outskirts of a city called Zantaayer in a region known as Zotola," Fraxino now informed them. "Our city is nestled at the base of several mountains."

"Wow!" Andrew commented. "That sounds pretty good."

"What sort of vehicle is that craft of yours down there?" William wanted to know.

"That's a hybrid land craft-space craft," Rinto replied. "They're really neat."

"A lot of people use them for travel," Fraxino added.

"What sort of power source do you use in it?" William wanted to know.

"It runs on hydrogen and other sources as well," said Rinto. "The controls of the craft are operated through a crystal known as Ulexite. After we explore the cave, Fraxino and I will be glad to show it to you in more detail."

"Sounds good to me," said William.

"How many people settled your planet when they fled from Atlantis?" Andrew wanted to know.

"Our historical records put the figure at around 65,000 settlers from Earth at that time," answered Rinto.

"That's a fair amount," said Andrew.

"A few of them never left Earth," Rinto went on, "and it's been rumored that they settled different parts of your planet Earth and passed on the Atlantean culture."

"Yeah, that sounds about right," Robert now said, "seeing that Egypt has the large pyramids and seeing that there are historical artifacts all over the world."

"That's right," said Rinto. "Did you know that the three pyramids of Egypt are arranged in the same configuration as the three stars of the Orion Belt?"

"No, I didn't," Robert admitted.

"I believe the same is true for the pyramids built by the Aztecs near Mexico City," Morris added.

"Oh really?" Chris responded.

"Yes, that's true too," said Rinto. "Our star, Al Nitak, is the bottom star of the three stars of the Orion Belt."

"Oh, is that right?" Robert responded. "Isn't that something."

They continued talking and eventually reached the cave's entrance. Even though the wind hadn't blown much, they were cold by this time, and the warmth of the cave was a welcome relief to them. The walls of the cave were made of limestone and some sandstone, and the cave appeared to go back quite a ways.

"Man, am I glad to be out of that cold!" Paul exclaimed.

"Right on dude," Fraxino agreed.

"I wonder where this cave leads to," Chris commented.

"Let's explore it and find out," Rinto offered.

All of them took flashlights out of their packs and proceeded.

"So, you say you've come here to research your roots?" Robert asked Rinto.

"Right, I'm doing a history project on the origins of the human beings on Artenia."

"For school or something?"

"That's right," Rinto continued, "and I figured I'd go above the normal call of duty and come here to Antarctica to research Atlantis myself. What about you guys? Why are you researching Atlantis?"

"We're just curious," Robert replied. "It's all in the interest of fun and adventure."

"That's why I chose to do this and why I came here," said Rinto. "My brother came along to accompany me and also because of his interest in rocks and crystals."

"Yeah, dudes," said Fraxino, "I really like rocks. I have a good collection of them back at home. I hope we find some really cool stuff in here."

"What was that crystal like that you guys found on Aleyone?" Rinto wanted to know.

"It was literally grown in the shape of an egg, according to what Tom told us," Morris explained, "and the egg is made of green Fluorite while inside of it was grown an orange Calcite crystal in the shape of a pyramid, and no matter which way the crystal egg is turned, the pyramid maintains an upright position because it is weighted and allowed to freely move within the egg's smooth inner walls."

"Wow, dudes!" Fraxino declared. "That's really cool!"

"You two really use the words *cool* and *dudes* a lot," Robert commented. "Where did you learn those words from?"

"From being in your state of Tennessee," Rinto answered.

"We don't actually use those words that much," said Robert, "but you're right. A lot of Tennesseans do."

They were now well within the cave and were proceeding down the corridor.

Soon, they came to some stairs which appeared to descend beyond sight into the darkness. For half an hour, they descended until they reached the bottom of the steps. Another corridor now led them slightly uphill, and fifteen minutes later, they came upon a wall of ice on the right side of the corridor. Every now and then, they heard creaking and cracking sounds as the ice way above them shifted.

"Oh wow!" Paul suddenly exclaimed as he noticed the solid ice-free wall to his left.

"What?" Robert asked Paul.

"Cool!" Fraxino exclaimed.

There on the wall were rows and rows of hieroglyphs and inscriptions of various things. In addition to that, there were numerous and various rocks and crystals decorating the wall.

"That is really cool!" Rinto declared.

"Yeah, but not as *cool* as the ice on the other side of this corridor," Paul added with a smile.

All of them laughed at his clever comment.

"What do you make of this?" Robert asked Morris.

"Very impressive display of what is probably an accurate historical record of Atlantis. My feeling is that this could be what they wrote just before they fled to Al Nitak, as Rinto and Fraxino have now informed us."

"I'd say you're probably right," said Chris. "Can you two read it?" he now asked Rinto and Fraxino.

Suddenly, the look on Morris' face changed. The others noticed. "What is it, Morris?" Robert wanted to know.

"I just suddenly got a strange feeling," he replied. He turned and faced Rinto. "There's something about this place that gives me chills down my back. I have a very strong feeling that I'm not supposed to know something that I'm about to find out if I don't get out of here right now. Rinto, I'll tell you this. You're very familiar to me. I've known you before, but you're linked to something I'm not supposed to know about, something to do with a pact made before we were born. It's weird, really. I can't put it in words, but I really must go." He now turned and faced Robert.

"But Morris, wait," Robert requested. "Wh . . .What do you mean you're leaving? You're the one who does all the astral travel. We need you on our future adventures."

"Yeah really, Morris," Paul agreed. "You're the one who got us all started."

"My purpose has been served. I've got dolphin research to do now and have a book to write, and I best get at it while the knowledgeable ones are still alive before they get killed by tuna fish nets."

"Morris, this is absurd!" Andrew declared.

"No, it isn't," Morris stated. "It's my next calling. I have a purpose to serve and karma to fulfill and balance with a former world renowned dolphin."

"What?" Andrew asked. "You're off your rocker!"

Morris, ignoring Andrew's comment, turned and faced Robert. "You and the others won't be seeing me anymore. I've got a lot of work to do." He took out of one of his pockets the green Fluorite ball that Michael on planet Aleyone had given him and handed it to Robert. "Here, Robert. Take this green Fluorite ball with you. Somebody you will meet is supposed to have it. You'll automatically know who he is when the time is right. I will say this, that it will be sometime soon."

"We're never going to see you again, ever?" Chris asked.

"Well, I will take that part back," Morris admitted. "I'll be back in school with you this fall."

"And where until then?" Robert wanted to know.

"On Delikadove, the dolphin's old home world."

"35 million years ago?" Paul now asked. "How in the world are you going to do that?"

"That's just it, Paul. It's not this world, is it!" Morris cleverly remarked with a touch of anger in his voice. "I can't be giving out details."

Paul hesitated, slightly taken aback.

"Well . . . have fun, Morris," said Steven.

"Thanks, Steven." Morris now turned and faced Rinto and Fraxino. "Sorry if I don't seem very hospitable, but I must follow my instincts. It was nice knowing you, brief as it was."

"Oh, that's okay," Rinto assured him. "Call your dolphin friends. We'll take your friends back to Al Nitak with us and show them around."

"That's very kind of you two," said Morris.

As Morris continued to speak for a few minutes with Rinto and Fraxino, Robert quietly made a comment to Chris. "What do you think of Rinto's comment, Chris? 'Call your dolphin friends,' he said."

"Huh! That is really strange," Chris admitted. "He really understands what Morris is supposed to do. Strange . . . It's as if Rinto already knows it ahead of time."

"Could be," said Robert.

"That's his subconscious mind at work," Chris added.

Morris, now finished talking with Rinto and Fraxino, turned and faced Robert and his friends. "These two have offered to take you all to their home world and show you around. I know my leaving you all is a sudden surprise, but that's how things are meant to be sometimes. Life's a strange experience, isn't it. Enjoy the rest of your travels." With that, he placed his hands on either side of his waist and slowly moved his hands and arms up and down, and he thought the certain way, bringing on the pink glow and the sound of whirring wind. In seconds, he dematerialized and disappeared, followed by the disappearance of the pink glow and whirring wind.

"Wow, dudes!" Fraxino declared. "That is really cool!"

"Is that how your transport procedure works?" Rinto asked.

"That's it," Robert calmly answered.

"That is really neat!" Rinto exclaimed. "How did you learn that?"

"It came to me in a dream," Robert explained. "Then the next day, it was really true because Tom gave it to me and my friends, according to the deal he and Morris made that same night."

"Interesting," Rinto commented.

"Well, mates," James now brought up, "now is as good a time as any."

"What?" Robert asked. "You too?"

"Suzanne, isn't it," William calmly stated.

"Yep, mates. You guessed it," James admitted. "I'm going to return to Aleyone."

"I just *knew* you'd be lovesick," Paul declared.

"Yep, I know it," said James. "I feel like I belong there. I miss her like you wouldn't believe."

"I don't doubt it," William remarked.

"At least you know where I'll be if you want to visit," he offered.

"Golly!" Robert exclaimed. "That's two. Does anyone else want to bail out?"

"I'm staying," Andrew stated. "I like the fun and adventure."

"Me too," Paul agreed.

"I'm not bailing out," Chris assured them.

"I might have felt guilty about travelling, but not anymore," said Steven. "I thoroughly enjoy it!"

Although William didn't show quite the enthusiasm, he stated that he was staying with them, especially because of his interest in Rinto and Fraxino's craft parked outside at the foot of the mountain.

"Well, so long, James," said Robert. "We'll come to Aleyone before the summer's over and visit you, Suzanne, and her family."

"All right, mates. I'll keep in touch." With that said, James proceeded to transport himself away. He had forgotten to speak to Rinto and Fraxino.

Robert, somewhat taken aback at what had just happened, came around to say, "So, Rinto and Fraxino, what do you think the inscriptions say?"

"Well, let's see here," Rinto began. "I can read a little bit of the Atlantean language." He and Fraxino stared at the inscriptions. "I know it says this much, that the Earth's crust evidently slid over the globe and sent Atlantis to its doom near the new south pole. It says here," and he pointed to a certain section of the inscriptions, "that they knew the seas would soon rise, and that they came here to this cave to write this historical document." He now pointed to the tail end of the inscriptions. "It says here that they fled to the Orion Belt, as you know it. Look at the arrangement of these three pieces of crystal," and he pointed to them. They were arranged nearly in a line, similar to the arrangement of the three stars in the Orion Belt. "Up here, it indicates that much of Atlantis got flooded and would likely be covered with lots of ice and that the main center was closer to the coast than we are now."

"So, this cave served as a storage facility to store their historical data," William speculated. "Interesting."

"Oh wait," said Rinto, and he pointed to another section. "This section says that there are other caves and mines throughout the world where historical information is also hidden, to be discovered much later by the next advanced civilization when the time is right."

"Huh!" Chris remarked. "That's really weird. Do you think they really did all that?"

"Yes, right here," said Rinto, and he indicated. "It says that there is an excellent storage and data base deep in a mine in the continent north of here."

"Probably South America," Andrew commented.

"Way up in the mountains, too," Rinto added. "Fraxino, hand me your orange Calcite." Fraxino handed it to him while the others looked on with interest. "Thanks." Rinto took the orange rock, and over the next several minutes, he scanned the entire surface on which the inscriptions were written.

"What are you doing?" Chris asked with interest.

"Something Morris is not yet supposed to know about, dudes," Fraxino answered for him in a joking manner.

"Yeah, that's probably why he ran off and left so quick," Rinto added with a smile on his face.

"You're kidding," said Steven.

"I don't know, Steven," said Robert. "There may actually be some truth in what they just said."

"After all," Paul added, "Morris did take off and leave rather suddenly."

"How does that work, what you're doing, Rinto?" Robert wanted to know.

"All I do is scan the written data with this orange Calcite crystal in my hand, and it telepathically receives the data. Later when we return to the craft, it will telepathically communicate the data to the Ulexite controls crystal on our craft."

"Wow!" Steven declared. "But how?"

"It's all done through energy field manipulation," Rinto explained to them. "That's why these crystals are fastened to the wall here and interspersed throughout the hieroglyphic text. My crystal is actually communicating with these crystals."

"The Atlanteans knew that one day in the future, people like us would come here to read this," Fraxino added.

"Huh!" Chris remarked. "Weird!"

"To you all, it is," Rinto admitted, "but to us, it's more normal. It's part of what got passed down from the Atlantean culture, only most of you on Earth lost faith in them."

"In what?" Robert asked.

"In the crystals and what they can do," Rinto replied. "Good thing we didn't come any later. That wall of ice may still be advancing and may well destroy what's written on this wall. So, you guys want to come with us to Artenia?"

"Sure," Steven eagerly replied. "Let's go."

"Wait," said Chris. "Aren't we going to be able to see any of the remains of what was Atlantis?"

"You mean buildings and ruins and things like that?" Robert asked.

"I don't see how," Paul pointed out. "It's under probably half a mile or more of ice."

"I wish Morris hadn't rushed off like he did," Chris remarked.

"I know," Robert agreed. "He probably could have figured out a way for us to get down there and see it."

"Yeah, but you know Morris," said William. "He has his things he's gotta do."

"This is probably all we're going to find for now, dudes," said Fraxino.

"Yeah, I'd say you're right," Andrew admitted.

"So, Andrew," Chris asked, "do you still believe that continents can't move?"

"I don't know. It looks like to me something really happened. Maybe continents really do move, at times, at least."

"So, you guys ready to come with us?" Rinto asked again.

"Yeah, sure," Robert replied. "How far away from here is Al Nitak?"

"It's 1,132 light years from here," Rinto replied.

"That's further than Aleyone by more than double," said Robert.

They continued talking as they walked out of the cave the same way they came in. The cold air greeted them outside as they left the cave and made their way back down the mountain. Around 30 minutes later, they were back on the icy plains of the valley floor. Rinto and Fraxino led the way as they walked the few hundred meters to their craft.

"This really is a neat looking rig you've got here," William commented.

"Thanks. Yes, it serves us well." said Rinto.

"The body of this craft looks like something out of the future," said Robert.

"I would imagine so," Rinto agreed. "This body's made out of a mixture of various metals, including Vanadium, and mixed with a silicone base. Actually, the body of the craft is grown over a period of several months."

"Oh, yeah," Robert recalled. "We actually saw some of that going on in a spacecraft factory on Aleyone."

"Oh, okay. Then you've seen it," said Rinto. "That's exactly how it's done."

Fraxino reached for the metal handle and slid the door open sideways. "Welcome to our craft," he said.

"Wow, dudes!" William exclaimed. "This is remarkable."

"Now *you're* also saying dudes, William," Paul remarked.

Inside the craft were several seats and a table fixed to the metallic looking floor. At the front were two seats, and the controls were very similar to an automobile's controls. It even had a steering wheel and a windshield. Between the two seats was a most unusual looking crystalline object in the shape of a cube, and it was half a meter in diameter.

"Huh!" Steven remarked. "This isn't so different from a typical van."

"Like I said," Rinto pointed out, "this is a hybrid land craft-space craft. It's made by a Zotolan company called Velosa, and as best as I can translate it into English, this vehicle is a Velosa cruiser craft. At the very front of the craft sits a Richmond in-line 6-cylinder motor with a 5-speed manual gearbox behind it, much like many of your trucks here on Earth have."

"No kidding!" Steven remarked. "I suppose then you have gasoline or diesel to run it?"

"No, it runs on hydrogen and has zero emissions," Rinto answered.

"Huh! Hydrogen!?" Steven exclaimed.

"That's right," Rinto verified.

"But that stuff's highly explosive," Paul stated.

"No more than gasoline," said Rinto.

"Well, I will say!" Robert commented. "I wish our planet would use hydrogen."

"It would definitely be better for the environment," Rinto agreed, "but as you all would put it, there's too much red tape with Earth's oil companies."

"How did you overcome it there and switch over to hydrogen?"

"We've never had any oil," Rinto replied.

"We never had a coal age on Artenia," Fraxino added. "I'm glad, too. Coal and fossil fuels do nothing but pollute when they're burned."

"Yeah, you're right," Paul admitted. "Changing over would be too costly. That's why our oil companies haven't done anything about it."

"One day they'll have enough sense to realize that the environment is more important than money," Fraxino pointed out.

"Yeah, when it's too late," said Paul.

"Maybe not," said Fraxino, "but if they do wait too long, then we may have a *few more* settlers coming to our world from yours."

"Anyway," said Rinto, getting back to the subject of the craft and pointing to the crystalline cube-shaped object between the seats, "this Ulexite crystal cube is the main controls crystal of this craft when we're flying through space." He took the orange colored crystal out of his pocket and placed it on the large cube. "I'm entering the data I collected from the cave into the main controls crystal, and it will process and analyze it."

"Did you say that was Ulexite?" Andrew asked.

"That's right, dude," Fraxino confirmed.

"How does it work?" Andrew wanted to know.

"What it actually does is to keep everything in line throughout the craft. As you look at it, you will see that it consists of many in-line fibers vertically arranged. It's really cool to look down through it and read text because it causes the text to jump out at you or appear elevated. Some call it TV rock, and some use it for aiding them in astral travel. Here on this craft, it's useful in guiding the craft through space and keeping it in line."

"So, it's like a computer," Steven remarked.

"Exactly," Fraxino verified, "only its process is on the mental etheric level instead of on the physical which uses transistors and electronic devices like your actual computers use."

"Huh!" Steven remarked.

"Interesting," Andrew commented.

"You said the text jumps out at you when you look through Ulexite?" Robert asked.

"That's right." Fraxino took a small piece of Ulexite out of his pocket and handed it to Robert. "Put this over a piece of paper with text, and you'll see what I mean."

Robert took a piece of paper out of his wallet and placed the flat rock over it. "Wow! Look at that!"

"Here, let's see," said Chris. Robert handed it to him, and Chris looked through it. "Oh, neat! That is really strange."

The rest of them looked through it and were impressed.

"Anyway, go ahead and take your backpacks off," Rinto offered, "set them in the back, and we'll be off." Everyone did so, and Rinto got in the driver's seat and started the engine of the craft. They watched as he started off from a stop and drove it like a normal car or van. As he picked up speed, he pulled back a lever, and the craft levitated upward. They were now airborne. He switched off the engine, now using the power of the crystals.

"Wait," said Robert. "How can you fly this thing without the engine running?"

"Oh, that's only for land use," Rinto replied. "The power of levitation and propulsion now comes from the anti-gravity crystal pack or crystal array situated under the Ulexite cube."

"It's really cool how it works," Fraxino added. "The crystal pack is made out of quartz crystals arranged in a certain grid or configuration, and they were each grown with slight impurities added which are needed to give the crystals their capacity for intelligence so they know how to counter gravity and fly."

"You're kidding!" Steven remarked.

"Far out!" Paul added.

"It's for real, dudes," Fraxino insisted.

"Yes, with the right combination of added impurities," Rinto explained, "their etheric minds become very clear as they are fine tuned to the right vibrational frequencies."

"Well, I will say!" Robert remarked. "I didn't know that was possible."

"This year," William commented, "we're finding out all sorts of things that we didn't think were possible."

"Lot's of things are possible that one wouldn't think are possible," said Fraxino. "This crystal array is in constant communication with the main controls crystal, the cube of Ulexite, which keeps the crystals focused on the task at hand, maneuvering the craft."

"That is impressive," said Robert.

"That *is* really strange," Chris added.

They were now flying well above the ground, and Rinto added comment. "If you think that's impressive, watch this," he said with a smile. A forcefield which accompanied a faint green glow suddenly overtook them. They felt as if they dematerialized but only for a moment. Before they realized it, they were restored to normal, but when they looked out of the window, the scene had completely changed.

CHAPTER 3

THE TRIP TO ZANTAAYER

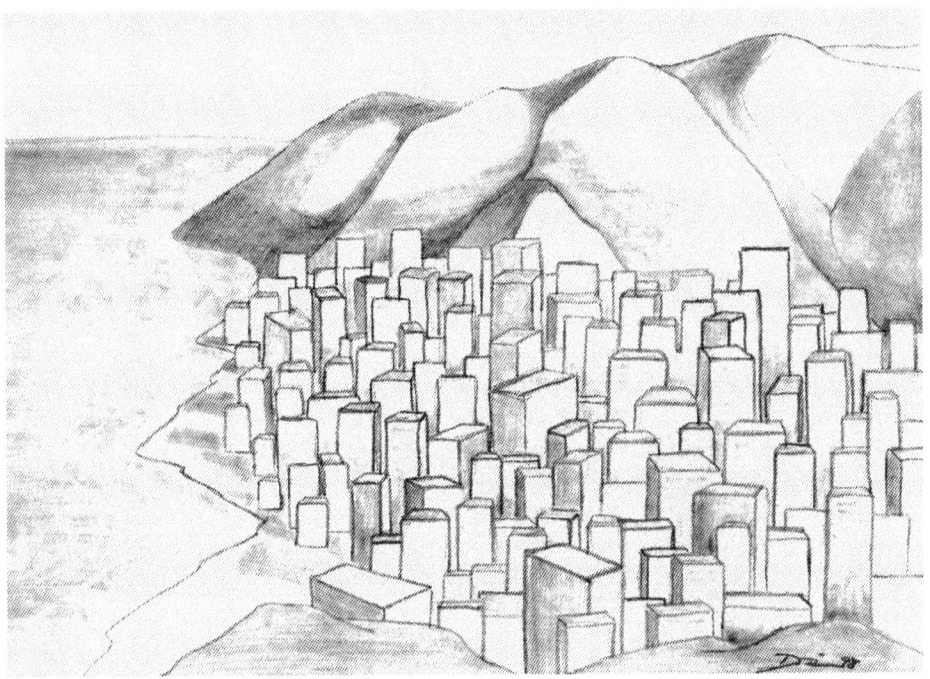

They were no longer flying over Antarctica but were now flying around 100 kilometers above a blue-green planet which they knew wasn't Earth, although similar in appearance at a glance.

"Golly!" Paul exclaimed. "What was that?"

"A form of teleportation," Rinto replied.

"That crystal array is so smart," Fraxino explained, "that it knows how to teleport us wherever we want to go. All we have to do is think of the place we want to go, the crystals read our thoughts, and they activate and teleport us and the craft there."

"But how?" Paul wanted to know.

"The power of thought is more effective than you realize," Rinto informed them. "It's not so different from your method with the pink glow and whirring wind, only it's the crystal array that activates the process instead of your mind alone."

"That is really neat, dudes!" William remarked.

"Are we already flying over Artenia?" Steven asked.

"Right on, dudes!" Fraxino enthusiastically answered.

"So, Fraxino," Rinto said, "do you think my research report on Atlantis will be a smashing success?"

"Indeed it will," said Fraxino. "I'm sure your teacher will be most impressed, along with your classmates."

"I hope so," said Rinto. "That was really lucky for us to find those inscriptions. I can't wait to enter it into my crystal base computer at home and process the data."

"You have a computer at home, too?" Steven asked Rinto.

"Yep, sure do," he answered, "only it operates on crystals, as you might have guessed. It's a very interesting setup because it literally transmits visual images to the mind of the person using it along with the text that it formulates through its own built-in translator."

"Huh! Interesting!" Steven remarked.

"Tell us about Artenia," Robert requested as he looked out of the window at the blue-green world below them.

"Well, as you can see, it's very similar to Earth," Rinto explained, "nearly a duplicate as far as temperature, vegetation, and climate are concerned. Around 50% of the surface is covered with water, 15% with ice at the poles, and the remaining 35% is land. We live in a city called Zantaayer, population 120,000, located at a latitude of 40° north and situated on the northern coast of a region called Zotola. We have nice warm summers, and our winters are fairly mild, thanks to the currents of the sea to the north and west of us which we call, as it could best be translated to English, the Elizabeth Ocean. It almost never gets below freezing in the winter. Zantaayer is nestled within a range of mountains on its other three sides, and they are called the Ciruclar Mountains."

"Tell us about the technical data of Artenia," Andrew requested. "How far is it from your sun and so on?"

"Our star, Al Nitak, is larger and brighter than your sun," Rinto continued. "You can see it above us through the window," as he indicated to them. "Artenia is located 260 million kilometers from Al Nitak, and its diameter is 11,500 kilometers. It takes 423 of our days for our planet to orbit Al Nitak, and our days are $25^1/_2$ of your hours long. So, in your days, that comes out to be 449.4375, assuming 24 hours to the day."

"What about gravity?" Robert wanted to know.

"It's nearly the same as your Earth at 98%. You'll feel slightly lighter here than on Earth and therefore more energized. Anyway, you'll see when we arrive."

Rinto operated the controls accordingly, and the craft began to descend into Artenia's atmosphere which was more of a turquoise color than Earth's normal blue sky. They were flying over a sea of water, and ahead of them could be seen the range of mountains on the coast. Zantaayer sat nestled in among them just like Rinto had said. Clouds covered the peaks of the mountains, and the scenery was most attractive.

As they were approaching the coast, Fraxino took a holographic disk out of a box and inserted it into what looked like some sort of a player. Music was soon heard to play, not too different from the normal pop music of Earth. It was a very moving piece, and the beat was so invigorating to Robert and his friends that their emotions were gripped with an uncanny sense of familiarity, even though they knew they had never heard the song before.

"What's that song about?" Steven asked with considerable curiosity.

"It's about taking charge of your life and living it to the fullest," Rinto answered, "to best explain it in English."

"So familiar! I feel like surely I must have heard it before," said Robert.

"It's one of our favorites," Rinto answered.

"It's really cool!" Fraxino added. "It's from a recent holodisk album by a group of young pop artists called *The Hydragyros*. They're from Zantaayer."

"*The Hydragyros*," Steven repeated. "*That's* an amusing name."

"Really an impressive melody," said Paul.

"I really like it, too," Robert told Rinto and Fraxino.

They continued to let the holodisk play as it went through the album's songs.

As Rinto steered the craft lower, they flew over the mountains bordering the western side of the city and came in for a landing near the top of the range above the edge of the city. Trees and scenery whizzed by as he brought it in for a landing on a narrow winding gravel backroad which went through a forest. Rinto laughed as he landed, just missing trees, and he almost didn't make the curve ahead of them.

"Golly boy!" Chris exclaimed. "You scared me to death! I thought you were going to crash into those trees for sure."

"Don't worry, dudes," Fraxino assured them. "Rinto's an experienced driver. He lands here every time we come back home."

"Yeah, I don't want to disturb the neighbors, landing in the middle of the city," Rinto explained. "So, I always land up here out of the way."

"Besides," Rinto further explained, "the crystals make all necessary corrections for whatever errors I may make, and they correct my course."

Rinto started the engine, the craft now moving slowly, put the gearbox in second gear, engaged the clutch, accelerated to an appropriate driving speed, and drove the craft down the gravel road.

"You've got a smart crystal array," Paul remarked. "That it knows how to correct your course is amazing!"

"Yes, I will say this crystal array is a little unusual, especially to those from Earth," Rinto admitted.

As they continued along the forested road, they caught glimpses through the trees of the city of Zantaayer well below them. It appeared to be mid afternoon. Rinto made a left turn on another gravel road, and they descended rather steeply with plenty of hairpin curves to the foot of the mountain. The drive took half an hour.

"I can see all the way across the city to the mountains on the other side," Robert commented. "There's not a bit of haze nor air pollution."

"That's the advantage of hydrogen fuel and zero emissions," said Rinto.

"Your cities on Earth are full of white and brown smog," Fraxino added.

"If Earth's oil company people were to come here and see this," Paul declared, "they'd quit using fossil fuels in a hurry."

"Right on, dudes!" Fraxino remarked.

"What types of trees are these up here?" Robert asked. "They look like Beeches in a way."

"They are," Rinto confirmed. "These trees used to grow in Antarctica, or that is, Atlantis, and our ancestors brought them here. They've established themselves pretty well here, after 12,000 years, haven't they."

"Yes, I agree," said Robert. "It looks like a pure stand of them."

"What used to grow here?" Andrew wanted to know.

"I'd say it was treeless with just grassy fields and meadows before," Rinto speculated.

He carefully maneuvered the vehicle-craft through all of the curves, and when they reached the foot of the mountain, he took the gearbox out of second gear, put it in a higher gear, and proceeded to normal driving speed as the road straightened and the pavement began. Soon, they entered a residential area and were passing houses on both sides of the road. They weren't very different from houses back home on Earth, and in some ways, this particular area could have passed for Tennessee.

"Fraxino and I live around two kilometers from here," Rinto informed them, "not too far from the foot of the mountains. We'll take you all to our house and introduce you to our family." He proceeded down the paved road and eventually made a left turn, after which he soon turned left into his driveway.

"Yep, looks like Mom and Dad are home," Rinto stated with assurance, upon seeing his father's car parked in the driveway. Rinto and Fraxino's father drove an antique classic, a turquiose colored 4-door Tolejo sedan with a straight 6 engine and a 3-speed on the column. It very much resembled a late 1950's Ford Edsel, and Mr. Zapatero kept it in immaculate condition.

Once Rinto parked at the end of the driveway, everyone stepped outside and looked around.

"So, dudes, how does it feel to step out into a new world?" Rinto asked them.

"The air feels so crisp and clear," Paul remarked.

"You're right, Rinto," said Robert. "I do feel lighter and more energized here."

"That's 98% Earth's gravity for you. Come on inside everyone," he offered.

They followed Rinto and Fraxino into their house. "Mom, Dad," Fraxino called out in their native language of Artenia. Rinto and Fraxino's parents soon came from another room and greeted Robert and his friends. Their parents didn't speak English, so Rinto and Fraxino served as interpreters as they spoke with their parents in their native Artenian language, explaining how they happened into them soon after landing in Antarctica.

Robert began to have a sense of familiarity with the place but couldn't figure out why. He decided to keep that thought to himself as they continued talking. After around twenty minutes of conversation, Rinto and Fraxino took them back outside.

"Come on, and I'll show you guys the engine under the hood of our craft," Rinto offered.

At that moment, the sound of crunching gravel could be heard at the neighbor's house as its resident's car pulled in. Rinto noticed and looked left in that direction. "Looks like Chispo has just arrived," he commented. "Come on. Follow me over to his house. I'll introduce you to him."

Robert and his friends followed Rinto and Fraxino through the back of their yard, through a row of tall bushes dividing their yard from Chispo's, and through his backyard to the back of his house. Chispo was just stepping out of his car, a smooth, futuristic-looking golden-yellow one. "Hey Chispo," Rinto called out to him in the Artenian language. "I've got a group of Earthlings here from Tennessee," he now told him in English.

"Wow, man!" Chispo declared enthusiastically.

"Yeah dude, Rinto and I found them in Antarctica earlier today," Fraxino added.

"What's going on, dudes?" said Chispo as he introduced himself to them and shook hands with all of them. He faced Robert and said, "Man, did Rinto tell you all that he's such a guru that he specially rigged up that crystal array of his so that he could teleport and fly to and from Earth?"

"No, he didn't quite put it that way," Robert admitted. "You mean it's unusual?"

"Rinto, you modest genius you," Chispo said to him with a smile and chuckled. "Yeah, you got it, dude," he now said to Robert. "Man, that was quite a project he did last year, causing that pack of crystals to think. He grew them himself, man."

"Where?" Robert wanted to know.

"In a secret cave way up in the mountains," Rinto answered for him. "Chispo, I was just about to show them my craft in detail and tell them when I heard you pull your car into here. So, we came over here instead."

"Oh, all right, man," said Chispo.

For some unknown reason, Robert found Chispo very familiar. He had a vibrant, lively personality, and he was energetic as well. It was strange. He recognized Chispo right away, possibly on a soul level, as if he was someone he had known all of his life. It was only the second or third time in his life that he had experienced this sort of sense of familiarity. In addition to Chispo, the whole place had a sense of familiarity. Again, he kept his thoughts to himself.

"Anyway, Chispo," Rinto offered, "come with us. I'm going to show them my craft, and then we're going to go cruising on the roads up in the mountains."

"All right, dudes," Chispo agreed. He walked with them back over to the Zapateros.

"We're going to do some rock hunting, as well," Fraxino added.

"What did you say your last name was?" Robert asked Chispo.

"Colancha. Actually, it's Colancha-Pachanga, even though my last name is Colancha. Colancha comes from my father's last name, and Pachanga is my mother's last name. Rinto's full name is Rinto Zapatero-Rodiga, and mine is Chispo Colancha-Pachanga. Our last names work similarly to the way the Spanish speaking cultures do it back on your world."

"Oh, I see," said Robert. "So, each person attaches the maiden last name of his or her mother to the last name of his or her father."

"Exactly," said Chispo. "Man, I was surprised when Rinto said you dudes were from Tennessee. I've actually spent some considerable time there."

"Oh really? Where?" Robert wanted to know.

"This is who I was earlier telling you about," said Rinto. "He actually lived there for a year."

"Well, I will say!" Robert declared.

"Oh yeah, Rinto," Paul recalled. "I do remember you'd said a friend of yours had spent quite a bit of time there in Tennessee."

"Yeah, man, I was an exchange student in Nashville for a year," Chispo informed them.

"Nashville?" Robert asked. "When?"

"Last year, dudes," Chispo continued. "I've only been back home a month. That's a wild place you all got down there on Earth."

"Wait," Paul asked. "How in the world did you become an exchange student in Nashville?"

Chispo laughed at his question and then said, with a twinkle in his eyes, "Man, we fooled 'em. All we had to do was fabricate some documents. Rinto had just finished his project on his Velosa cruiser craft, and he took me and my parents down there. We told the school system that we were visiting the United States from Spain, and they believed us 100%, man. They sent out a search and located a host family to accommodate me for the school year. You all have a great place, Tennessee, except for the air pollution and smog."

"Yeah, I can imagine so," Paul admitted, "seeing how crisp and clear your air is here on Artenia."

"I'm glad we never had a coal age here on Artenia, or we'd be doing the same as you dudes back on Earth," said Chispo.

By this time, they had walked back through the bushes and were approaching Rinto and Fraxino's vehicle-craft. "I'll start by showing you guys the engine under the hood," said Rinto. He raised the hood.

"Huh!" Steven declared. "Richmond. Never heard of it."

"It's a straight six," William commented.

"Yes, as you guys already know, it runs very smoothly," Rinto added. "Richmond makes all of the internal combustion hydrogen engines on Artenia."

"Interesting," said Robert, "but wait. That's a name in English. How can that be?"

"Good question," Rinto admitted. "Richmond is a would-be manufacturing company on Earth, but the idea never materialized there while it did here."

"We are about as far advanced as you dudes are on Earth," Chispo added. "Like your geniuses there, our geniuses here on Artenia got their ideas from the same source."

"Same source? What source?" Robert wanted to know.

"People get ideas all the time," Chispo explained. "They come from higher levels of thought from the astral world. It's all in the mind."

"You mean there's a central source of information available somewhere?" Andrew now asked.

"That's right, man," Chispo verified. "Since your planet and our planet are equals on levels of advancement, we tapped into the same source of ideas."

"But where?" Robert insisted.

"It's all out there in the ether," Rinto now answered.

"Weird," William commented.

"That's part of what Morris, who ran off and left you, tapped into," said Rinto.

"So, how does this rig run on hydrogen?" William asked, changing the subject.

"Back on Earth, there are some vehicles that run on propane or butane," Rinto answered. "It's almost identical to that."

"But hydrogen is highly explosive," said William.

"Like I mentioned earlier, no more explosive than your gasoline and propane," Rinto reminded. "Even still, our hydrogen tanks are well within the vehicle and protected by thick metal on all sides in case of a collision."

"Well, that's good," said William.

"So, how many cubic inches is this engine?" Steven asked.

"276 in your units, or around 4.5 liters," Rinto answered.

While Rinto continued showing them the engine, Chispo called Robert over to see Mr. Zapatero's car.

"Take a look at this immaculate automobile," Chispo proudly boasted. "This is a rare collector's classic, a *Tolejo* sedan, complete with an early model Richmond in-line 6-cylinder motor and a 3-speed on the column. The body's made of stainless steel. Dude, this car will *cruise*. Rinto and Fraxino's father takes super care of it, and he takes us riding in it several times a year. It's a lot of fun," and he laughed.

Meanwhile, Fraxino opened the side door of the vehicle-craft and said for everyone to come inside and take a look. Rinto closed the front hood, and they walked around to the side and entered. Fraxino removed a side plate and revealed the crystal array situated underneath the main controls crystal, the cube of Ulexite.

"Wow!" Andrew declared. "That is really something."

"And you mean this pack of rocks here can do all that you said it can do?" Paul asked.

"You guys saw the results," Rinto answered. "We got here, didn't we?"

"We did that all right," Paul admitted.

"Rinto's more into engines and motors than I am," Fraxino commented. "He and I both did the project of growing and creating this crystal array."

"Dudes, you'd have laughed if you'd seen what all these two brought in from the mountains," Chispo declared. "They brought in all different types of rocks, plant material, metals, and crystals and extracted the impurities for use in growing these crystals. I rode up there with them several times and helped them mine some of it."

"Is that right?" Robert asked.

"That's right, man," Chispo verified. "I couldn't believe it when it worked! I was really impressed by it, especially when they took me to Earth on a test run."

"I'd say," Robert commented.

"How did you get these crystals to think?" Andrew wanted to know.

"That information is also available from higher levels of thought," Rinto answered.

"We listened to our dreams, figured out what combination of impurities we'd need, worked together, and grew this array," Fraxino informed them.

"That is really strange," Chris declared.

"It's like I said," Fraxino reminded them, "lot's of things are possible that one wouldn't think are possible."

"Rinto and Fraxino are geniuses, dudes," Chispo remarked. "There are actually very few of these rigs that can fly, let alone, teleport to other worlds like Earth!"

"Really?" Paul responded. "You mean this isn't an everyday thing here on Artenia?"

"Not at all," Rinto replied.

"That's why they land on a backroad way up in the mountains," Chispo said with a smile.

"Oh, I see," said Paul, laughing a little. "To not be seen by the general public."

"Exactly," said Chispo.

"Wait, Rinto," said Robert. "I thought you said you landed way up there so you wouldn't disturb the neighbors."

"He didn't want to say too much, man," Chispo replied. "Modesty."

"Oh, okay," said Robert, now realizing.

"If we were to tell everyone," said Rinto, "we'd have 500,000 visitors a day wanting to know how this rig works."

"Who's ever going to find out if we land and take off from a backroad way up in the mountains?" Fraxino asked them.

"Very few, if any," Paul answered.

"And whoever sees them way up there will probably just count it off as a UFO sighting," Chispo added.

"You have UFO's here on Artenia too?" Andrew asked.

"Yeah, man, just like you have them back on Earth," Chispo answered.

"So, dudes," Fraxino offered, "what do you say we go up in the mountains and cruise around, maybe find a few neat rocks or something?"

"Yeah, sure!" Steven replied with enthusiasm.

About this time, Mrs. Zapatero came outside. "Rinto, are you going to have time to mow the lawn and clean out the gutters before the day's out?" she asked in Artenian.

Rinto and Fraxino exited the vehicle-craft. "Yes, I will," Rinto answered back in Artenian. "Fraxino and I are going to take our new guests cruising up in the mountains."

"You all bring back *more* junk from those mountains," she complained. "You've got a huge pile of stuff back there. I wish you'd haul it off and get rid of it instead of hiding it all back there in those bushes."

"Mom, don't worry so much," Rinto requested. "It's all hidden back in the bushes anyway, and it's not taking up any yard space."

"Besides, we need that stuff for future projects, anyway," Fraxino added.

"Okay, whatever," she said as she gave in. "Just see if you can get to the lawn before the day's out."

"I will," Rinto assured her.

"What did you all just say?" Robert asked Rinto and Fraxino when they returned to the vehicle.

"That these two geniuses have crate loads of junk that their mother would *love* to get rid of," Chispo answered with a smile, "and that Rinto's been a lazy bum and hasn't mowed the lawn."

Everyone laughed because of the way he said it, in a joking manner.

"Let's go, dudes," Fraxino told everyone.

Everyone took a seat, and this time, Fraxino drove the vehicle-craft. Before going to the mountains, they made a side trip to the main highway to fuel up with hydrogen. Fraxino drove them into the service station where other similar looking vehicles were also fueling up at the pumps. An attendant came to the pumps and filled their hydrogen tank for them. All of the road signs and business signs posted were unreadable with hieroglyphic-like characters, except for the name of the fuel station.

"Exxoll," Steven commented. "Is that the brand name of your fuel stations?"

"That's it, man," Chispo answered. "Like the name Richmond, the name Exxoll never materialized into reality on Earth."

"But it was close with the name *Exxon*," Rinto pointed out.

"How much does your hydrogen fuel cost on this world?" William wanted to know.

"Right now, it's 11.6 duocibols per liter," Rinto answered.

"Our unit of currency is the Zotolan zúbola," Chispo informed them, "worth just over 6 of your U.S. dollars. Instead of having cents, we have duocibols, and there are 144 duocibols to the zúbola."

"It's all base 12 here," Fraxino told them.

Steven and the others noticed how similar to Earth Artenia was, a planet with human beings descended from those of Atlantis, living on nearly the same level of technological advancement as those on Earth. They all felt a strong connection to their new friends: Rinto, Fraxino, and Chispo.

Fraxino paid the attendant 7 zúbolas for the fuel.

"All rights, dudes," Chispo declared with enthusiasm, "Let's make for the mountains!"

"And we're off!" Fraxino exclaimed. He pulled out of the Exxoll station and accelerated rather rapidly, going through the gears quickly to attain normal driving speed. He took a different road which later put them on the same road they had been on earlier when they had descended the mountain. For the next half hour, Fraxino negotiated the hairpin curves on the gravel road and ascended to the top of the ridge once again. He turned left on the same road they'd earlier landed on and proceeded along the forested ridge.

During this time, Robert and his friends had a chance to tell Chispo about Tom, the galactic salesman, their travels, experiences, and adventures.

Al Nitak was now getting lower in the sky as Fraxino drove them for the next 15 minutes along the winding gravel road which followed the ridge top of the mountain range.

"Okay, we're almost there," Fraxino announced as he made a right turn and began to descend into a gully. He soon pulled the vehicle-craft over and parked it in a wide spot of the road on a curve and said for everyone to walk from here.

Fraxino and Rinto now indicated the direction, and Fraxino said, "The secret cave we discovered is down this narrow gully below us. Just follow us. It takes around 20 minutes to get there. Has everyone got a flashlight?"

Chispo, Robert, and his friends all followed Rinto and Fraxino through the forested gully which was somewhat difficult going because of large boulders and other shrubs in the way. Some had leaves, and others didn't. Birds of various colors flew above the trees and gave out their calls in the cool mountain air.

After they let themselves down a very steep and treacherous section of the gully with rock walls on each side, via a rope Rinto and Fraxino had earlier installed, they arrived at the cave whose entrance came into view when they reached the bottom of the dropoff. It was tucked underneath the wall of rock literally underneath the small, dry creek bed.

"This is it, dudes," Fraxino announced.

"Huh! Underneath a creek bed," Steven commented. "How interesting."

"Welcome to our secret cave," said Rinto. "Our research room is about ten minutes back, then up, and to the right."

As they entered, Paul asked, "Aren't you worried about other people discovering this cave and finding you out?"

"People here aren't like they are back on Earth," Rinto replied. "They don't come up here to party, vandalize, and leave beer cans and trash all over the inside."

"Dudes," Chispo added, "when people here visit the mountains, they come for useful and responsible reasons, and most of all they respect the environment."

"Yes, unfortunately, it's true," Paul admitted, "that caves and the wilderness back on Earth bear the brunt of such littering and irresponsibility, but still they could discover your secret project."

"Oh, we've got that safeguarded," Rinto assured him.

"Rinto and Fraxino got it all figured out, man," Chispo boasted in a friendly manner. "Their research room is accessible only via a high ledge well within the cave, and if that's not enough, the room is well recessed from view from below the ledge. They have to scale the ledge by a rope."

"And each time we enter and leave," Fraxino added, "we attach the rope and take it down."

"And I suppose you hide the rope somewhere in the cave as well?" Paul asked.

"We do indeed," Rinto verified. "In fact, we're just about to reach the rope now." Everyone stopped while Rinto reached behind a large boulder, gathered the rope and slung it over his shoulder.

"If that's not enough security for you," Fraxino added, "we've programmed our crystals to cause unwanted intruders to simply lose interest and leave the area before they even reach the room."

"That's right, man," Chispo added. "The crystals transmit telepathic messages to the energy field of any would-be intruder that there are other areas of the cave much more interesting, and he or she simply decides without realizing it to always go to other areas. It's much more effective protection than the doors and locks your people on Earth use."

"How can that possibly stop every would-be intruder?" Steven wanted to know. "You'd think some would be immune to such methods of protection."

"Well, I will admit," said Rinto, "there might be a select few, but the way our crystal protection works is effective for just about 100% of the population. People act according to instincts more than they realize, and since our crystals, being as intelligent as they are, communicate directly with the instinct level or portion of their energy field, their conscious minds therefore never realize it."

"That's really ingenious!" Steven declared.

"We're pleased with it," said Rinto. "Even still, very few people here on Artenia would intrude to do purposeful harm, but it's a good feeling to have such crystallized protection for our cave's research room up here in the mountains."

After they had walked through winding corridors and up and over ledges and boulders, Rinto and Fraxino both shined their flashlights on a ledge a little bit ahead of them.

"Here we are, dudes," Fraxino announced.

Rinto took the rope off of his shoulder and proceeded to sling the end loop of it to the top of the ledge where it caught on a hook they had previously installed. "Come on up, everyone."

"Are your crystals going to let us?" Robert wanted to know.

"Oh yes," Rinto assured him. "I've already telepathically communicated to them our intentions and that you all are okay."

"Oh, okay. That's good," said Robert.

One by one, they climbed the rope, treacherous and scary as it seemed to some of them.

"Whew!" Steven declared, relieved once he reached the top of the ledge. "I'm glad I got up that one without mishap."

"Yeah, me too," Andrew agreed.

Once everyone had climbed up, Rinto and Fraxino led everyone down more winding corridors for several minutes and came to an opening.

"We're here, dudes," Fraxino announced.

The room was approximately ten by ten meters with the ceiling being an average height of three meters. All around the walls were various sizes of crystals of different colors, the majority of the ones being clear quartz. They were securely fastened to the walls. The vibrant energy from the crystals could be felt within the room. In the far end of the room was a metal platform, its sides encased in glass, and to its left was a large shelf with all different types of minerals and flasks and bottles of liquids.

"This is where we grew the special crystals in our crystal array that we use in our craft," Fraxino announced, pointing to the platform. "We placed each base crystal on our platform. Next, we programmed our base crystals to be grown in just the right form and fashion, and with the help of our meditation and concentration at the right times and the right amount of added impurities, we were accurately successful with just what we needed."

"To grow the crystal array in our craft," Rinto added, "we telepathically communicated to our crystals around the walls what we needed accomplished, and with their expertise in knowledge, they caused the base crystals to take on and incorporate the right amount of impurities during their growth such that they would accomplish the wanted tasks in our craft."

"The power of the mind within these crystals is radical, dudes," Fraxino declared.

"Why are crystals hardly more than ordinary rocks back on Earth?" Paul wanted to know.

"Yeah, why aren't more people on Earth able to do this?" Andrew added.

"Well, dudes, in actual fact, there are only very few of us here on Artenia who can do this," Fraxino replied. "Most people on Earth, and here on Artenia as well, haven't yet achieved the right level of telepathic communication required to properly communicate with crystals. Rinto and I are blessed with that gift, and through practice, we have achieved the right frequency of communication with these crystals, and we've brought forth amazing and favorable results."

"Chispo here also has that rare gift," Rinto pointed out, "only he's not yet fine-tuned his abilities to the point that Fraxino and I have."

"No, I haven't been able to make crystal packs think and cause teleportation or anything to that extent," said Chispo, "but I can read crystals pretty well and can pick up a lot of insight through them."

"How did you all get blessed with your ability?" Robert wanted to know.

"Fraxino and I got it from Mom's side of the family," Rinto answered. "My grandfather had the same ability, and our family history says that the Rodigas right back as far as we can trace them had nearly the same special abilities that we have."

"My dad's aunt has special abilities above and beyond the norm," Chispo added. "It runs in my family."

"Isn't that lucky that you all are neighbors," Chris commented.

"Yeah, that is nice," Chispo agreed. "It's convenient, man. Rinto and Fraxino are like brothers to me. We all grew up together, and we run around and do things together all the time, don't we dudes?" He looked at Rinto and Fraxino as he said this last part.

"That's true indeed," Fraxino agreed. "Destiny or fate worked in our favor."

"Anyway," Rinto concluded, "that's about how our setup works. Mom wants me to mow the lawn. We need to go back home before it gets too late."

Everyone exited the room, and they made their way back to the ledge, descended the rope, took the rope with them, later hiding it in its place behind the boulder, and they walked back outside and into the dry creek bed.

On the way out, Robert asked Rinto and Fraxino, "Where did you get all of those crystals you attached to the walls of your research room?"

"Fraxino and I are, as you call it on your world, rock hounds. We've been gathering and collecting rocks and crystals all of our lives. We search the mountain slopes, creek beds, and go to rock and mineral shows and trade them for more desirable crystals for us.

"Most of our supplies," Rinto continued, "come from a place around 100 kilometers south of here in a huge, mostly flat, open terrain of boulders on the other side of the mountain range. There are loads of neat rocks and crystals in all shapes and colors. It's like someone just dumped them all there, but I don't know."

"I keep telling you, man," Chispo insisted to Rinto and Fraxino. "My feeling is that it's an ancient galactic dumping site from bygone days. My theory is," now talking to everyone, "that they used those dumped rocks and crystals for a short while for whatever they needed them for, but as their equipment and/or their needs became obsolete, they just dumped them in that remote area way away from any and all and left them there."

"I don't know, Chispo," Rinto disagreed. "It seems to me like such a waste for them to have just tossed those crystals instead of finding a better and newer use for them."

"Okay, man. Fair enough," said Chispo. "It's just that the area gives me that feeling every time I go out there with you guys."

"Where did you get that huge slab of Ulexite that you have in your craft?" Andrew wanted to know.

"Good question, dude," said Fraxino. "There's a large Ulexite mine in a canyon around 1,600 kilometers south of here on the other end of Zotola. Within the layers of bedrock, there's a huge vein of Ulexite. It's one of the few locations on our entire planet where Ulexite is available, as most of the sites of Ulexite are protected for ecological reasons. They sell the Ulexite by the cubic meter. Many people use it for clarity of the mind and for astral travel, but our main use for it is in our cruiser craft, needless to say."

"Instead of just astral travel," Chispo added, "we believe in physical travel."

"Yes, it's clearer and more definite," Rinto agreed. "Our controls Ulexite crystal is one-eighth of a cubic meter in our craft, plenty enough to accomplish all we need."

They had left the cave and climbed the rope up the wall to the upper part of the creek bed, now well above the cave entrance, and they were making their way back up the gully to the ridge top. Al Nitak was nearly on the horizon behind them, and its light somewhat penetrated the trees and forest canopy. A cool breeze blew in from the west behind them.

Upon reaching their vehicle-craft, they climbed in, and Rinto drove them back along the narrow winding gravel road and then made the descent back to Zantaayer, returning home. Al Nitak had just set when they arrived, and it was now dark.

As soon as they pulled into their driveway, Mrs. Zapatero immediately emerged from the house to talk to Rinto in her native Artenian language. "Where have you boys been all this time? We've had supper waiting on the table for nearly an hour! How are you going to mow the lawn now? It's already dark! Why did you all stay gone so long?"

"Mom, Mom, enough!" Rinto yelled, calming down her ranting and raving. "What's the big fuss about? We have our guests from Tennessee, and we needed to properly show them the cave up in the mountains. Don't worry, I've got headlights on the mower, anyway."

"Well, okay," she consented. "Tell your friends to come join us for supper."

"Okay thanks, Mom. We'll be right in."

Rinto told the others what they just talked about, and everyone stepped out of the vehicle-craft and went inside. Chispo joined them also. His parents were usually gone and nearly always ate out at night. So, it was a common occurrence for him to eat supper with the Zapateros. While Mrs. Zapatero had the tendency to rant and rave, Mr. Zapatero was a calm and easy going man.

Rinto and Fraxino's father had been a school teacher for numerous years at one of Zantaayer's high schools, and he had taught Chemistry. He was well liked by the community and by the students he had taught. For his unique interests, he knew a lot and kept up with events, including researching and investigating different topics at Zantaayer's central library.

"So, fellows," Mr. Zapatero inquired, "how do you like our planet, so far?"

"Oh, it's excellent," Robert answered. "Your sons and Chispo are a lot of fun."

"Yeah, they are intelligent, energetic souls," Mr. Zapatero agreed. "Isn't their craft the most unique thing you ever saw?"

"I'll say," William answered. "Those crystals are really . . ."

"Dad!" Rinto broke in. "When did you learn English?!"

"Just now, son."

"Now? But how?" Rinto wanted to know. "You never spoke it before."

"Well, I understand your surprise, son," he answered, "but it's suddenly easy for me. I just picked it up off the minds of your friends, here. Suddenly, I just know English like it's second nature. It kind of surprises *me*, now that you mention it."

Mrs. Zapatero looked at her husband with shock and surprise, evidently not having had the same knack or luck at picking up English like he just did. "How did you just up and suddenly learn English in the blink of an eye?" she asked him in Artenian.

"I just picked it up," he answered her in Artenian. "You might be able to do the same if you'd just calm yourself down, quit ranting and raving all the time, and relax, Sosta."

She gave him an angry look for that comment and marched out of the room.

"You don't have to go to such extremes about it, Sosta!" he yelled into the next room where she went.

"Oh, never mind her," he now said to the others in English. "She'll get over it. What were you saying to me?" now directing his question to William.

"Oh, let's see. Oh, yeah. Those crystals are really neat, both in that vehicle-craft and up in that cave in the mountains."

"Have you been up there to see Rinto and Fraxino's setup?" Robert asked Mr. Zapatero.

"Oh yes, several times," he answered. "My sons and I have been in on this somewhat together, and they've consulted me at times along the way."

"Yes, father-son relationships are important," Rinto added.

"I guess you were surprised to see," Mr. Zapatero now said to everyone, "that all of our fuel stations carry their name in your alphabet from Earth, the name Exxoll."

"Yes, we noticed that," Andrew replied, "and the name of the engine in their vehicle-craft is Richmond."

"Rinto said those names come from would-be manufacturing companies on Earth," Steven added comment. "The geniuses on each world of equal technological advancement get their ideas from the same source out there in the ether, from higher levels of thought."

"While that does bear some truth," Mr. Zapatero (Glecko) added, "that's not . . . Rinto, why didn't you tell them the *real* reason behind the origin of those names?"

"It's his modesty, dudes?" Chispo said to everyone. "He didn't want you all to freak out since you're from Earth."

"Chispo's right, Dad," Rinto admitted.

"Tell us, Mr. Zapatero," Robert requested. "What is the real story?"

"By the way, fellows, you can call me by my first name which is Glecko. My wife's name is Sosta. To answer your question, though only a few of Earth's top officials know this, Earth has been secretly conducting galactic trade for the better part of two centuries now. I'm sure you all have heard of the *Esso* or *Exxon* oil company, haven't you?" They nodded yes. "Well, they secretly expanded to a galactic level some 15 years ago and bought a monopoly on our hydrogen fuel companies here on Artenia and set up business under the name of Exxoll. They are an Earth-based fuel company, and it's in their interest to monitor from their Earthly business standpoint the selling of hydrogen fuel, in hopes to eventually do the same back on Earth. Even though they won't admit it on a public level, they know and realize that your fossil fuels pollute and won't last many more years anyway.

"As far as the name Richmond being stamped on all of our engines, while Rinto is right about that brand name never materializing on Earth, what he didn't tell you was that one of your major car manufacturers . . . I can't remember which one right now . . . behind the public's eye, met with some of the members of the galactic trade group and sold some of their engine and vehicle designs to them. It was decided that here on Artenia, all of the engines of that design at that time would bear the Richmond brand name. Since then, newer Richmond designs have been implemented and made here. My Tolejo was one of the first automobiles to carry the Richmond design engine."

"How long ago did that take place?" Chris asked.

"That's been some 35 to 40 years ago, I believe," Glecko answered.

"I don't see anything wrong with that," Paul stated. "If a few smart Earthly businessmen want to expand their ideas and designs and their business to a galactic level, then more power to them."

"I agree whole heartedly," said Glecko. "It's all in the name of worldly relations and friendship, isn't it?"

"That's right," Paul agreed.

"You know," Chris brought up, "why didn't Tom tell us about this?"

"Well, you know Tom," Paul commented. "There's a lot of stuff he doesn't know about Earth, since he's from Sirius B."

"Even though he's a galactic salesman," Steven added, "you can't expect him to know all of the secret galactic trading deals that take place."

They continued their discussion. Rinto soon got up from supper to mow the lawn.

"You're certainly welcome to stay with us," Glecko offered to Robert and his friends. "There's plenty of room on the floor inside, or if you want to camp outside in the yard, it won't be any problem at all, either way."

"Thank you," Robert answered for everyone.

"What are your plans tomorrow?" Glecko asked everyone.

"I don't know," said Robert. "Fraxino, Chispo, what do you suggest?"

"What about that old galactic dumping site south of here?" Chispo suggested.

"I was going to suggest the same, fellows," Glecko agreed. "That sounds like a good idea. There's an abundance of crystals out there."

"That's what your sons were telling us," Andrew commented.

"What about it, man?" Chispo asked Fraxino. "The galactic dump site tomorrow?"

"Sure, that sounds cool, dude," Fraxino agreed. "Let's go for it."

"Yes, let's go there," Steven added.

"All right, it's settled," Fraxino concluded. "When Rinto finishes mowing, we'll tell him."

"Go ahead and bring your backpacks and equipment in from the vehicle-craft," Glecko offered, "and you can spread out your bedrolls on the floor if you like."

While the others went to the vehicle to get their packs, Chispo motioned Robert over to the side. Robert was somewhat surprised, and immediately he was overwhelmed by the sense of familiarity he had earlier experienced. There was something about Chispo's voice and his way of speaking which kept reminding Robert of certain people he knew back on Earth, but he couldn't quite put his finger on who they were. Robert gave Chispo a glance, implying for him to wait up a minute. Then he got his backpack out of the vehicle while everyone else did the same and purposefully waited for all of them to go inside the house. Robert propped his backpack against the side of the house and walked over to Chispo. "Yes, what is it?"

"You're pretty much the leader or instigator of your group, right?"

"Yes, that's right," Robert replied. "Well, actually Morris was also, only he suddenly left our group today for details he wouldn't tell us."

"Come on over to my house," he offered. "I want to show you something."

"Yeah, okay," said Robert, his interest and curiosity quickly rising.

As they walked through the bushes dividing the Zapatero's and the Colancha's yards, Chispo said, "I don't know, but it's strange, man. I've got a feeling you're a little different from the others in your group. You're very familiar to me." This really surprised Robert that the feelings of familiarity were two way. They were now walking through his backyard.

"You're familiar to me, too," Robert admitted. "Like you said, it's strange. I can't quite figure it out."

"I pick up or sense that you have quite an interest in trees and plantlife," he said to Robert.

"Yes, how did you know?"

"I'm just that way, man," Chispo explained. "I can just sense a lot of things about people. Wasn't there another one in your group keenly interested in trees?"

"Yes, indeed there was," Robert verified, astounded at Chispo's accuracy, "but he also suddenly left us today. He's in love with a girl on Aleyone."

Chispo gave out a hearty laugh at that comment. "Just typical. That's lame, dude. People fall in love, and they just don't follow through with what they're really intended to do, man."

"I know what you mean, Chispo," said Robert. "The rest of us are mostly interested in travel and adventure. The girlfriends and falling in love can wait till later."

"I agree, man. I like the fun and adventure. When I'm ready to settle down, I'll find a girlfriend and maybe later marry, but that's going to be a while yet."

By now they had reached Chispo's house. "Looks like my parents haven't come home yet. They eat out most of the time. They're hardly ever home in the evenings. Come on in." He opened the door, and he and Robert entered the house.

"I'm willing to bet that Morris in your group fled the scene because of something he was afraid to know about," Chispo speculated.

"Yes, he *did* tell us that," Robert verified, again astounded. "He said Rinto was linked to something . . . Aw, Rinto and Fraxino told you, didn't they?"

"No, honest man, they didn't," Chispo insisted. "I just sensed it. You know they didn't. You've been with them the whole time since you all arrived here."

"Yeah, that's true," he admitted. "You really are perceptive, aren't you?"

"It's like Rinto said, man. I have special abilities, only not as fine-tuned as his and Fraxino's. The way I read you is the same way I read crystals, which brings me to the reason I brought you over here. Wait up a minute." He walked to his bedroom and returned with what looked like an egg-shaped piece of glass.

"What's that?" Robert wanted to know.

"One of my most interesting finds from that old galactic dump site I was telling you about."

"Oh really?"

"Yeah, take a look at it, man." He placed it in Robert's hand.

"Wow!" Robert exclaimed as he stared at it spellbound. "You found *this* at that galactic dump site?"

"Honest, man, I did. It's quite a piece, isn't it? It has quite a bit of meaning to it, too."

"I can imagine so," Robert agreed.

What Robert was looking at was an egg-shaped polished piece of clear quartz crystal with seven engraved white lines running around its equator. Numerous tiny stars were also engraved on it and dotted its surface. It measured ten centimeters from end to end. As Robert looked within, and as he turned the crystal in certain ways and viewed it at certain angles in the light, he could see a ghostly white outlined image of a hard Pine cone within, very much the appearance of a Virginia Pine cone.

"It's a Pine cone!" Robert exclaimed. "What an image to install within this crystal!"

"That's right, man," Chispo verified. "That's why I called you over here, because of your personal interest in trees. What do you make of it?"

"Well, I mean . . . This type of Pine tree whose cone is imaged within this crystal grows in Tennessee and in neighboring states as well."

"I noticed that last year when I was there, too."

"Does this type of Pine tree grow here on Artenia, also?" Robert asked.

"Yes, it does, up in the mountains, and it was likely brought from your Earth via galactic trade a long time ago. People also plant them in their yards here."

"The same is true in Tennessee, as I guess you noticed last year."

"I did, man."

"As far as what I make of it, Chispo, who did and how did they get that ghostly image of a Pine cone in there?"

"That crystal you're holding is at least 100,000 years old, and my best idea is that it came from Earth, judging by the Pine cone image. Some civilization back then was very technologically advanced, and they artificially grew crystals on a regular basis. Evidently, they could transmit image thought patterns into what they grew, and during the growing process, a ghostly outline of whatever image they thought into each crystal manifested because the appropriate molecules would align themselves in a different pattern or direction and cause the image to appear within when viewed at certain angles in the light."

"How interesting!" Suddenly a rush of thoughts entered Robert's mind, including the exotic crystal he and his friends had located on Aleyone and what Tom had told them of the ancient civilization on Earth.

"They were one smart civilization," Chispo added.

"Suddenly, Morris' last words entered Robert's mind. *Here Robert. Take this green*

Fluorite ball with you. Somebody you will meet is supposed to have it. You'll automatically know who he is when the time is right.

"He's the one!" Robert suddenly blurted out to himself.

"What?" Chispo asked.

"Oh, yeah . . . Uh . . . Wait here just a minute, Chispo. I've got something to show you, too. I'll be right back."

"All right, man."

Robert ran back over to the Zapateros and dug out of his backpack the green Fluorite ball that Morris had handed him and took it over to Chispo's house. As he entered his house again, he said to Chispo, "Morris sent me here with this crystal, saying someone I will meet is supposed to have it. I've figured it out. You're the recipient." He placed it in his hand.

"Wow, man!" Chispo exclaimed. "I'm really impressed by this! Thank you." He thought for a moment. "*That's* why we found each other so familiar. We've been meant to do this all along. This green crystal chose to come to me. Wait a minute! This came from the place James went to, right?"

"Yes, exactly," Robert verified. "You even picked up *that* information from that crystal?"

"I did indeed, man. Morris and you were the chosen couriers to bring it to me, and . . . Wait up a second." He paused as he continued to look at the crystal and concentrate. "Morris wasn't supposed to come because there's certain information here that he's not yet ready to find out until he's done some certain and specific types of research . . . about dolphins."

"Golly! How did you know that, Chispo?" Robert wanted to know.

"It's all recorded in the mind of this crystal, man. I just pick up information from them, just like that. Obviously, this green Fluorite ball and this clear quartz crystal have remotely telepathically communicated with each other and caused us to meet each other and to find ourselves familiar to each other, which brings me to what I was going to do next." He picked up the clear quartz egg-shaped crystal. "I am now placing this in your hands for you to take back to Earth with you. It's now yours." He handed it to him.

"Oh wow! Thanks, Chispo."

"No problem, man. I've been wondering what I was supposed to do with it since I found it two years ago, and now I've figured it out."

"Well, I'm really glad to have it," said Robert. "I appreciate this."

"I figured it was intended for someone I would meet in Tennessee, but I never found anyone who I thought was the recipient the whole time I was there. It's strange, man. Suddenly you guys turn up with Rinto and Fraxino, and you're the one! Destiny is really cool the way it works sometimes."

"Yes, it is," Robert agreed. "You said this crystal is at least 100,000 years old, didn't you?"

"That's right, man. I picked up that information from that crystal."

"Well, it's strange," said Robert, "but Tom, that galactic salesman we were telling you about, told us a story about an ancient race of technologically advanced people around 100,000 years ago on Earth. They lived in what is now Antarctica, and they grew an exotic green Fluorite egg with an orange pyramid grown within. That's the crystal my friends and I located way up in the mountains on Aleyone and took to Earth and placed on Mt. Timpanogos in Utah."

"Dude, that's got to be the same civilization that grew this one with the Pine cone," Chispo declared. "I feel sure of it. That's no easy process, growing a pyramid of a different color crystal within that egg-shaped piece of Fluorite. I'm sure there's got to be a lot more interesting stuff out there at that galactic dump site. Rinto, Fraxino, and I discovered it. Most of the general public is not really aware of it, man."

"Oh, really?" Robert asked. "Why don't more people know about it?"

"It's never been publicized, and it's well off the beaten path. Besides, most of the people here don't care to venture that far. The government here has no real interest in it. It's just wasteland to them."

"Do you think that . . ." Robert began.

Suddenly, the phone rang in the next room. Robert hadn't even noticed that Artenia had phone service. He hadn't even thought about it until this very moment.

"Excuse me, man," said Chispo. "Let me get the phone." He went into the next room, answered it, and chatted with the caller in Artenian. After a few minutes, he finished and returned to Robert.

"You didn't tell us that you all have phone service on Artenia," Robert mentioned.

"Oh yeah, man. Most people here have a telephone."

"Is that right?" Robert asked with surprise. "Isn't that something! So, Earth is not the only planet with an extensive phone system for communication. We need to get Tom to connect this world with Earth."

"Man, that would be cool! I could call up all my friends in Tennessee. We'll have to check that out."

"Okay, I'll tell Tom the next time I see him," said Robert.

"All right, man. By the way, that was Dad on the phone. He said he and Mom are out of town and are going to spend the night out on the road. What were you about to ask me earlier?"

"Let's see," said Robert. "Oh, yeah. Do you think that some top officials possibly know what that wasteland really contains?"

"They probably do, but to them it's just worthless archaeological junk, and they don't want to take the time to fool with it."

"So, they don't realize the value in it like you, Rinto, and Fraxino do."

"Exactly," Chispo agreed. "Well, truthfully I won't say that we are the only ones. There are other people from here who go out there rock hunting. They bring back various rocks and crystals and trade them here in the city, but they don't realize the true archaeological value of that galactic dump site. You heard what Rinto was saying earlier. Even he doubts it."

"Yes, I noticed. Why?"

"I don't know. Rinto's just like that sometimes," Chispo explained. "I feel that once we turn up some more interesting stuff out there, and I feel sure we are, he's going to be convinced, man."

"Oh, yeah," said Robert as something came to mind. "Chispo, what were you saying earlier about Morris and me being the chosen couriers?"

"You and Morris were the chosen ones to get this green Fluorite ball to me. These two crystals remotely telepathically communicated with each other to cause us to meet each other and to find ourselves familiar to each other."

"You mean crystals can cause that?" Robert asked.

"Oh yeah, man," Chispo verified. "They have their own way of thinking, and like Rinto and Fraxino's crystals in that cave cause people to visit other parts of the cave instead, this clear quartz crystal and this green Fluorite ball instilled thoughts in their unique way into both of us without our realizing it and caused us to find each other familiar. Of course, now we realize it. In truth, we've probably never seen each other before, but because the crystals made us think we were familiar to each other, the task they desired got accomplished. We've exchanged crystals."

"I just never realized that crystals could cause all of that," said Robert.

"Well, you see what Rinto and Fraxino have caused to happen with their abilities. When you have special abilities oriented toward communicating with crystals like they and I have, you can accomplish a lot with them."

"I want to tell you something about the exotic crystal that we placed on Mt. Timpanogos."

"Yeah, what?" Chispo wanted to know.

"Well, right before we transported ourselves to Antarctica when we were still on Mt. Timpanogos, Morris got a strange telepathic message about Antarctica, and it told him about the past civilization that used to be there, that it got catastrophically flooded, and about a few of them that never left. I suppose those few settled other continents there on Earth. What was really weird was the next thing Morris heard from the crystal."

"What was that?" Chispo wanted to know.

"It said, '60375 . . . Go meet him.'"

Chispo's mouth dropped open in surprise. "Wow, dude! That's unreal! That's my phone number, man."

"Really?!" Robert exclaimed.

"That's right, man, and you mean the exotic crystal that you guys dug up on Aleyone and moved to Mt. Timpanogos in Utah on Earth communicated *that* to Morris?"

"It did," Robert verified.

"That proves it, man," Chispo declared. "We were definitely meant to meet, and that large exotic crystal already knew it. Wait a minute . . ." He paused. "Morris had this green ball with him then. There's a link. It could be that the exotic crystal figured out the needs of this green ball by telepathically communicating with it and therefore remotely located me here, probably through communicating with the clear quartz crystal I just gave you, found out my telephone number in the process, and communicated that piece of information to later be used as verification by us. That's brilliant, man. What a coincidence!"

"You got that right, Chispo, and I'll tell you that as soon as Morris told me that number, it surprised me because I had earlier had a dream where I had called Morris on the phone but dialled 896-0375 instead of his true number of 896-0278."

Chispo thought for a few seconds and then said, "Our subconscious minds had already established a link on that level, and it was only a matter of time and destiny before we would truly meet up like we've done today. That's amazing, man! I'm really impressed by this coincidence and how well it worked. The minds of crystals and higher levels of thought and what they set up is truly a wonder to me sometimes."

"Something just came to mind," said Robert as he recalled something. "One of the first things you said to me was that Rinto caused his pack of crystals to think, but it looks like crystals think already."

"That's true, man," Chispo admitted. "I'll clarify that to say that while his pack of crystals could already think on one level, he actually grew them in such a way that he could program them to think to such a directional level that they could cause his craft to fly and to teleport to other worlds. It's sort of like he trained the crystal array to do what he needed to get accomplished."

"Oh, okay. That makes sense."

"The power of thought really works when you properly tap into it," Chispo added.

"Yeah, you're right. Back on Earth to most of us, it seems like magic. By the way, Chispo, what do your phones look like here on Artenia?"

"Not too different from yours on Earth. You can come on back. I'll show you."

Robert followed him into the next room and soon saw it sitting on a table. It was a dial phone but appeared to have more holes than normal in the fingerwheel. He counted them. In addition to that, each hole had an unrecognizable character corresponding to it.

"Twelve holes?!" Robert asked with surprise. "How?"

"We're on base 12 here, man."

"For your telephones, too?" Robert asked.

"That's right, man," Chispo answered. "Our currency is on base 12, our telephones, and a lot of other things."

"Huh! Base 12. Interesting," Robert remarked. "What are those characters corresponding to the holes? Are they numbers or what?"

"Those are our number characters or digits 1 through 12. Your '0' on the phones back on Earth is like our '12' here on the phones of our world, the last digit on the dial."

"So, you don't even use the same number characters that Earth uses?"

"No, man. We don't," Chispo replied. "Our base 12 is a carryover from our long-ago ancestors of your Earth's Atlantis. Several of your early cultures descended from the Atlanteans that stayed on Earth continued to incorporate base 12 into their society. One of them was Babylonia."

"Oh, yeah. They invented the clock. They liked the numbers '5', '12', and '60'."

"That's right, man, and your geometry and trigonometry uses base 12, like 360° to a circle."

"That's true. Did you all here on Artenia come up with this type of phone design, a dial phone, separately, or did the idea come from Earth?"

"Your Alexander Graham Bell of Earth invented the telephone, and via the galactic trade that Glecko was just telling us about, since we are close to equals on technological advancement, we started a phone system here on our world not long after you all did on Earth. Today, we have a worldwide telephone system, and it's all under one company called Astrelcom."

"What about your telephone exchanges?" Robert asked. "How do they work?"

"They're all on step-by-step, man," Chispo proudly replied, "every last one of them."

"Is that right? You mean they've not cut over to digital?"

"No, man, and they're not going to. Your Almon Strowger on Earth invented what became the most durable, trouble-free telephone line connecting switches of all the types that were ever invented. You can't find any better. Your Earth had some smart geniuses, man."

"But that must be a fantastic amount of wiring, especially in the larger cities."

"Yeah, but we accommodate that with subexchanges," Chispo pointed out. "It's not too bad, especially since we operate on base 12. We have 144 contacts per switch instead of the 100 that your Strowger switches on Earth use. So, we save a lot of space there."

"How many people does Artenia have, then?"

"Around 250 million, and that's enough for this world, man. Your Earth's gone wild on population growth with several billion people!"

"You're right, Chispo," Robert agreed. "Earth's way too overcrowded. How did you all not overpopulate this world?"

"Ever since we came from Atlantis, we've made conscious responsible efforts to keep our population from going, as you would call it, haywire."

"That's smart," said Robert.

"Man, we gotta be, or we'd deplete our natural resources faster than our world could replenish them. That's one of the worst problems with Earth. Most of your people don't realize nor consider the long term future. Come on outside, man," Chispo offered, now changing the subject. "I'll show you my car." They got up and walked outside.

"Yeah, I saw your car when you arrived this afternoon. What type is it?"

"It's a Velva Dibe as best as I can translate it to English for you."

They walked up to his car, a two-door, smooth, futuristic-looking, golden-yellow one. Chispo raised the front hood, revealing the engine.

"It looks like a V-8," Robert commented, "and it's got that name Richmond on it."

"Right you are, dude. These V-8 engines are not that common. About 90% of all cars here have the in-line 6-cylinder, but I like this V-8. It's got a lot of pep and

I mean it will flat get up and go, man!"

"I'd say so with that V-8," Robert agreed.

"Zantaayer is where they make numerous products used throughout Artenia," Chispo explained, "including cars like this Velva Dibe, Rinto and Fraxino's Velosa cruiser craft, their father's classic Tolejo, and also other types, such as the Skiivona. Come on back, and I'll show you the inside."

They walked around to the side of the car. Chispo opened the door, and Robert looked inside. It didn't look much different than what a car would have looked like back on Earth, only more futuristic.

"4-speed!" Robert remarked. "A sleek, fancy car like this has a stickshift in it?"

"All cars in this world do," Chispo informed him. "We like to feel in control of the vehicle we're driving."

"Personally, I do too, but you mean there are no automatics at all?"

"None at all, man. Some places on your world are the same way. Like go to Spain or France sometime. Automatics are next to none there."

"Yes, I've heard that from people who live over there," said Robert. "I think a bunch of European countries are the same way."

At the Zapateros across the bushes, the sound of the lawnmower ceased.

"Looks like Rinto's just finished mowing the lawn," said Chispo. "Let's go back over there."

They walked over, and Rinto saw them approaching when he emerged from the garage after storing the lawnmower.

"Hey, Robert and Chispo," he called out to them. "What have you guys been up to?"

"We've been chatting, dude," answered Chispo. "I finally found the right one to give that clear quartz Pine cone crystal to."

"Oh, really?" Rinto responded.

"Yeah, I traded him the green Fluorite ball for it," Robert told him.

"Oh, yeah," Rinto recalled. "You mean the one that Morris handed you right before he took off and left us?"

"Right."

"That's cool. That sounds good," Rinto commented. "Fate and the power of thought cause amazing things sometimes."

"Boy, you got that right," Robert remarked.

"Dude, let me tell you what we just discovered," Chispo began. "You won't believe the coincidences that took place . . ." and he proceeded to explain everything to Rinto as they walked inside the house. Fraxino and Robert's friends were swapping stories back and forth, and Chispo now did most of the talking as he and Robert related to the others the coincidences and synchronicities they had just discovered.

"So," Chris commented, "that weird message with that number Morris received was Chispo's phone number. Huh! That *is* really strange."

The others were very surprised that the number Morris picked up ever led to or had any connection to anything. Rinto and Fraxino, with their experiences with crystals and the power of thought, took Robert and Chispo's story with a grain of salt, but even they showed some surprise at this impressive coincidence.

"Well, what do you all make of this coincidence," Steven asked Robert and Chispo, "aside from it being an impressive synchronicity?"

"I don't know how you dudes handle it back on Earth," Chispo replied, "but whenever I experience a coincidence this far out which involves the meeting of people, I take it as a sign that we were brought together for a major purpose, that we are supposed to spend time together, and to be good friends for always."

"Well said, Chispo," Fraxino commended. "I agree, man. That's an excellent way of looking at it."

"By the way, everyone, in case you didn't know it," Rinto informed them, "Fraxino, Chispo, and I attend the equivalent of what you would call on your world . . . university. Chispo's going to begin his first year, and Fraxino and I are going to begin our second year. We just got out for summer vacation a week ago."

"Yeah, and we were going to travel around, anyway," Fraxino added. "Rinto and I went to Antarctica and found all of you, and now Robert, with the major coincidence between you and Chispo, I think we're meant to spend our summer or at least the next several weeks running around together."

"Or possibly doing research," said Rinto.

"Dudes, it could be that we all met to figure out more about Atlantis," Chispo speculated.

"I think you could be right," Robert agreed.

"We'll start with the galactic dump site, as Chispo calls it, tomorrow," Rinto offered. "Come on, I'll show you my computer setup. I've got to download the information I scanned in from those inscriptions in that cave on Antarctica."

Everyone followed him into another room. "Actually, I call it my crystal base," as he began to point it out to them, "and as you probably guessed, the base or central crystal is another large piece of Ulexite."

"It's not too different from what's out there in our craft, dudes," Fraxino added. "There's another assorted crystal array aligned and situated under the Ulexite, and the array serves as the information processor. Whatever it receives and sends is channeled through the Ulexite cube's many in-line fibers, numbering in the millions."

"I've also connected and interfaced a computer monitor and keyboard for more conventional use, as you guys would see it, since Fraxino and Chispo and I have more dealings with Earth than the usual Artenian. Over to the left of the cube," as Rinto indicated, "is an electrical converter box which serves to translate the data to and from the crystal array via the Ulexite cube. Through that, we're able to see the data on the screen of this monitor." Rinto touched a few buttons on the keyboard. "Let's see. Enter, store, translate to English, display information . . . There. That's got it." A few seconds passed, and then paragraphs of text in English started showing up on the screen. "There it is, guys," Rinto announced. "It says just what we discussed in that cave when I scanned it in."

"That is just incredible!" Steven remarked.

"I'm really impressed," Andrew added.

"You mean that Calcite crystal you used," Robert asked, "to scan in the data from the crystals interspersed with those hieroglyphics has already communicated to your main crystal array and has now translated it to English?"

"There it is on the screen, dudes," Fraxino indicated.

Robert and his friends read the English text on the screen, and sure enough, what it said matched what Rinto had earlier read on the spot when he had scanned in the data in the cave.

"This type of computer is very versatile," Fraxino told them.

"You see," Rinto explained, "when you have a crystal base computer working on the mental etheric level instead of the physical, you don't have to worry about the incompatibility between different programs, formats, or various sizes of disks and hard drives. Your Earth uses a very cumbersome computer system with the extremely complicated electronic circuitry and magnetic disk hard and soft drives."

"So, I'm assuming your crystal array serves as your hard drive storage facility?" Andrew asked.

"That's right," Rinto answered. "This crystal array stores appropriate information within it, and the rest of it is stored in the mental ether around it, in other words, the energy field. Actually, it works on a similar principle to the way a human brain works and remembers information."

Rinto and Fraxino continued to show them more features of their computer setup, all of which they found very interesting.

They looked at their watches. Earth time, it was 11 PM, June 29. It had been a long day for them: leaving the slopes of Mt. Timpanogos, visiting Antarctica, meeting Rinto and Fraxino, discovering the cave, then going with them to their home planet of Artenia around the star Al Nitak, meeting Chispo, and then having adventures there also.

"What time is it here?" Robert asked Rinto.

"From your time of reference, it's around 11:30 PM since it's been dark for two hours now."

"As far as the date goes," Chispo added, "we're on the tenth day of the sixth month of our year here on Artenia of 10130."

"Where did you get 10130?" Steven wanted to know.

"That's how many Artenian years ago it was when our ancestors settled here from Atlantis," Chispo replied.

"In your Earth years, it's around 12,500," Rinto informed them.

"How many months are in your calender, here?" Andrew wanted to know.

"We have 12, like you do on Earth," Rinto answered, "only each of our months has either 35 or 36 days, since we have 423 Artenian days to our year."

"According to historical legend," Chispo explained, "there was a hero from Atlantis who helped our Atlantean ancestors come to this world. His name was Cresma, and he was a leader in his day. Through galactic trade deals he made at the time, he arranged for more than 65,000 of his people to be brought here after the natural disaster on Earth. They arrived in a fleet of huge spacecrafts provided by the galactic trade union of that time.

"For his wisdom and good deeds," Chispo went on, "our world started a new calendar when the fleet of Atlanteans arrived 10,130 of our years ago. On the first day of every year, which is the middle of winter for us here in Zotola, all of the people have a festive celebration in honor of who he was. We call it the day of Cresma. It's a world holiday, man. All of the shops and businesses are closed for the day. Some people gather in public places while others gather and have family reunions, all to remember and celebrate his life.

"It's a time for looking back on the past and appreciating where we came from. There has been a book compiled which contains ancient legends and stories, many of which were orally handed down through the generations. It's called *The Book of Cresma* because Cresma is the central figure of many of the stories."

"So, you all meet and talk about Cresma while we on Earth meet and talk about Jesus?" Andrew asked.

"You could compare it that way," Chispo replied. "Jesus was a good man on your world like Cresma was, here on our world."

"That is interesting," Chris commented.

"Almost like a church," said Robert.

"In a way, that's true," Chispo agreed, "but on this world we don't so many of us dress up and take our finest cars to a specially constructed building like you do it on your Earth. Here, only a small percentage of our people actually go regularly, and they usually meet in office buildings, warehouses, or even private homes. Further, they don't worship the man like a lord. They just meet and talk about Cresma, and they discuss and interpret his various teachings, covering a different section of *The Book of Cresma* each time."

"Do people give each other presents on the day of Cresma like we do for our Christmas?" Steven wanted to know.

"Oh yeah. They do," Chispo answered. "Here, we gather with family members and friends, and we swap gifts as a gesture of showing appreciation for each other."

"Right, dudes," Fraxino announced, "we've got an adventurous day ahead of us tomorrow. Let's all get some sleep."

Everyone, almost everyone, felt sleepy, and they returned to the room where they had spread out their bedrolls. Chispo returned to his house for the night. Robert was unable to get to sleep for a long time. He really felt energized and excited after his coincidental meeting with Chispo. Everyone was impressed with the good character that Rinto, Fraxino, and Chispo possessed, and they looked forward to their adventures and exploration tomorrow.

Morning arrived perfectly sunny with clear blue-green skies. The Zapateros served them a good breakfast of food not too different from what they would have been served back on Earth.

Glecko was reading Zantaayer's newspaper. "Guys, here's a report from Earth about butyl chloride being used to ripen apples."

"They're ripening with *chemicals*?" Rinto asked with surprise.

"That's right. They can store the apples green for up to a year in huge kilometer-square warehouses, and right before shipment to the markets, they spray them with butyl chloride to ripen them."

"Dad, that sounds terrible!" Fraxino told him.

"They say the chemical evaporates off during transit," Glecko explained.

"Yes, but still . . ." Fraxino began.

"Wait, here's the good part," Glecko continued. "Through galactic trade, some of Earth's apple companies made efforts to break into the market with their butyl chloride laden apples. Some star systems accepted, but Artenia's agricultural representative from Zantaayer refused them on the grounds that they were not fresh enough, in addition to their failing the organic growing requirements for them to be granted entry to our world."

"Well, good," said Rinto. "We don't need to be eating apples like that."

"That's right," Glecko agreed. "No matter how much butyl chloride evaporates off, there's still going to be some residue left on the apple, and . . ."

They continued talking about it while eating breakfast.

Chispo soon arrived, ready to join them. Rinto and Fraxino gathered some lunch and supplies to take with them for the day. Robert and the others got food out of their backpacks and made some lunches.

Paul suddenly made an announcement to everyone. "Well, fellows, I just had a disturbing dream last night. I dreamed that my father had a major crisis at the plant and needed my help."

"What plant?" Rinto wanted to know.

"That's what we call our factory," Paul explained. "My father's company fabricates aluminum boxes and brackets for industrial use."

"What happened in the dream?"

"That's all I remember," said Paul. "I better transport myself home and find out. It may be true."

"You mean you may have to quit travelling with us this summer?" Robert asked with concern.

"I don't know until I find out, but I feel a strong urge to return home and make sure."

"Remember, Paul," Robert reminded him, "Once you show up, you're going to have to explain to your parents the real truth of our trip. If you turn out having to stay and help, you and your dad might as well go and recollect your trailer attached to the back of my station wagon, hidden behind the haybales in our barn. If you do tell them, please don't tell anyone else, and ask them not to also."

"Believe me," Paul assured Robert, "it won't go beyond me and my parents. I'll get them to believe me somehow. Later today, I'll return here and tell the Zapateros either way, once I know something. I have a feeling I'm going to have to stay and help out Dad."

"Well, okay," said Robert. "Good luck, Paul. I hope everything is okay back home."

"Yeah, you and all of us," he agreed.

As everyone began to see Paul off, William came forth and said, "Paul, wait up. I'm going to come with you. My parents know the real story. We'll transport to my house, and you can call your parents from there. Then we'll figure out how to get you home without your parents being suspect of our true travels."

"Good thinking, William," Paul told him. "Okay, we'll go to your house."

Everyone, including Mr. and Mrs. Zapatero gave them their best wishes. They stepped outside, and Paul and William proceeded to transport themselves away back to Earth. Glecko and Sosta and also Chispo expressed their amusement at their transport procedure with the pink glow and whirring wind since they had never seen that type of teleportation before.

"Well, dudes," Chispo announced, "I guess between you and us, that now leaves seven of us. Let's make for the galactic dump site."

Everyone followed his timely suggestion, climbed into Rinto and Fraxino's vehicle-craft, and they left. Rinto drove, and they passed through the central region of Zantaayer as Rinto, Fraxino, and Chispo pointed out landmarks and told them about their city. Most of the streets were two lane and narrow as they passed between mostly square-shaped buildings averaging ten stories in height. They turned right and left the central district and passed through the section of commercial establishments and stores. Further out, by the foot of the mountains on the south side of the city, they passed by several factories. Rinto pointed out the Velosa Cruiser Craft Company that grew and made their vehicle-craft.

The narrow two-lane concrete highway was busy with traffic as they reached the foot of the forested Ciruclar Mountains and began to climb on what, to Earth standards, was a narrow, winding, dangerous road.

"Is this the main highway leaving the city?" Steven wanted to know.

"This is it, dudes," Chispo answered. "We don't have big, wide superhighways like you all do back on Earth in the United States. I was amazed at the waste of space caused by unnecessary shoulders on many of your two-lane highways, and I just couldn't believe the grand scale of your interstates, man!"

"We operate more conservatively here on Artenia," Rinto told everyone. "We build just enough roads to accommodate travel needs and no extra. We believe in minimal impact, and narrow two-lane highways are much more conservative and respectful of the trees and the environment."

"Yeah, that's true," Robert agreed.

Rinto whizzed up the mountain and took the hairpin curves seemingly with the greatest of ease. There was plenty of traffic including transport trucks. For much of the ascent, the highway passed through thick stands of deep forest with plenty of tree limbs hanging over the road, making it seem as if they were going through a tunnel. It was very scenic. To their north was a clear view of the city and the ocean beyond.

The forest was dominated by Southern Beeches, but there were other trees as well. Many of them were Earth varieties like the Black Locusts, Hemlocks, Oaks, Poplars, and surprisingly, Acacia and Eucalyptus trees, evidently brought in from Earth's Australia. Higher up, there were Pine trees.

After 20 minutes of ascending, they crested the ridge, which was not as densely populated with trees, and they descended into a large dry plain ahead of them. It stretched out as far as the eye could see, and there were very distant mountains and mesas seen on the horizon. The highway descended in a much straighter and direct manner with only a few curves at first near the ridge top as the highway came out of a small, dry gorge and entered the sloping landscape to the plains below.

"If you look way out there and to the right," Chispo indicated, "almost to the distant mountains, that's where the ancient galactic dump site is."

CHAPTER 4

THE ANCIENT GALACTIC DUMP SITE

For the next half hour, Rinto drove them across the barren plains along the narrow highway which followed the terrain with humps and dips. For the whole stretch, there was a fair amount of traffic. Fraxino played some more Zotolan pop music in their holodisk player. The only types of plantlife in these plains were various types of Cactus and scrub bushes resembling Mesquites. Finally, they reached an intersection and made a right turn, drove for fifteen minutes, made another turn, drove another few minutes, and then stopped.

"We're here, dudes," Chispo announced.

The scenery around them was a huge boulder field of mostly brown colored rocks. To their southwest could be seen a mesa nearby, and further southwest was another range called the Placatera Mountains. The mountain range they had just crossed to leave Zantaayer now sat barely visible in the distant horizon to the north.

As everyone stepped out of the vehicle-craft, Robert said, "You weren't kidding, Chispo. This place is remote!"

"That's right, dude," Chispo proudly said with a smile on his face. "That's why so few people are interested in coming out here and also why we have such great pickings of what can be found."

"Right on, man!" Fraxino remarked. "Let's get to searching."

"Okay, fellows," Rinto directed, "the site is mostly west of here and further along the base of that mesa more to the south." He indicated by pointing in that direction. "We need to stay fairly close to each other so we don't lose each other, or if you're pretty good with landmarks, you can meet us back here at our vehicle-craft before it gets dark."

They put daypacks on their backs, followed his advice, and headed in a westerly direction, walking and hopping over various sizes of boulders. Cactus plants and other shrubs grew between some of the rocks, and they had to watch their step as they made their way closer to the mesa. As they proceeded, they began to notice various bits and pieces of crystals of different colors, and their quantities increased as they continued. In addition to that, some of them were large enough to draw their attention.

"Oh, neat! Look at this one," said Chris as he picked up a rock with white and orange and layers. It was the size of his hand.

"We're just getting started," Chispo informed him. "The good stuff is still further ahead."

As they continued, the ground between the boulders became increasingly covered with more broken pieces of quartz-like rock, the dominant colors being white, orange, and clear. As the richness in selection increased, Rinto, Fraxino, and Chispo began to pick up some pieces of interest and place them into their daypacks.

"Many of these rocks are broken like they've been dumped from the air," Robert commented.

"Yeah, I know, man," said Chispo. "That's been my thought on it, too. They really had a liking for this orange and white stuff. It's all over the place here."

"Have you all been digging to find rocks and crystals," Andrew brought up, "or just picking stuff up off the surface?"

"No, we never have done any digging here," Fraxino admitted.

"There's enough interesting stuff on the surface," said Rinto, "that we never saw a need to dig."

"If this is a dump site like Chispo says it is," Andrew suggested, "there might be a lot more interesting stuff buried underneath the surface."

"Chispo," Robert wanted to know, "did you find that Pine cone crystal lying on the ground, or was it buried?"

"Actually both, man. I found it further ahead between two large boulders," as he indicated and pointed further ahead, "and it was barely sticking out of the ground with one end exposed. The rain or erosion must have just uncovered it."

"It's amazing it didn't get broken or chipped," said Robert.

"I know," Chispo agreed. "They probably didn't dump everything from the air, probably just this orange and white stuff, seeing that's what mostly covers this area."

"So, it could be that they brought much of it in here by some sort of vehicle and dumped it that way?" Robert asked.

"Or buried it, too," Andrew added.

"You know, Fraxino," Rinto said as he paused and thought about it. "Of all the times we've come out here, we've never actually done any digging. Go back to our craft and get our pick and crowbar out of our tool box in the back."

"Right on, dude!" Fraxino eagerly responded. "I'll be right back." He made his way back to the vehicle-craft, walking quickly and sometimes hopping from boulder to boulder. The others continued toward the mesa.

Nearer the mesa, the orange colored rocks were not so dominant. There was a mixture of all different crystals and rocks from quartz to Fluorite to Calcite to name some of them. Robert and his friends were collecting some of the interesting specimens to later take back to Earth with them.

"Can you all read any information from these crystals?" Steven asked Rinto and Fraxino. "Like can you tell what they were used for or what information they might hold?"

"Dude, most of the information these crystals contained has been worn off over time," Fraxino answered.

"The rain and sitting out here over time like this just saps the information right out of them," Rinto added.

"Really? But you read those crystals in that cave in Antarctica," Steven pointed out.

"Yes, but those are protected by being in that cave," Rinto answered, "and they retained their information."

"Oh, okay," said Steven. "So, nothing ever cleaned them."

"That's right."

"Chispo, where did you say you found that Pine cone crystal?" Robert asked. "Maybe there's some more interesting stuff over there."

"Over that way, dude," he said as he pointed near the mesa. "It's between those two large boulders."

"Oh, okay. I see it."

"Come on over there with me," Chispo offered.

As he and Robert walked and hopped from boulder to boulder, the others went to areas nearby. When they reached the site, Chispo pointed between the two large rocks and said, "I found it right there in that low spot in the ground."

"Let's see if we can find any more," Robert suggested.

"All right, man. Good idea," Chispo agreed.

They began to search between all the rocks in the area. Nothing more than broken pieces of quartz and other crystals were visible. They turned over some smaller rocks, hoping to find something under them.

After a while, Robert said, "Well, I guess nothing else turns up." He turned over one last rock before moving on, and the sight of what he revealed caught his eye. It looked like a smooth, round piece of glass, and only the top of it was visible, the rest of what it was being buried. "Hey, Chispo. Look at this."

"Wait up, dude," he responded from a couple of boulders away. "I'm coming." As he came over, he looked where Robert pointed. "Wow, man! I believe you found one. Let's get it uncovered."

They spent a couple of minutes scraping away the dirt with the help of other nearby pieces of rock. Excitement and wonder built up in both of them as they finally and carefully pried it out of the ground with their fingers. Robert picked it up and got the dirt off of it. It was another egg-shaped piece of clear quartz crystal the same size as the one Chispo had given him.

"What's it got in there, dude?" Chispo enthusiastically wanted to know.

"Let's see," said Robert. He wiped the remaining dirt off with his shirt, and as he held it up to the sky and turned it at certain angles, he saw that it had a different type of tree cone, a very familiar one. "Hmm . . . Where have I seen that type of cone before?"

"Let's see it, man," said Chispo. Robert handed it to Chispo, and he looked inside of it and soon saw the tree cone image within it when the light hit it right. "Dude, if I'm not mistaken, I believe this type of cone belongs to your state tree."

"You mean the Tulip Poplar?"

"That's right," Chispo verified. "Here on Artenia, we call it the Flowering Sun Tree."

"Really? Let me see it again," said Robert with increased interest. Chispo handed it back to him, and Robert looked within it a second time. "Huh! What do you know! You're right. That *is* the Tulip Poplar cone. I just couldn't place it at first. What did you say you all call it here?"

"The Flowering Sun Tree, and you don't know your own state tree when it shows up on another star system," Chispo jokingly said as he poked him in his side.

"Oh, don't get me wrong," Robert responded. "I know my trees pretty well. It's just seeing that cone by itself, I couldn't quite place it. Had it been a leaf . . ."

Suddenly, they heard a shout in the distance nearer the mesa from one of the others. It was Fraxino.

"What?!" Chispo shouted back to them.

"Dudes, you're not going to believe what we just found!" Fraxino exclaimed.

"Yeah, what?!"

"A bunch of holographic plates or film, the best I can make of it," he shouted back.

"Cool! We're coming!" said Chispo. "Put that in your pack, Robert. Let's go see what they've got."

Robert quickly placed his new find in his daypack, put it on his back, and they went over to Rinto, Fraxino, and the others, quickly hopping from boulder to boulder as they went. In five minutes, they reached them. They were now almost at the base of the mesa's cliff.

"Yeah, what did you find?" Chispo asked just as they were arriving.

"Dudes, you're just not going to believe this stuff," Fraxino declared.

"Wow!" Chispo declared, his mouth dropping open. "Dudes, that's really far out!"

Robert looked on with quite a bit of interest and surprise.

There before them with Rinto, Fraxino, Andrew, Chris, and Steven standing around it, was a large, tarnished bronze metal box the size of a footlocker. They had already removed the lid, and it was stacked full of a bunch of black metal plates likely made out of bronze as they were heavy. There were twelve stacks altogether. Each plate had a bluish-purple smooth surface on one side, and the metal of each plate came up and made a lip on the four sides of each bluish-purple image in the same manner as a normal picture frame would on its picture. There was a large hole and a big pile of dirt next to the box, as they had just dug it up.

"Golly!" Robert exclaimed. "Who found this thing and how?"

"Steven found it," Rinto replied.

"Yes, we were just searching the ground," Steven explained. "Suddenly, I noticed a piece of metal sticking out of the ground, and when I reached for it, it wouldn't move. Obviously, it wouldn't because it was part of this whole box!"

"The next thing we did was dig it out of the ground," Andrew added.

"Guys, fate works like clockwork at times," Rinto commented. "It's strange that Andrew had just mentioned to us about more stuff possibly being buried. As a result, Fraxino went for our pick and crowbar, and we've already used them. Nice work on your intuition, Andrew."

"Thank you," he said. "It just seemed the practical thing to me."

"Look what I just found over there with Chispo," Robert said to Andrew as he took the egg-shaped quartz crystal out of his daypack and handed it to him.

"Oh, it's another one!" Andrew declared as he looked at it and then looked within it. "Hmm . . . It looks like a Tulip Poplar cone. Interesting," and he handed it back to Robert.

"He guessed it right away, dude," Chispo quietly said to Robert.

"Yeah, I noticed," Robert admitted. "I don't know why I didn't recognize it immediately. How did you know it right away, Andrew?"

"We have several of them growing in our yard," he replied.

"What do you make of all these plates?" Steven asked, bringing everyone's attention back to the box.

"Yeah, let me check them out, man," said Chispo as he reached for them. He picked up one of them, and he began to laugh in amazement as he inspected it. "Dudes, this is really far out! This could be some sort of ancient data storage, the best I can make of it." He continued to look at it and turn it at different angles to view its holographic surface. "Wow, man! It looks like it's holographic. Well, what about you, Rinto? You're the modest genius here."

"From what I could tell about this," he told everyone, "my feeling is that these plates were used for either image processing or for data storage as Chispo just said."

"Do you think it might possibly be some ancient historical data?" Chris asked everyone.

"I don't know," said Rinto. "It could be. It would be interesting if it is."

"Is it telling you anything telepathically?" Robert asked Rinto.

"No, I haven't been able to get much from these," he admitted. "Not everything works that way. Let's get this box back over to our craft. Maybe our crystal base in the craft, or better yet at home, can read and interpret these plates."

"Wait up a minute," Chispo said to everyone. "I'm just getting something." He paused as he continued to look at the plate in his hands. "I believe some of these plates were used to give instructions, sort of like a modern disk drive does for a computer back on Earth."

"You think these plates were used in conjunction with some ancient computer system?" Andrew asked Chispo.

"Dude, that's exactly what I'm thinking," Chispo enthusiastically replied. "Rinto, Fraxino, I don't know what it is, but I suddenly have a strong feeling these plates came from Earth."

"Really? From Earth?" Andrew responded.

"I believe so, man," Chispo went on. "Chris, I believe you're right on what you said. Some of these plates may actually tell a history of Earth's earlier civilizations, maybe Atlantis, or even further back."

"Huh!" Chris responded.

"Chispo, you're reading these plates better than we are," Fraxino declared.

"You just got to probe yourself into it, dude, like plunging or extending your mind into it, and when I do, the thoughts just come to me." He continued to look at it. "Wow! This plate must be the index plate for this whole set in this box, man! I believe we've just laid our hands on quite a treasure of information. I mean, if my thoughts are correct, part of this could be like an encyclopedia telling about Earth and its history, and this box was brought here via galactic trade to keep the residents of this world informed about its Earthly cousins, sort of like an information packet."

"Cool, dude!" Fraxino told Chispo. "We'll soon see what our crystal base reads from these plates."

"When do you think these plates were brought from Earth, if that's where they came from?" Robert wanted to know.

"Probably when the Atlanteans fled Earth and came to this world, or it could have been earlier," Chispo replied.

"Why would they have just dumped this treasure of plates here?" Steven asked everyone.

"This stuff probably became obsolete and probably forgotten about," Rinto answered, "and they had other means of storing the information. So, they probably didn't realize what they were tossing."

"It's like I've suspected for a long time, dudes," Chispo pointed out to them. "This is an ancient galactic dump site. They brought obsolete stuff out here and just dumped it."

"In case you dudes don't realize it," Fraxino explained to Robert and his friends, "we've been through rises and falls throughout our history like you all have back on Earth, and there's a lot that's been forgotten, especially the history of Earth's Atlantis."

"As well as the long-ago stories on this world," Chispo added.

"Yeah, that's the main reason my brother and I went to Antarctica to research it," said Rinto.

"Dudes, I don't know how you all feel about it," said Chispo, "but we need to keep this information to ourselves within our group and thoroughly analyze it before letting Zotola's news media get hold of it."

"That's right," Rinto told them. "Once they find out, they'd take these plates away from us for *proper analysis*, as they would call it."

"So, we'll do all the analyzing before they do," said Chispo.

"That doesn't sound too different from the way they'd handle it back on Earth when someone makes a major find," Andrew commented.

"Let's go ahead and take this box to the craft," Fraxino directed.

"How heavy is it?" Chispo asked.

"Very," Rinto answered. "It took all of us to drag it out of that hole."

"Let's each carry an armful of plates," Steven suggested.

"Good idea," said Rinto. "Let's just keep them in order, and be careful with them. We don't want any of these surfaces broken." Everyone lifted plates out of the box.

"I believe we're going to have to make two trips altogether," said Chispo.

"I think so, too," Robert agreed.

They more than halfway emptied the large box and took plates to the vehicle-craft while Rinto stayed at the site so they wouldn't lose its location. On the way back when they had nearly reached the site again, Robert spotted a piece of what looked like orange Calcite sticking out of the ground between two boulders.

"Huh!" he said to Steven who was nearby at the time. "What's this?" He picked it up, wiped the dirt off of it, and looked at it. From end to end, it was approximately 15 centimeters in size. When he turned it over, he got a real surprise when he saw several rows of what appeared to be some sort of holographic film in sections or frames firmly attached to a smooth, flat side of this piece of orange Calcite. "Hey, everyone!" he called out. "Look what I just found."

"Let's see it, Robert," Steven requested. Robert handed it to him. "Huh! How interesting!" Steven remarked as he inspected it. "It looks like some sort of film strip stuck in layers on this rock." He paused. "Now why would anyone paste strips of film on a rock like this?"

"Good question," said Robert.

Everyone else came over to see what he just found. Rinto came over from the box nearby.

"What did you find, Robert?" Chispo wanted to know.

"Here, take a look at this," Steven said to Chispo as he handed it to him.

Chispo began to inspect it and started laughing in amazement. "Wow, dudes! We're finding all kinds of artifacts today. This is part of an ancient holographic filmstrip!"

"Really?" Robert responded.

"Yeah, man. I've heard about these before . . . always wondered what one would look like. They come from Lyra, or as you would call it, Vega."

"Vega? Is that right?" Robert responded in a surprised manner.

"You know about Vega?" Steven asked Chispo.

"Oh yeah, man," he replied. "Legend has it that the ancestors of the Atlanteans came from Vega and colonized Earth long before Atlantis was founded. Isn't that right, Rinto?"

"That's right," Rinto answered. "They taught us that in history class a few years ago, a course which discusses the possibilities of our ancient human history based on historical artifacts."

"A few of these types of Calcite holographic filmstrips have been unearthed in other parts of this world," Fraxino informed them, "and they were determined to be from Vega."

"But we've never actually seen one before," Rinto added.

"How old do you think they are?" Chris asked.

"The ones that were unearthed were dated at around 150,000 to 200,000 years old," Fraxino replied.

"It is thought that people back on Vega used them for displaying in a special place in their homes," Chispo told them, "because each one seems to tell a sacred story. That's why they were attached to these pieces of orange Calcite, so they would look presentable."

"Orange does seem to go with the color of Vega," Andrew remarked.

Chispo began looking at the holographic filmstrip with concentration. "Oh, far out, man! Robert, what is it with you and those Tulip Poplars, your state tree? This particular filmstrip relates a sacred story about them!"

"What?!" Robert responded. "You're kidding! All I saw were a bunch of pink and purple colors on it."

"Take another look at it, man," Chispo directed as he handed it to him. "All you need to do is concentrate on each frame. Just insert your energy or probe the etheric part of your mind into each frame. Use your telepathy in that manner, and you can extract the story by reading the holographic images. You can also feel the sacred story empathically."

Robert looked at it with concentration as everyone else looked on. "No, I can't see any more than pink and purple colors."

"Turn it at different angles and look at it."

Robert did as Chispo suggested, and after a few seconds, an image flashed through his mind. "Oh, yeah. There. I just saw a quick flash of a Poplar forest."

"Concentrate, Robert," said Chispo. "Probe your energy and feelings into each frame."

Robert continued concentrating. Another image flashed through his mind. "It's a scene from what looks like Vega . . . mostly desert like. That's all I get."

"That's okay, man," said Chispo. "You're not accustomed like we are to reading things like this, but that's a good start."

"What all does it say or relate?" Robert asked Chispo as he handed it to him.

"Let me concentrate on it a few minutes."

"How or by what method did they make those holographic filmstrips?" Andrew asked Rinto and Fraxino.

"According to historical speculation," Rinto answered, "that ancient human race on Vega gathered a lot of experience with crystals, and some of them later settled Earth and founded a colony on Earth over 100,000 years ago, later becoming Atlantis. To make these holographic filmstrips, they probably used sophisticated digitalized holographic imprint machines, or you might call them developing machines. Actually, it works on a similar analogous principle to your typical camera film developing on your Earth. The telepathic thought processes of the story are holographically impregnated into the film, and then the strips are pasted onto Calcite for durability and pleasing appearance to the Vegans. After all, most of them contained sacred stories. Anyone with the right telepathic mindset can read them."

"I believe I've got it, man!" Chispo enthusiastically declared. Everyone turned to face him. "Dudes, this really is a far-out sacred story."

"Yeah, what is it?" Robert wanted to know.

"As best as I can translate it to English," Chispo began, "it says that the Flowering Sun Tree, or as you call it on Earth, the Tulip Poplar, is a sacred tree endemic to Vega, and that the early modern humans that first colonized Earth 1 to 2 million years ago took that tree species with them. They arrived in an area . . . Wait up a second. I'm getting an image in my mind." He paused. "The image appears like your southeast Asia. That would be China. That's where they arrived with the sacred Flowering Sun Tree. The early Lyran humans from Vega brought it with them because it's very fast growing, grows to great size, taller than native Earth hardwoods, lives several hundred years virtually disease free, and was a reminder of their home world. The wood is easily workable and is as soft and as light as Pine. Even in its old age, the tree maintains itself free of decay and keeps its vividness at the same time. In comparison to Earth's native hardwoods, the Flowering Sun Tree is superior in many respects!"

"You're getting all this information from that rock?" Robert asked in disbelief.

"Wait up, man. There's more," Chispo went on. "It even goes on to describe the way the leaves grow. Each new leaf comes out of a bud that looks like a seed or a seed pod. It's like a new beginning for each leaf, the way the buds of each twig grow one leaf at a time, stacked above and out from the previous one, a weird way of growing by Earth's standards since nearly all the rest of Earth's native hardwoods send out a tightly packed bundle of leaves from each bud. There is no close comparison to Earth's native hardwoods in that respect because the Flowering Sun Tree is truly extraterrestrial, being Lyran, or that is, Vegan.

"Here on the second row of holographic frames," as Chispo indicated and continued, "it gives a sacred legend about the flower." He paused. "Oh, cool! So *that's* why they call it the Flowering Sun Tree. That makes sense."

"What? Tell us," Chris wanted to know.

"It's a whole legend about the flower, saying that each flower holds a sunshine in its cup. From the inner part of the flower to the outer part, the colors change from yellow to orange to green. The sun in its yellow center gives forth through its orange flames to the green of life, the forest. To early humans on Earth, this was very significant and sacred." Chispo paused and then burst out laughing.

"What is it?" Robert wanted to know.

"This next part's hilarious, man," Chispo declared. "It relates here that while the species migrated into Europe in a normal manner over time even though that branch of them later got wiped out by ice ages, the Flowering Sun Tree arrived to Earth's North America by a much more exotic method because some guru among those first human colonists in what is now China conducted an experiment and accidently caused a whole forest of this new species to disappear. It wasn't till much later, many years later, that the end result of that blunder was discovered."

"What was that?" Andrew asked.

"Man, they were teleported there from China!" He paused. "According to the image of North America I'm picking up, it looks like the location was in what is now your Mississippi, and from that point, the tree migrated and flourished in nearly all of eastern North America."

"Wait a minute," said Andrew as he appeared to realize something. "That just made me think of something."

"Yeah, what?" Chispo asked.

"I just remembered . . ." Andrew began. "Something in the back of my mind tells me." He paused. "Yeah, now I remember. Near Vicksburg, Mississippi, there's a section of land with lighter colored sand, and they don't know how it got there because the only other land that matches it as far as the type and color of sand is concerned . . . is in China!"

"Dude, I'll bet that's exactly where that Chinese forest was teleported to!" Chispo declared with enthusiasm. "How did you know about a mysterious piece of land like that?"

"I went down there with my family when I was a child, and the locals told us," Andrew replied.

"Oh, wait!" Chris suddenly said as something came to his mind. "Robert, what did you tell us the scientific name of the Tulip Poplar is?"

"Liriodendron tulipfera."

"That's what I thought," said Chris. "Is it not a coincidence that since the Tulip Poplar came from Vega that the word Liriodendron would have some similarities to the word Lyran, which is the name of the constellation Vega is in?"

"You know," said Robert, "I think you're onto something, Chris." He paused. "Actually, that word Lirio comes from the Greek work Leirion which is even *more* similar to the word Lyran. Wow! What a coincidence!" as he realized it. "How did they do that, those that scientifically classified that species?"

"Sometimes," Rinto pointed out, "the older languages have more sense to them than you realize."

"They must have," said Robert. "By the way, Chispo, there's another interesting point about the Liriodendron."

"Yeah what, man?"

"There are only two species of it on Earth: one in southeastern China and the other in eastern North America, and that genus Liriodendron literally sits by itself in its classification. It's very unique."

"Then what this holographic filmstrip is saying is true, man," Chispo declared.

"I believe you hit it right on the head, Chispo," Robert told him, "and that's a *very* interesting story about its flower, too."

"Yeah, you're not kidding," Chispo agreed. He handed the piece of Calcite back to Robert.

"Anyway, guys," Rinto announced, "let's get the rest of the plates carried to our craft. Fraxino and I will bring the empty box."

Robert placed his new find in his daypack. He was amazed and felt somewhat stunned at the information that had just been revealed about the Tulip Poplars. They walked the short remaining distance to the box, gathered the rest of the plates, and carried them to the vehicle-craft with Rinto and Fraxino carrying the box behind them.

"Dude, I can't wait to see what this box of holographic plates has to tell us," Fraxino told his brother.

"You're not the only one," Rinto responded. "This is by far the most awesome thing we've ever turned up out here."

"Hey Chispo," Robert called over to him.

"Yeah, what?"

"Why would anyone dump any pieces of Calcite like this from Vega, seeing they have sacred stories on them?"

"That's what I want to know," said Chispo. "The same goes for that large box of holographic plates."

"Yeah, really," Robert agreed.

"The most logical reason I can come up with," Chispo explained, "is that some of those sacred pieces of Calcite must have been taken to Earth from Vega by possible later settlers. They must have been handed down through the generations, and somewhere down the time line, their true value was forgotten, and they got traded off and eventually brought here and tossed out."

"That sounds about right," said Robert.

"At the same time," Rinto pointed out, "fate let you find it today."

"Well, maybe it did," Robert admitted, "seeing that I also found that clear quartz egg-shaped crystal with an image of a Tulip Poplar cone in it."

They now reached the vehicle-craft. Rinto and Fraxino loaded the empty box onto the floor of the craft right behind the front seats, and they carefully placed all of the holographic plates back in the box in the same order they had found them, after which they placed the lid on it.

"What's up there on that mesa?" Robert wanted to know.

"We'll go up there sometime," said Rinto, "but for now, let's go directly back to our house with our precious cargo and see what it has to tell us."

Everyone followed his suggestion and climbed into the vehicle-craft. It was now early afternoon, and with Al Nitak now sitting high in the sky, it had become warm in this desert valley. Rinto started the engine and drove them back to Zantaayer along the same route they had used earlier this morning.

"You know, when we were on Vega," Robert said to Chris, "why didn't Ingra tell us the Tulip Poplars were from there?"

"Probably didn't know anything about them."

"She was somewhat indifferent, anyway," Andrew added.

"Yeah, I know," Chris agreed, "and she didn't mention a *thing* about sacred story stones."

"She probably didn't know anything about that either," said Andrew, and he laughed a little.

"I'd say not," Robert agreed, "or she just didn't care to tell us."

"How do you all have so much free time to run around and do your different projects?" Steven wanted to know, changing the subject.

"We come from a moderately wealthy family," Rinto answered.

"Enough that we don't have to work during our summer vacations," Chispo added.

"As you already know, we go rock hunting and collecting," Fraxino also answered, "and we swap, trade, and sell rocks, minerals and crystals at different rock shows and trade fairs."

"For the months of the year we are in school," Chispo informed them, "we also sometimes take jobs and save zúbolas that way."

"Here on this world, you don't have to work your tail off to make a living," Rinto explained. "The economy is designed such that a person can work part of the year and have enough money left over to enjoy life, pursue the arts, or do whatever hobbies he or she wants."

"That's great," said Steven.

Fraxino popped a holodisk into the on-board player, and they listened to some more Zotolan pop music on the way back to Zantaayer. They also continued talking.

An hour and a half later, they were pulling into the Zapatero's driveway.

As everyone stepped out of the vehicle-craft, Rinto said, "All right, guys. Let's all carry this box into the house and let my crystal base read them."

"These plates most certainly have got to have a wealth of information on them, dudes," Fraxino commented.

"Just be sure our media doesn't hear a peep about it," Chispo advised.

"Our lips are sealed in that respect," Steven assured them.

All seven of them heaved the heavy bronze metal box out of the craft and with difficulty, carried it into the house. Glecko and Sosta at the same moment entered the room from a different part of the house.

"Hi, guys. What have you got there?" Glecko asked.

"Oh, law!" Sosta exclaimed in Artenian. "What have you all drug home to clutter our place with this time?"

"A whole crateload of holographic metal plates," Fraxino answered her in Artenian.

"Robert here found two artifacts both having to do with the Flowering Sun

Tree," Chispo informed them.

"Oh, really?" Glecko responded. "That's one of the finest tree species known. It's got the best wood known for its workability. It's a bit strange how its wood always has those two tones in it of the colors blond and brown."

"Look what I found, Mr. Zapatero," Robert said to him as he unzipped his daypack. He took out his two finds and handed them to him.

"Oh, yeah," Glecko remarked as he looked at the egg-shaped quartz crystal. Then he looked at the orange Calcite. "Ohh . . .would you look at that! It's a sacred story stone from Lyra. I've never seen one before . . . always wondered what one looked like."

"That's what Chispo was saying," Robert told him.

Glecko stared at the holographic frames with concentration. "My goodness! It's a sacred story about the Flowering Sun Tree and how they got to Earth from Lyra. How interesting!"

"Anyway, Dad," Rinto said, "we're going to read these plates with our crystal base computer. Come on back with us. We're kind of anxious to get started."

"Right, okay," said Glecko. He handed the two pieces back to Robert.

"I'll leave you all to it," Sosta said in Artenian. "I need to return to what I was doing." She walked out of the room.

All of them heaved the heavy bronze metal box into the next room, set it next to the crystal base computer, and Rinto took the lid off.

"Wow!" Glecko remarked with surprise. "You guys *really* made a find this time!"

"Yeah, and we better keep it away from Zotola's news media until we've thoroughly examined it," Chispo added.

"Right you are," Glecko agreed.

Rinto took the first holographic metal plate out of the box and placed it on a tray just underneath the crystal array which began to read and process the data and channel the information through the large Ulexite cube situated above it. He switched on the monitor and the converter box, and in seconds, frames of images and various hieroglyphic characters started showing up on the screen. He touched some buttons on the keyboard, giving the computer some commands, and soon it began to display English text on the screen for Robert and his friends to read.

"Yes," Rinto verified, "this is an index plate for the whole set, just like you suspected, Chispo, and there are 144 plates altogether."

"Oh wow, dude!" Fraxino remarked. "Look at what all this set contains!"

"You got that right, man," Chispo said as he looked on.

"Sons," Glecko told them, "you really hit the jackpot this time! I can feel it."

As Rinto and his brother viewed the index list on the screen, Rinto said, "Based on what the contents on this index list says, it looks like this whole box is indeed from Earth's Atlantis and was brought here 10,130 of our years ago when they had to flee Atlantis and come here. The best I can tell, an Atlantean historical society dedicated to preserving its heritage and technology, put this set together right after Earth's natural disaster, the devastating crustal displacement."

"So, that really did take place," Andrew admitted.

"According to this documentary," said Rinto.

"And also according to what the hieroglyphic inscriptions said in that cave in Antarctica," Fraxino added.

"So, the last 44 plates," Rinto commented, "numbers 101 through 144 are entirely dedicated to programming instructions for their state of the art computers of that time."

"Wow, dudes!" Chispo remarked. "So the Atlanteans basically backed up all of their software onto some of these plates."

"In case someone in the future might have a use for some or all of it," Andrew added.

"Huh! Look at that one," said Chris as one of the listings caught his eye. "*Origin of the Hieroglyphics.*"

"Yeah, that looks interesting," Rinto admitted. "Plate number 36. Let's have a look at that. Reach in the box and find number 36 for us, Chispo," as he was standing nearest the box.

Chispo soon laid his hand on it. "Here it is, man," as he handed it to him. Rinto placed it on the tray next to the index plate, and after several seconds, information started showing up on the screen.

"Oh, cool!" Fraxino declared.

"Wow, man!" Chispo remarked. "So, it originated from mental telepathy and visualization."

"That and from pictures or visual scenes," Rinto added.

"Interesting, dude!" Fraxino remarked. "It says that there came a need to find an alternate way of telepathically communicating with those that had lost the natural ability to do so."

"I don't guess I've ever thought about how hieroglyphics originated," Andrew commented.

"I haven't either," Robert admitted.

"Huh!" Steven remarked. "What an amusing concept, how hieroglyphics originated."

"I suspected there had to be some good reason to their existence," Glecko stated.

"According to this," as Rinto began to narrate the text, "it says that early humans that colonized Earth from Lyra, or Vega, as you call it, communicated mostly by mental telepathic imagery. In other words, they transmitted visual images back and forth to each other to communicate. Very little speech was used. At the same time, the Lyrans were a sophisticated technologically advanced culture and also had interests on Earth, but there was something about the mental status about Earth which caused one Lyran culture after another to lose sophistication. The Lyrans kept having to recolonize Earth numerous times over a period of several million years and re-install their sophisticated technology.

"Around 150,000 years ago, they discovered that a different line of humans was being born with a slightly altered genetic setup, and among some of them, their minds were basically feeble when it came to communicating telepathically and visually. While all Lyrans had their telepathic abilities intact, this newly mutated branch of humans on Earth lacked the same ability. As it turned out, this new line of humans was genetically dominant in other respects over the original version of humans known as your Neanderthal man, and as they inner bred over the generations, the new version began to replace the original, purely telepathic Neanderthal man. This was a tremendous problem for the Lyrans, and they came and set up a new technology center in Antarctica which later became Atlantis.

"As a result of the loss of telepathic powers, people began to communicate by sound, and the Lyrans had to derive a basic language for their Earthly cousins to use. Their technology already had computers which operated on a holographic data storage principle, and they set up many of Earth's residents with computer systems or telepathic translators according to what it says here. These computers or translators served the purpose of telepathic communication between users who were lacking in the natural ability because the users could communicate by visual image transmission through these computers which were connected to a central network.

"The ingenious Lyrans set up their Earthly cousins with quite a list of icons or pictorial imaging representations that they could choose from, and they would set them up in any order or you might say, made sentences out of icons to communicate with each other. These icons were pictorial representations of around 2000 of the most common visual images and symbols that the original line of humans used to telepathically transmit to each other in communication. As they well knew, since a picture says a thousand words, communication by icons was much more efficient than verbal language. However, since not everyone had the luxury of these types of computers, the remaining individuals, the lower class, of the new line of humans had only the verbal language with which to communicate. So, it wasn't long before many humans were writing to each other and writing documents in the form of drawing icons. Over the generations and over time, the image detail of the icons was simplified, and eventually, hieroglyphics became the standard written text of communication, and hieroglyphics were widely used during the times of Atlantis.

"It goes on to say here that by 20,000 years ago, which is now around 32,500 years ago, the last of the original line of humans, the Neanderthal man, became replaced by the new line of humans, leaving only a small percentage of humans with decent telepathic powers intact, even though they were also of the new line. For this small percentage, some of the telepathic powers from the past Neanderthals must have carried through to those who were lucky enough, by chance, to inherit them."

"So, Earth's Neanderthals didn't die out after all," Glecko commented. "A mutation occurred, and the new dominant gene was powerful enough to replace them over thousands of years."

"That's right," Rinto answered and continued. "According to this document's predictions, it says that Earth's future cultures and civilizations will likely further simplify hieroglyphic text into a standard set of characters with numerous varieties of alphabets, written and spoken languages. As we all know, that's what happened."

"What an interesting concept," Robert commented.

"Yes, I'll say," Steven agreed.

"I had never realized that before either," Rinto admitted.

"That really is a wild concept!" Chispo enthusiastically remarked. "It does make a lot of sense, now that I think about it."

"Oh, wait," Rinto announced. "Here comes some more." Everyone became silent. "It says that after the Lyrans set up a spoken and written language among their Earthly cousins, they liked the idea so much that they took the language back home with them to use on their world. In fact, it wasn't long before non-telepathic humans began popping up on Lyra, though not in the vast numbers as they did on Earth."

"I wonder why that new line of humans showed up?" Chris wanted to know.

"I'd say it was a tradeoff," Rinto answered. "While there are advantages to the efficiency of hieroglyphics, there must have been a destined plan to incorporate written text languages like your English and other Earth languages to accommodate and meet the technological demands of Earth's future civilizations. It is true that a picture can say a thousand words, and while bunching together a group of icons can tell quite a story, it's not as precise nor as specific as the evolved written text which your Earth's later cultures would require through the time line. While in one sense, hieroglyphics degenerated, in another sense, they evolved and were modified to meet the peoples' needs."

"Evidently," Fraxino brought up, "telepathic communication with visual images served enough precision in earlier times, because based on our own telepathic experience with crystals, not only do you see images in your mind, you also pick up a whole array of mental thoughts and feelings with each picture."

"So, what you're saying," Chris commented, "is that when most humans lost telepathic communication capabilities, the visual images or icons no longer carried the mental thoughts nor feelings and therefore no longer carried the same meaning they used to."

"Exactly," said Rinto. "Evidently, Earth's later cultures, including our own here in the Orion system, needed a more precise written form of text which, as they saw it, was a vast improvement over hieroglyphics, especially since they had forgotten which mental thoughts and feelings went with each hieroglyphic character."

"Then why didn't the Atlanteans use alphabet languages like we do?" Andrew wanted to know.

"They probably didn't need to in those days," Chispo replied. "They were still accustomed to their past and had a better understanding of the meaning of the icons and hieroglyphic characters they were using."

"That was part of their culture in those days," Rinto explained, "and after most of them came here to Artenia and since only a few of them remained on Earth and spread their culture to other continents, in addition to a severe loss of population due to the natural disaster, the future generations did the best they could with hieroglyphics. Soon much of their meaning became forgotten, and they soon evolved into the different alphabets of today."

"What does your written language of Artenia compare to?" Andrew asked.

"It's also derived from Atlantean hieroglyphics," Rinto replied. "As far as which Earth language our Artenian compares to, I'd say it's most similar to your Earth's Indian language."

"You mean the native American Indians?" Andrew asked.

"No, the country of India," Rinto clarified. "I believe they call it Sanskrit."

"Oh, yeah," Andrew recalled. "I've heard that name before."

"How many languages does Artenia have?" Steven wanted to know.

"We have one standard language," Chispo now answered.

"That's all?" Steven remarked with surprise. "Just one?"

"That's right, man. Just one," Chispo replied. "We had a worldwide campaign of standardization some 50 years ago to facilitate communication and technological advancement since we are going through fairly rapid changes like your Earth is."

"In addition to galactic trade requirements," Fraxino added.

"I just couldn't believe the numerous varieties of languages your people on Earth use!" Chispo went on. "I don't mean to be critical, but your Earth's citizens take a lot of pride in their domestic cultural heritage, and they were basically too stubborn to give in to one standard language for the whole planet. That's what happens when you have several billion people on a world instead of 250 million, like here."

"You're right, Chispo," Robert admitted. "Most of us are too stubborn to standardize to one language. That's just the way we are."

"That would be a good thing for your Earth to accomplish," Glecko suggested, "to just turn the page and standardize."

"I know," Andrew commented, "but we Americans can't even properly accept Earth's metric system, let alone a worldwide universal language." He laughed a little.

"Hey, everyone. Where are Paul and William?" Robert brought up, suddenly remembering them.

"I don't know," Andrew replied. "Did they come back yet?" he asked Glecko.

"I haven't seen them," he answered.

At that moment, they heard a knock on the outside door. Glecko went to answer it. "Here they are right here, guys."

"Oh, really?" Robert responded. He went to greet them and brought them to where the others were gathered around Rinto and Fraxino's crystal base computer.

"How are you doing?" Rinto asked them.

"What's going on, dudes?" Chispo asked them.

"Look what we found," Fraxino told them as he pointed at the large box of holographic metal plates.

"You mean to tell me you just *found* that?" Paul asked in disbelief.

"What is it, dudes?" William wanted to know.

"A box of holographic metal plates," Fraxino answered.

Everyone proceeded to tell Paul and William about the box and brought them up to date on what they had missed today.

"I'm telling you what," William remarked. "That is really cool!"

"Man, I'm saying the same," Paul agreed. "That sure is an interesting find."

"So, can you stay with us, Paul?" Robert wanted to know.

"No, I was just about to tell you," he replied. "Dad's in a crisis at the plant, just like I felt."

"Oh, really? What happened, Paul?" Robert asked.

"Well, it's like this. Dad's behind on the plant's manufacturing of boxes, and we have customers on back order. Furthermore, Cabinet World, a major manufacturing chain, has offered to buy him out, but he wants to hold out and not sell. He's too proud to give in to a major chain, and I can't much blame him. He needs my help in managing his employees so he can get out there and travel to promote the business."

"So, you're not going to be able to travel with us anymore," said Robert.

"No, I've got to go back home. Dad needs my help right away."

"We went ahead and told his parents," William informed everyone. "They were shocked, but once we demonstrated how we transport ourselves, they were convinced, and they've promised to keep the secret among themselves."

"I guess it was necessary under the circumstances," Robert admitted.

"I'm going to go back home, too," William now told them.

"You too?" Robert remarked.

"Yes, my father's asked me to work with him for the phone company, and I've realized I need to begin saving money to go to college. It's only a little more than a year away."

"Well, okay William," Robert said to him. "I guess you know what you want to do."

"William, since you're returning home," Andrew requested, "can you take the cold weather clothing back home with you?"

"Sure," William answered. "I don't think you all are going to need it, here in Zotola."

Andrew, Chris, Robert, and Steven went to their backpacks and dug out the snowsuits and other warm clothing and returned them to William and Robert for William to take home with him and keep at his house for the rest of the summer. It had slipped Robert's and William's minds to recollect the loaned snowsuits and warm clothing from Morris and James when they had suddenly left the group when they were in the ice cave in Antarctica. They would sort that out at the end of the summer.

Then they recalled the crystals that Michael from Aleyone had given them. Andrew decided to send with William his Amethyst crystal. Chris decided to hold onto his piece of Hematite, and Steven sent his green Malachite home with William. He was glad to take them home for the others and keep them at his house for the rest of the summer. Robert also sent with William his Amethyst crystal and his piece of green Fluorite with Pyrite specks. However, he decided that for the while, he would store at the Zapatero's house the more recently acquired pieces, like the orange Calcite sacred story stone and the two clear, egg-shaped quartz crystals, each with a tree cone image within. They had also collected a few pieces at the ancient galactic dump site, and they sent them home with William, as well. He ended up having so much to carry that he divided the load with Paul for their transport trip home.

Robert and his friends continued talking with Paul and William for a few more minutes. Rinto, Fraxino, and Chispo wished them well, and everyone walked outside to see Paul and William transport away. It was sad for Robert to see two more of his friends part from the group, now reaching a total of four over the last two days.

"Well, like you told us this morning, Chispo," Robert commented, "that leaves seven of us."

"I know, man, but under the circumstances, they have other things they have to do."

"We're still here, Robert," Andrew reminded him. "These summer travels are too interesting to just quit and go home."

"There's no way I'm quitting," Steven insisted. "These travels have really enlightened me."

"Along with what those holographic plates say," Chris added.

"Don't worry, man," Chispo assured Robert. "We'll enjoy the summer with you, even though four of your friends just cut out on you."

"Yeah, we'll show you around Zotola and Artenia and join you guys on your travels," Rinto offered.

"Sure, that sounds great," said Robert, already feeling better.

"Dudes, let's look at some more of those holographic plates," Fraxino suggested. They returned to the crystal base computer and looked at the index.

"Huh! Here's one I'd like to see," said Rinto. "*End of Atlantis, Leaving, Reminiscent of the Human Beginnings.* Plate number 44." He reached for it in the box, took plate number 36 off the tray, and replaced it with number 44. Hieroglyphic-like characters appeared on the screen, followed by English text upon Rinto's typed commands. "Yep, that agrees with the writing on the cave's walls in Antarctica."

He began to narrate the text. "As many residents of Atlantis were experiencing premonitions that a major natural disaster was soon inevitable, they started making preparations to leave and flee to another world. They knew that one of the original cradles of human civilizations lay in the Orion System, and through galactic trade with some of the original humans that never left the Orion System, some 65,000 Atlantean residents decided to return there via spacecrafts capable of teleportation.

"Most of Earth's colonists had arrived via a former human colony, called Lyra, or as you call it, Vega. In fact, there were literally hundreds of human civilizations throughout the galaxy as the human race is far more ancient and dates back further than most people would think . . ."

"72 million years!" Chispo suddenly blurted out, reading the number on the screen.

"How's that possible?" Robert wanted to know.

"That's even before the dinosaurs of Earth got wiped out," Steven commented.

"Wait. Here's the answer on the screen," Rinto announced as more text appeared. He continued to narrate. "The original human stock naturally evolved on the third planet out from the star Al Nitak, the bottom of the three stars of the Orion Belt . . ."

"Dude, that's here!" Fraxino exclaimed.

"Yeah, I realize that," said Rinto. "Let me finish narrating, and then we'll discuss it." He continued. ". . . three stars of the Orion Belt, and when they achieved technologically advanced status, they began to travel to other star systems, one of them the Sol System where your Earth is. After its major disaster which wiped out the dinosaurs, they took many varieties of plant and animal life including primates and restocked Earth but decided not to settle it as a colony until some 60 million years later due to a galactic trade agreement made with other non-human intelligent civilizations, in addition to giving Earth's ecology a chance to properly stabilize itself.

"However, they were conducting a long-term experiment to see if some of the primates they took to Earth would evolve into apes or some humanoid form. Their reasoning was that if this occurred, Earth would prove favorable for human civilizations in the future. Besides, this evolved stock of apes could then later be genetically modified and improved upon and still carry certain evolved inherited genetic traits necessary for survival on Earth.

"Reminiscent of their original homeland, the Atlanteans came to an arrangement with Al Nitak's or Artenia's original inhabitants, and 65,000 people moved there, leaving around 400 residents on Earth to spread their culture around that planet. Many of them were top scientists and were very skilled in the crafts and art of levitation. They engineered and built the great pyramids in Egypt and in other parts of the world, leaving the mark of the Orion Belt in their work. They engineered the pyramids so well as to create a precise mathematical puzzle for Earth's future civilizations to figure out. A major shaft was built within the great pyramid to point precisely at Al Nitak, 76.3 light years away . . . Wait a minute . . . 76.3? How can that be?" Rinto momentarily said and continued narrating. ". . . precisely at Al Nitak, 76.3 light years away, at certain times as it crossed the 45° line of Earth's latitude which it did around 12,500 Earth years ago, and this was to signal to later civilizations the location to where the Atlanteans fled. At the same time, they set up a complex on Mars as an information backup system in case Earth's later cultures might destroy theirs, the pyramids on Earth. Eventually, Earth's future civilizations would figure out where to find us and re-establish contact."

"Looks like you all already have," Fraxino told Robert and his friends.

"Wait a minute, dude," Chispo declared. "Did you say 76.3 light years for the distance from Earth's Sol System to here?"

"Yes, according to this," said Rinto, "but I just always assumed that it was 1,132 light years, according to Artenia's scientists."

Robert and his friends watched as Rinto, Fraxino, and Chispo discussed the obvious discrepancy.

"Well, that's just it, Rinto," Chispo declared. "Maybe our so called accurate and modern day faithful scientists made a slight error on purpose and swept the truth under the rug, man."

"I don't know, Chispo . . ." Rinto began.

"Well, you know," Glecko brought up, "we depend on our scientists to do their job. I don't think they'd lie to the general public."

"I have to disagree, man," Chispo insisted. "I've never felt like we were so far apart from Earth as 1,132 light years, anyway. I'm inclined to believe Atlantean data long before I'd believe some of the data our modern day scientists tell us. I mean, really, how big would Al Nitak have to be to show up like it does, so big and bright in Earth's skies, and be 1,132 light years away?"

Rinto and Fraxino stopped and thought. "Well," Fraxino began, "we know Al Nitak is 1.6 times larger than Earth's sun, and if you viewed a star like Al Nitak at a distance of 1,132 light years . . . Wait. It would be a tiny speck, hardly visible! Something's wrong!"

"That's what I'm telling you, man," Chispo went on. "Think about it. For Al Nitak to be so clearly visible in Earth's skies, it would have to be a massive supergiant, which we know it isn't. So, there's only one possibility, that it has to be a lot closer to Earth."

"Al Nitak and the other two stars in the Orion Belt are certainly a lot brighter than the Pleiades Cluster," Steven pointed out, "and the Pleiades are around 360 light years away from Earth. So, the Orion Belt has to be closer than that."

"How many light years do your Earth's scientists list for the Orion Belt?" Fraxino asked.

"Well," Andrew answered, "according to our star books, they are listed as 1,100 to 1,400 light years away, the other two being Al Nilam and Mintaka, and I believe all three are classified as supergiants."

"That's it, man," Chispo declared. "I'll bet it's a galactic trade agreement secret, a scientific conspiracy to hide the truth!"

"Probably to keep the general public from freaking out," Chris speculated.

"Wait, Rinto," Fraxino said to him as he realized something. "What about the information from that cave in Antarctica? Did it give Al Nitak's distance from Earth?"

"I don't know. Let me pull it up." Rinto took plate number 44 off the tray, typed in a few commands on the keyboard, and pulled up what he had earlier downloaded from the piece of orange Calcite. "Let's see . . . distance to Al Nitak from Earth's Sol System." After a few seconds, information popped up on the screen. "Huh! Look at that . . . 76.37 light years."

"We're onto the truth, man," Fraxino declared.

"It seems to me," Chris speculated, "that the scientists lied on purpose about the true distance and size of Al Nitak so that people on Earth would look the other way and would not suspect that human life could be here."

"How do people here think about Earth?" Robert wanted to know. "Does the general public believe that people live on Earth, and do they know about Atlantis?"

"Oh yes. The general public of Artenia is aware of it," Rinto answered. "After all, our calendar is based on how many Artenian years ago it was when some 65,000 Atlanteans came here and settled: 10,130 of our years ago."

"Oh, yeah. That's right," Robert recalled.

"Actually, I think our scientists here on Artenia did tell us what they thought was the truth," Glecko pointed out. "It was probably an honest discrepancy on their part."

"Then what you're saying," Chispo said, "is that the distance misinformation fed by the galactic trade agreement to Earth's scientists accidently got taken for the truth here on Artenia and that most of us here have never bothered to check its validity for accuracy."

"It looks that way," Glecko agreed.

"I must say I never thought that one through before," Rinto admitted.

"I just got an idea in my head," Steven brought up. Everyone listened as he began. "You know, if the three stars in the Orion Belt really were supergiants, they would be unstable since both Earth's Sol System and the Orion System sit near the edge of the galaxy."

"How's that?" Rinto asked.

"Basically, supergiants belong in the center of the galaxy," Steven explained. "The centrifugal force of our slowly rotating galaxy would have long since slung the three stars of the Orion Belt far out of the galaxy during the last few billion years of their existence, into the remote nothingness of space between galaxies, had they been supergiants. Since they are normal size stars, that hasn't happened, needless to say."

"Steven, I believe you're right," Fraxino declared. "What would supergiants be doing on the edge of the galaxy?"

"Exactly," said Steven.

"You know," said Rinto, "I just wonder what information Zantaayer's central library has listed for the distance to Earth's Sol System, especially some of the older documents."

"Good idea, man," Fraxino told him. "Let's go and research it. Besides, we can show our friends some of Zantaayer's central district and give them a tour."

"Or if you like," Chispo offered, "I can take you all for a tour around the area if Rinto and Fraxino end up spending a lot of time researching this discrepancy. Knowing these two, they probably will," he said with a smile.

"That sounds good," said Robert.

"Well, guys," Glecko commented, "that's quite a wealth of information you all have found there. I'd keep those holographic plates to yourselves if I were you, and take only a *copy* of the data to the appropriate sectors of Zotola's news media."

"That's a good idea," Rinto agreed, "but that's for later, after we've thoroughly examined it."

"Oh yes. Certainly, son. Anyway, it gets dark in around four hours. We'll have supper ready for you then."

"Thanks, Dad."

"I'd better get back to what I was doing," Glecko told them. "See you all tonight." He walked out of the room.

Rinto and Fraxino closed down the crystal base computer and properly stored the holographic plates back in their box. Everyone went outside, climbed into the vehicle-craft, and Fraxino drove them to Zantaayer's center.

They arrived in 15 minutes, and he parked in front of the central library.

"Here's the key, Chispo," Fraxino offered. "Take them on a tour. Rinto and I will probably be here the rest of the day."

"All right, man," Chispo replied.

Rinto and Fraxino got out of the vehicle-craft and walked inside the library.

"Okay, dudes," Chispo announced. "Let's take a whirlwind tour."

"How about the beach?" Andrew suggested.

"Right on, dudes! Let's go!" Chispo announced with enthusiasm. He drove them through the central district. There were several streets with markets set up flea market style. They stopped and walked through some of them.

Robert bought a holodisk of the *Hydragyros*, the group whose songs Rinto and Fraxino had played at the time Robert and his friends were arriving to Artenia. He had no idea how he was going to play the songs once back on Earth, but he would figure that out later or better yet, buy a holodisk player to take back home with him. No matter what, it was an exotic souvenir with a great picture of the five pop artists on the holoalbum cover. The album was quickly becoming a success, already achieving many sales throughout Zotola.

Next, Chispo drove them northeast, leaving the central district, arriving at the beach ten kilometers away. There were plenty of people on the beach this afternoon.

"I don't know about you guys, but I'm going swimming," Robert announced.

"I guess I'll just walk the beach," said Steven. The others also decided to go walking.

The waves of the Elizabeth Ocean were fairly big as he rode them to shore numerous times. He soon got out of the water to join the others. As he ran down the beach to catch up with them, he noticed that several people called out to Chispo and that he was introducing his friends to them. The beach went on for several kilometers and basically lined the north border of Zantaayer between the two mountain ranges on the east and west sides.

After a couple of hours of walking and chatting with some of Chispo's friends, they returned to the vehicle-craft, and Chispo drove them to Zantaayer's university.

"You'll be impressed with our university, dudes," Chispo declared. "It's got a lot of modern facilities. Let's go over there, and I'll show you around."

The University of Zotola was just east of Zantaayer's central district. They arrived in ten minutes. The buildings were made out of stone and were very well constructed, and the grounds were beautiful with plenty of large trees and numerous varieties, now native to Artenia. Chispo led the way as they got out of the vehicle and walked through the grounds. He showed them the buildings where

Rinto and Fraxino take classes.

As they approached the dormitories on the grounds, Chispo announced, "Here's something that will probably get your curiosity up. Cloak Hall, as it could best be translated to English."

"What's that?" Andrew wanted to know.

"It's the name of one of the dormitories, man," Chispo answered. "There's a strange, ghostly legend about it that you can actually feel a change in energy as you walk through the corridor between these two buildings," and he indicated ahead of them.

"Hmm . . . That's weird," said Steven. "Is it like a vortex or something?"

"That's what I suspect, dude," Chispo agreed. "Many students suddenly receive telepathic thoughts and ideas from spirit as they walk though here, and they feel a little bit energized, as well."

As Robert and his friends accompanied Chispo through the corridor, all of them could feel the energy with a slight tingling in their bodies, almost like some form of fear. It was a unique feeling indeed.

Suddenly, Robert saw a flash of an image in his mind and heard a voice within his head say something. "Huh! Did you hear that?"

"No, what?" Andrew asked.

"I just saw a flash image of a piece of clear quartz crystal with an image of a mountain range within it, and a voice just said the word *Hichicera* to me."

"Wait a minute, dude," Chispo suddenly said. "I just heard something . . . Oh, yeah. The civilization of the green ones . . . Hichicera, Zotola . . . That's a small town in southern Zotola. There's supposed to be an ancient race of humans, way up in the mountains there, tucked in some remote, nearly inaccessible valley between two mountain ridges. It's not too far from the town of Hichicera."

"Do you think that image of a clear quartz crystal I just saw has anything to do with them?" Robert asked Chispo.

"Oh yeah, man, definitely. Legend says that they are an ancient and wise race of humans and that past human civilizations have learned a lot from them. It's very likely that such a crystal could be residing with them."

"Are you just now finding this out, Chispo," Andrew asked, "or did you already know it?"

"I've known there was a legend. They taught us that in history class a long time ago, but I've never known the details until just now. Somebody's telepathically sending me those thoughts."

"Hmm . . . That sounds interesting," Andrew commented. "I'd like to go find and meet them."

They proceeded through the corridor, and upon reaching the end of it, the tingly feeling went away.

"It must be some sort of telepathic vortex," Steven remarked.

"Yeah, it's a weird one, man," Chispo agreed. "Who knows how long it's been there. Let's go and see if the two geniuses are done at the library, and we'll go home."

They walked through the grounds back to the vehicle-craft, climbed in, and Chispo drove them the short distance back to the library.

"I wonder why you were given telepathic information about an ancient race of humans near Hichicera, Zotola?" Robert asked Chispo.

"I don't know, man, but there's got to be a good reason for it. We probably need to go down there and find them . . . probably a part of our mission this summer."

Chispo parked in front of the library, and everyone got out of the vehicle and walked inside. They soon found Rinto and Fraxino going through stacks of books in the basement.

"Hey, dudes. How's it going?" Fraxino called out.

"We took a tour of the central district, the beach, and the university grounds including Cloak Hall," Chispo informed them.

"That Cloak Hall is a wild anomaly, isn't it?" Rinto commented.

"So, dudes, what did you all find out?" Chispo asked.

"Well," Rinto answered, "it looks like nearly all the books that were written are based on scientific misinformation. All newer sources we've looked through say that Earth's Sol System is around 1,132 light years away. However, we also searched through some books which are much more ancient, and they do indeed say that the Sol System is around 75 to 80 light years away."

"Really?" Chispo responded. "What did I tell you? Somewhere along the time line, scientists swept the truth under the rug."

"I believe you're right, Chispo?" Rinto admitted.

"That's really weird," said Robert. "I'm going to believe the Atlantean data of 76.3 light years."

"Me too," Andrew agreed, "especially considering Al Nitak's size and brightness in comparison."

"Oh, by the way, Steven," Rinto brought up, "what you earlier said about supergiants being slung out of our spinning galaxy is actually incorrect. The laws of physics allow for supergiants to reside on the outer fringes of a galaxy."

"How can that be?" Steven wanted to know.

"It's easy," Rinto explained. "The center of mass or total combined mass of the galaxy is so many times more massive than the mass of any particular star regardless of its size, that any star will basically have the same orbital speed and be exposed to the same gravitational attraction by the galaxy's center of mass. So, the supergiants on the edge of the galaxy will be contained just as easily as normal size stars."

"Hmm," Steven commented and thought. "Yeah, you're right, now that you put it that way. Of course! I don't know what I was thinking about."

"It's okay," Rinto told him. "All people are subject to thinking erroneously at times."

"Such is life, sometimes," said Fraxino.

"You dudes ready to go back to the house?" Chispo asked.

"Yes, let's go," Rinto agreed. "Oh, by the way, we came across some interesting literature about a legend of an ancient human civilization living up in the mountains near Hichicera, Zotola."

"That's wild," said Chispo, "because as we walked through the corridor of Cloak Hall, a voice told me about the same thing!"

"Really?" Rinto asked with surprise. "What a coincidence!"

"And I saw a flash image of a quartz crystal with the image of mountains within it," Robert added.

"Let's go home," Rinto told everyone, "and go through our plates and see if we can find out more about them." He laid his hand on the book which discussed it. "Here, Fraxino. Go check this book out, and let's go."

They left the library. Fraxino soon joined them and drove them back home. As they pulled into the driveway, Glecko was outside and walked up to their vehicle as they parked.

"Supper's ready, everyone," he announced. "You're just in time. So, what did you guys find out?"

Rinto started to explain as everyone stepped out of the vehicle. "All the books which were written anywhere near the range of recent times say that Earth's Sol System is from 1,100 to 1,200 light years away, but we did locate some very ancient books in another part of the library which are in agreement with Atlantean data that it's only 75 to 80 light years away."

"How interesting!" Glecko remarked. "That doesn't add up. Something's fishy about that."

They all walked inside and related other stories of the afternoon including the revelation when they walked through Cloak Hall.

After supper, Rinto announced, "Let's see if those holographic plates say anything about an ancient race of humans in the mountains of southern Zotola."

They walked into the room where Rinto and Fraxino kept their crystal base computer. Rinto switched on the controls, placed the index plate on the tray, and soon pulled up the index list on the screen.

"What do you want to look at first?" Rinto offered as he pointed at the screen.

"Let's see," said Robert. *"Speculation on Future Human Philosophy Based on Atlantean Views.* That sounds interesting. Plate number 45."

Chispo located that particular plate and handed it to Rinto who placed it on the tray. After several seconds, information started popping up on the screen, and seconds later the crystal array automatically translated the text to English.

Rinto began to narrate. "Since it is a known fact that the human species is not originally indigenous to Earth, they were therefore instilled with a residual idea in their subconscious minds that Earth was only a temporary location for them to live and that they are not really from Earth. The Atlantean society was a highly technological society with considerable luxuries, and the general whole of that society was used to being cared for, pampered, and cleaned up after, like having a maid.

"Based on the combined thinking of their subconscious thoughts of not really being indigenous to Earth and their thoughts and views on the technology side of things, it was theorized that the Atlanteans were subject to faulty thinking because they relied too much on technology and as a result lost their true sense of ethics.

"For those people of Atlantis who are staying behind on Earth, the Atlantean Historical Society is predicting that since their conveniences and luxuries will be removed upon the evacuation and fleeing of some 65,000 Atlanteans to Al Nitak, they will endure with the residual idea of being wasteful in certain ways. They will have the feeling that their maid was taken away.

"They will develope the idea that they don't need to care since they are not really from Earth. Well into the future, they will have consciously forgotten that their ancestors settled Earth from another world, but the residual idea will have already been instilled in their subconscious minds from their long past Atlantean ancestral heritage, and they will therefore continue to treat Earth as if it is not really theirs, that they are only temporary residents of Earth, and that there is a better world to soon go to.

"This philosophy of the future human species of Earth will likely become so entrenched in human understanding and behavior that they will likely develope numerous religions and belief systems based on one of Atlantis' flaws in that society: that humans don't need to care, can pass the responsibilities on to others, and that they will one day move on to another world on which to live. While there will be some humans who truly care, the majority will likely follow the above said trend."

"Wow!" Steven commented. "It seems to me that it's explaining some of the origins of Earth's present day religions."

"That's just what I was thinking too," Robert agreed.

"Oh, look at that title," said Chris. "*Destiny, Alternate Realities, and Dreams.* Plate number 98."

"Yeah, I've got to *see* that one," Rinto agreed. He swapped plates on the tray. Information soon popped up on the screen, and he began to narrate.

"While it is a known fact that some of the past ancient human civilizations arrived to Earth by teleporting themselves from their world existing in alternate realities, it has been theorized that destiny originates from higher levels of thought in alternate realities. Quite often, humans have dreams, and though they don't always realize it, they are actually visiting those alternate realities in their mind and spirit, sometimes so clearly that they feel like they've actually been there. In truth, some of those alternate realities are where their long ago ancestors came from.

"In the true sense of reality, there are multiple levels of consciousness, and some of the higher levels are mentally out of reach or out of range. At these higher levels of thought in alternate realities, there are minds which operate and think and cause us on this level to experience coincidences and various synchronicities which cause us to think many actions are predetermined or destined. Through the complex system of multiple levels of consciousness, there is truth to this. As those beings at higher levels of reality plan their lives and thoughts, we at lower levels are sometimes affected by their actions."

"Huh! That's really interesting," Steven remarked. "So, what is actually going on are higher levels of thought, and since they know more than we do, they therefore cause our destiny to occur on this level."

"Exactly," Fraxino agreed. "In truth, when you really look at all the levels, there is no destiny. Each being on whatever level plans his life and causes his own destiny as a result."

"I don't know," said Rinto. "I believe in destiny. I mean, we are affected by higher levels of thought and by their plans. By definition, that is destiny."

"I'm telling you, those dudes from Atlantis were smart!" Chispo declared. "That's a really good definition of how destiny works."

"There's more still," Rinto announced.

"Oh, all right man. Go ahead," Chispo consented.

"It has been a long proven fact that each living human being has a soul or more precisely, a life force which causes the body to live and function. Many humans through their souls are linked to other worlds and parallel worlds in alternate realities. In actuality in some cases, the same life force can be maintaining multiple human bodies or even more generally, multiple bodies, and through sleeping and dreaming, communication takes place. In other words, a soul can live multiple lifetimes even though they may exist in the same linear timeline, and through dreaming, memories are swapped back and forth between the physical counterparts.

"In fact, many Atlanteans have reported experiencing memories of things they've done or of people they've known, and though it is very true and very real in the dream as if it were true to life, when they wake up, they realize that those memories are not true to the real world of this life, nor are the people true to this level of reality. It is therefore theorized that they are communicating mentally with their parallel world counterparts existing in alternate realities."

"Well, I will say!" Robert exclaimed. "I know exactly what they are talking about. I've actually experienced memories in dreams that seem very true to life until I wake up and realize that it was just a dream."

"There are probably more reasons why humans sleep and dream than we realize," Chris stated.

"It's probably very necessary for humans to sleep so their minds can communicate with those other levels of reality," said Rinto.

"It's probably a life force requirement," Chispo speculated, "that humans communicate with other levels of reality so that they can do their job properly such that the human body can be kept alive."

"And that's done through sleep," Andrew added.

"Oh wait," Rinto announced. "Here's some more." He continued to narrate.

"One human civilization, an original and ancient race always having lived on the original seed planet of the human beings, the third planet out from the star Al Nitak, is very knowledgeable and experienced in the ways of multiple levels of consciousness and alternate realities. Some of them in the ancient past have come to Earth and have trained our society in the above mentioned art. They are a wise society with a true sense of understanding the life and of conservation. They have never been very numerous, and they remain in one group, living a moderately inconspicuous lifestyle in one of the mountain ranges on their original homeworld. They have long been known as guardians of that world."

"Dudes, that's got to be the ancient race of green men!" Chispo declared.

"I don't doubt it, man," Fraxino agreed.

"That's three separate sources or reminders in a day," Robert pointed out.

"You know," said Rinto, "there's got to be a good reason why we've discovered these holographic plates."

"Somebody on a higher level of reality planned this out for us," Chris stated.

"I agree," said Steven. "I believe our destiny is to go find this group, meet them, and see what they have in store for us."

"It wouldn't surprise me if they are already aware of us," said Andrew.

"And already have plans for us," Chris added.

"You don't think they've set some trap for us, do you?" Robert asked.

"No, man," Chispo assured him. "According to our sources of information, this race of humans is entirely good. I pick up no bad feelings or vibrations."

"That's good," said Robert. "Actually, I don't either."

"Well, there you are, Robert," Chispo pointed out. "People who are true to themselves have true feelings, and those who properly pay attention to their feelings are able to make the right decisions and can nearly always avoid problems and danger."

"A person's feelings can serve him very well," Fraxino added. "Your feelings are always reliable and tell the truth of a situation."

"Well, what do you say, everyone?" Rinto offered. "Let's take a trip to southern Zotola."

"Yes, I'm for that," Andrew agreed.

"It looks like the signs are telling us to go there and meet them," Steven admitted.

"Especially seeing that I saw that flash image of a crystal as I walked through the corridor of Cloak Hall with you all," said Robert.

"Yeah, I wonder what that crystal flash image was all about?" said Chispo as he pondered.

"I'm sure it must have something to do with them," said Robert.

"Hmm . . ." said Chris, changing the subject. "*Feelings, Personality, and Friendships*, plate number 83. I'm curious to see that one."

"Yeah, let's take a look at that," Rinto agreed. He soon had it on the tray and began narrating the text that popped up on the screen.

"Throughout Atlantean society and human society in general, it has long been known to be a fact that human feelings are a form of telepathic communication and that when properly paid attention to, serve as a flawless warning device in times of potential danger. Without any spoken words, humans can telepathically transmit and receive feelings through the use of appearances, actions, or even through sleeping and dreaming. Empathy is a very sensitive method of communication.

"The Atlanteans frequently communicate empathically, and it is likely that those who stay behind on Earth may do the same, but it is possible that its importance may become forgotten or suppressed. Survival and personality will become important to the future generations of those who remain on planet Earth, and feelings may become considered less important. Since various luxuries of human society will no longer exist, and since it is suspected that humans will subconsciously consider Earth a temporary place to live, they may not see the need to consider and analyze their feelings nor their personality. They will just want to get through their life and move on to the next one on a better world.

"As a result of their subconscious ideas, they will for the larger majority of them consider friendships temporary and of little value, that friendships are to be taken for granted without appreciation. However, there will likely be some people who will rise above their subconscious instilled ideas who will discover the true value of friendships and the rewarding possibilities that come with true friends for life.

"While the 65,000 Atlanteans who are fleeing Earth are believers in the importance of the trueness of friendship, it is predicted that the majority of those who remain on Earth will generally come to consider friendships of little value and of little importance."

"Not a very good outlook for us, is it," Robert remarked.

"Well, it's only true," Rinto stated. "Look at all the wars your world has had, especially this century."

"Yeah, I know," Robert admitted.

"Well, at least among our group," Andrew pointed out, "we consider ourselves true friends and valuable friends."

"I know, and that's good," said Chris. "Of course, we all know that most people on Earth are just not true friends."

"Dudes, I noticed that when I stayed in Nashville last year," said Chispo. "I learned that most people are your friend if it's convenient to them and if they have a use for you."

"And if you have a falling out with one of them," Fraxino added, "they'll forgive you *only* if they need you or if they can think of a way to *use* you."

"Man, it's rare that an Earthling will forgive you simply to be your friend again," Chispo stated.

"Yeah, I have to admit you're right," said Robert.

"Here on this world," Chispo informed them, "when you have a friend, that person is your true friend, and for life! He will help you when asked and will defend you in times of danger, and he will confide in you, as well."

"That's really noble," said Steven.

"I've had people on Earth tell me that people need to love each other and forgive each other," Chispo explained. "The Bible says to, they tell me, but the truth is that many people forgive in theory after some falling out or fight, but they almost always feel the hurt after that and hold grudges. Think about it, man. How many times have you heard of people forgiving each other and completely forgetting the bad that happened in the past and restoring their friendship 100%?"

Robert and his friends thought for a few moments and said nothing.

"That's what I thought," said Chispo. "True forgiveness is completely forgetting the falling out and restoring the friendship just like nothing bad ever happened. It's like I tell you, man. Very few people on Earth know how to properly forgive. Even if someone has completely forgiven, the other person will usually bring up old grudges *way* on down the road and will cause the falling out all over again."

"I know what you're talking about," Robert agreed.

"I guess that's the way people are on Earth," Andrew added.

Robert and his friends continued discussing concepts with Rinto, Fraxino, and Chispo. They looked at more holographic plates. Several hours went by, and they went to sleep. Robert had a vivid dream that Morris came to talk to him.

"Uh, Robert? Are you there?"

"Morris, is that you?"

"Yes, it is indeed," he verified. "What have you all been doing?"

"Oh, lots," Robert answered. "We met Rinto and Fraxino's friend Chispo, and you won't believe their perceptibility of crystals, and their computer setup is out of this world. Well, you know what I mean."

"Oh yes."

"And we went to an ancient galactic dump site and found a box of holographic metal plates full of ancient history and philosophy, in addition to finding some really interesting crystals, including an ancient sacred story stone telling that the Tulip Poplars originated from Vega."

"How interesting!" said Morris. "Listen, have you found the right person for that green Fluorite ball I sent with you?"

"I sure did and right away. It was Chispo, Rinto and Fraxino's good friend and neighbor. It was obvious to me that he was the one to receive it. He had just given me a clear quartz crystal with an image of a Virginia Pine cone within. Well, the coincidences that went with the exchange made it obvious."

"Excellently done!" Morris commended. "It never ceases to amaze me how synchronous events can be sometimes. I knew you'd find the right recipient, and it was soon, just like I told you, wasn't it?"

"It certainly was. So, what's it like on Delikadove, the dolphin world?"

"I'm getting quite a bit of research done, and it's going well. Oh, this might interest you. In case you didn't realize it, in addition to the Tulip Poplar whose origin you've recently discovered, there's another oddball tree species on Earth."

"You mean the Eucalyptus or something else?" Robert asked.

"Well, there's a distant cousin to the Eucalyptus which the dolphins also brought to Earth from Delikadove. It's the *Platanus*, or you would know it as the Sycamore tree."

"The Sycamore tree? Really?"

"That's right. Pay attention to the bark and to the leaf buds just as the leaves begin to emerge each spring. It will be instinctively obvious to you."

"Is that right?"

"That's right. Listen, I'll tell you the real reason I didn't come with you guys. Yes, it's true I have dolphin research to do, so it's time well spent, and while I knew I wasn't supposed to meet your new friend Chispo, at least not quite yet, the real reason I reacted so suddenly and strangely in that cave on Antarctica was that I sensed a very strong feeling that the Orion Belt stars are blocked, and I knew I wouldn't get in."

"Well, we got here with Rinto and Fraxino. Why couldn't you come also?"

"Maybe I could have done, but I had to obey my instincts for my own safety. It would have been too risky for me to have come along. I might not have arrived. Besides, this is your trip now and is for you to deal with. You and your friends are one of very few Earthlings behind the scenes there. It's your destiny, not mine. You all are very privileged that you got in. Not even my essense can get in, being spiritually blocked from Earth."

"Then how are you able to talk to me now?" Robert wanted to know.

"I located your dream essense around in the ether, and I therefore accessed you in your dreams."

"That's very clever. So, communication is possible through dreams?"

"Oh yes, communication through the dream level is open. Listen, I'm glad I found you because Tom has another project for you guys if you want it."

"What project does he have for us?"

"I just paid Tom a visit, and he informed me that he suspects there is an abnormal amount of tension and stress among the people on Earth due to some very subtle and cleverly placed transmitter devices, likely some form of crystal, placed at strategic locations around the world by the Atlanteans when they fled planet Earth 12,500 years ago. Tom and I suspect that they were placed in order to block certain forms of access to the Orion Belt where the Atlanteans fled. They were supposed to last only around 500 years, but at least one transmitter is still very much active, and one aspect of its blocking and subduing power is that it is transmitting negativity and is causing people who live nearer to it to be more violent and aggressive. It could be that one or more of the transmitters were built to endure on purpose as a means of foul play by one or more unscrupulous Atlanteans and was placed as a long term experiment on the descendants of those who stayed behind on Earth. The location is northern Mexico."

"Northern Mexico?" Robert asked with surprise.

"That's right," Morris verified. "You might want to pay Tom a visit. He's at home on Sirius B right now. I'm beginning to lose you, Robert. You're starting to fade."

"Wait, I was going to tell you about an ancient race of green men here in Zotola."

"Find them. That's part of your mission. They can tell you about . . ." Morris faded from Robert's dream, and he woke up. He felt somewhat stunned with amazement, and he wondered, *Did Morris and Tom already know about the race of green men?* It seemed like they did. Robert now knew that he and his friends needed to find those unique people up in the mountains near Hichicera, Zotola, and now a discussion with Tom was in order, as well.

CHAPTER 5

HICHICERA, ZOTOLA

It was the morning of July 1, a crisp clear morning with no clouds in the sky. Robert had gone back to sleep after his surprising dream, and it was now four hours later. His friends were getting up and stirring around, packing up bedrolls and backpacks in preparation for the trip to southern Zotola. Now, better than later was a good time to tell his friends about his dream.

"Hey Andrew, Chris, Steven, everyone. I've got an announcement."

"Yes, what is it?" Andrew responded. Everyone became silent and listened.

"I had this dream about talking to Morris," Robert began. "He said Tom, the galactic salesman, is looking for us . . . wants us to do another project . . . something about this system being blocked from Earth since the days of Atlantis. He wants it cleared, and Morris said something about northern Mexico."

"Northern Mexico?" Chispo commented in a surprised manner.

"Yeah, and I also mentioned that I'd given you the green Fluorite ball, and he said that was excellent."

"Did you mention anything about the ancient race of green men?" Rinto asked.

"Yeah, that too," Robert answered. "As soon as I mentioned them, Morris said to go and find them, that it's part of our mission, and my dream ended."

"Part of our mission," Chispo commented. "Dudes, we're *definitely* going there now."

"Oh, yeah," Robert added. "Morris also told me why he didn't come here with us. He said he felt like it was blocked and that if he had come, he probably wouldn't have arrived."

"I don't understand," said Chispo. "Why would he have been blocked?"

"Morris just told me that was his feeling when Rinto and Fraxino offered to bring us here. He told me last night that not even his essense could penetrate the block, but last night he saw my essense floating around away from here, and he accessed it and entered my dreams that way."

"That's pretty smart going," Chispo remarked.

"Anyway, we need to to talk to Tom and see what's really up," Robert suggested. "Morris said Tom's at home on Sirius B right now."

Everyone agreed to it. Glecko and Sosta Zapatero served some breakfast to everyone, and they ate cereals and fruit.

"Well, guys," Glecko told Rinto and Fraxino. "You've really had a lot happen for you since you brought your new friends here from Earth."

"I know it, Dad," Rinto agreed. "Everything's falling in place just like clockwork."

"That's your special talent at work, sons," Glecko complimented.

"Thanks, Dad," said Rinto and Fraxino both.

They finished breakfast and loaded the vehicle-craft with their backpacks and other supplies. While Rinto and Fraxino checked over their vehicle, Robert decided to go visit Tom on Sirius B. Andrew, Steven, and Chris were comfortable talking with Glecko and therefore didn't want to go.

"Well, Robert, it looks like all your friends are going to play lazy on you," Chispo remarked in a joking manner. "I'll come with you. I'm curious to see what Sirius B looks like anyway."

"Okay, Chispo," Robert consented. "Let's go." As they walked into the backyard, Robert realized something. "You know, I just thought of something. Do you know how to transport yourself or teleport yourself?"

"No, man. I've never done it on my own, just inside Rinto and Fraxino's craft."

"That's what I thought," said Robert. "Here, stand in front of me. I'm going to take you. I'm going to put my arms and hands on either side of you, and as I think of the location on Sirius B, I'm going to transport us. It's been a while since I've taken someone else, so bear with me and remember how it feels so you'll be able to transport yourself from now on."

Chispo did as Robert said. Robert thought the certain way, and soon the pink glow and whirring wind overtook them. They disappeared from the Zapatero's backyard and in seconds made their appearance on the hill near the telephone station on planet Sirius B, 68 light years from Al Nitak. The weather was hot and sunny which was usual on Sirius B. Chispo successfully arrived with Robert. Needless to say, Chispo was considerably startled.

"Dude, I'm telling you that was far out!" he exclaimed. "How did you do that?"

"That's the special gift Tom gave me and my friends," Robert replied. "All you have to do is think of and visualize the location you want to go to, and then transport yourself there by the method I just showed you."

"I guess that must be the telephone station down the hill from us?" Chispo asked.

"It is," Robert verified. "Let's go call him and tell him we're here to see him."

They walked down the hillside which was sparsely covered with Cypress-Pine and Tamarisk shrubs and various Cactus plants. These shrubs dotted the surrounding hillsides which were also full of many red rounded boulders.

"Man, it's hot here, isn't it!" Chispo remarked.

"That's right," said Robert. "Such is life, here on Sirius B. Hot and dry, like Australia's Outback on Earth."

As they approached the telephone station, a lady in a white robe came outside to greet them. She was Manta, the same woman who had greeted Robert and his friends the first time they had come here one month ago. She telepathically sent for Tom whose residence was 20 kilometers away. After several seconds, Tom suddenly appeared on the scene, arriving by instantaneous teleportation.

"Hello, Tom," Robert called out.

"Hello, Robert. How are you?" He walked over to greet Robert and Chispo.

"Doing fine. How are you?" Robert responded.

"Just fine. Who's your friend with you?"

"This is Chispo Colancha from the Orion Belt from the star Al Nitak."

"Is that right?" He walked over to Chispo and shook hands.

"I take it Morris must have succeeded in contacting you," Tom now commented to Robert.

"He did. He came into my dream last night and told me you have another project for us."

"That's right," Tom verified. "Morris paid me a visit yesterday. I had meditated earlier in that day and called for you all. Morris was the only one who responded, and he informed me that he had separated from the rest of you so he could do research on the dolphins and that you all took off in a craft with two natives from the star Al Nitak."

"Right, that's what we did," Robert verified.

For the next ten minutes, Robert and Chispo related to Tom what they had done, from the exchange of crystals to the trip to the ancient galactic dump site, the treasure find of the box of holographic metal plates, and the clues they kept getting about Hichicera, Zotola. Tom listened to them attentively and with interest.

" . . . and Morris said there's a problem with the Orion Belt, that it's blocked from Earth."

"Yes, that's what I've discovered." Tom responded. "Robert, how did you and your friends succeed in getting in there, successfully arriving on that planet around Al Nitak?"

"We just hopped a ride with Rinto and Fraxino Zapatero in their craft. We had no idea there was any block in place, except now looking back on it, Morris suddenly felt strange and wouldn't come with us."

"Yes, Morris is very perceptive, as you well know, Robert," said Tom. "He knows a lot more than he lets on. That block was placed when the Atlanteans fled Earth, and it was not supposed to last over 500 years, but there's at least one of them still going strong as ever in northern Mexico, and it's having negative repercussions on those living near it."

"That's what Morris told me in my dream last night," said Robert.

"The Galactic Federation and I have discovered that it is very difficult to communicate with the Orion Belt with that block in place. We've tested out telephone signals, and the gravity waves become so distorted that the sounds are scrambled and undecipherable."

"How strange!" Robert remarked.

"I cannot teleport there since I've never seen it, but now that you've been there, would you be able to take me by your transport procedure?" Tom requested.

"Well certainly, Tom. Let's go," Robert consented. "Do you think you'll be allowed to arrive, or will the block prevent you?"

"I'm not sure. Let's go for it."

"Chispo, are you comfortable transporting yourself back home?" Robert asked.

"I don't know, man. Not yet. Take me back home and then return for Tom."

"Okay," said Robert. "I'll be right back, Tom."

Tom consented, and Robert took Chispo back to the Zapatero's backyard and immediately returned for Tom on Sirius B.

"I hope this works," said Tom.

"Me too," said Robert. "I'm going to concentrate very well." As the energy of the pink glow and whirring wind overtook them, both Tom and Robert successfully disappeared and seconds later appeared in the Zapatero's backyard.

"Well, I . . . I will say," Tom faltered and said. "We got by it! That's incredible! There are ways through and around anything."

Rinto and Fraxino and Robert's friends were waiting around the vehicle-craft, packed and ready for the trip to southern Zotola. After Tom got over his surprise at having successfully physically arrived, he walked over to meet everyone.

"This is Tom, the galactic salesman," Robert said to Rinto and Fraxino as he introduced him. They greeted each other and talked for several minutes. Tom was most impressed with their vehicle-craft and with the cube of Ulexite serving as the main controls crystal of that craft.

"Rinto and Fraxino, you two are brilliant!" Tom declared. "Never have I seen such a unique setup in all my days with the Galactic Federation. This crystal setup must be so smart that it knew how to penetrate that block without your even knowing about it."

"We never had any idea that there was such a block in place," Rinto admitted.

As Tom looked around, he realized that some of Robert's friends were missing.

"Robert, did some more people in your group go their separate ways?"

"Yes, James went to the Pleiades because he's fallen in love with Suzanne. Paul and William just went home yesterday. Paul's father had a crisis at his place of business, and he needed him, and William ran out of free time and decided to work with his father in the phone company and save money."

"That's the way things go sometimes," said Tom.

"At least Andrew, Chris, and Steven say they're staying with us," said Robert.

"It's probably for the better," Tom said reassuringly. "Now you have Chispo, Rinto, and Fraxino in your group, and I'm sure there's a good reason you've met and become friends with them."

"That's true. I'm sure there is," Robert agreed.

"Anyway," Tom began, "let me tell all of you at the same time what I've discovered." Everyone became silent and listened. "The Galactic Federation has requested that I add your star system to our inter star system telephone system, and the federation knows full well that there is a civilization here and that they are the descendants of those that fled Atlantis 12,500 years ago. They are fully aware of some of the trade deals that have taken place over this past century as your world here has advanced technologically, almost the same as Earth's. Like for example, you have a telephone system on this world. You have cars in agreement with federation design, and you more recently sell hydrogen at your fuel stations, all under contract and agreement with the intergalactic fuel company called Exxoll.

"The federation and I have been testing out gravity waves with some of your world's top officials, and the signals just don't properly arrive. They come through very distorted, scrambled, and quite literally in my view, time warped by whatever the blocking force field is that's installed. Evidently some or all of it exists as an

enveloping protector around the Orion Belt since we on Sirius B are also blocked, but what I suspect is that the subtle transmitter device is sitting on Earth and is booming some sort of a forcefield to the Orion Belt.

"Those transmitters by secret agreement with the Atlantean government were . . . and I say those transmitters because there were 12 of them installed at strategic locations around the world of Earth, shortly before the Atlanteans fled Earth and came to this world. Evidently, the Atlanteans wanted to be left in peace here on their new world for several generations, which is why they had the blocking devices installed, to last for 500 years and to keep the 400 or so Earthlings who stayed behind from accessing them. The agreement was that those who stayed behind could not seek help nor advice from those Atlanteans who fled Earth, according to Galactic Federation historical records.

"What we've discovered is that some of the scientists who stayed behind were somewhat dishonest and unscrupulous, and after the Atlanteans fled, they tampered with one or more of the devices, reprogramming them and causing at least one that we know of for sure to endure *far* longer than the agreed 500 years. We've scanned the Earth and pinpointed the location of the most problematic live transmitter to be hidden somewhere in the mountains of the region known as northeastern Mexico, and there are negative repercussions occurring there as a result.

"If one or all of you can pinpoint its exact location in northeastern Mexico and can neutralize it or switch it off or even destroy it if possible, there is a reward for the equivalent of Earth currency of U.S. $25,000, because we've got to set up telephone communication with the Orion Belt as soon as possible. The time has come, and the federation had recently forgotten that such a block existed, or they just didn't take it into account, until we proposed telephone communication and tested out signals and discovered it. Sure enough, when we checked our historical files on Atlantis, we discovered that such devices were actually installed 12,500 years ago when the Atlanteans fled Earth to come here."

"Tom, you know what I'm thinking?" Chispo brought up.

"What?"

"Seeing that Robert and his friends got here easily enough, and seeing how you just got here without any problem, it could be that people can physically come and go as they please and that it's not actually a block on the physical level."

"So, what you're suggesting," said Tom, "is that this block operates on other levels, blocking communication, telepathy, astral travel, and anything non physical while at the same time it freely allows physical travel entering and leaving this star system."

"Exactly," Chispo confirmed.

"That's a good point," said Tom. "You're probably right. I hadn't thought of it that way. Yes, that does make sense as I think about it. Galactic Federation members have been travelling to and from here for well over a century. Well, actually according to historical records, physical travel and teleportation to and from here has been occurring off and on right through the time line."

"So, the truth is, there's not a physical block," Chispo stated.

"That's very likely the truth," Tom agreed. "Yes, that's a very cleverly designed block indeed, one that permits physical travel entering and leaving but prevents the rest that is non physical."

"So, you mean Morris would have arrived if he had come with us in Rinto and Fraxino's craft?" Robert asked Tom.

"He may very well have been able to," Tom admitted. Then he hesitated. "No, not Morris, according to what he told me," Tom corrected himself.

"What?" Robert wanted to know. "What did Morris tell you?"

"Well, he didn't want me telling too many details about his real reason for his having been blocked."

"Aw, come on. Tell us," Chris urged him.

"Okay, I'll say this much," Tom consented, "in view of the possibilities that it may ease your methods of locating and eliminating the transmitter device. Morris, as I'm sure you're aware, is a very perceptive individual, much more so than any of us here, even including myself. Communication as far as mental telepathy, spiritual and astral travel to this star system is blocked from Earth and as a result, from Sirius as well. Morris will later inform you at the appropriate time of his specific reasons why he could not physically come, but I will say as much to the effect that physical travel to this star system is possible for the majority of people. Further, communication with this star system is possible through the normal dream level because dreams operate at much lower vibrational frequencies than spiritual and astral travel and mental telepathy. According to Galactic Federation rules, the historical records show that the agreement made with the Atlanteans was that the device would always allow dreams to pass through, along with physical human beings . . . except for people like Morris."

"That sounds discriminating," Steven remarked. "I just don't understand why he wouldn't be able to come here."

"Morris has his reasons for not telling," said Tom.

"I just remembered something else Morris told me in my dream last night," Robert informed them. "In addition to what he said that he might not have arrived, he also told me that it would have been too risky for him. That's all I know."

"Well, I guess we'll have to leave it at that," Steven admitted.

"Tom, did I hear you right that there's a reward for $25,000?" Chris asked.

"Yes, that's right," he answered.

"Golly! That's pretty good!" Chris remarked. "I know I'm in on the project."

"Me too," Andrew enthusiastically agreed.

"Everyone else, needless to say, agreed to take on the project of pinpointing the device in northern Mexico and eliminating it.

"Anyway, Tom," Rinto announced, "we're all loaded up and ready to drive to southern Zotola to search for the ancient race of green men near Hichicera. We got several signs yesterday that this is what we're supposed to do."

"Especially after my dream of talking to Morris and his telling me that's part of our mission," Robert added.

"Yes," said Tom, "my feeling is that's a necessary step for you to pursue to guide you toward pinpointing the device in Mexico. They probably can provide you with some insight and some clues."

"Do you want to come with us, Tom?" Rinto offered.

"Thanks, but I need to return to Sirius B. I have some business transactions to conduct with the federation this week, but if you could take me part of the way and turn me loose in the countryside, I'll teleport myself home. That way at least I'll see a little bit of your world."

"I wish you'd come with us," said Robert.

"I know, but I'll let you all take control of the project now. If I didn't have those business transactions I would come."

"Well, okay Tom. You know what you want to do."

"Anyway, hop in, Tom," Rinto offered.

Everyone boarded the vehicle-craft. Rinto started the engine and began to back out of the driveway. Glecko and Sosta must have heard them because they rushed out of the house at the same moment. "Wait, wait, Rinto!" Glecko shouted. Rinto stopped. "Could you take me to the city center and drop me off?" Glecko requested.

"Sure, Dad. Let's go." Glecko hopped in. Sosta waved as Rinto backed out of the driveway.

Glecko turned around and noticed Tom. "Oh! Who's this? You've got another person."

"This is Tom, the galactic salesman from Sirius B," said Robert as he introduced him.

"From Sirius B? So, you're the galactic salesman," said Glecko. "Nice to meet you." They began talking and carried on pretty good conversation until Rinto delivered his father in the central district.

"Yes," Glecko concluded, "that's all very interesting about the block that's been placed around our star system. I don't doubt it a bit. Tom, it's been a real pleasure conversing with you." They shook hands, and Glecko stepped out of the vehicle-craft onto the street. "Have a good trip, fellows." He waved at everyone as Rinto drove away.

He took them on the same highway out of town that they had taken yesterday when they travelled to the ancient galactic dump site. Tom was impressed by the scenery of the winding road as they climbed the Ciruclar mountain range leaving the city behind. The clean crisp air afforded them impressive clear views of the city and the Elizabeth Ocean beyond. Rinto crested the mountain ridge and proceeded down the two-lane highway into the outstretching desert valley beyond.

"Tom," Andrew brought up, "I remember you had told us that you thought Atlantis was where the Bermuda Triangle now is."

"That's right," said Tom. "I used to think that until I looked at the Galactic Federation historical documents about Atlantis. It surprised me that Antarctica is the location."

"Since we'd spoken to you on Aleyone in the Pleiades," Andrew told him, "we found out the truth of its location, too."

"And a whole lot more since we located those holographic plates just ahead at the galactic dump site," Fraxino added.

"Tell me about the holographic plates," Tom requested.

For the next half hour as Rinto drove south along the highway, they spoke about the contents of the holographic metal plates, their meaning and purpose, and they speculated on why the plates would have been dumped like they were.

"Rinto, do you think it's okay if we show Tom the galactic dump site?" Fraxino asked.

"Yeah, I don't see why not. I pick up no bad feelings at all about him. He comes across to me as a trustworthy and honest man."

A few more kilometers down the road, Rinto turned right and drove them to the site. Tom stepped out of the vehicle with everyone else, and they walked over to the interesting spots and showed him where they had found the large metal box and other interesting rocks and crystals. He was impressed with the site and picked up some interesting crystals to take back to Sirius B with him.

"All right, that's good," said Tom. "Let's go."

"Do you want to continue with us or teleport back to Sirius B?" Rinto asked him.

"I'll ride a little ways further. You can let me out on the side of the highway, and I'll teleport home."

They walked back to the vehicle-craft. Rinto continued driving. They took the side road back to the highway, turned right, and continued south. Soon they came to the Placatera mountain range on the south side of the large desert valley. Juniper-like shrubs dotted the scenery along the highway as the curves began, and they climbed uphill through a canyon with tall mountains on both sides.

"This spot looks good," said Tom. "I'll look around here a little bit, and then I'll go home."

"Okay," said Rinto. He pulled over at the next available turnout and stopped. Everyone else got out to look around. Tom wished them all well on their adventures.

"So, we'll contact you on Sirius B when we've identified and eliminated the blocking device in northern Mexico," said Robert.

"That will be fine," said Tom. "I'll notify the federation to allot funds for the reward. Best of luck everyone."

"Thanks, Tom," said Steven, speaking for everyone. "We'll see you later."

Tom left the highway, walked into the meadow, and disappeared behind some shrubs.

"Right, let's get moving," Rinto directed. "We've got a long ways to go."

They boarded the vehicle-craft and continued down the highway as it climbed through the canyon, finally cresting at a forested ridge, after which it descended into another large desert valley. Hichicera, Zotola was a 22-hour drive from Zantaayer, and it was around 1,600 kilometers away. Since the entire trip was along two-lane highways, which in some places commanded slower speeds for the mountainous curves, they could only average 75 km/h. Nevertheless, the trip was interesting, and they enjoyed it.

Half an hour after leaving Tom in the mountainous canyon, they entered the small town of Efforestow at the base of the south side of the Placatera mountain range, the northern end of the Salatrillo Desert. It was a pretty town with plenty of hardwood trees of Oak, Hickory, and Sycamore. One of the streams out of the mountains fed the town. So, it was like an oasis. They stopped to have a look around town and also ate lunch since it was now the middle of the day.

When they boarded the vehicle-craft again, Rinto pulled out a map which he had under the driver's seat. "Let's see, Fraxino. Which way do we want to go from here?"

"Dudes, let's take them by the west coast," Chispo suddenly suggested. "It's only a little bit longer that way. We can camp overnight there, too."

"Good idea, Chispo," said Fraxino. "Let's do that, Rinto."

"All right, agreed," Rinto consented. "So, we'll take this highway across the desert valley to Harkelrhodes, cross the Colerene mountain range, go through the town of Pilares, and go around another 100 kilometers to arrive at the coast town of Lominac. We'll camp near there and go on to Hichicera tomorrow."

"Sounds like a good plan, dude," Fraxino approved.

"Right, let's be off," Rinto announced. "It's around 85 kilometers to Harkelrhodes. We've still got plenty of hydrogen fuel left. We'll fill up at the Exxoll station there." He started the engine and drove them out of town.

"That was a nice town, Efforestow," Robert commented. "It's right at the base of the mountains, and it looks like a tranquil place to live."

"Efforestow is one of the best towns in Zotola, man," Chispo informed him. "Sometimes, I come down here just to kick back and relax. It's a cool place to get away from it all. There are some neat trails that go up in the mountains, too."

"Really?" Andrew suddenly responded. "Let's all go sometime."

"All right, dudes," Chispo consented. "When we finish our project in Mexico, we'll return here sometime."

"Consider it planned," said Steven.

Along the way, they listened to Zotolan pop music from the on-board holodisk player.

The desert crossing was flat with sparse vegetation of shrubs and Cactus. The narrow two-lane highway was straight as an arrow as it gradually descended to the center of the valley 35 kilometers away, flattened out, and slowly made the gradual climb up the other side for an additional 30 kilometers and then entered some lowland hills. The highway made a right turn and entered a canyon and climbed in altitude, reaching the medium-sized town of Harkelrhodes at the upper end of the canyon situated at the base of the Colerene Mountains.

Rinto pulled over at the Exxoll station at the entrance to the town.

"Golly, man!" Rinto said to his brother. "Gone up again!"

"11.7 duocibols per liter," said Fraxino as he read the price on the pump.

"Man, it only stayed at 11.6 for a month," Chispo complained.

The attendant came to the pumps and filled their hydrogen tank for them. There were vendors on foot carrying knick knacks and other items, and they walked from customer to customer, offering to sell what they had. One man was selling miniature glass encased cabinets displaying various types of rocks and crystals.

"Oh neat, dudes!" Fraxino exclaimed when he saw the cabinets. He immediately stepped down from the vehicle, made a deal with the man, and bought all three of his cabinets. Fraxino came back grinning from ear to ear, glad to have what he just purchased. "Look at these rocks in these cabinets, dudes. They only cost me one zúbola each! Some of them are just *perfect* for our collection. Here, Robert. This cabinet is for you and your friends. I'm keeping one. Here, you can give this other one to Tom." He handed two of the cabinets to Robert.

"Thanks, Fraxino," said Robert. "This is great!" Inside were three rows of five rocks and minerals each. "We'll treasure this, a souvenir from Harkelrhodes, Zotola."

After filling up with fuel and paying for it, Fraxino now did the driving. They left the station and drove through Harkelrhodes. The highway went right through the center of town, and the streets were narrow and considerably crowded with people, shoppers, and vehicles, including trucks parked in front of shops for loading and unloading.

After they made it through the congestion, Chispo took out another holodisk, popped it into the player, and they listened to some more music.

The highway climbed through the canyon with plenty of hairpin curves for an elevation gain of 2,500 meters. The Colerene Mountains were the great dividing range between the desert interior to the east and the greener, coastal plains to the west. As they climbed, the trees increased in numbers from Ponderosa Pines and Junipers near Harkelrhodes to other versions of Pines higher up, along with Firs and Spruces. It was surprising to Robert that the trees were the same as he would have seen on planet Earth, but then this star system and Earth had been conducting galactic trade for many millions of years.

After crossing the ridge of the Colerene Mountains, they descended for a few kilometers and entered the mountain village of Pilares. It rested on a large table or plateau on the west side of the mountains, and there were crystal clear views of the green coastal plains way below them with a view of the ocean on the horizon.

"Way out there and to the left," Chispo indicated, "over where you can see that mountain range touching the coastline, is the town of Lominac."

Pilares only had 500 residents, and almost before they realized it, they had passed through the town and were now descending the thickly forested slopes of the mountain. Everyone noticed the increase in air pressure to their ears as they descended to the green plains which were nearly at sea level.

At the bottom of the mountain, Fraxino finished the last curve, and the highway straightened. The scenery was a mixture of forest and farmland with pastures and various crops. The terrain was nearly flat with a few ups and downs. As they neared the coast, the traffic volume slowly increased with cars, trucks, and sometimes various farm machinery.

After 70 kilometers of driving through the plains, they arrived at the coastal highway where Fraxino turned left, pulled over, and let Chispo drive. Lominac was 20 kilometers south of the intersection. As Chispo drove them toward Lominac, the Elizabeth Ocean could be seen in places. Much of the terrain was sandy, and there were sand dunes in places along the highway on the ocean side.

One of the ridges of the Colerene mountain range extended from the main dividing ridge to the ocean, and Lominac was situated at its base along the coastal highway. As Chispo approached the town, the highway entered the foothills of the mountains, and there were numerous curves as well.

Lominac was a medium sized town with around 3,000 residents. There were several docks, and people were fishing from them. The smell of fish was prevalent in the breezy ocean air, and Chispo pulled over and parked at the Exxoll station just north of the town center. "Let's have a look at the town," he announced.

Everyone got out of the vehicle and walked down the highway which was the main street through town. The mountains towered above them on their left, and the ocean was on their right. There were several shops and restaurants in the central district, and no one would have known that it wasn't a typical coastal town on Earth, aside from the fact that the signs were written in Artenian script and that Artenian was the language that was spoken.

"Huh!" Chris commented as he looked in a restaurant window. "That looks like fish and chips."

"It is, man," Chispo verified.

"Right, let's eat some fish and chips," said Andrew.

They entered, ate supper, and then walked around town, saw the docks, and then returned to the vehicle-craft. Rinto and Fraxino had the vehicle refueled, and Rinto now did the driving.

"Okay, everyone," he announced. "We'll go a little further south and camp for the night."

It was already evening, an hour before sunset. Al Nitak's rays could now be seen reflecting off of the ocean's waters to the west.

Just south of Lominac, the mountains literally met the sea, and the highway became dangerously narrow with plenty of curves as it wound its way along the base of tall cliffs. In some places, the highway gained altitude and was up to 100 meters above the sea.

"We'll get through this dangerous section in a minute," Rinto assured everyone, "and then we'll turn left and camp just on the north side of this mountain range."

"Sounds good," said Robert.

For the next ten kilometers, the highway continued to wind its way along the coastal mountains, and as the road began to straighten out, Rinto took a left turn and followed a gravel road for five kilometers and found a large turnout at the base of the mountains. Higher up, the slopes were forested, and to the south were more coastal plains.

"Yeah, this spot looks good," Andrew approved.

Robert and his friends stepped out of the vehicle and set up their tents in the open meadow just uphill from the turnout. Rinto, Fraxino, and Chispo did the same.

Soon it became dark. It was a clear night, and now away from Zantaayer's city lights, they could see the stars very clearly. Rinto and Fraxino pointed out where planet Earth's sun was located, near Sirius A in the sky.

"Huh! They're right next to each other," Steven commented.

"That's right," said Rinto. "In your skies on Earth, Sirius is nearly in the same direction as our star Al Nitak. So, it would make sense. They're only 8 light years apart from each other."

"Yeah, that sounds right," Steven agreed.

"If you look in the eastern sky," Chispo pointed out to Robert who was standing by him at the time, "that bright star is called Al Nilam. It's 3.2 of your light years away from here."

"Is that all?" Robert responded. "That's pretty close."

"That's one of the Orion Belt stars, isn't it?" Andrew asked.

"That's right," Chispo answered. "It's the middle star of the three from Earth's vantage point."

"It's also the closest star to us," Rinto added.

"Now, if you look a little bit below it," said Chispo as he indicated, "that second brightest star is called Mintaka, and it's 5.8 of your light years away from here. In Artenian light years, that would be 2.75 for Al Nilam and right at 5.0 for Mintaka."

Robert stared at the stars, wondering if their planets also had life on them.

"You don't think anybody's going to bother us here tonight, do you?" Chris asked, changing the subject.

"No, man. Not a chance," Fraxino assured him.

"We have little or no crime on this world," Rinto explained. "Well, think about it. Even if we were to camp in a remote spot like this, say, in the western United States, the chances would be next to none that something would happen to us."

"Yes, that is true," Chris admitted. "Most of the crime happens in the cities."

"I wish I could say planet Earth has little or no crime," said Robert.

"I know, man," said Fraxino. "In nearly all of your larger cities, there are robberies and assaults every day."

"Dudes, when I stayed in Nashville last year," Chispo informed them, "I walked in on a robbery once."

"You did?!" Steven asked with surprise. "What happened?"

"Man, I was driving a car belonging to the family I stayed with. It was night time, and I pulled into a convenience store fuel station, and after filling up, I walked inside to pay. Suddenly I heard two men yell out, 'Hit the floor!' and I did. The next part surprised me, man, because they began fighting with each other over which one was going to hold up the cashier. I watched them out of the corner of my eye, and they really got into it, man! I got so scared they were going to kill me and everyone, that I perched myself and suddenly bolted out of there as fast as I could go. My fists hit the glass double doors so hard that the glass cracked. I was scared to death that one of them would shoot me in the back, but I ran like a scalded cat right across the street and literally dived over a limestone rock wall and landed on the ground on its other side. I stayed there several minutes, and then I remembered and said to myself, 'Oh, yeah! My car, and I left my keys in it.' I peeped over the wall, and the robbers were already gone. The police were arriving, so I jumped back over the wall, walked back to my car, and described the men to the police officers."

"No kidding!" Steven remarked. "That really happened to you?"

"Oh yeah, man, and I was scared to death."

"I'd say you were," said Robert.

"Did the police comment on the broken doors?" Andrew asked.

"Yes, they did, and I told them, 'It was my fault, sir. I broke them when I bolted out of here and ran for my life!'"

"What did they do to you for that?" Robert asked.

"They understood and excused me. The store's insurance paid for some new doors."

"That's good," said Robert.

"Your world has too many people, man," Chispo told them. "There's just too much stress and tension, and for that reason, there's crime."

"Some people are just not brought up right," said Chris.

"So, how much further is it to Hichicera from here?" Andrew wanted to know.

"We did ten hours today," said Rinto. "So, tomorrow it's going to take us twelve more hours to get there."

"Are we going to follow the coast or go an inland route?" Robert asked.

"We'll follow the coast highway south for around 200 kilometers," Rinto explained, "and then we'll turn inland and cross the mountain ranges and cut through two desert valleys, cross another mountain range, and arrive at Hichicera which is at the foothills of the Cloerinne Mountains and only 30 kilometers from the ocean in southern Zotola."

They continued talking, looked at the stars in the clear night sky, and eventually went into their tents to sleep for the night. The faint sound of the ocean could be heard several kilometers to the west, and the night was moderately warm.

Since they had a long day ahead of them, they got up early, loaded the vehicle with their tents and backpacks, and set out shortly after the crack of dawn. Chispo started out driving and drove them back to the coast highway, turned left and headed south. The majority of the terrain was farmland, and most of it was flat.

An hour later, they passed through the medium sized coastal town of Jande. They stopped and ate some breakfast, had a quick look around town, and proceeded south for another 100 kilometers where they turned left and went inland. They passed through more farmland and arrived at the great dividing range again, the Colerene Mountains.

The straight highway suddenly reached the steep, forested slopes of the mountains, and immediately the curves began. Chispo continued driving and took the curves and the mountain grade of the highway with the greatest of ease for the next ten kilometers until they reached the coniferous ridge, leveled out, and continued along the now level and straight highway through a Pine and Fir forest until they arrived at the town of Sentaha. There were higher mountain slopes to the right and behind the town.

"This is a cool ski resort in our winter months," Chispo informed everyone. "I came down here once with my family when I was growing up, and we stayed here for a whole week and went skiing. Rinto, you came with us, didn't you?"

"That's right," he answered. "We had a blast."

"It was a lot of fun," Chispo agreed.

They continued east along the highway and began descending the eastern slopes of the mountain range into the Whevosa Valley way below them. Since they were now inland, the valley, as expected, was semi-arid. It was a large valley, well, actually two valleys because there was a small range of lowland hills separating them. In 80 more kilometers, they arrived at the town of Carencro which was situated within those lowland hills. Chispo pulled into the town's Exxoll station and refueled.

"Man, I believe that's enough driving for me for today," he announced. "Here, Rinto. You take over."

The weather was hot, as it was now the middle of the day. No more than they filled up with fuel and ate lunch than they left and drove southeast through the second half of the Whevosa Valley, and in 80 more kilometers, they crossed the Golondrinas Mountains. They were now officially in southern Zotola.

They had yet another valley to cross and another mountain range as well, the Cloerinne Mountains. As they crested the forested summit of those mountains, they could see the Zuehl Sea, an inward extension of the Elizabeth Ocean which separated Zotola from the next continent south of them. Rinto continued driving as he drove them down the narrow winding highway, complete with hairpin curves and forest canopy above them. The trees were various types of Eucalypts and Acacias. One would have thought this was Australia.

At the base of the mountains, Rinto turned left and drove east along a highway which followed the base of the Cloerinne Mountains, and 50 kilometers later, they entered the town of Hichicera, Zotola. It was a small town with around 1,500 residents, and it had the luxury of a mixed culture from those who liked the mountains to those who liked the ocean.

It had been twelve hours since they left the spot where they had camped near Lominac, and it was now late afternoon with around two hours of daylight left.

"Good," said Robert. "We're finally here."

"I'll say," Steven agreed.

Rinto drove into the town center and parked the vehicle-craft at the plaza. Everyone got out and had a look around the town's shops and other sites. A warm breeze was blowing in from the south.

Even though Hichicera was situated at the base of the mountains, and since it was at a latitude of 32° north, it was semitropical which was the known climate for southern Zotola. The warm ocean breezes coming off of the Zuehl Sea kept the coastal plains south of the Cloerinne mountain range a warm and steady temperature year round. This made the south coast of southern Zotola a favorable place to live, and Hichicera was one of Zotola's favorite vacation spots.

Rinto, Fraxino, and Chispo inquired at several shops about the mountains and where the best hiking trails were located. Robert and his friends tagged along, just listening as best as they could to the Artenian which everyone spoke. At one of the shops, Chispo decided to casually ask if they happened to know about an ancient race of endemic people living way up high in the mountains.

"Yes, as a matter of fact I do," the man answered in Artenian. "There's a man in the next sport shop who goes every other month and visits and trades with them. He's writing a book about them, as well. You would do well to pay him a visit. In fact, I believe he's going to set out tomorrow morning for another trip to visit them."

"Really? Where's this store?" Chispo asked him in Artenian.

"Just go up this road for three blocks. The store's on the left, and it's on the corner."

"Thank you," said Chispo.

Everyone continued walking up the street.

"Oh cool!" Chispo suddenly commented when he noticed what appeared to be a fancy looking sports car.

"What is it?" Robert wanted to know.

"It's a *privately owned* Skiivona Zetna," Chispo answered. "I haven't seen one of these in more than a year!"

"Skiivona Zetna," Steven commented. "Now *that's* a name!"

"You got that right, dude!" Chispo agreed. "Man, you don't see *these* cars every day!"

"Except for the ones used by the police to patrol our highways," Rinto added.

"That's right," Chispo went on. "This is the only type of car used by the highway police. If you think my Velva Dibe has pep, this Skiivona Zetna will leave it like it's standing still, man!"

"No kidding!" Steven responded.

"I'm serious!" Chispo insisted. "Throughout Zotola we nickname the police the Zetna Force."

"Hmm...The Zetna Force," Steven repeated, and he laughed. "I like that name."

"Dudes, the Zetna Force never has a bit of trouble catching speeders along the highway!" Chispo proudly boasted.

"Except our cruiser craft when we put it in high gear and fly away from them," Fraxino told everyone with a smile.

"Which we've never had to do yet, thank goodness," Rinto added.

After walking several blocks up the street, they found the store and walked inside. A lady was at the counter.

"Good afternoon," Rinto said to her in Artenian. "We were wondering if we could speak to a man who goes into the mountains."

"Oh, right," she answered in Artenian. "That's my husband. Wait here just a minute, and I'll get him for you." She walked into the next room in the back.

He soon came forward. He was a young man appearing to be in his thirties, and he looked at everyone with interest. He introduced himself as Doulos, and Rinto, Fraxino, and Chispo introduced themselves and also introduced Andrew, Chris, Robert, and Steven.

For the next 20 minutes, they chatted in Artenian, and Rinto, Fraxino, and Chispo explained why they had come to Hichicera and that their mission was to find an ancient race of endemic people supposedly residing in the mountains up from Hichicera.

"Very interesting reasons indeed," commented Doulos in Artenian. "So, why don't you all come with me tomorrow when I leave. I'm away at the crack of dawn."

"Thank you, Doulos," said Rinto for everyone. "We'll meet you here in the morning with our vehicle. How far up the road did you say the campsite was?"

"Go straight out this same road here, and follow it for five kilometers until it terminates at the foot of the mountains."

"Very good," said Rinto. "It was a pleasure meeting you."

As everyone left, Chispo remarked, "Rinto, how do you always manage to pull it off so well?"

"That's just timing and destiny working like clockwork," he modestly answered.

"And if we'd shown up here a day later?" Robert wanted to know.

"Then we would have missed our chance," Rinto answered.

"Or at least the easy route," Fraxino added.

"Doulos said it's a three day hike up into the mountains from the road's end where we're going to camp tonight," Chispo informed everyone. "That's where the ancient race of green men live."

"Yeah, I didn't think it would be a short distance," said Chris.

"Me neither," Robert agreed.

They arrived back to the vehicle-craft parked at the plaza, and Rinto drove them out of town and up the road to the campsite at the foot of the mountains. The site was by the side of a large creek. There were plenty of Eucalyptus trees and Acacias in the area, and there were River She-Oak trees (*Casuarina cunninghamiana*) growing by the creek side. Most of the lower slopes of the Cloerinne mountain range were covered with forests of Eucalypts and Acacias, and in certain areas, there were Palm trees.

In ten minutes, they set up their tents in the area. There were no other campers at all. Only half an hour of daylight remained, so everyone took advantage of the time to prepare and eat supper.

"Hey, everyone?" Andrew called out. "How much food do each of you still have left?"

"I'm not sure," said Chris. "Let me check."

"I have about two days of food left," Robert answered.

"And how many days is this hike going to take round trip?" Andrew asked.

"Probably a week," Robert answered.

"Aren't we going to need more food?" Andrew reminded everyone.

"Yes, we are," Robert admitted.

"I guess it's time to go back to Coles New World and Roelf Vos supermarkets in Devonport for more food," Andrew suggested.

"You know," Chris reminded everyone, "we haven't restocked since the time just before we went to the Pleiades, and that was well over a week ago."

Robert looked at his watch. Earth time, it was 1 AM, Wednesday, July 3 which meant that it was 4 PM, July 3 in Devonport, Tasmania. The stores were indeed open.

"It's four in the afternoon there," said Robert. "Oh, yeah. James isn't with us anymore. Here, I'll go for everyone. What do you all want, the same as last time?"

All of them made arrangements with Robert and handed him some leftover Australian cash out of their wallets. Rinto, Fraxino, and Chispo had sufficient food supplies since they had just stocked up yesterday at their homes. Robert transported himself to Devonport and was gone for over an hour, after which he returned with a week's supply of food for the four of them.

Since it had been a long day on the road, they didn't wait long before they entered their tents and slept for the night.

An hour before daylight, Robert awoke and got up. He awakened everyone else, and they soon got themselves up, packed up the vehicle, and drove back to Hichicera to collect Doulos. They pulled up in front of his shop right at the crack of dawn. Doulos heard them arrive and came around the side of the store from the back. He was carrying his backpack with him.

"Good morning," he said to everyone in Artenian. "Looks like we're all ready to go."

"That we are," Rinto replied.

Doulos boarded their vehicle, and Rinto drove everyone back to the campsite and parked. They took their backpacks out, closed the doors securely, and began the long climb up the mountain slopes. The trail ascended alongside the creek.

"So, Doulos," Chispo asked in Artenian, "you say you come up here and visit this endemic race of people every other month?"

"That's right," he replied in Artenian.

"And you're writing a book about them?" Fraxino asked.

"Yes, I am," Doulos replied. "The chief of their group is an older man by the name of Zocanto, and the group lives up in a nearly inaccessible mountain meadow above the Makeeseldruff Gully. They live in such a place on purpose so that the general public won't bother them. In fact, many of Artenia's residents have accepted the falsehood that this group of people is merely a legend."

"Yes, that's true," Chispo admitted. "Most people back where we live in Zantaayer believe it's just a legend. In fact, little is known about them."

"That's why I'm writing a book about them."

As they ascended along the well used trail beside the creek, Doulos continued to relate stories to them about the group whom he called the Atascosa people. The River She-Oaks made for pretty scenery, and some of the Eucalyptus trees were quite large with trunks up to a meter in diameter. Higher up, the trail became steeper, and the Eucalypts, Acacias, and She-Oaks, all originally having been brought in from Earth's Australia 12,500 years ago, gave way to Southern Beeches and other hardwoods which were more prevalent at higher altitudes.

Doulos led the way as they eventually crossed the creek and continued on the trail as it traversed the hillside and reached a ridge. They turned left and continued ascending the ridge top until it intersected another ridge, on which they continued ascending. It was a long and fairly steep climb, and they felt tired by the end of the day.

They found Doulos to be a nice companion. He certainly had the stamina and experience of a mountain hiker since he had made frequent visits to his friends, the Atascosa people.

The ridge on which they ascended for several hours finally brought them to the main ridge or backbone of the Cloerinne mountain range. When they reached the crest, it was late afternoon. They had hiked some 20 kilometers, and they were now at 3,100 meters in altitude. The ridge top was partially forested with Pines, Cedars, and Spruces, and a trail ran along the entire ridge of the Cloerinne Mountains. It was called the Cloerinne Way, which ran for some 300 kilometers and was a popular walking path among mountain enthusiasts. It was on this trail that Doulos turned right and headed east.

The views behind them of Hichicera, the coastal plains and the Zuehl Sea beyond them were excellent and crystal clear. To the north of them could be seen more groups of mountains as far as the eye could see. Doulos indicated to everyone which mountain gully contained the Atascosa people. It appeared to be around

30 kilometers distant.

After walking a short while, Doulos chose his usual spot to make camp, and they all set down their packs, pitched their tents, and set up camp. They prepared and ate supper. Rinto and Chispo and Doulos found some of the food from Coles New World interesting and different, so Robert and his friends traded some of their food with them.

The weather had been perfect with clear skies all day. Here on the ridge of the Cloerinne Mountains it was cooler, especially after Al Nitak set on the horizon and night arrived. The stars could be seen very clearly.

The next morning Doulos was up at the crack of dawn. The others started stirring and soon got up, ate some breakfast, packed up, and they all left. Doulos led the way as they walked east along the Cloerinne Way.

The going was mostly level with some ups and downs as the trail wound its way along the ridge, passing through meadows with partial forests of Pine, Spruce, and Cedars. They followed this route for ten kilometers until late morning, after which Doulos made a left turn and led them along a ridge to the north.

In a few kilometers, they began descending, and several hours later they arrived at the bottom of a mountain valley that was thickly forested with Hemlocks, Southern Beeches, Poplars, Acacias, and other hardwoods. It was a beautiful virgin forest, and many of the trees were quite large. They had descended some 2,000 meters from the ridge top and were now next to the medium sized, fast flowing Makeeseldruff River, named for the nearly inaccessible gully from which it flowed. They had hiked well over 20 kilometers today.

"We'll camp here for the night," Doulos announced in Artenian, "and tomorrow we'll arrive at our destination 15 kilometers upstream from here."

Everyone set up camp. Around three hours of daylight remained. Doulos decided to relax at the campsite. So, the others explored the area and had a look around the hillsides, explored the riverbanks, and played and swam in the river as well.

When it was nearly dark, they ate supper, chatted with Doulos for a while, and went to sleep. The sound of the rushing river dominated all other sounds.

It was now their third day of this walk, and Doulos was again up at the crack of dawn. Everyone soon got ready and left camp, and he led the way as they walked the trail alongside the Makeeseldruff River following it upstream. At first the going was easy, and the trail only gently ascended as it passed through thick forests of Hemlocks, Southern Beeches, Poplars, and other hardwoods.

After several kilometers, the trail ended when they arrived at Makeeseldruff Falls. They were tall and massive, and their total height must have been over 200 meters. There appeared no earthly way to advance any further as both sides of the river were sheer cliffs ahead of them.

"So, this is why it's nearly inaccessible," Chispo commented to Doulos in Artenian.

"How do we continue?" Rinto asked him.

"Over there to the left," Doulos explained, "behind that group of trees is a secret cave entrance, and inside of it is a stairway which will take us to the top of the cliff."

He now left the trail and led everyone through a large group of Hemlocks and shrubs until they arrived at the bottom of the cliff. Sure enough, at the base of a small mound of dirt and obscured from view was a cave entrance. They took their flashlights out of their backpacks and entered.

Doulos led them down the dry, narrow winding corridor for some 150 meters. They arrived at a man-made stone spiraling staircase that spiraled counter-clockwise and took them straight up a long vertical shaft. There must have been a thousand steps to go up, and they finally arrived at the top of the cliff.

Much of the terrain was solid rock with patches of Shortleaf Pines and Hemlocks with other hardwoods as well. Now at the top of the falls, they were well above the forested valley they had just left, and they could see for many kilometers.

Ahead of them, Doulos continued to lead the way for five more kilometers along a narrow, winding and steep trail as it ascended the narrow, forested gully. In some places, it reminded Robert and his friends of the Savage Creek gorge of Savage Gulf State Natural Area in Tennessee. To their right, the Makeeseldruff River was fierce and dangerous as it raced and plunged down the steep gorge. If one had fallen into the river, he would have been quickly swept downstream with no chance of saving him. In some places, the narrow trail hugged the edge of the cliffs with dropoffs which would have plunged them straight into the dangerous river! Fortunately, in the most dangerous sections, there were cables attached to the cliff's walls.

"Whew!" Steven declared. "Now I understand what they mean by nearly inaccessible."

"You got that right," Robert agreed.

After two hours of ascending this narrow and dangerous gorge, they reached its top, and the scenery opened up into a beautiful wide grassy meadow with nearly level terrain. They were now at 1,800 meters in elevation, and the Makeeseldruff River gently passed through the large meadow, which was in stark contrast to the manner in which it descended through the gorge. The change in scenery was so abrupt that it surprised everyone, except of course, Doulos. On either side of the large meadow were forested hillsides consisting mostly of Shortleaf Pines, Cedars, and Hemlocks. While most of the trees were conifers, there were also some Poplars and some other hardwoods.

"This is where they live," Doulos announced.

CHAPTER 6

THE ATASCOSA

On the other side of the meadow, they could see a few of the Atascosa people walking from one place to another. They did indeed appear to be slightly green. As Doulos led them into the meadow, leaving the dangerous gorge behind, everyone could see small stone houses tucked into the forested slopes on either side of the meadow. Doulos had told them that around 450 of the Atascosa people live in this meadow, and it was a most beautiful place indeed, ideal for a peaceful and tranquil lifestyle. Further up the hillsides and upstream from the meadow, they could see some terracing where the residents grew their crops for food.

It wasn't long before their chief, Zocanto, saw Doulos and his new friends entering the meadow, and he walked toward them to greet them.

"Well, hello Doulos," Zocanto said in Artenian. "How are you? Who have you brought with you?"

"These are my new friends," he answered in Artenian. "They have come from Zantaayer to know your people. Four of them are originally from planet Earth in the Sol System."

"Is that a fact?" Zocanto remarked. "How interesting! Come. Bring your friends with you, and let's visit."

Zocanto led the way as they crossed the meadow and entered the forest on the upper end of the meadow. Within the group of Pines, Cedars, and Hemlocks was a moderately sized stone house where Zocanto lived with his wife and family. Upon reaching the house, he opened the door and immediately welcomed everyone inside.

He now spoke in his native mountain dialect and called for his wife, Cawrenfra, to come from what she was doing and meet them. She soon came into the room and greeted everyone in her native mountain dialect that Doulos called Atascosan. It was early afternoon, and she served everyone a lunch of mixed vegetables, bread, fruit, and native nuts. All of it was, needless to say, grown and prepared locally.

Also on the table was a small jar of what appeared to be honey or molasses. As Zocanto put some of it on a slice of bread, he informed them that it was called Colorajorm, a native honey made by bees of the Atascosa. It was very nutritious, complete with a touch of chlorophyll.

Zocanto and his wife had two children: a daughter, Govianna, and a son, Zahiyo. They soon arrived for lunch and were introduced. Both of them appeared to be the age of Rinto and Fraxino, and they were about the same height as well.

It was true indeed that the Atascosa people had a green tinge to their skin, a genetic trait that was a remnant of bygone days many millions of years ago when some of the genetic characteristics of trees were combined with the genes of their long ago ancestors, giving this group the ability to manufacture their own food from direct sunlight, a method very similar to the photosynthesis process in tree leaves. As a result, this group of humans was more closely related to trees than all other humans on Artenia.

Doulos had explained the whole story during their three-day walk that this genetic trait was installed as a long term experiment in some of the humans to increase their chances of survival during possible future times of food shortage crises. At the same time, there were some side effects that had resulted from such a genetic combination, and many of them died of various, unexpected diseases, leaving only a few lucky ones who carried the correct genetic characteristics within their own bodies to accommodate the photosynthetic genes, and they reproduced and furthered the new race of green humans.

As Doulos had explained, there were never very many of them, and a positive side effect was that they were very environmentally conscious and appreciated nature with utmost care. They were a very wise race of people who had a lot to offer, and in ancient times they came to gather and made their home in this meadow along the banks of the Makeeseldruff River, a fine location so removed from the general public, that the Atascosans became considered a legend.

Rinto and Fraxino, Chispo, Robert, and the others looked around the room of Zocanto's stone house, or cottage would be a more appropriate name. Things appeared more old fashioned. There were antique appearing artifacts hanging on the walls. Since the Atascosans had no electricity, the inside of the room appeared darker since it was only lit by candlelight and whatever remaining amount of forest filtered sunlight that entered through their small glass windows.

Nevertheless, it was a beautiful home in an excellent location of woods.

Among the Atascosa people, peace and tranquility were among their top qualities. It made sense that they were calm and peaceful because all versions of trees also carried those same characteristics. Through their genetically inherited ability to be peaceful, the Atascosans were also a very reasonable society with a sense of fairness and appreciation. They were always known for these positive traits in the legends throughout the world of Artenia.

Both Govianna and Zahiyo were in the process of learning the worldwide language of Artenian, and most of the younger generation of the Atascosa people could now speak at least some Artenian. None of them knew English, so Rinto, Fraxino, and Chispo served as translators so Robert and his friends could understand them. As they were eating lunch, they enjoyed talking with Govianna and Zahiyo.

"So, Doulos," Zocanto requested in Artenian, "tell me what brings these seven young fellows here with you?"

"They have a mission with a galactic salesman named Tom from the Sirius B star system, and he wants to set up telephone communication with this world, and there is a problem with a transmitter device in what they call northern Mexico . . . Here, you all explain it," he now said to Rinto, Fraxino, and Chispo.

"Basically, what's going on," Chispo explained in Artenian, "is that when the Atlanteans fled planet Earth to come here 10,130 years ago, they left 12 transmitters on that planet so they wouldn't be able to communicate with this world. While they were supposed to last only 500 years, at least one is still going strong and is having negative repercussions on residents in northern Mexico on that world.

"A galactic salesman named Tom who, as Doulos told you, is from Sirius B, recently informed us of the problem, and his mission is to have this still active transmitter located by us and either switched off or destroyed so that telephone communication will no longer be inhibited between this world and other worlds."

"If I gather your story correctly," Zocanto said, "that transmitter device is still blocking communication to this world."

"Exactly," Chispo verified.

"Yes, very ingenious, those from Atlantis were," Zocanto remarked. "It sounds like they were using remote transmission of forcefields. It's a form of teleportation, and the power supply can be anywhere with the actual forcefield and blocking process taking place in a remote location, in this case, our world of Artenia. They literally boomed the blocking forcefield to our star system."

"That's somewhat how we suspected they did it," said Chispo.

Zocanto sat and thought for a few moments with everyone looking on, and then he got up from the table, walked over to a shelf by the far wall, laid his hands on an object, returned, and placed it on the table. The next thing he did was to instinctively look straight at Robert, and he indicated for him to pick it up. Robert took one look at the object and couldn't believe his eyes! His mouth dropped open in astonishment. There before him was the same piece of clear quartz crystal that he had seen in his mind when he walked through Cloak Hall. It was rounded on the top and had a flat base, and within it was the ghostly image of a range of mountains just as it had appeared in his mind. He reached forward and took it off the table.

"That's just like I saw in my . . ." Robert began. He paused and then managed to say, "But how did you . . . know?"

Chispo translated to Zocanto what Robert said and explained what Robert had seen during their experience at Cloak Hall the other day, along with the coincidences that followed, which prompted them to come here and visit the Atascosa people.

Zocanto explained that many generations ago, several thousand years ago, this crystal had been brought to them by a visitor from another part of Zotola, and the courier said that it had originally come from Atlantis and had come from one of their unique libraries in that society. Zocanto said that this crystal portrayed information about the blocking devices that were installed on Earth at the time of their evacuation and that the scene of the mountains within it could well be telling the whereabouts of the most problematic transmitter.

"What else do you know about that area," Rinto asked Zocanto, "or put it another way, what more has this crystal told you?"

"Well, to put it this way," Zocanto explained, "this crystal has helped verify some of the ancient stories handed down over many generations within our people, one of them being that some of our most gifted ones visited the Atlanteans and helped them make that move from their world to this one. There are paintings and artifacts throughout your world which are symbolic of the technology Atlantis once had on your world, and I believe that if you can find some ancient paintings done by the native peoples in your region of interest, you will most likely be able to figure out how to pinpoint that device and eliminate it."

"Hmm . . . That's a clever idea," said Rinto.

"Interesting," Chispo commented. "We'll have to check them out."

"Ancient paintings," Fraxino remarked. "I hadn't thought of it like that before."

"What do you read from this crystal, Chispo?" Robert asked, and he handed it to him.

Chispo held the crystal up to the light coming in through the window and concentrated as he stared into it. "Let's see here," he said. He turned it at different angles until he could clearly see the image of the mountain range within it. "Dudes, this was definitely grown by the Atlanteans in Antarctica. I can feel it, man! . . . Wait . . . I believe I've got it. This crystal is one of the necessary links that we need to solve our problem. It's a guiding crystal. From the thoughts I'm receiving from this, these mountains portrayed within this crystal are both near the paintings and the transmitter device. Wait a minute, I just . . ." He paused. "I thought I just heard two words. Yeah, there they are. *Chiquihuitillos . . . atasco.*"

"What are those words?" Robert asked.

"They sound like Spanish," Andrew commented.

"I don't know, man," said Chispo, "but that second word *atasco*, according to the thoughts I'm getting, has something to do with being connected to this group, the Atascosa. Look how similar the two words are: *atasco* and *Atascosa*. Anybody here know Spanish?"

"I do, but I don't know that word," said Robert.

"I know what it means," Andrew replied. "The Spanish word *atasco* means obstruction or block."

"Really, man?" Chispo responded. "It means block?"

"That's right," Andrew verified.

"Wait a minute," Chispo went on. "That device we're looking for is doing the same, blocking communication with this star system. That's really wild!"

"What is the origin of the name of your group, the Atascosa people?" Rinto now asked Zocanto in Artenian.

"That name goes back many generations, at least as far as the length of time this crystal has been residing with us."

"Do you think this crystal may contain the reason your group is called the Atascosa?" Rinto asked.

"It may very well," Zocanto answered in Artenian. "Yes, it's very possible that the name Atascosa was derived from this crystal in more recent times since its arrival several thousand years ago. I don't know what our people called themselves in ancient times before that. Languages change and evolve over time, you know."

"That's true," Rinto admitted.

Meanwhile, Chispo translated to Robert and his friends what Rinto and Zocanto had just said.

"I just realized something." Chris brought up. "Is it not a coincidence that the Spanish word *atasco* means block or obstruction since the Atascosa people are living here in a remote area of the mountains and are nearly inaccessible, which means they are basically blocked from society?"

"Yes, that is an interesting comparison," Robert admitted.

"Words do have hidden meanings," Andrew commented.

"Think about it this way," Steven brought up. "It could be that the Spanish word for obstruction originated from here from the more ancient name of Atascosa through interconnecting thoughts through telepathy. After all, the Spanish language hasn't been around all that long."

"Words have all kinds of origins," said Andrew.

"That's possibly so," said Chispo. "As for the word Chiquihuitillos, it probably has something to do with those paintings of interest."

"Really?" Rinto responded. "If that's so, then we're really onto a good start."

"Dudes, it looks like all we need is to do some research in northern Mexico," Fraxino suggested, "and if we can turn that name up, then we'll know where to look."

"Good thinking, man," said Chispo.

Rinto, Fraxino, and Chispo next explained in Artenian to Doulos and Zocanto what they had just discussed.

"You fellows are most impressive with your abilities of discernment," Zocanto praised them. "Chispo, it looks like you have just read that crystal better than anyone among us ever has. Some of the information you just received from that crystal has never been realized by us before."

"Thanks, Zocanto," said Chispo.

"That brings me to realize," Zocanto continued, "that you seven fellows are the chosen ones to solve the problem of that blocking transmitter device in Mexico. Some of you are better telepathic receivers than you realize. There are always higher levels of thoughts and ideas floating around in the ether, and they can be received into the mind by any concentrating person with the correct frequencies to receive them. As they are received, the person thinks of those ideas as a result, translates them into words within his mind according to the languages he knows, realizes them, and says them."

"That's what channeling is all about," said Rinto.

"That's pretty similar to how we read crystals and the information they contain," Fraxino told Zocanto.

Meanwhile, Chispo was translating to Robert and his friends what was being said.

"That's a fine gift you have," Zocanto went on. "The mission you are about to undertake requires people of your caliber and philosophy. I will advise that you remember to keep an open mind as you go about your project. Take that crystal with you. I feel that it will help you locate the device more easily." He now looked at Rinto and Fraxino and said, "If you have some other crystals that you think may facilitate this project, then by all means take them with you on your mission."

"That we will," Fraxino assured him.

Doulos sat back and listened and found the conversation most interesting. He realized that he would definitely be adding a new and different chapter to the book he was writing about the Atascosa people.

"So, how do we want to do it?" Chispo asked everyone. "Do we want to leave right now? Robert can transport us back to the vehicle in a matter of seconds, man, or do we want to stay here and walk back with Doulos when he leaves?"

"Well, Chispo, we just got here," Rinto pointed out. "Let's have a look around the place before we go. Besides, I don't feel comfortable being transported like that. Doulos, how long are you going to stay here before you walk back?"

"Tomorrow I rest, and the next day I leave."

"Yeah, that sounds good enough," said Rinto. "We'll stay here and leave when Doulos does, and we'll walk back with him. Is that agreeable to everyone?"

Everyone agreed that it was the best solution, and besides, they were curious to stay a little while and have a look around.

"Zahiyo and Govianna will be glad to take you on a tour of our area," Zocanto offered.

They finished lunch, thanked Cawrenfra, and then she went to another part of the house to do other things.

Zocanto and Doulos had some other business to attend to, so Zahiyo and Govianna took the seven of them on a tour. They left the house, turned left and walked upstream along the gently flowing Makeeseldruff River. Along the way, they saw several stone houses within the forests on either side of the meadow.

Next, Zahiyo and Govianna turned and left the meadow, led them uphill through the forest, and ten minutes later arrived at the gardens. They passed several other Atascosans who were carrying baskets of their harvest. The gardens were beautifully terraced and maintained, and there were numerous varieties of vegetables, plants, and trees. Other terraced areas had wheat and other grain plants growing.

Zocanto's son and daughter were not fluent in Artenian, so communication was at best troublesome, in addition to the fact that Chispo, Rinto, and Fraxino had to translate so Andrew, Chris, Robert, and Steven could understand. Nevertheless, Zahiyo and Govianna were friendly and were good tour guides.

The scenery from the terraced gardens was magnificent. They could see the whole meadow well below them. Way over to the right and in the distance, they could see the beautiful, forested Makeeseldruff Valley where they had camped last night. To the left, they looked upstream and could see numerous sheer cliffs in the distance with mountains above them. Reaching the upper sections of those mountains looked impossible without special climbing gear. From all sides, accessing the area in which the Atascosa people lived was truly difficult.

After an hour's walk through the various terraced gardens, Zahiyo and Govianna returned to the meadow at its furthest point upstream. They were now at the base of the cliffs, and there before them was the source of the Makeeseldruff River. Its waters charged out of the cliff's base from a cave whose tunnels reached back for several kilometers, according to what Zahiyo and Govianna told them. The river gathered its sources from various underground streams originating in the highest reaches of the mountains above them.

Next, they walked alongside the river downstream and arrived at Zocanto's house 45 minutes later. They passed by the social center, town hall, and the market center along the way.

It was now late afternoon. Zocanto was gone, and Cawrenfra prepared beds and floor space for everyone to sleep for the night. They were tired after their three days of hiking into here with Doulos, so they rested for a while. Some of them took naps inside, and the others went outside and sat under the Pines, Cedars, and Hemlocks and chatted, discussing possible plans for Mexico.

In a couple of hours, Zocanto and Doulos arrived. Doulos had been visiting other friends with Zocanto and had traded some goods from Hichicera. Cawrenfra had supper prepared and fed everyone basically the same types of food that they had eaten earlier.

Everyone had been going pretty much full speed ever since they had come to Artenia with Rinto and Fraxino, and the discovery of the holographic plates had added to the excitement. With that and the three-day walk into here, they were feeling the exhaustion, and they decided to go to sleep early.

At the crack of dawn, there were various birds calling out and small squirrel-like animals making scratching sounds as they raced among the trees and branches. It was a clear morning and was moderately cool, and there was plenty of dew on the meadow. Al Nitak appeared above the opposite forested hillside at mid morning.

Even though it was morning, since Artenia's days were 25½ hours long, the times of day had shifted out of phase since their arrival to Zotola last week. Earth time, it was 6 PM, Saturday, July 6. They now felt well rested, after their long night's sleep.

Zahiyo and Govianna had gone to the gardens at the crack of dawn to pick fruits and vegetables, and when they returned, everyone had eaten some breakfast and was ready to go with them for the day. They packed a lunch into their daypacks and left with them at mid morning. The weather soon became warm, and the skies remained clear all day.

For the morning they visited the market center. There were several stalls, all manned by native Atascosans selling useful items for their society. There were tools, cookware, clothing, blankets, and even furniture. The blankets looked most interesting with their unique designs sewn into them. Among the seven of them, Andrew and Robert couldn't resist buying one blanket each to take back to Tennessee with them.

Zahiyo and Govianna introduced them to several of their friends, all of whom found it very interesting that four of them were from planet Earth. It was unusual enough that the Atascosans had visitors from other parts of Zotola but most unique indeed to have visitors from Earth.

One of their good friends whose name was Orolizo was most interested in the mission that the seven of them had awaiting them in Mexico. He spoke a decent amount of Artenian and was one of the more gifted people of the Atascosa.

"How interesting that you seven are the chosen ones to go to planet Earth's northern Mexico," Orolizo told them in Artenian.

Meanwhile, Chispo translated to Robert and his friends throughout the conversation.

"A part of me knew that you would be coming here . . . instincts, I believe. Ever since I was a young child, I have had numerous dreams about a cultural society in what is most likely your Earth's northern Mexico. I feel fairly certain that one of my soul links is living his lifetime in that region, as my soul is presently maintaining my body and also his. We have communicated often when I'm dreaming, and sometimes I dream that I am that fellow. I experience his memories, only to find that when I wake up, I realize that I'm not physically that person."

"That's wild, man!" Chispo remarked in Artenian to Orolizo. "Listen, dude, we came across a whole crateload of holographic metal plates in an ancient galactic dump site, obviously dumped by Atlantean descendants soon after their arrival to this world. We've been looking through those plates with Rinto and Fraxino's crystal base computer, and one of the plates actually discusses that sort of stuff you're experiencing: dreams, alternate realities, souls maintaining multiple human bodies on different worlds."

Feelings of excitement ran through Orolizo as Chispo informed him of the holographic plates, and the fact that they related to what Orolizo was experiencing surprised him even further.

"Listen, since you are about to go to that region," Orolizo requested, "there is something I would like you to take to my counterpart and deliver to him." He paused. "I see I have a customer here. Come by my house this afternoon. Zahiyo and Govianna know where I live. They can bring you. I'll see you then." He immediately attended to his customer.

Once a week the markets were set up like they were today with all the stalls open. They were open for the morning, and they closed in the early afternoon. Three hours remained until closing.

Meanwhile, Zahiyo and Govianna took them on a walk through the forested hillsides on the opposite side of the Makeeseldruff River from where they walked yesterday. On this side of the meadow, it was totally forested right up to the base of the cliffs. There was a trail that ran along its base for the entire length of several kilometers. In places as they walked along that trail, there were beautiful views of the meadow below them. At various places along the trail, there were waterfalls that were surrounded by Hemlocks which were the dominant trees. In other areas, there were small caves, some of them being lived in by native wildlife.

For the entire length of the trail, the walls of the sheer cliffs were from 100 to 200 meters high, and they looked most inaccessible unless one had some technical climbing gear. For those who knew about them, and most of the Atascosans did, there were a few secret passageways that would take them to the higher reaches of the mountains. A few of them would go up there searching for plants, herbs, rocks, and minerals.

They ate lunch by one of the larger falls. Some of the Hemlocks were fairly large and had trunks up to two meters in diameter. Birds flew among the trees and perched in their limbs, and small squirrel-like animals ran from tree to tree, hopping along limbs and branches. The sounds of the falls were dominating, and Zahiyo and Govianna informed them that this was one of the favorite areas for the Atascosans to come, relax, and enjoy nature.

After lunch, they continued along the trail until they arrived at the source of the Makeeseldruff River at the base of the cliff where they had come yesterday. Next, they followed the same path they had used yesterday, following the river downstream through the meadow toward Zocanto's house, only they made a right turn a short distance away from the river's source, walked uphill into the forest for a few minutes, and arrived at a stone house on a small knoll.

"This is where Orolizo lives," Zahiyo announced.

He knocked on the door. His younger sister answered the door, and an *attractive* looking young lady she was. She had a beautiful facial complexion of light, olive green color. Zahiyo and Govianna asked for Orolizo, and she said that he had not yet arrived from the market. At that moment, they saw him walking up the path. He was glad to see them.

"How good that you've come to visit," said Orolizo in Artenian as he greeted everyone. "This is my sister, Lumela." Everyone introduced himself to her and shook hands. Andrew found her to be very attractive. Steven, even more so, found her attractive, and he was at a loss for words as he looked at her and admired her features.

"Come in," Orolizo offered. They entered and had a seat on various chairs and window ledges around the main front room. "Let me bring you the item I want to send with you on your mission." He walked into one of the back rooms and returned with a clear quartz crystal sphere around five centimeters in diameter. It was clear on one end, and the other end had what appeared like a base of tiny internal cracks and other interference. As light struck its surface, rainbows were reflected off of the internal fractures. He handed it to Chispo.

"Wow! That is quite a piece!" Fraxino exclaimed.

"You're not kidding, dude," Chispo agreed, as he peered into it. He then placed it on the table.

"I didn't get to tell you this, but all along I have felt that my physical counterpart on your world is troubled by something. From my dreams I've been having, he comes across as a very fine, well mannered, emotionally tuned fellow, but at times, for insufficient reasons, he loses control and becomes very angry and is quite dangerous. His emotions come through since I am his soul's other physical counterpart, his soul link, and some of my dreams are quite disturbing to me as a result.

"It is my feeling that you will come across him one day in the town you will visit, and you will likely experience or notice a coincidence that will serve as verification that you've located him. He's a young fellow around my age, and if

there is not an obvious coincidence, your experiences that you will have with the people there will guide you to the right fellow instinctively. My feeling is, as you get to know people, one of you will trigger a reaction which will cause you to identify who my soul link is.

"I am also in agreement with you and your galactic salesman friend," Orolizo went on in Artenian, "that there is an Atlantean transmitting device that is still active and is hidden in the mountains near the town where my soul link lives, and based on the dreams I have been having, that device is blocking communication to this star system and is causing adverse reactions to the residents who live in the regions near it."

"Wait a minute," Chispo broke in and asked. "If that transmitting device is actually blocking communication with this star system, then how in the world are you able to communicate with your counterpart in Mexico on planet Earth?"

"Good question," Orolizo replied. "When I dream at night, my dream essense leaves my body and goes to planet Earth, gathers its experiences, and then returns home to me since my body resides here."

"Hmm . . . that's very clever," Chispo commented. "Rinto, what good is that blocking transmitter device anyway? It looks like there are so many ways around it."

"The galactic salesman did say it is definitely blocking telephone communication via gravity waves with this world," Rinto reminded.

"And Tom told us the dream level was never blocked," Fraxino added. "Spiritual and astral travel and mental telepathy are the types that got blocked."

"Oh, yeah. That's true, man," Chispo admitted, now recalling what Tom had earlier said.

Next, Chispo translated to Robert and his friends what he and Orolizo had just discussed.

"Has Zocanto shown you fellows the crystal with the view of the mountain range within it?" Orolizo asked.

"Yes, he showed us that," Rinto replied. "Chispo here read it pretty well."

"I did, man," said Chispo. "It's definitely from Atlantis, and I read two words out of it: *Chiquihuitillos* and *atasco*."

"Oh, yeah," Orolizo recalled. "I've actually heard that word, Chiquihuitillos, from my dream memories. My soul link knows about it. Wait, let me think . . ." He paused. "Yes, that's the name of some ancient Atlantean paintings done by some of the people that were left behind in that region of Mexico. They exist on the sidewalls of some cliffs on some lowland hills in the middle of a remote desert valley."

"You *know* all this?" Chispo asked with enthusiasm.

"I do through my soul link's memory."

"Wow, man!" Chispo exclaimed. "That's more verification. Dudes, we're that much closer to solving the puzzle."

"Right on, dude," Fraxino remarked.

"Cool!" Rinto added.

"And that word atasco means blocked . . ." Chispo went on and explained.

They stayed and visited for the rest of the afternoon, as it turned out, talking and relating stories of their experiences, including their visits with the galactic salesman, the telephone exchange they built, about Morris who was no longer with them, and about their past adventures to Tasmania, Great Britain, Sirius B, Vega, and the Pleiades. While Chispo, Orolizo, Rinto, Fraxino, Andrew, Chris, and Robert were busy talking, Zahiyo, Govianna, and Lumela had long since gone over to another part of the room and were talking about things of their interest.

Their having retired themselves to another part of the room was unnoticed, except by Steven who could hardly take his eyes off of Lumela. He admired every shape of her beautiful face and body, and it was for certain that the love bug had bitten him. It was taking a stronghold of him in a hurry. Steven contributed precious little to the conversation with Orolizo. In fact he was totally oblivious to the conversation since he was concentrating on Lumela.

"Well, it's starting to get dark outside," Rinto announced. "I guess we better leave."

"Wow, man!" Chispo exclaimed. "We've been jabbering for three or four hours!"

"I know, man," Fraxino agreed.

"Orolizo, it was truly a pleasure getting to know you," Chispo told him. "I've really enjoyed the chat."

"The pleasure was mine," said Orolizo. "Come back anytime."

"I will, man."

Zahiyo, Govianna, and Lumela saw the others getting up to leave. So, they stopped their conversation. Everyone wished each other well, and Zahiyo and Govianna walked out of the house with the seven others.

As they were walking down the hill toward the meadow, Andrew said, "That Orolizo certainly is a character. He knows a lot."

"Yes, he's a good natured, easy-going fellow," Robert commented.

"He's definitely one of the links we needed to help us find that device in Mexico," Rinto stated.

"Dudes, with you, everything falls in place like clockwork," Chispo told Rinto and Fraxino. "How do you two do it?"

"I never told you this," said Rinto, and he did his best to keep a straight face, "but I threw a destiny program into the crystal array of our vehicle when I grew those crystals."

"Really, man?" Chispo responded.

"No, I'm just joking," said Rinto. Everyone started laughing.

"You modest genius, you," Chispo remarked.

"No, Chispo, that's just how fate and destiny work," said Rinto.

"Then you've got the destiny program up in your head," Chispo told him.

"Probably do," Rinto admitted.

"Fellows, I've got to tell you something," Steven brought up.

"Yeah, what?" Robert asked.

"I'm telling you, I just could not take my eyes off of her!"

"Who, Lumela?" Chris asked.

"Is that right?" Andrew responded. "I will admit she is a pretty one."

"Yes, I noticed you weren't with us on our conversation," Robert commented.

"I don't even know what you guys were talking about," Steven admitted. "All I could do was look at her. I mean it was love at first sight!"

"Well, Robert," Chispo said to him, "it looks like another one in your group has fallen in love."

"Looks like it," Robert admitted.

"What do you suggest we do, Rinto?" Chispo asked. "Do we want to go back and tell Orolizo?"

"No . . . no, don't do that," Steven requested. "That would be too much. I don't think I could handle all that. Besides, I don't speak Artenian, let alone Atascosan."

"All right, man," Chispo agreed.

"Let's go back to Zocanto's house, and we'll all leave tomorrow," Steven suggested.

In 30 minutes, they were at Zocanto's house and Cawrenfra greeted them and let them in. Zocanto was inside and was talking with Doulos.

"How was your day?" Zocanto asked them.

"We had a great time, today," Chispo answered for everyone. "Your son and daughter took us along the Base Cliff Trail, and then we spent the whole afternoon visiting with Orolizo at his house."

"Excellent!" Zocanto remarked. "He's a fine fellow, and his sister Lumela is most attractive."

"Yes, we saw her," Chispo told him. "In fact, one of Robert's friends here couldn't take his eyes off of her."

"Is that a fact?" Zocanto responded, and he gave out a hearty laugh. Somehow he instinctively knew which one he was, and he looked straight at Steven and said to him in Artenian, "Doulos and I have been discussing it and we, the Atascosa people, would like to offer one of you the chance to stay here with us for a 30-day program to learn our way of life and then take your knowledge back to your home of Earth in the format of legends."

Chispo translated to Steven what Zocanto just said.

Steven's mouth dropped open in surprise. *How did Zocanto instinctively know so fast?* he thought. "Well . . . I just don't know," Steven managed to say.

"Aw, come on Steven," Chris urged him. "This will give you a chance to know your *chick*," and he leaned toward Steven and gently poked him in his side as he said the last word.

Steven returned Chris a weird look for that comment, but he knew Chris was only joking.

"I don't know," Steven continued. "Let me think about it a few minutes."

The others talked to him and explained the benefits of the program and how it would be a unique education for him in his life.

"Hmm . . . tempting," said Steven. He paused. "No, I don't think so. I like being with my friends. Besides, I can't speak any Artenian nor Atascosan. Further, the galactic salesman has offered a hefty reward for the detection and elimination of that transmitter device in Mexico."

About that time, they heard a knock on the door. Zocanto answered it, and Orolizo walked in. He was carrying the clear quartz sphere in his hand.

"Oh, my goodness!" Steven quietly exclaimed in a startled manner.

Chispo saw the sphere in Orolizo's hand. "Oh, yeah. The crystal ball. Sorry, man, I guess we got so carried away jabbering all afternoon that it completely slipped my mind."

Orolizo handed it to Chispo. "That's okay, Chispo. It was my fault too."

"Man, I don't know if you realized it," Chispo explained to Orolizo in Artenian without Steven knowing what they were talking about, "but one of Robert's friends has really fallen for your sister. He couldn't take his eyes off of her."

"You know," Orolizo admitted, "I got so carried away talking with you, Rinto, and Fraxino that I didn't even notice. Well, that's very nice of him that he finds my sister so attractive. Which one is he?" and he looked at Robert's friends and immediately instinctively looked at Steven. "Oh, yeah. I see him. Steven, right?"

Steven got wind of what the conversation was about and said, "Now, wait a minute! I didn't say that I wanted to . . ."

"Don't worry. It's okay, Steven," Chispo assured him. "We're only talking, man."

"I don't know if you noticed that my sister is a bit shy," Orolizo explained. "She's more of the quiet type who makes conversation with those she knows. Nevertheless, I take it as a compliment that Steven finds my sister so attractive."

"Man, Steven didn't want me to tell you," said Chispo.

"Oh, by the way, Orolizo," Zocanto broke in, "Doulos and I have been discussing a program where one of the fellows from Earth could stay here with us, the Atascosa people, for a duration of 30 days to learn our culture, way of life, and then take stories in the format of legends back to Earth with him at the end of his stay. Would you be interested in hosting Steven if he were to stay?"

Orolizo perked up with interest. "Sure! That would be an ideal choice. I view that as a great opportunity to host an Earthling. Yes, he can stay at my place. My sister needs another friend anyway, and since Steven likes her looks, he can get to know her. That will work out splendidly." He looked at Steven as Chispo translated what he said.

The desire for Steven to stay with the Atascosans increased, and again he said, "Hmm . . . tempting . . . but the language barrier?"

"Oh, that's no problem, Steven." Chispo assured him. "You'll have that licked in a week."

Steven's memories of Lumela's perfect attractiveness invaded his mind. Excitement at the possibility of knowing her built up in him. He could no longer refuse the offer.

"Yes, okay yes. I'll stay," Steven told everyone. Chispo translated his answer to Orolizo.

"Excellent," said Orolizo. "You'll be a welcome member of our family for your stay. Do you want to come with me now, Steven?" Orolizo offered. Chispo translated to Steven.

The desire had built up so strongly in Steven that there was just no way he could have done differently. He picked up his backpack, faced everyone, and said, "I don't know what it is, but I just have this very strong urge to take this offer and stay."

"It must be your destiny, Steven," Rinto said.

"There must be a good reason," Chispo assured him. "Good luck with your stay here."

"Okay, see you, Chispo," said Steven. "Fellows, I've really enjoyed my travels with you all. Don't worry. I'll join you for more later."

"Have a good time, Steven," Robert told him.

Everyone wished him well, and he walked out the door with Orolizo.

"Have a great trip to Mexico," Orolizo called out to them. "Thanks for carrying that crystal ball with you, Chispo."

"No problem, man. See you around, Orolizo."

Once they left, Zocanto looked at everyone with a little bit of surprise and said, "It never ceases to amaze me the force with which destined activities do occur! One of you is already staying with our people. Rest assured, he is in good hands with our group. He will have an excellent stay and will learn so much. I feel sure of it."

That made everyone feel better because Robert and his friends were feeling a little bit of shock at the suddenness with which Steven had acted. Not even James had acted that way when he had met Suzanne in the Pleiades.

Cawrenfra fed everyone some supper, after which they chatted with Doulos and Zocanto. They took a short walk in the meadow and looked at the night sky. The stars could be seen very clearly, and they soon found and pointed out the Earth's sun. Nearby to it in the sky was the star Sirius A.

Tomorrow was going to be a long day of hiking, so they went to bed before it became too late.

As they were drifting off to sleep, Chris said, "That is strange how Steven suddenly left us."

"Yes, I agree," said Robert. "There's something not right about it."

"Steven will be fine," Andrew reassured everyone. "Don't worry about it."

That night, a stormfront of clouds moved into the region. For several hours in the middle of the night, it rained. There was thunder and lightning, and the wind blew fiercely at times.

By the time morning arrived, the storm had moved out, and the skies had cleared. Water was standing in areas, and the Makeeseldruff River had nearly overflowed its banks. It was flowing down the meadow at a considerable rate, and its waters were somewhat muddy.

"Dudes, that must have been more of a rain last night than we realized," Fraxino remarked.

"I'll say it was," Andrew agreed. "Look at that river. It's up."

They rolled up their sleeping bags, loaded their backpacks, and ate some breakfast that Cawrenfra served them.

Suddenly, there was a knock on the door, and Zocanto answered it. It was Steven, and he had a look of terror on his face! Immediately, he walked inside and set down his backpack.

"Steven, what happened, man?" Chispo asked him.

"I'm coming with you guys. Let's go."

"What happened to you, Steven?" Robert asked. "You look scared to death."

"I'm telling you!" Steven declared.

"What . . . what happened?" Rinto wanted to know. "Did somebody attack you?"

Steven stared at Rinto a moment, then said, "No, but I dreamed it. Let's get out of here now!"

"Dude, calm down," Chispo urged him. "Tell us what happened."

Steven sat at the table, calmed himself, and then he began talking.

"Well, to start with, it's nothing bad about Orolizo. I find him a very kind and reasonable person, but we were unable to communicate for the language barrier, and when we arrived at his house and entered for the night, I was so overwhelmed with emotion for Lumela that I didn't know what to do. Even though she's pretty, she's so shy that there was nothing for us to do together, and to top it all, we couldn't communicate for the language barrier! I quickly realized that any relationship with her would have been impossible under the circumstances.

"Orolizo and I slept in the same room last night, and I'm telling you, I had a dream that scared the wits out of me! I dreamed that I was in Mexico and was cornered by a mean looking Mexican guy. He was hopping mad and was rough with me as he kept asking me a question over and over. The ferocious look on his face told me that he was about to kill me, and in the dream I was doing my best to figure out a way to escape from his clutches. He jabbed me several times, and when I realized there was no other solution, I gave out a loud scream that woke me up. Orolizo heard me and came to my side to be sure I was okay. I was shuddering with fright!"

"Golly, Steven!" Robert exclaimed. "That's terrible!"

"Dude, that had to be Orolizo's soul link who you dreamed about!" Chispo declared.

"Well if that's so, now I understand why Orolizo is having disturbing dreams," said Steven.

"Did you see him clearly?" Rinto asked.

"Yes, of course," Steven replied.

"Good. That may come in useful for us," said Rinto.

"What did you do next?" Robert wanted to know.

"Well, needless to say, sleep was impossible. I wanted to leave right then, but it was pouring rain. So, I remained awake in the bed. This morning, everyone was still asleep. So, I sneaked out of there and walked straight over here."

"What about Lumela?" Chris asked him.

"Never mind her! I just wanted to get out of there!"

"Steven, can you remember what the guy kept telling you?" Andrew asked.

"Let's see." He thought for a moment. "I know it was in Spanish, and I couldn't understand it. I think it was something like . . . *Kay deeheest ober me* . . . and then the word, *Eh!* and he emphasized that word. He said another phrase, but I can't remember it."

"Hmm," said Andrew as he thought. "It sounds to me like he was saying, 'What did you say about my . . .' and in Spanish, that would be, 'Que dijiste sobre mi . . .'"

"Yeah, that's it!" Steven quickly responded.

"Can you remember the rest?" Andrew wanted to know.

Steven thought briefly. "No, I can't."

"Well, that's okay," said Andrew.

"Steven, we did think it was strange how you just up and left us last night," Chris told him.

"I know," he admitted. "As I look at it now, I don't know what came over me."

"Wait a minute," Chispo said. "Didn't Orolizo say that one of us would trigger a reaction which would cause us to identify who Orolizo's soul link is?"

"Yes, that's true," Rinto recalled.

"Steven, would you be able to identify him if you were to see him in Mexico?" Chispo wanted to know.

"Yes, of course," Steven replied. "I can see his ugly, ferocious face just as plain as day."

"Good," said Chispo. "Man, I know it may be unpleasant for you, but don't forget what he looks like. We'll probably need your accurate memory so you can identify him and warn the rest of us so we can know where to be cautious."

"That's right, man," Fraxino added. "The dude's probably an emotional case, especially knowing what Orolizo told us yesterday. People like that do not reason, and they can be very dangerous at times."

"That's one of the reasons your planet has so much violence," Rinto pointed out.

"You know," Chris speculated, "it looks like to me that Steven's attraction for Lumela was set up, possibly by Orolizo's subconscious mind even though Orolizo didn't realize it, so that Steven would be at the right place at the right time to have that disturbing dream to help us identify who Orolizo's soul link is in Mexico."

"Good point, Chris," said Rinto.

Since the whole conversation was in English, Zocanto, his family, and Doulos were looking on. They knew that something was wrong with Steven and asked about it. Chispo, Rinto, and Fraxino turned their attention to them and explained what had happened. They reacted with concern.

"I'm sorry for Steven's disturbing dream," said Zocanto, "and considering the recent circumstances, I believe it's best that he stay with you and not stay here with us."

About this time, Orolizo showed up and knocked on the door. Zocanto greeted him and let him in. He carried a folded up piece of paper with him and, needless to say, had come to find out what happened to Steven.

"Dude, let me tell you what happened to Steven last night," Chispo began, and he explained the whole story to Orolizo in Artenian.

"Yes, I suspected that's what happened," Orolizo responded. "Steven gave out a terrible scream in the middle of the night, and I came over to him to be sure he was all right, but because of the language barrier, he couldn't tell me."

"I know, man," said Chispo.

"I will admit that I was curious why Steven took such a strong attraction to Lumela," Orolizo went on, "but the circumstances it created will help you identify who my soul link is, when you get to Mexico. Steven's dream may have been a premonition. So, my advice to all of you is to be cautious. If you meet him, don't let on that you know about his underlying dangerous emotional side. Act normal around him, but for your own safety, don't separate or do things individually. Stay in groups of two or more at all times."

"That's smart thinking, Orolizo," Chispo told him. "We'll follow your advice." He translated the advice to the others.

"There's something else I would like you to take to him," Orolizo requested. He handed Chispo the folded up piece of paper. "This is a letter explaining to him who I am and how I'm connected to him. If he seems open to extraterrestrial matters, and if that sort of thing interests him, then hand it to him and tell him about me. But if he's not, then hand it to him at the moment you all leave Mexico."

"What about the quartz crystal sphere?" Chispo asked.

"You can hand that to him anytime you like. I've already installed some energies into that crystal which will subconsciously help him without his realizing it. Just be very casual as you deliver it to him. Don't tell him where it really came from. My letter explains that. Just hand it to him as a gesture of friendship."

"All right, man," Chispo agreed. He unfolded the letter and looked at it. "Man, it's written in Artenian."

"I know," Orolizo admitted. "Although I've heard my soul link speaking their language of Spanish in my dreams, I cannot speak or write it."

"Don't worry. We'll translate it for you," Chispo assured him.

"Thanks, but please do also hand him the original, written in Artenian script."

"All right, I will, man."

"I will give you one more bit of advice," Orolizo continued. "I would be very careful about who I talk to about your true reasons for being in that part of Mexico. Use your own judgment, but I wouldn't just tell anybody that you're down there to locate and eliminate a mysterious device hidden in the mountains. From the feelings I've picked up through my soul link, the town he lives in is small, and the people like to gossip. They could take your intentions in a weird way."

"Oh, by all means we'll be very subtle," Chispo told him. "You can be sure of that." He now translated to Robert and his friends.

"I think it would most certainly be better if Steven stays with you and goes to Mexico with you," Orolizo advised. "His remaining with you will be to your benefit."

"I agree, man," said Chispo. "As for Lumela, I believe his feelings for her have disappeared."

"That's also for the better," said Orolizo. "There was a purpose for that, and it's been served."

Zocanto, his family, and Doulos had been listening, and Doulos now made a gesture that he was ready to leave. The others reached for their backpacks and put them on their backs.

"Like I said, man," Chispo told Orolizo, "it was a pleasure knowing you."

"The same is true for me," he replied. "Come back and visit."

"You can be assured that we will."

Orolizo said goodbye to everyone, wished them well, and left.

Zocanto got up from the table and walked over to Doulos and the others.

"Doulos, as always, it's a pleasure having you visit our people. I've enjoyed meeting your friends, and I wish them the best of luck with their mission in Mexico. I hope they are successful. They are always welcome here in the future."

"Thank you, Zocanto. The pleasure has also been mine."

Chispo, Rinto, and Fraxino translated to Andrew, Chris, Robert, and Steven. They expressed their thanks to Cawrenfra, Zahiyo, and Govianna, said goodbye to them, and walked out the door. As they walked toward the meadow, Zocanto and his family waved. In a way, they were sad to leave, but it was time to move on and make preparations to go to Mexico. The kind, peaceful, hospitable mannerisms of the Atascosa people had made a lasting impression upon them.

They soon entered the meadow and walked downstream along the banks of the swollen Makeeseldruff River. In a short distance they reached the bottom of the meadow and entered the top end of the gorge. Since the river was up, it was really roaring as it violently plunged its way down the steep and narrow gorge! Doulos advised everyone to use extreme caution, especially in the sections where the trail hugged the edge of the cliffs. In other areas the waters were lapping the edge of the path, which made the going even more dangerous!

All of them breathed a great sigh of relief when they reached the top of the falls at the bottom of the gorge. They descended the great stone spiral staircase through the vertical shaft, walked through the corridor, and emerged at the bottom of the cliff near the falls. Makeeseldruff Falls was quite a spectacle with the volume of water that was plunging over the cliff top, now way above them.

They walked the several kilometers alongside the river and returned to the bottom of the valley. The lower sections of the campsite were flooded, and they could see that a short while earlier the water had been higher. Although the ground was wet, it was still firm, and they pitched their tents on the higher ground.

It was late afternoon now. The temperature was considerably warmer here than it was in the high mountain meadow where the Atascosa people lived, and the day had remained clear and sunny. They did some more exploring, and that night they talked with each other about their experiences with the Atascosans.

They took two more days to finish the walk with Doulos, and they followed the same route they had used when they entered. On the final descent, they passed some other hikers. It was late afternoon when they arrived at the road's end where Rinto and Fraxino's vehicle-craft was parked. The weather had been warm and sunny for their entire walk.

"We made it back," Steven declared.

"Back to civilization," Andrew commented.

Everyone including Doulos threw his backpack into the back of the vehicle-craft. Rinto started the engine and drove them the few kilometers back to Hichicera and pulled up to Doulos' residence behind his sport shop. He unloaded his backpack and invited everyone inside to eat supper with him and his family. They entered his residence through the back door.

His wife was just starting to prepare supper. They were glad to see each other, and she asked him how their trip went.

"This is my wife, Clarinda," said Doulos as he introduced her. All of them greeted her, and then Doulos began relating the whole story of their past week's adventure. At times, Chispo, Rinto, and Fraxino added comments. By the time they were finished relating their story, she had supper prepared, and she served everyone.

There were various types of mixed vegetables along with fish from the Zuehl Sea. They were hungry after their full day of walking, and they ate well.

"You fellows are certainly welcome to stay here overnight," Doulos offered.

"Thanks, but I kind of want to return home as soon as possible," Rinto answered. "We'll get several hours of driving done tonight."

"Right then, as you wish," Doulos responded. "Anyway, have a safe journey, and all the best with your mission in Mexico."

"Thank you, Doulos," said Rinto. "It was a pleasure getting to know you, and I appreciate your taking us into the mountains to meet the Atascosa people."

"Not a problem. I enjoyed having all of you along."

Clarinda also wished them well as they walked outside and boarded the vehicle-craft to leave. Rinto started the engine, and he drove them out of town toward the east. It was now evening, and between two and three hours of daylight remained.

Earth time, it was 12 noon, Wednesday, July 10.

"Are we going to take the same route home or take a different route?" Robert asked Rinto.

"We're going home a more direct route," he answered with confidence.

"More inland?" Andrew asked.

"Dudes, we're *flying* home!" Rinto exclaimed enthusiastically. He pulled back a lever and switched off the engine. The vehicle-craft left the ground.

"Oh, yeah," said Chris. "I didn't think about us flying home."

"Dudes, sit back in your seats," Chispo enthusiastically told them. "Rinto's going to put this craft in high gear, and we're going to zoom directly home in three hours, man!"

Under the command of the on-board crystal array, the craft swiftly accelerated with such a force that they were pressed into their seats and could not even reach forward. In short order, they cleared the crest of the Cloerinne Mountains, and

Rinto briefly levelled out the craft at a cruising speed of 900 km/h.

They could now leave their seats, and they looked out of the windows and saw the Makeeseldruff River below them. Rinto caused the craft to briefly swoop into the large valley. Then he made a left turn and quickly gained altitude. They were soon flying over the dangerous Makeeseldruff Gully and then a brief moment later, over the meadow where they had just stayed. As Rinto had gained sufficient altitude, they were well above the meadow and could not make out details.

"We've just done in five minutes what took us three days on foot," Fraxino commented.

Rinto caused the craft to gain even more altitude, and they cleared the highest point of the mountains north of the meadow. He levelled out the craft and maintained an even cruising speed of 1,000 km/h. They were now headed directly for Zantaayer, which in a straight line was 1,200 kilometers due north of them.

They played more music in their on-board holodisk player during the flight.

A huge desert valley stretched out ahead of them into the horizon and beyond that was another range of mountains. They flew over two more valleys and mountain ranges, and then Rinto steered the craft toward the western ridge of the Ciruclar Mountains and brought it in for a landing on the narrow, forested backroad on the ridge top.

"We're back!" Rinto exclaimed as he touched down on the gravel road.

Al Nitak was just setting in the western sky, and as Rinto made the descent into Zantaayer on the mountainous road, they could see the lights of the city in the twilight.

CHAPTER 7

MEXICO, THE ANCIENT PAINTINGS

As Rinto finished the descent on the gravel road, night arrived. In a short time, they were pulling into the Zapatero's driveway. As everyone was getting out of the vehicle, Glecko came outside to greet them.

"Hi, fellows. How was your trip?"

"We had a great time, Dad," Fraxino answered.

"Your mother's at a meeting right now," Glecko informed them. "She'll be home later tonight. Sorry I haven't got any supper for you guys. If I'd known you were coming . . ."

"Oh, that's okay, Dad," Rinto reassured him. "We just flew our craft in from Hichicera, and we ate supper with a new friend of ours there."

"That's good. Tell me all about your trip."

"Well, Dad, we had a nice two-day drive to get there, and we visited Lominac . . ."

"Did you really?"

"That's right, and when we got to Hichicera, we met this guy named Doulos who visits the green people every other month. By the way, they're called the Atascosa . . ."

By now they were unloading their backpacks from the vehicle-craft, and they walked into the house as Rinto and Fraxino told their father the whole story. Chispo and the others also walked in with them and added their comments.

". . . and let me tell you," Chispo related. "We met this really neat dude named Orolizo who says he's got a soul link counterpart living in Mexico where we're going to go . . ."

Suddenly, there was a knock on the door. It was Mrs. Colancha.

"Chispo, looks like your mom's found you," Rinto remarked.

"Come on in," Glecko told her in Artenian.

"Oh, hi Mom," said Chispo.

"Hi, Chispo. How are you?" she said to him in Artenian. "I understand you've been to southern Zotola. How was it?"

"We had a great time, visited a town called Hichicera, and we walked into the mountains and visited the Atascosa people."

"Well good," she commented. "Listen, I need you to do some things around the house."

"Don't worry," Chispo reassured her. "I'll do them tomorrow. By the way, Mom, these are my new friends from Tennessee. I don't believe you've met them."

"No, I haven't. Hi, I'm Vironga Colancha-Pachanga, and I'm Chispo's mother."

Chispo translated to Andrew, Chris, Robert, and Steven what she said, and they introduced themselves to her.

"Guys, I guess I'd better go on home," Chispo told them in English. "Mom wants some chores done. I'll have them licked in a heartbeat. I'll be back first thing in the morning. See you around, dudes." He and his mother left, and they walked home through the backyard.

As they were leaving, Rinto overheard what Vironga said. "They're not having a bad influence on you, are they?"

"No, not at all, Mom," he answered. "I really enjoy them. They're the . . ."

The rest of them continued to relate their adventures to Glecko. He was really impressed about the way of life of the Atascosa people.

Fraxino proudly showed his father the display cabinet he had purchased for himself. Chispo showed Glecko the two quartz crystals as well.

It wasn't much longer before they spread out their bedrolls and sleeping bags and settled down for the night.

"So, what are we going to do tomorrow?" Andrew asked everyone as they were drifting off to sleep.

"Dudes, I'm going through my rock and crystal collection to choose out certain ones that will serve us in Mexico," Fraxino told everyone.

"Chispo and I are going to look over my craft and be sure it's all ready to go," said Rinto.

"What about the holographic plates?" Steven asked.

"We're going to have a quick look through those too," Rinto answered. "More importantly, I'm going to have our crystal base read in those two crystals we brought back from Zocanto and Orolizo."

"Good thinking," Chris told him.

They talked a few more minutes and then went to sleep. All of them slept peacefully for the entire night.

The next morning was partly sunny with some clouds in the sky. Sosta had come home late last night, well after everyone was asleep, and she was sleeping late. Glecko came into the room where everyone was sleeping and announced that breakfast was ready. They got up, rolled up their sleeping bags and bedrolls, and came into the kitchen to eat.

"It looks like it's going to rain by late afternoon," Glecko informed everyone, "seeing how the clouds are building up in the sky."

"I hope we get everything ready for us to go before it starts," said Rinto. "Packing up the vehicle for a trip while it's raining is a nuisance."

"Man, I hope Chispo doesn't take too long with his mom's chores," Fraxino mentioned.

Rinto leaned over and peeped out of the window. "There he is. I see him through the bushes. Looks like she saddled him with weeding her flower beds."

"Robert, go over to Chispo and get those two crystals from him," Fraxino requested. "We need to go ahead and read them into our crystal base."

Robert had just finished eating. "Okay, I'll be back in a few minutes." He got up from the table, walked out of the house, and went over to Chispo's house, crossing under the row of bushes on the way. He found him still weeding the flower beds in the backyard.

"Hey, Robert," he called out to him. "What's going on, dude?"

"Good morning, Chispo. How's everything?"

"Man, she's got me weeding the flower beds. This will take me about another hour, and I'll be right over."

"Good," said Robert. "They sent me over here for the two crystals we brought back. They want to read them with their crystal base computer."

"Oh, all right, man. You can go on in the house and get them. My backpack's in my room, and they're both in the top compartment. I'd go in there for them myself, but Mom's got me doing this."

"That's no problem," said Robert. "I'll go in and get them."

"Don't worry about Mom," Chispo told him. "She's already gone for the day."

Robert walked into the house, found Chispo's backpack, got the two crystals out of its top compartment, and walked back over to the Zapateros with them.

"Good, just what we need, man," Fraxino said to Robert as he walked into the house and handed them to him. "Let's take them straight to the crystal base and have them read in. Rinto, have you got a clean piece of orange Calcite so we can do a duplicate reading and take that rock with us?"

"Let me go check." Rinto went upstairs to the attic and picked through his rocks. "Hey, Fraxino!" he called out from the attic.

"Yeah, what?"

"Come on up here and sort through your collection. You've got more rocks than I do."

Fraxino set the two crystals on a table in the room and went upstairs to help Rinto sort through their rocks. Robert returned to the kitchen where Andrew, Chris, and Steven were still seated at the table.

"So, do you have any feelings for Lumela now?" Chris asked Steven.

"None at all. I'd rather travel with you guys and enjoy the adventure," he told them. "The bug that's bitten me is the travel bug, not the love bug."

"That's good," said Andrew. "Travelling is a lot of fun, isn't it?"

"I'm telling you . . ." Steven agreed.

It was nearly an hour before Rinto and Fraxino came down from the attic. They brought down a briefcase with them, and they opened it up and showed it to everyone. Inside of it they had carefully placed some crystals of various colors, including a beautiful specimen of Purple Rainbow Fluorite, the center piece of the array.

"We put that one in the center," Fraxino explained, "because it is known for causing positive changes in people without their even realizing it. Hopefully that will serve to counter the adverse effects the transmitter device is having on the town's residents."

"That's good thinking," Andrew told him.

"Okay, Fraxino," Rinto directed, "let's get those two crystals read in."

"They're on the table in there," Fraxino told him and indicated.

"I'm going to let the main controls crystal of our craft read them in first," said Rinto. "It might be able to glean some information as to the whereabouts of the Atlantean paintings. That way our controls crystal will have the knowledge to teleport us straight to that region." Rinto walked into the next room, found the two crystals and walked outside to the vehicle-craft.

At the same moment, Chispo came over.

"Oh, hey Chispo. How's it going?" Rinto called out to him.

"I just finished all the chores, man. Mom had me weeding her flower gardens."

"Yes, we saw you," said Rinto. "Chispo, give the engine a checking over. I'm going to read these two crystals into the main controls crystal. Maybe it will glean the knowledge on where to take us."

"All right, man."

In five minutes, Chispo had checked all the fluid levels and said everything looked fine.

"Thanks," said Rinto. "Okay, that gets them read in to our controls crystal. Oh wait! I almost forgot." He took a piece of orange Calcite out of a side compartment on the inside of the craft. Next, he slowly moved the Calcite piece over the top of the crystal that had the mountain scene within it, and he turned the Calcite piece at different angles as he did so. "There. That stores the data in this piece of Calcite. That's our backup copy." He returned the piece of Calcite to its compartment.

"Smart move, man," Chispo told him.

"Okay, now let's go into the house and see what the crystal base computer reads from these." Rinto walked into the house with both quartz crystals in hand. Chispo followed. They walked through the main room, and entered the room where they kept the crystal base computer. Fraxino and the others now joined them, and Rinto placed the two crystals on the tray. He turned on the controls, and they waited for information to pop up on the screen.

"Read error?" Rinto remarked. "That's weird."

"Take the crystal sphere off the tray," Chispo suggested. "I believe it's causing interference, and your reader can't differentiate the two."

"Good point," said Rinto, and he removed the sphere. "There we go. Now we've got something."

"Wow, man!" Fraxino exclaimed. "Look at that."

First, an outline image of the desert valley came up on the screen with a view of the same range of mountains as what appeared within the crystal itself.

"Let's see," said Rinto. "Zero in, closer range . . . There." The image on the screen zoomed in on some lowland hills, a pair of mesas, in the central part of the desert valley. Next, the image disappeared, and images of different drawings appeared on the screen.

"Oh my goodness!" Steven declared. "It's even got the images of the paintings recorded."

"How did they record all that in that crystal?" Chris wanted to know.

"Since the information exists," Rinto explained, "this crystal provides the right avenues or keys so that our crystal base can literally access the information and latch the data from the ether."

"The information is not actually in the crystal itself," Fraxino added comment. "That crystal is telepathically programmed and telepathically connected to that area, and anyone reading the crystal is connected straight to that location where the information is recorded in the rocks and the ether around them."

"Very interesting," Steven remarked.

"Lots of localized information is telepathically accessible with the right crystals from anywhere in the universe," Rinto told them.

"Yes, but what about the spiritual and telepathic block between Earth and here?" Robert asked.

"Oh, yeah. Good point," Rinto responded.

"Either the crystals intelligently know how to penetrate the block," Fraxino explained, "or the information may be repeated in the ether on this world so that it can still be accessed."

"No matter what," Rinto pointed out, "our on-board crystals do know how to penetrate that block and take us to and from planet Earth."

"That's true," Robert admitted.

"Wow, dudes!" Chispo remarked. "Look at those drawings."

"Look at all those figures," said Steven. "Some of them look like rockets or something."

"Some sort of spacecraft," Andrew agreed.

"Some of the drawings look like DNA," Chris mentioned.

"That or numerical charts," Chispo suggested.

"Tools and other smaller figures," said Steven.

"This is really interesting!" Rinto remarked.

They viewed other drawings, and then Rinto swapped the crystal containing the mountain scene for the quartz crystal sphere that Orolizo had handed them. He placed it on the tray.

"Read error again!" Rinto exclaimed.

"He must have put a telepathic lock on it, dudes," Fraxino commented.

"Could be," said Rinto.

"I just got to thinking," Chispo brought up. "Maybe we're not supposed to be reading that one. Orolizo intends for that crystal to go to his soul link."

"You're probably right," Rinto admitted. "Here, Chispo." He handed him the sphere. "You be the guardian of this crystal until we may find him, and you can hand it to him."

"All right, man."

"What about the holographic plates?" Robert asked.

"Yeah, let's have a look at the index plate." Rinto reached into the bronze box for it and placed it onto the tray. The index list popped up on the screen, and Rinto examined the contents. "I don't really see anything of interest. Chispo, what about you?"

He looked over Rinto's shoulder at the screen. "No, man, nothing pertaining to what we need to know about for this trip."

"I don't know about you guys," Rinto announced, "but I'm kind of anxious to go ahead and travel there. We need to leave before that rain comes this afternoon. There's no hurry on the rest of these plates. You all ready to go?"

"Okay, let's go," said Fraxino. "So, we've read the pertinent information into our craft's control crystal. The crystal array in our briefcase is ready. We've viewed the mountain scene crystal on our crystal base computer. Anything else we need to do?"

"Not that I can think of," Rinto answered.

"What about food and water?" Robert asked everyone.

"Good idea," said Fraxino. "I'll get some jugs and fill them." He left and went to the kitchen.

"I'll shut down our crystal base," said Rinto. He switched it off. "You know, we are low on food." He walked into the kitchen to join Fraxino.

"What about us?" Robert asked Andrew, Chris, and Steven. "How much food do each of you have?"

"Oh, a couple of days," said Andrew.

"About the same," said Chris.

"Same here," Steven replied.

"All right, we can wait until we get to Mexico, right?" Robert asked them. They answered yes.

"I believe I better go to my house and restock," Chispo told them. "See you in a few minutes." He walked out of the house.

In half an hour, everyone had the vehicle-craft loaded, and they were ready to go. Chispo had returned. They checked to be sure they had all necessary items, and once they were sure, Fraxino started the engine. Glecko and Sosta came outside to see them off and wished them a safe journey on their mission. They didn't know how long they would be gone, possibly for several weeks.

Fraxino backed them out of the driveway. They left, and he drove them up the mountains to the ridge top. Once they were on the ridge road, Fraxino turned off the engine and pulled back the lever. The vehicle-craft left the ground, and they were soon flying over the tree tops. The craft accelerated, and they flew west, leaving the Ciruclar Mountains behind.

"We're out of here, dudes!" Fraxino exclaimed.

For a brief moment, a forcefield accompanied by a faint green glow overtook them. They began to feel as if they were dematerializing. Then suddenly, they were fine, and they found themselves flying around 5,000 meters above a huge desert valley in northern Mexico. It was the crack of dawn, and the Sun was just making its appearance on the eastern horizon.

As Fraxino caused the craft to descend in preparation for landing, they could just make out, in the distance, a small range of lowland hills, a double mesa, on the desert floor due south of them.

"Yep, I believe we got it, Fraxino," Rinto declared. "There are the two mesas in the middle of the desert valley with the mountain ranges on both the east and west sides."

"Man, it looks just like it did on your computer screen," Chispo remarked.

There were several straight and narrow dirt roads crossing the desert in different directions, and as they neared the mesas, Fraxino began to look for a suitable road on which to make the landing. He lowered the air speed of the craft, and he chose one of the two north-south roads that appeared to head for the mesas. He prepared for landing and was now cruising only a few meters above the road.

"Watch it, Fraxino!" Rinto warned him. "This road looks rough."

Fraxino steered the craft and touched down at a speed of 100 km/h. Immediately, he swerved to the left to miss an upcoming pothole, and some scrub bushes scraped the left side of the vehicle-craft as he briefly left the center of the road. He jerked it back and slowed the craft as quickly as possible. It was a rough landing, to say the least, and they were bounced around inside somewhat.

"Golly!" Robert exclaimed.

"Law, Fraxino!" Chispo remarked. "What kind of stunt man are you?"

"Whew! That scared me to death!" Steven exclaimed.

"Fraxino, I believe I better do the landing from now on when we touch down in foreign lands," Rinto told him.

"Sorry, guys," Fraxino told everyone. "That's the best I could do with that stupid surprise pothole!" He brought the vehicle-craft to a stop, and he and Rinto stepped outside to check the tires and the suspension for possible damage.

Everyone else stepped out of the vehicle and had a look around. It was still the crack of dawn, and the desert valley was not yet fully lit. The morning temperature was mild, and the skies were clear. All around them, the desert floor was covered with Mesquite shrubs and other bushes including Yucca plants. Interspersed throughout the region was also a tree-sized version of Yucca that looked very similar to the Joshua Tree, only the blades were wider and thicker.

"Mexico, aquí estamos," Andrew commented.

"Yes, we are here," Robert agreed.

Five minutes later, Rinto and Fraxino announced that everything was fine and survived the shock of the landing. Everyone got back inside. Rinto now did the driving. He started the engine and drove them for around a kilometer along the narrow, bumpy road until they arrived at the foot of the mesas. It was now fully daylight. The time was 6 AM, Thursday, July 11. Rinto parked in a wide spot on the side of the dirt road.

"Man, I keep forgetting how blue the skies are, here on Earth," Chispo remarked as everyone was stepping out of the vehicle-craft.

"Yeah, you're right," Andrew agreed. "Your skies back on Artenia have a slight green to them, sort of a turquoise color."

The mesa pair now stood clearly before them with its cliff walls clearly visible. From the base of the cliffs, the land sloped steeply to the desert floor. The whole valley appeared to be uninhabited, but in actual fact there were a few ranches here and there and the occasional farmhouse.

Rinto and Fraxino opened their briefcase and examined their crystal array.

Luckily everything was still intact since they had packed them with cushioning. Rinto now took a piece of orange Calcite out of the array and placed it in his pocket to take with him. He was the last one out of the vehicle.

"Okay, ready to go," Rinto announced as he closed the door.

They walked down the lane and decided to climb up to the northeast face of the mesa on the left, and they would work their way around, following along the north face of the cliff. Then they would advance to the second mesa to the west. The dirt lane veered to the left and headed south as it passed by the east side of the mesas. They left the lane and immediately climbed the steep slope to the base of the cliff.

In addition to having to dodge various thorny bushes, Cactus, and Yucca plants, the soil was loose, and at times they slipped and fell. After some considerable effort and offering each other helping hands to make their advance, they arrived at the base of the brownish-beige cliffs. Sure enough, there the paintings were.

"Wow, dudes!" Chispo exclaimed. "This is far out!"

Steven's mouth dropped open. "I'm not believing this!"

"Pretty amazing," Andrew commented.

"Guys, these drawings are really unique," Fraxino remarked.

"Hey, look at this one," Robert announced. "It looks like a depiction of a person next to a serrated horizontal platform."

"Wonder what that means?" Chris asked.

Most of the drawings were done with red paint, and some of the depictions contained orange as well. There were drawings of what appeared to be people, tools, plantlife, animal representations, suns, and moons. There were also drawings of more exotic things like concentric circles, chains of diamond-shaped cross hatched squares, spacecrafts, and other vehicles.

Rinto advanced along the base of the cliff. "Here are some more drawings over here, guys," he called out. He took his piece of Calcite and briefly scanned the surfaces of the drawings as they went along. The others followed.

"Oh, neat!" Chris exclaimed as he spotted a drawing next to Rinto. "It looks like some sort of a gyroscope."

"It looks more like a drawing of a vortex to me," said Robert.

"Look at all those diamond-shaped squares under it," Steven indicated.

"What do you think all those diamonds mean?" Andrew asked Rinto and Fraxino.

"I think some of those could represent some sort of dating technique," Rinto answered, "seeing how they're pretty much lined up in rows or columns."

"Like I was saying earlier, man," Chispo reminded him, "they look like numerical charts."

"In some ways, these drawings look amateur," Andrew commented, "but then I believe there must be a lot of hidden meaning in them."

"Oh wow, man! Look at this one," Chispo remarked and pointed upwards. "That one looks like some people about to go up a ladder to a platform."

"And look at that image to its upper left," said Andrew as he indicated. "It looks like it could be a TV screen, maybe an oscilloscope."

"Hey, everyone," Steven called out. "Here's an interesting one. It looks like your typical, everyday military tank."

"Yes, it does," Andrew agreed as he looked at it.

"But wait," said Chris. "If you look at it more closely, it looks like a fort with seven houses within it."

"And that mast above it was probably a receiver/transmitter tower," Chispo speculated.

As they moved on to the next area, the path along the base of the cliff was narrow and difficult. They had to negotiate Prickly Pear Cactus, Yuccas, including Lechuguilla, and other thorny shrubs, and in places they had to climb over rocks and go up and down ledges.

"Golly!" Robert remarked as they arrived at another section of paintings. "Look at that one. It looks like a rocket for sure."

"Huh! Sure enough," Chris remarked.

"The image looks like a multistage rocket," Chispo commented.

"That is really cool!" Rinto declared.

They moved on a few more meters to another cliff wall.

"Dudes, I don't know quite what to make of this set of drawings," Fraxino told everyone.

"Well, let's see," said Rinto as he scanned his piece of Calcite over the drawings. "I see two different drawings of the Sun. That drawing on the upper left looks like some sort of small animal." He pointed further to the right. "There are some jagged lines. They probably represent some sort of energy."

"There are some more of those strings of cross-hatched diamond squares," Robert indicated.

"Hmm . . . three columns of eight and one of ten," said Steven.

"Some have cross hatches. Some don't," said Rinto.

"Different colors too," Chris added.

"Do you think they might represent electronic circuitry or circuit boards?" Andrew asked.

"That's possibly so," Rinto answered. "Maybe they're numerical storage systems."

"I'm telling you, man," Chispo insisted. "I think they are."

They advanced a few meters to the next wall.

"Wow! This one's got all kinds of depictions!" Fraxino remarked.

"Look at those four drawings up at the top," Robert announced and indicated.

"They look like some sort of craft in its hanger," said Rinto.

"What are all those jagged lines surrounding them in each depiction?" Chris wanted to know.

"They probably represent the energy or forcefields of the crafts themselves," Rinto answered.

"Dudes, it could be representing a time sequence," Fraxino brought up. "Look at the different stages in each of the four drawings. They're probably depicting its arrival."

"Yes, that's a good point," Rinto admitted.

"There's a whole slew of tiny marks under one of them," Fraxino remarked. "Four rows of them."

"Those drawings on the left look like plants," said Andrew.

"Chispo, here's another one of those numerical charts, as you call them," Robert said to him.

"Seven columns of them," Chispo commented. "That's weird, man! They're hanging down from a horizontal line, and there's only half a diamond at the top of each chain."

"Count them," Andrew suggested.

"Four and a half cross-hatched diamonds on the first column," Chispo mentioned to himself. "Five and a half in the next six columns. That's a total of 37.5."

"37.5 . . . You know, Chispo," Rinto pointed out. "If you take out that decimal, you get the last three digits of your phone number."

Chispo stared at it and recounted the diamonds. He started laughing. "Far out, man! That is really far out! We *are* the chosen seven to come here and perform this mission."

"Hey, Chispo," Robert said to him. "Look how many columns there are . . . seven."

He hesitated. "Dude, this has really got me beside myself. This depiction has definitely got some hidden meaning to it!"

"And the coincidence we experienced when we exchanged those crystals shortly after we met each other?" Robert brought up.

"That too, man. It's all connected to this in some way," said Chispo.

"Whoever drew this probably knew subconsciously that we were coming," Fraxino remarked.

"Man, I have to declare this depiction was drawn so that one day we would come here and read it," Chispo stated.

"I'd say," Rinto agreed. "I have to admit that is an interesting coincidence."

"That is pretty interesting," Chris remarked.

"Look at this little orange figure over here," Robert announced as he pointed to it. "It looks like a dolphin leaping out of the water."

"No kidding!" Steven responded.

"It looks like the people who drew these depictions had to be from somewhere else," Rinto explained. "I mean, how is a native ancient tribe of people going to know about dolphins? We're not that near the ocean here."

"And all these other depictions of spacecrafts and that rocket we saw earlier," Fraxino added.

"These people must have known a lot," Rinto declared.

"Definitely Atlantean descendants," Chispo remarked.

"Look at that round orange image depicted above the 37.5 diamonds numerical chart," said Andrew as he indicated.

"It looks like a sun with those red flames coming off the top of it," Robert mentioned.

"Do you think it might represent a dying sun somewhere?" Steven asked.

"Well, it is interesting that there's a depiction of a dolphin in this same group of drawings," Chris pointed out. "Didn't Morris say Delikadove, the old home world of the dolphins, got destroyed millions of years ago?"

"35 million years ago, if I remember correctly," said Robert.

"When their star Danetar died," Chris stated.

"Hey, Chispo," Robert asked. "Do you think we've got some connection to the dolphins?"

"Not that I'm aware of, man, but subconsciously who knows. Your friend Morris got that telepathic message about, '60375 . . . go meet him,' right before you all came to our world. Then he took off to the world of the dolphins. There could be some link, but there's nothing I'm aware of, except for the hidden meaning of these depictions. Dudes, I am really impressed by this coincidence, I'll have to admit."

"Of course, it could be irrelevant or trivial," Andrew suggested.

"Yeah, but still, the numbers are there in that depiction," Chispo insisted.

"No matter what, like I said, this is an interesting coincidence," Rinto stated. "I don't know what's in it for us, but it does make for an interesting puzzle to ponder."

"Hey, look at this," said Robert as he pointed to an image above the dolphin image. "It looks like a plant, actually very much like a Eucalyptus twig."

"Oh, yeah," Chris recalled. "Morris told us the Eucalyptus trees also came from Delikadove with the dolphins 35 million years ago."

"That's true," said Robert. "Isn't that something that there would be a drawing of that right above the dolphin!"

"I'll say," Chris agreed.

Chispo stared at the drawing. "Man, that's wild! Whoever drew this actually knew that."

"How could they have known something like that?" Steven asked.

"The Atlantean society knew a lot since they were involved with galactic trade," Rinto explained. "A lot of information has been lost since their days on this world."

"Man, I have to declare these depictions on this wall were put here for us," Chispo insisted. "They must have been intended only for us and to be interpreted only by us."

"You're probably not kidding, Chispo," Robert agreed. "This is truly amazing!"

"Ready to move on?" Fraxino asked everyone.

They advanced along the bottom of the cliff, and the going became difficult. They arrived at a drop off, and to advance any further, they would have had to carefully pick their way through a thick stand of Lechuguilla plants.

"I believe that's all the paintings for this mesa," Rinto announced. "Let's go to the other one."

They turned back, retraced some of their steps, and descended the steep sloping terrain to the north. As they passed by some large boulders near the bottom of the slope, they discovered some designs etched into the surface of one of them.

"Huh!" Chris remarked. "It looks like they used an engraver on this one."

Everyone stared at the boulder.

"I don't know what that depiction is on the right," Rinto told them, "but those concentric circles on the left represent a universal symbol."

"Dudes, that's a clear sign that the people who lived here had galactic trade," Chispo declared.

"What's the name of that symbol, Fraxino?" Rinto asked him.

"Let me think . . . Universa Ciruclar, as best as I can translate it to English."

They continued the descent and arrived at the dirt lane near the spot where their vehicle-craft was parked, and they walked to the vehicle. Although it was only mid morning here in northern Mexico, it was already well into the afternoon in Zotola, and everyone was hungry. They took food out of their backpacks, prepared, and ate lunch.

When they finished, Rinto closed the vehicle-craft again. They walked over to the second mesa and climbed the steep, treacherous slopes to reach the bottom of the cliff walls. There was a section of the wall that was lighter in color, and it was to that area that they made their ascent. They found more depictions. Although they were also painted with red and orange paint, they were of a different style. Rinto immediately began scanning his piece of orange Calcite over the drawings.

"Oh my goodness!" Steven declared. "This wall is full of paintings and drawings."

"Some are really faded like they're in the background," said Andrew, "and others stand out."

"I know," Chispo responded. "Look at this one, dudes. This chain of diamonds has two strings and then a third one branching off the left one."

"Some of them are filled in with red, and some are not," Rinto mentioned.

"And this arm and elbow with orange and red bands," Chris brought up. "What could it mean?"

"Maybe it means a turn of events," Fraxino replied.

"A lot of these depictions look like local tools they used," said Rinto.

"There aren't so many jagged lines over here like there were in that first group," Robert mentioned.

"That's true," Rinto agreed. "These drawings are of a different style."

They moved to a different wall a few meters to the left.

"Dudes, there's that Universa Ciruclar symbol again," Fraxino pointed out.

"Look what's to the right of it," said Robert. "It looks like a whale."

"It really does," Andrew agreed.

"Here's a bunch more of those tiny marks," Chispo informed them as he pointed to another area. "This one has three rows."

"What's that to the upper right of them?" Chris wanted to know.

"It looks like some sort of a net," Rinto replied.

"Hey, there are some more jagged lines," Andrew brought up and indicated.

"Oh, yeah. So, there are some over here also," said Robert.

"Well, that's about all there is in this area," Rinto announced. "Let's check out the rest of the wall west of here."

With considerable difficulty, they made their way along the base of the cliff. Some parts of the path were dangerously narrow, and dodging Cactus, Lechuguilla, and thorny bushes didn't make it any easier. In some places, they had to descend and make their way along the upper portion of the steep and treacherous slopes. It was some time before they came across more paintings, but finally, on the last section of cliff wall, now on the west face of the second mesa, they discovered some more paintings.

"Yep, here are some more paintings with jagged lines," Rinto announced.

"Huh! Look at that orange, barrel-shaped object," Chris brought up and indicated.

"Cool!" Chispo responded. "Four red feet underneath it and three more of them on top. That's wild!"

"Probably some sort of weird craft," Fraxino speculated.

"Here's another depiction of diamond chains," Robert indicated.

"It looks like part of it is gone or broken away," said Rinto.

"Look straight above the diamond chains," said Andrew. "It looks like a couple of pyramids."

"And all those lines criss crossing inside the two triangles," Steven added.

"Whoever drew these definitely knew some things," Fraxino commented.

"Dudes, look at this drawing over here," Chispo announced. "It looks like a couple of mountain ranges."

"Well, I will say!" Robert exclaimed. "The top range has what looks like some sort of a beam or ray taking off at an angle from the second peak."

"Now that is far out!" Rinto remarked.

"It seems to say that some visitors from space teleported in and left the same way," Fraxino speculated.

Rinto scanned his piece of Calcite over the drawing. He was also carrying the quartz mountain scene crystal that Zocanto had given him. He took it out of his daypack and looked within it and made comparisons with the mountain range to the west of them.

"Perfect match!" Rinto declared. "Perfect match."

"Really, man?" Chispo responded.

"Look at that second peak over there," Rinto told everyone as he indicated. "That could very well be the location where they teleported in and out, and this depiction actually tells us that."

"Wait a minute. A thought just came to me," Chispo announced. "The strangers came and spoke. They'd never seen this type before."

"What's that about?" Robert wanted to know.

"It must be a telepathic thought recorded in that depiction," Chispo answered.

"It's like I was saying earlier," Fraxino reminded everyone. "Information is recorded in the rocks and the ether around them."

"I'm telling you, dudes," Chispo assured them. "That depiction is clear proof that alien civilizations visited this area."

"Or the Atlanteans," Rinto commented.

"Well, I'd say some of both," said Fraxino. "Galactic trade is a fact, and the Atlanteans were definitely active in that respect."

"How old do you think these drawings are?" Steven asked.

"The thoughts I'm getting," Rinto answered, "are that these drawings are 12,000 years old, done shortly after the Atlanteans fled to Al Nitak. It looks like a small group of them settled here to live right after the big disaster in their native land of Antarctica."

"Wait a minute," Chispo broke in. "I just got to thinking about something. You know that boulder we just saw with the universal symbol and the other drawing we couldn't discern?"

"Yes, what about it?" Rinto responded.

"It looks like a map of Antarctica, the past homeland of the Atlanteans."

Everyone else recalled the image in his mind.

"Yeah, you're right. It does," Robert agreed.

"Good thinking," Rinto told Chispo.

"Do you think these paintings have any connection to Mars?" Chris asked.

"It's possible," Rinto answered. "There are some pyramids on that planet, likely a duplicate of what's in Egypt, and in case something happens to the ones on Earth, the pyramids on Mars contain a backup copy of the information recorded by the Atlanteans before they fled to Al Nitak."

"Well, guys," Fraxino announced. "I guess this is the last section of paintings."

"Probably so," said Rinto. "This is the end of the cliff and the rest of the mesa seems to gently slope to the west with no cliffs at all."

They made their way down the slope and followed a hot dry gully to a large riverbed on the west side of the mesa. They crossed the dry riverbed and picked their way through and around plenty of thorny shrubs, crossed a riverbank, and came upon the ruins of an old adobe farmhouse. A windmill stood on the site. They found the dirt road, turned right, and walked along it for half an hour until they got back to the vehicle-craft.

By now it was early afternoon. It had become hot, but the temperature didn't affect them due to the arid climate. Rinto opened the door to the vehicle-craft, and everyone entered.

"That was really an interesting collection of drawings on those cliffs," Steven commented.

"Yes, I enjoyed looking at them," said Robert.

"Do you think any of them have to do with that transmitter device that's blocking communication with Al Nitak?" Chris asked them.

"I don't know, man," Chispo answered, "but that second peak on those mountains west of us might hold some clues."

"What about those four drawings we saw of what looked like a craft with the jagged energy lines around them?" Andrew asked.

"Possibly, Andrew," Fraxino answered, "but I can't determine a connection that would cause us to pinpoint the device."

"Right, hop in, fellows," Rinto directed. "Let's fly over to those peaks and take a look."

They boarded the craft. Rinto took his piece of orange Calcite and let the Ulexite main controls crystal read it. Then he opened the briefcase, placed the Calcite back in its spot, closed the lid, and got in the driver's seat.

"Ready, everyone?" Rinto checked.

They answered yes. Without his even starting the engine, the craft left the ground under the power of the crystal array. Rinto steered the craft around to face west, and the craft swiftly accelerated as they made a straight course for the mountain range west of them. They gained altitude and reached the mountain in a matter of minutes.

Its slopes were rugged and had numerous sheer cliffs. Normal access by foot would have been considerably difficult, but with the luxury of flying to the ridge top in Rinto and Fraxino's craft, they were upon the top with the greatest of ease. The second peak was actually a small mesa that was sitting on top of the mountain ridge, and all sides of it were sheer cliffs with dropoffs of 60 to 70 meters in height.

"This appears like it would be an ideal location for extraterrestrial crafts to come and go," Rinto commented.

"Yes, I agree it is a pretty secure location," said Steven, "seeing that it's got dropoffs on all sides."

Rinto gently brought the craft down for a landing and touched down on the flat top of the mesa. It was approximately 100 by 100 meters in size, and much of the terrain was dominated by limestone bedrock. There were various types of Yuccas, Lechuguillas, Cactus plants, and other shrubs growing between the rocks, and there were Juniper shrubs as well. The views of the surrounding countryside were fantastic, and the double mesa now sat well below them in the desert valley to the east.

"Let's see if we can find any clues," Rinto suggested.

Everyone stepped outside and explored the top of the mesa. They went in different directions. Robert and Chispo walked over to the north side of the mesa and looked over the edge of the cliff. Below them was a small gully of Oak and Hickory trees, and there were Fan Palm trees as well.

"Hey, Robert. Look at this," Chispo suddenly said to him. He pointed to a section of bedrock on the cliff's edge near him.

"Yes, what is it?" Robert asked.

"Do you see those scorch marks?"

"Yeah, I sure do," Robert replied.

"That's probably the direct result of rockets or spacecrafts taking off from here."

"Oh, wait! Look over there, Chispo," said Robert as he just noticed a different section of bedrock. "That rock looks a little bit melted on top, doesn't it."

Chispo walked over and inspected the surface. "Hey, Rinto, everyone! Come over here!"

Rinto was the first one to arrive.

"Take a look at this, man," Chispo told him.

"Now, that is something of interest," Rinto commented as he stared at it. "Good going, guys."

The others arrived by now.

"Oh, cool!" Fraxino exclaimed. "It looks like an ancient landing pad, dudes."

"I believe it is," Andrew agreed.

They inspected the site and looked for other clues in the area, including physical artifacts.

"It doesn't look like we turned up anything," Rinto announced after searching for a while.

"I've been looking between rocks and everything," said Andrew.

"Are we ready to go on over to the town and see what we can find out?" Robert proposed.

"Yeah, sure. Let's go," Rinto agreed.

"Too bad we didn't find any more artifacts," Fraxino commented.

"That doesn't necessarily mean there aren't any here," Steven pointed out.

"If need be, we'll come back here later," said Rinto.

He opened the door to the vehicle-craft, and everyone entered. Rinto drove again, and once everyone was safely inside, the craft quietly left the ground. Under Rinto's direction, they flew off the east face of the mesa and back over the desert valley, passing by the double mesa well below them on their right.

Rinto decided to take them on a flying tour, looking for clues. They flew east and reached the other mountain range. It was also rugged with numerous cliffs and inaccessible areas. As they cleared the range and began to enter the next valley, they were suddenly afforded a view of a town way below them at the foot of the mountain range.

"Oh wow, dudes! That must be it!" Chispo exclaimed.

"Quick! Turn around, Rinto!" Fraxino ordered. "There's no telling how that town may freak out if they see us flying around up here."

"Oh, yeah. Good point," Rinto admitted. He immediately turned sharply to the left and flew back over to the western side of the ridge top.

"Well, we found the town, I believe," Robert said to everyone.

"Yeah, that's an understatement," Steven added.

"Rinto, let's cruise on up this valley and choose a place to land," Chispo suggested.

They flew by the left side of another mesa, and it appeared to be the highest point of the entire range. A little bit further north they noticed an opening in the range, actually a canyon, allowing access to the east, and they could see a road passing through it. Rinto caused the craft to descend, and he steered it in for a landing. Next, he lined up with the road, cruising a few meters above its surface.

"Dudes, this road's worse than the other one!" Chispo remarked.

"Yeah, I see it," Rinto responded. While still several meters above the road, he slowed the craft until they were almost stopped, and he carefully brought it in for a gentle landing. Next, he started the engine, shifted the transmission to first gear, and proceeded at a crawl. The one-lane road was considerably bumpy with plenty of large rocks, potholes, and dips as it made its descent through a thick stand of Mesquite shrubs and other bushes. On both sides of them were tall mountains, their sheer cliffs and slopes clearly visible.

Suddenly, the scenery changed, and they came upon a large spring and pond of water on the left. It was situated in a beautiful woods of Anaqua, Ash, Mesquite, and Sycamore trees. Some of them were quite large. As they looked beyond them, the whole canyon continued the same way downstream along the river.

"Oh, cool!" Fraxino declared. "Check that out. It's a spring."

"Let's stop and take a swim, fellows," Rinto suggested. He drove into a turnout on the left side of the road and parked.

There were no other people in the area, mainly because of the bad condition of the road. The only people who used this road were a few ranching families driving to and from the nearby town and their ranches in the desert valley to the west.

"I don't know about the rest of you," Chispo brought up, "but let's go ahead and camp here. It's already late afternoon, anyway."

"Sounds fine to me," Steven agreed.

"Me too," said Robert. "Let's go swimming." He was the first one out of the vehicle, and he ran to the water's edge and jumped in the 20 by 20 meter pond.

The others soon followed and jumped in. They played, raced each other, splashed each other, and enjoyed the afternoon. An hour later, they got out of the water, dried off, and began to prepare supper next to their vehicle-craft.

"Well, Rinto, how do you like Mexico so far?" Fraxino asked.

"It's a lot of fun and interesting, as well."

Suddenly, they heard a vehicle approaching from the desert valley, and they could hear it bouncing along as it descended the bumpy road.

"Oh my goodness!" Steven quietly declared.

"Quick, what do we tell them if they ask us?" Andrew wanted to know.

Rinto thought for a few seconds. "Just tell them we're American tourists, and we're driving a futuristic prototype vehicle. We're down here testing it out."

"Good thinking," said Andrew.

In half a minute, the vehicle came into view. It was a rancher, and he was driving an old Ford pickup truck. He pulled up beside Rinto and Fraxino's vehicle-craft and stopped, and he definitely had a look of curiosity on his face.

"¿Qué tal, jovenes? ¿De dónde vienen?" he called out to them in Spanish, greeting them and asking them where they were from.

Andrew and Robert knew a fair amount of Spanish. Both of them had always been interested in the language and had already studied two years of it in high school. In addition to that, Andrew had spent part of his early childhood in Spanish-speaking Peru, since his parents were missionaries. They decided to walk over to the rancher and chat with him, and Andrew did the talking.

"Somos de los Estados Unidos, y somos turistas," Andrew answered, telling him that they were American tourists.

"¿Y vienen en eso?" the rancher asked, wanting to know if they actually came in Rinto and Fraxino's craft.

"Sí, es un vehículo de prueba de un tipo futuristico," Andrew replied, telling him that it's a futuristic prototype vehicle.

"¿Sí verdad?" the rancher responded with surprise, asking if that was true.

"Sí."

"¿A qué vienen?" the rancher inquired, wanting to know why they had come to Mexico.

Andrew answered that they had come to see the sights, that they had seen the ancient paintings earlier in the day, and that they were going to visit the mountains. They chatted a couple of minutes. The rancher's name was Jesús Lucio, and each day he drove to his ranch in the desert valley to tend to his cattle.

"Está bien," he responded, saying that was good. "Bueno, jovenes, ya me voy. Que les vaya bien," telling them he was now going to proceed down the road, and he wished them well.

Andrew and Robert shook hands with Sr. Lucio, and as he drove off, they returned to the others and continued preparing supper.

"So, what did the rancher think of our Velosa cruiser craft, dudes?" Fraxino wanted to know.

"It looks like he took it pretty well," Andrew replied.

"Good, then I believe we can go ahead and drive this craft into the town," Rinto commented with a sense of relief.

"I don't think anything bad will come out of it," said Chispo. "I mean, they'll probably look at it in a weird way, and then they'll get used to it."

"Did the rancher tell you anything about this place?" Steven asked Andrew.

"No, not much. He did tell me that this place is called Ojo del Agua. That means water eye or spring."

"So, how do you suggest we go about searching for the blocking transmitter device?" Steven asked everyone.

"Would it be better to tell the residents the real reason we've come," Chris asked, "or to not let on what our real purpose is for being here?"

"I believe we better play it safe," Rinto replied.

"It's going to be strange enough showing up in this craft," Fraxino pointed out. "They'd freak out if we told them the real reason."

"Dudes, it's like Orolizo told us," Chispo reminded. "We need to be very careful about who we tell."

"Which means we can tell a few trusted individuals," said Robert.

"And those who would understand the concept," Andrew added.

"So, everyone," Rinto suggested, "the plan is for us to arrive as American tourists and that we are driving a futuristic prototype vehicle."

"Sounds good," said Robert.

Evening arrived. They ate supper, and afterwards they explored the upper sections of the small river and also climbed the lower slopes of the mountain to get a better view of the canyon.

It became dark at 8:30 PM, and they pitched their tents for the night.

The next morning was perfectly clear and warm, and the air was still. Birds called out and flew among the trees by the spring. All of them got up around an hour after sunrise. They packed up their tents and belongings and boarded the vehicle-craft.

Chispo did the driving. The one-lane gravel road was rough, narrow, and winding as it followed along the right hand side of the canyon, sometimes hugging the cliff walls towering above them on their right. The canyon forest was beautiful, and the road passed through stands of massive Ash, Pecan, and Sycamore trees. Sometimes, their branches covered the road like a canopy. The route was very scenic.

For ten kilometers, they followed this road, and as the river canyon became wider downstream, the road left the woods and entered some scrubland of Mesquites and other shrubs. There were plenty of Cactus plants, Yuccas, and Lechuguilla plants. The road briefly climbed a hill and then descended into the town they had seen yesterday from the air. On the edge of town, the pavement began.

"Bienvenidos a Bustamante," said Robert as he read the sign. "Welcome to Bustamante. That must be the name of the town."

"Bustamante," said Rinto. "Interesting name . . . sounds familiar."

CHAPTER 8

BUSTAMANTE, NUEVO LEON

As the road entered town, they saw a park on the left, and it was situated in a grove of large Pecan trees. As they proceeded, they were passing numerous houses made of adobe and of concrete blocks. Nearly every street corner had a small place of business. The road they were on appeared to be the main street through the town, and it was called Calle Mier. Numerous streets intersected and crossed the main street. Since nearly every house came right up to the sidewalks, Calle Mier was quite narrow. In some places it was difficult for two vehicles to pass by each other, and they would soon discover that nearly every street followed the same style.

Bustamante was a small town with around 3,000 residents. In some ways, the whole town was like a large family. Most of the residents were lifetime natives, and they were related and connected to each other in various ways. There were no banks, no law offices, no fast-food restaurants, and no convenience stores. There were no traffic lights. Bustamante did not even have a fuel station. The nearest one was a Pemex station ten kilometers away.

As Chispo proceeded for at least a kilometer through the town, the others were looking to the left and right as they passed the intersecting streets. They certainly received some strange stares from some of the residents that saw them driving by.

"How about let's turn here?" Chispo announced as he came upon an intersecting street called Escobedo.

"Go for it, dude," Fraxino approved.

He turned right and drove them down the street for a block and saw a bakery on the left. There was a speed bump right in front of their place of business. A lady was hand throwing water onto the street from a bucket she was carrying, a sacred daily ritual that all business owners did when they opened each morning.

"I don't know about you guys, but this looks like a good place to stop," Chispo told them.

"Looks like they just opened," said Robert.

Two other ladies were carrying a large sign, and they displayed it on the sidewalk in front of their house next to their place of business. It read: *Pan de Bustamante, N.L., cocido con leña*. The business had several display tables, and they were selling various types of bread, their specialty. In addition to that, there were local crafts, ceramic statues, cookware, and even some rocking chairs.

"Let's check it out, dudes," said Chispo as he parked on the right hand side of the street.

"Good idea. I'm hungry," said Andrew.

"All seven of them exited the vehicle-craft and walked across the street.

"Buenos días. Pásen," the young woman told them, welcoming them to their place of business.

"Buenos días," Andrew said to her. "¿Venden pan aquí?" asking her if they indeed sold bread here.

"Sí, tenemos pan dulce, empanadas de piña, de calabaza, y semita," she answered, telling about the various types of bread they sold. She seemed to take no notice of Rinto and Fraxino's very unique vehicle-craft parked across the street.

About this moment, they saw a young fellow around their age walking toward them from their patio behind the business. They overheard him saying to his mother, "Mamá, en la maleta mía, traigo muchos calcetines y otras . . ." By this time, he had reached the vendor's area. He stopped and stood spellbound, mouth dropped open!

"Buenos días," said Robert, breaking the silence.

The young fellow started laughing with a look of amazement on his face as he looked at the seven of them and also at Rinto and Fraxino's vehicle-craft.

He finished his laughing. "¡Válgame Dios!" he exclaimed. "¿Qué es eso, un ovni?" he asked, wanting to know if their vehicle was a spacecraft.

"No, no es un ovni," Andrew replied, telling him that it wasn't a spacecraft, and he explained that it was a futuristic prototype vehicle and that they were American tourists.

Andrew and Robert carried on conversation with him, telling him that they had just visited the ancient paintings on the other side of the mountains in the desert valley. Meanwhile, the others motioned to the young woman which types of bread they wanted and purchased them with American money.

The young fellow introduced himself as Paco Casso de Luna, and he offered to give them a tour of their bakery. They followed him through the back patio to another building. As Robert and his friends were munching away, Paco took them into the building. The two ladies who had earlier displayed the sign were kneading a large amount of dough, nearly ready to divide the lot into around 100 units, after which they would bake it on many flat metal sheets in an igloo-shaped adobe stove outside behind the building.

Next, he took them further back into their backyard to a large pole barn. "Este es mi negocio de hacer sillas," he told them, explaining that he ran his own business of making chairs. He had various rocking chairs and upright chairs, and all of them were made to look rustic according to the older and traditional styles of the past. All of the chair bottoms were woven with an ever continuous strand of twisted Fan Palm leaves from the local mountains. Some of the chair backs were also woven with Palm leaves while others had wooden backs.

"Me gustan tus mecedoras," said Robert, telling Paco that he liked his rocking chairs. He asked him how much they cost. Paco told him, and the price was very reasonable. Robert said to him that before they leave town, he would buy one from him.

"Está bien," Paco told him, saying that would be fine. "Mira, mi papá sabe varias historias sobre las pinturas. Vengan y hablen con él. Está en la cocina," telling them that his father knows various stories about Chiquihuitillos and inviting them to speak with him in the kitchen. Paco also told them about a neighbor up the street named Sabastian Xavier who was an investigator of odd phenomena.

The Casso family had a decent residence situated within a grove of large Pecan trees (locally called Nogal) and Avocado trees (locally called Aguacate). In fact, most of Bustamante sat in the middle of an oasis, and there were Pecan trees throughout the town, except for the upper reaches nearer to the mountains. The center of the town sat five kilometers from the foot of the towering mountain range, and its main feature was the Lion's Head Mountain, elevation 1,860 meters, locally called Cabeza de León, because its outlines did indeed have the appearance of a lion resting and facing south.

They followed Paco into the small concrete block building on the edge of their patio. "Pásen," Paco's mother said to everyone as they entered.

His father, whose name was Sr. Lázaro, was seated at the table, and he was eating some breakfast. He was a man of stocky build and appeared to be in his seventies, and he was hard of hearing. "Pásen, jovenes," he told them, welcoming them. "Siéntense," he offered, telling them to have a seat. All of them situated themselves. Some sat in chairs, and others remained standing. Paco briefly explained to him that the seven of them had come to talk about the ancient paintings.

"Ah sí, que bueno. Es un lugar muy interesante y muy antiguo," Sr. Lázaro responded, saying that it's a very interesting and ancient place. Andrew and Robert translated to the others the best they could. For five minutes, Sr. Lázaro told them of ancient legends about giants having come and visited. He said the strangers came and spoke. They'd never seen this type before.

When Andrew and Robert translated that last part, it surprised Chispo considerably because those were the exact words he had heard in his mind yesterday!

Sr. Lázaro continued, and he informed them that those ancient paintings are unique and are not like paintings anywhere else. Much of it is intact, and some of the drawings, although authentically very ancient, appear as if they had just been painted. He said that there are, in places, groups of many one-centimeter tall figures and that the name of them is tatigrafia.

Andrew, Robert, and Paco chatted a few minutes, and then as Paco looked out the kitchen window, he noticed his three workers arriving for the day. As he left to greet them, the others followed. At the same moment, Sr. Lázaro got up and left the kitchen to tend to his goats, donkeys, and other animals in the backyard.

As Paco's workers were parking their bicycles, they walked over to them, and Paco introduced them. Their names were Alejandro, Juan, and Roel. Paco explained to the three of them that these were American tourists, that they were driving the futuristic prototype vehicle parked out front on the street, and that they were investigating the ancient paintings. Of the three of them, Roel showed the most interest.

Robert and his friends discussed with Chispo, Rinto, and Fraxino what they wanted to do for the day. They talked it over with Paco and his workers, and Robert asked Paco if he would be able to show them around town.

"Mira, lo que pasa es eso. Tengo varios mandados en Sabinas Hidalgo," Paco responded, saying that he had various errands in Sabinas Hidalgo, a large town 40 kilometers to the east of them. "Pero, lo que puedo hacer es dejar que mi trabajador Roel les acompañe," saying that what he could do was let his worker Roel accompany them. That sounded fine with them. In fact, Paco even offered to let Roel accompany them and hire him as their guide for their entire visit to Mexico. He would get along fine with just his other two workers, as work was a little slow at the moment, anyway.

"Muchas gracias, Paco," said Robert, telling Paco thanks.

"Sí, sí, no hay problema," Paco responded, saying that it was no problem.

Andrew asked him how much the going rate per day was, and Paco told him that it was 1,500 pesos per day, (around U.S. $5). They couldn't believe how cheap the wages were in Mexico! At that low rate, there wasn't a problem at all. They were glad to hire Roel to be their guide.

"Bueno, déjame. Ya me voy a Sabinas Hidalgo," said Paco, telling them to let him get on with things, that he was already going to go to Sabinas Hidalgo. "Que les vaya bien," he told them, wishing them well. He immediately got into his old Ford truck, started it, backed out onto the street, and drove away.

Alejandro and Juan walked to the pole barn and began work for the day.

Roel stood with the seven of them and had a look of irresistible curiosity on his face. He felt blessed to have been relieved of his hard work and was eager to begin his new job as a local tourist guide. He was 16 years in age, and he was tall and slender for a Mexican, standing the same height as Robert and his friends.

With a smile on his face, he said, "¿A ver su carro futuristico?" He was curious to see that futuristic vehicle-craft, as it was first and foremost on his mind.

Robert translated what Roel said, and Rinto and Fraxino led the way as they walked back to the street and returned to the vehicle-craft. Rinto raised the hood and began to explain about the motor. The name Richmond was unheard of by Roel, as was the name Velosa, but then it was understandable, as this was an "American futuristic prototype vehicle." Roel was most impressed with the vehicle-craft and especially liked the metallic body style with its color of green, tinged with yellow and brown.

"¿A dónde quieren ir?" Roel asked them, wanting to know where they wished to go.

"A visitar a Sabastian Xavier," Andrew answered for them.

They boarded the vehicle-craft. Rinto and Fraxino decided to keep it a secret about their Ulexite main controls crystal and their crystal array situated underneath it. They would tell him later. Rinto drove, and Roel sat in the front seat and gave directions. They proceeded for three blocks along the same street. The pavement ended, and a half block further on the right was the residence and business of Sabastian Xavier.

It was a simple concrete block building somewhat in the open with few trees. There was a sign displayed out front that said, "Taller de Artes, Bustamante." As everyone stepped out of the vehicle-craft, a fairly tall man stepped out of the house. His mouth dropped open with surprise at the sight of the vehicle-craft.

"Buenos días," Andrew called out to him.

He walked over to them and introduced himself as Sabastian Xavier. Andrew did the explaining about the unique appearance of the vehicle, and Sabastian welcomed them inside.

As they entered, there were three children doing artwork, painting images on rocks, and doing various drawings. Around the house were displayed numerous fine oil paintings with images from the local region and sites.

A lady came forward from the back of the house and greeted them. Sabastian introduced her as his wife, Bertha.

Robert explained why they had come. "Venimos aquí para platicar contigo sobre las pinturas antiguas, Chiquihuitillos," saying they had come to chat with him about the ancient paintings.

"Ah, sí verdad. Soy un investigador, y me interesan mucho las pinturas antiguas," he responded, saying that he was an investigator and that the ancient paintings interested him a lot.

Andrew and Robert translated for the others, and for the next hour they chatted about the meanings of the paintings. Sabastian was a very interesting man of unique and intriguing ideas, and as they discussed each depiction on those mesa side walls, he was very much in agreement with the ideas that the seven of them had gotten from them. Sabastian showed such an understanding with an open mind that they decided to tell him about the paintings' connection to Atlantis and also what they knew about that society.

With this information now being said to Sabastian, Roel, being their guide, automatically found out the truth about them and that Chispo, Rinto, and Fraxino were extraterrestrials from the star Al Nitak in the Orion Belt. Roel then said to them that he already knew that instinctively. He had his own input as well, and he expressed his belief that there was a connection to Mars with those paintings.

"¿Cuántos años tienen las pinturas?" Andrew casually asked, wanting to know how many years old Sabastian believed the paintings to be.

"Como dos mil quinientos," he answered, saying 2,500.

"¿Dos mil o doce mil quinientos?" Andrew asked to clarify because Sabastian's answer sounded very much like 12,500, but he wasn't sure.

"*Dos* mil quinientos," he clarified, saying 2,500.

"¿Es todo?" said Andrew, asking if that was all. "Es que nosotros pensabamos que tenían doce mil quinientos años," saying that they thought the paintings were 12,500 years old.

Sabastian explained that a team of experts had come from France a few years ago and had dated the paintings at 2,500 years old, and they had used the radio carbon-14 decay rate as their method. He asked them why they believed the paintings to be 10,000 years older, and Andrew explained that for what the paintings say and mean, they have to be that old because that was when the Atlanteans fled Earth and went to Al Nitak. There was just too much evidence in those paintings for their age to be otherwise.

Andrew and Robert translated to the others what Sabastian had said.

"Carbon-14 dating is not all that accurate, anyway," Rinto told everyone. "It surprises me how this world still uses it. There are so many factors involved with that method, which can result in very wrong conclusions. One accurate dating technique is the measurement of chlorine-36 rock exposure dating. By that method, you can determine how long a rock has been exposed to the atmosphere after having been quarried. We use that method on our world and achieve much more accurate results with it."

"That's right, man" Chispo agreed. "Not only that, would you believe that some of Earth's archaeologists actually date a building by the artifacts and utensils found inside them, and that can be totally in error."

"I know, man," Fraxino added. "Those artifacts and utensils could be thousands of years newer than the building itself."

Andrew explained to Sabastian what Rinto, Chispo, and Fraxino were saying. Sabastian said he wasn't familiar with that type of dating. However, with the evidence of their visit and what they had just discussed during the past hour, he now believed without a doubt that the ancient paintings were drawn by Atlantean descendants and that they were around 12,500 years old.

"Pues, mucho gusto haber platicado con ustedes," Sabastian told them, saying that it was a pleasure having chatted with them. They all shook hands and wished each other well.

"This town has all kinds of interesting people," Andrew commented as they were walking back to the vehicle-craft.

"I know," Robert agreed. "I like this place already."

"It gives us a chance to use our Spanish," said Andrew.

"¿Ahora qué hacemos?" said Roel, asking what they wanted to do next.

"Vamos a ver el pueblo," Robert replied, saying they wanted to see the town.

Everyone climbed in, and Rinto drove them along the streets of Bustamante as Roel gave directions. He felt very proud to be their guide, and he was thoroughly enjoying the status of cruising the town in such a unique craft. His new job was so much better than doing manual labor, making chairs for Paco. As a result, Roel showed a sense of true friendliness and appreciation for his new friends. They told Roel where they were really from.

After making two right turns over a distance of several blocks, Rinto drove them into the plaza in the town center. It was a large square with the government building and police station on the east end and the main church on the west end. There were residences within a continuous run of buildings on both the north and south sides, and there was a small market on the southwest corner. Streets intersected each corner of the square, and within the square was a grassy flat with park benches all the way around it and an outdoor dance stage in its center. Tall narrow Cypress trees, Pecan, Ash, and Sycamore trees grew throughout the plaza.

Roel requested that Rinto drive around the plaza several times, and as he did so, Roel rolled down the window of the vehicle-craft and enjoyed whistling and waving at several of his friends. All of them gave him weird looks of surprise.

On their third round, one of the members of the comandancia, the police, made his appearance on the corner of the square by the police station. He was a tall slender man and was wearing a brown uniform. He put his arm up in the air and waved them over by moving his hand and fingers in a downward motion several times.

"Ah, no! Es la policía. Que te pares," Roel said to Rinto, telling him to pull over. Andrew translated to Rinto, and he pulled over on the street side.

The man approached them. "Buenos días, muchachos. ¿Qué es eso en que andan?" he smiled and said, greeting them and asking what kind of vehicle this was that they were running around in.

Roel did the explaining and said that he was serving as a guide for these American tourists and that they were driving a futuristic prototype vehicle.

The man's name was Jorge, and he gave Roel a weird smile of disbelief for his answer. He stared at the craft and then looked Roel straight in the eyes and said, "¿No es un ovni?" asking if it was actually an extraterrestrial craft.

"No, no, es como te digo . . ." Roel insisted, explaining that it was an American futuristic prototype vehicle.

"Sí, pero las placas traen figuras que no se reconocen," said Jorge, pointing out that the two license plates carry unrecognizable characters. Though Robert and his friends didn't yet know it, Roel and Jorge were personal friends. "Roel, si es un ovni, me dices la verdad. No me eches mentiras," he told him, insisting that Roel tell him the real story.

"Sí, sí, es un ovni," Roel admitted, telling him that it was indeed an extraterrestrial craft. "Viene de Zantaller, Zotola," telling him where it came from.

He and Roel chatted several minutes. Robert and Andrew couldn't understand everything they said, as they were talking more of a local Spanish dialect containing slang. However, they did understand them when Roel admitted that it was an extraterrestrial craft, and that worried them considerably.

"Está bien, Roel," said Jorge, telling Roel that everything was fine. "Pásenle derecho," telling them to go ahead.

Rinto drove them north, leaving the plaza.

"¿Por qué dijiste que este vehículo es de otro mundo?" Robert anxiously asked Roel, wanting to know why he told Jorge that it was an extraterrestrial craft.

"No pude mentir. Vió las placas," Roel answered, saying he couldn't keep the truth from Jorge because he saw the license plates. "Pero ya arreglé todo. Ya no nos hace nada. Es mi amigo. Se llama Jorge," Roel explained, saying that he already took care of any problem.

"Whew! That's good," said Robert in English. "Roel said everything's fine. The police isn't going to do anything to us. That policeman is Roel's friend. His name is Jorge." Everyone breathed a sigh of relief.

Roel directed Rinto to drive around the block and return to the other side of the plaza so they could see the church. He pulled over and parked under an Ash tree, and they got out, crossed the street, walked across the front yard of the church, and entered the normal size building. There was a bloody statue of Jesus hanging on the cross above the pulpit at the front end of the aisleway.

They walked up the aisleway and saw that two hallways intersected, one from each side. Roel led them down the hall to the left and took them into a small room where they came upon a glass encased mannequin of Jesus. He related to them the story behind it, saying that it came from the Tlaxcaltecan Indians in the late 1600's, and in those days they used to call the town and region Boca de Leones, (Mouth of the Lions). The town then came to be called San Miguel de Aguayo in honor of Marqués de Aguayo. It was much later that the name Bustamante came about, having been named after one of Mexico's presidents, Gral. Anastasio Bustamante, of the early 1800's.

Roel further explained that every early August, they have a carnival in Bustamante, and on August 6, they have a big celebration where they have a devout marching procession and carry the mannequin of Jesus throughout the streets of the town. It is such an important event, that each year all of the residents are notified ahead of time so that they will know what streets are used, and they hang decorations on the front of their houses in honor of Jesus.

"Si quieren, ya nos vamos," Roel announced, offering them to now leave with him. They followed him back through the front aisleway, out the front door of the church, and they walked back to the vehicle-craft.

"Ya tengo hambre. Vamos a la tienda," Roel told them, saying that he was already hungry and requesting that they go to the store. He pointed toward the corner of the plaza. Andrew translated to the others.

"Oh, then let's just leave the craft parked here and walk over," said Rinto. They walked to the corner store in the plaza and entered.

The store had no name, and even though it was a small store, it was well stocked with a little of everything. They sold fruits, vegetables, cereals, beans, grains, various types of bread and flour, and tortillas. There was a shelf with cookware, household goods, and even shoes. In the back, they had a meat department with a bandsaw and a meat slicer. A man was back there processing meat for a customer.

Robert noticed a sign hanging on the back wall. It read: *No fío porque cobrar es un lío, y el negocio es mío.* (I don't sell on credit because charging is a complicated matter, and the place of business is mine.) He wondered why there was such a sense of mistrust. More than that, why would it be so complicated to charge clients later for what they purchase on credit?

"Buenos días," said the young woman at the counter as she greeted them.

Roel returned a reply and introduced his new friends to Mina Cantu. Her husband's name was Chilo, and he was the one who was processing meat in the back. He came forward to greet them. Robert and Andrew translated, and they had a nice chat while Roel took a packet of crackers and a Jumex drink off the shelf, returned to the counter, and paid Mina for them. Chilo and Mina wished them well as they walked out of the store and returned to the vehicle-craft.

"Vamos por Rudy, mi hermano," Roel announced, requesting they go to where his brother, Rudy, was working. They climbed in. Rinto drove south and left the plaza. They turned right and pulled up to a small building with a large open yard around it. The sound of saws buzzing could be heard along with other wood working tools. This was all part of a carpentry business, owned and operated by Felipe Hernandez.

Everyone stepped out of the vehicle-craft, and Roel led them inside. They walked through the front building and into a small patio with a large Palm leaf thatched roof gazebo. One of the workers saw them approaching, and he switched off the saw. His name was Marin, and he greeted them. He told them that Rudy and the other two workers were at the Hotel Ancira the next street over and that they were talking to Felipe at the moment.

Roel led everyone across the street and entered the hotel's long courtyard, and they walked the 100 meters to the front of the hotel where there was a restaurant and gift shop. As they entered the giftshop, they saw the various wooden crafts for sale. There were chairs, tables, rocking chairs, wooden plaques with designs and scenery etched into them, wooden crosses, and more. Felipe and his father, Felipe Sr., had a thriving business and regularly sold their goods to tourists from various parts of Mexico and the United States. They found Rudy and his two working companions talking over business with Felipe.

Rudy was age fifteen, a year younger than his brother Roel, and he stood nearly the same height and size. His face showed that he was of genuine character, and they instinctively realized that Rudy would become their friend.

"Buenos días, muchachos. Pásen," Felipe said, greeting them and welcoming them to his shop. Roel introduced his new friends to Felipe and introduced them to Rudy and his two companions, Juan Carlos and Sotero. Felipe knew some English, and he chatted with them as he showed them his shop and told them about his carpentry business.

Next, he closed up the shop for lunch and took them on a tour of his business. Rudy accompanied them while Juan Carlos and Sotero returned to work. Felipe had yet another building on another street where two more workers were operating a table saw and a band saw. They entered, and he introduced them to Pancho and Alfredo. On certain days, Marin and the others would come over here to work also.

"We have a fine business here," Felipe explained, "and we give jobs to some of the people in this town by operating this business. They make chairs, tables, cuadros, crosses, and other items, and they do fine work." He continued telling everyone about the business and then took them over to the building they parked in front of.

Felipe then noticed the vehicle-craft. "My, what sort of vehicle is that?" He stared at it with interest and surprise at the same time.

"We're driving a prototype vehicle from the United States," Chispo explained, "and we've come to see the ancient paintings and also to go up in the mountains to explore."

"Very good," Felipe commented. "I'm sure you'll enjoy your time here. Bustamante is a beautiful place to visit. Have you seen the caves?"

"No, we haven't seen them yet," Chispo replied. "Where are they?"

"Go to the road's end," and Felipe indicated by pointing to the mountains west of them. "Park at the cono, and follow the trail uphill for 45 minutes. There is a guide manning the entrance, and he will take you for a tour inside. The caves of Bustamante are some of the largest in the world."

"Cool! We'll have to check them out, dudes," Chispo now said to everyone.

Felipe took them inside the building and briefly showed them the various types of lumber stacked in the room. Next, he took them to the thatched roof gazebo and showed them the table saws, sanding machines, and routers.

Roel asked Felipe if Rudy could join them for the afternoon.

"Sí, sí, no hay problema, Roel," he answered, saying that would be no problem. Felipe was a fine man who was honest, understanding and compassionate. For that reason, he had a successful business, and he also had a very good reputation throughout the town of Bustamante.

"Anyway, fellows, I will go to lunch now," Felipe told them. "Nice meeting you, and have a nice stay in Bustamante."

"Yes, nice meeting you," Robert responded for everyone. "Thanks for the tour."

"You're welcome." He walked with them through the building, and they returned to the street. Felipe walked back to the hotel while Rudy joined the others. They all climbed into the vehicle-craft.

"¿Roel, dónde encontraste a tus compañeros, y qué es este vehículo curioso?" Rudy asked him, wanting to know where Roel found his new companions and what type of weird vehicle this was.

"Llegaron a los Casso esta mañana, y Paco me entregó a ellos para ser su guía," Roel answered, saying that they showed up at the Casso's bakery business this morning and that Paco turned him over to them to be their guide.

"Está bien," Rudy commented, saying that was really good. "Vamos a la casa. Tengo hambre," Rudy told them, saying for them to go to his house since he was hungry.

Felipe's workers were just getting off for lunch, and Juan Carlos and Sotero emerged from the building. Rudy saw them and asked if they could be given a ride to their homes. Rinto consented, and they climbed in.

"¿Dónde viven?" Andrew asked them, wanting to know where they lived.

"Vivo media cuadra de la casa de Roel, y Sotero vive en la otra cuadra," Juan Carlos answered, saying that he lived half a block from Roel and that Sotero lived on the next block.

Under Roel's direction, Rinto soon made a right turn and drove several blocks, made a left turn on Calle Gral. Naranjo, and proceeded for several more blocks. The pavement ended, and a block later they pulled up in front of Roel and Rudy's yellow house on the corner. All of them stepped out of the vehicle-craft. Juan Carlos and Sotero walked the remaining distance to their houses. Everyone else entered the house with Roel and Rudy. His mother was home preparing lunch.

"Mamá, ven a conocer a mis compañeros," Roel called out to her, telling his mother to come and meet his new friends.

She came forward from the kitchen and calmly introduced herself to them in a kind and hospitable manner. Her name was María. Next, her two daughters came, and María introduced them. They were attractive little girls, and their names were Nora, age 11, and Idalia, age 6.

Roel asked his mother if it would be all right if his new friends could eat lunch with them. She consented, saying that would be fine, and she and her daughters returned to the kitchen where she warmed up some more beans and rice and slapped some additional corn tortillas on the stove top.

Meanwhile, Roel and Rudy chatted with everyone as they took seats around the living room/bedroom. Andrew and Robert served as interpreters. They got to talking about the caves, and since Rudy had been freed up for the afternoon at Roel's request, they decided to go there. Roel explained that the caves were discovered in the early part of this century by a native of the town while he was manning his goats grazing on the mountain slopes.

María and her two daughters called them to come into the kitchen to eat. Everyone entered, and María served each one of them a plate and a glass of water. They took seats, some of them at the kitchen table, and the others at a table in the next room. She indicated for them to help themselves to the stack of hot tortillas, beans, and green hot sauce on the kitchen table. The food was well prepared, and while it was basic, it satisfied their hunger. Robert and his friends were experiencing Mexican hospitality at its best, and they were glad to be here with their new friends, Roel and Rudy.

Their sisters helped their mother with preparing and cleaning up after lunch, but since they were only young children, they were not the most efficient helpers in the kitchen. They laughed and played a lot, and at times they fought and cried.

They finished eating and thanked María for the lunch. Roel and Rudy prepared their daypacks for the afternoon tour of the caves in the mountains. María wished them well and invited them to return for supper if they wished. They left the house through the front door and climbed into the vehicle-craft.

This time, Chispo did the driving, and both Roel and Rudy sat up front with him and gave directions. He started the motor and proceeded down Calle Gral. Naranjo. Two blocks down the street, Roel saw two of his friends. They were on the corner chatting with each other.

"Que te pares. Son mis amigos," Roel said, telling Chispo to stop so that he could talk to his friends. Chispo instinctively understood and pulled over.

Roel's friends gave him some weird looks, and he stepped out of the vehicle and shook hands with them. They continued to have playful, questioning looks on their faces as Roel introduced them to the others. Their names were Alvaro and Pegaso. Alvaro was standard height for a Mexican, but Pegaso was quite big, had an imposing stature, and stood even taller than Roel.

"Oh my goodness! That's him!" Steven exclaimed.

"Who, Orolizo's soul mate?" Chispo asked.

"Yeah, the big guy," Steven verified. "That's him. I'm sure of it." As the memories of Steven's disturbing dream came back to him, he grew anxious.

"Calm down, man," Chispo reassured him. "He's not going to do anything to you. Besides, that was just a dream."

"Yeah, don't worry, Steven," Andrew added. "We'll protect you if something goes wrong."

"¿Qué pasó?" Rudy asked, wanting to know why Steven showed anxiety.

Suddenly, a group of thoughts raced through Chispo's mind, even though it was only for a split second. The thoughts had come from Rudy.

"Whew! ¿Qué fue eso?" said Chispo, reacting to what had just raced through his mind and asking what it was. "Es que Steven se acordó de un sueño malo," Chispo answered Rudy, saying that Steven just remembered a bad dream.

"¿Sabes español?" Rudy said with surprise, asking Chispo if he knew Spanish.

"Chispo!" Rinto said to him with surprise. "Since when did you know Spanish?"

"I don't know Spanish . . ." Chispo began. He paused briefly. "Well, I guess I do now. Wow, man! What a surprise!" He started laughing. "I know all kinds of phrases. Seems like Rudy just transmitted everything to me."

"Rudy *what*?" Robert asked in a surprised manner.

"You mean Rudy gave you the Spanish language, just like that?" Andrew asked.

"That's right, man," Chispo verified, "and it was in a split second."

"No way!" Steven remarked with disbelief.

"¿Dígame, qué sueño tuvo?" Rudy asked Chispo, wanting to know what dream Steven had.

"Es que . . . No, mejor no decimos. No mas que le molestó mucho," Chispo replied, explaining that it would be best if they didn't tell, no more than the dream bothered Steven a lot.

"Chispo, you're getting better with your abilities all the time," Rinto told him.

"I declare," said Steven, "with you guys, nothing surprises me anymore!"

"You're not kidding," Robert agreed.

"How did you do that, Chispo?" Fraxino wanted to know.

"Like I said, man, Rudy just gave it to me."

"Fraxino," Rinto reminded him, "don't you remember how Dad suddenly learned English soon after Robert and the others arrived?"

"Oh, yeah. That's right," Fraxino recalled. "He just picked it up off their minds."

"Exactly," Rinto told him. "That's all Chispo's done."

Rudy wasn't aware of the fact that he had just transmitted the entire Spanish language to Chispo. He had done it subconsciously without realizing it.

Meanwhile, Roel and his two friends were just finishing talking. "Bueno, nos vemos," he told them, saying they'd see each other later. He hopped back in the vehicle-craft. "Vámonos, ya," he told Chispo, saying okay, let's go.

"¿Cuánta distancia hay hasta el cono?" Chispo asked Roel, wanting to know how far away the cono at the end of the road was.

"Cinco kilometros," saying five kilometers. Then Roel suddenly realized. "¿Tú también, hablas español?" he commented with surprise, asking Chispo if he also spoke Spanish.

"Sí, desde ahora mismo," Chispo replied to Roel, saying since right now, and he explained to him that he had just suddenly picked Spanish up off the mind of Rudy in a brief split second while Roel had been chatting with his two friends. Roel showed some surprise.

He gave directions, and Chispo drove them east along Calle Gral. Naranjo until they reached the social center building. They took a right turn, passed the school, and entered the plaza, went halfway around it, made a right turn, and proceeded down that road. Its pavement later ended when they reached the edge of town. The road veered to the right and headed southwest in a straight line toward the cono at the foot of the mountains. The road was somewhat rough since it was gravel, but it was built up and was in good condition otherwise. As it gently climbed to the cono, it gradually steepened with the steepest part being last. Chispo cruised up to the east side of the cono building and parked under a Mesquite tree.

Everyone stepped out of the vehicle-craft. They were now around 200 meters above the elevation of Bustamante and were on the upper edge of the valley floor. From here, the route was by footpath, and the slopes of the mountain range began only 100 meters beyond the cono. To their right was a large, dry riverbed with a major dropoff to reach it.

All nine of them put on their daypacks. Rinto and Fraxino closed up the vehicle-craft, and they began the 45-minute walk. No one was at the cono which meant the guide was more than likely at the cave entrance instead.

It was a hot and sweaty climb. They ascended rather steeply in places, and they passed through various large shrubs of Mesquite and other local plants. Both

Roel and Rudy told them what the plants and shrubs were called. They had names like: Anacahua, Barreta, Buajillo, Cenizo, Chapote, Colorín, Coyotillo, Frijolillo, Granjeno, and Palo Blanco. Also there were Fan Palms.

In places along the first section of the trail, there were huge Agave plants, locally called Maguey (*Agave havardiana*). They sometimes sent up tall stalks of blooms up to ten meters in height, and they could also be seen growing throughout the desert valley and in Bustamante itself.

There were plenty of other plants, as well. There were Desert Spoons, locally called Zotól (*Dasylirion wheeleri*). There were plenty of Lechuguilla plants, Pita de Zabandoque, Zoyate, Espadín, and Huapilla.

In addition to that, there were plenty of varieties of Cactus plants, such as the large Prickly Pear Cactus, locally called Nopal (*Opuntia lindheimeri*). Other types were called Biznaga, Candelilla, Coyonostle, Peyote, Tazajillo, and Tesajo.

Oddly enough, the vegetation in this whole region was not too dissimilar from the vegetation growing throughout the desert valleys of Zotola.

As they continued ascending, they began to see a few Oak trees. Around 15 minutes up the trail, they took a rest and sat under a fairly large Oak tree situated next to a rock face. Then they ascended the steepest and most treacherous section of the trail. Under their feet was fairly loose rock and scree, and they had to watch their step as they proceeded. After another hundred meters, they were through it, and the rest of the climb was more moderate with switchbacks.

As they crested a rise, an open area came into view, and the cave's entrance was tucked into two rock faces on either side, almost like a crevice. They entered the crevice and descended steeply to an iron gate, which was open. As they looked inside, they could see that the lights were turned on. The cave's size was absolutely enormous, and they were amazed.

"Golly!" Robert remarked. "That is huge."

"Dudes, I've never seen a cave room that large," Chispo commented.

"You're not kidding," Chris agreed.

"I don't believe we have any caves that large on our world," said Rinto.

"I know," Fraxino agreed. "The cave where we keep our crystals is large, but not *this* large."

They could see a man down in the distance on the far end of the first large room. He was carrying a flashlight, and they could see him using it. Roel and Rudy called out to him, and he replied, saying that he would come up for them in a few minutes to give them a tour.

They returned to the open area and rested on different rocks in the area. Roel and Rudy took some apples and oranges out of their daypacks and began eating them. Everyone else also did the same. They were now at an elevation of 1,000 meters, 500 meters above the elevation of Bustamante, and the views of the town way below them were excellent. The temperature was a little cooler here than it was in Bustamante, and the skies were perfectly clear.

The guide emerged from the cave and called for them to come. He greeted Roel and Rudy since he knew them. Then he introduced himself as Ramiro Gomez, and he explained that there was a small entrance fee of 300 pesos, around 65¢, per person. He was a kind looking Mexican and appeared to be in his early 20's. He stood around the same height as Roel.

"Estas grutas son muy bonitas, y son unas de la mas grandes en el mundo," Ramiro told them, explaining that the caves were spectacular and that they were some of the largest in the world.

They took some money out of their wallets. Rinto, Fraxino, and Chispo had only Zotolan zúbolas and therefore couldn't use them. Andrew, Chris, Robert, and Steven paid for all nine of them, and Ramiro led them into the cave.

They passed through the small iron gateway, veered left, and made a fairly long descent on a footpath to the floor of the first room. They were really amazed at the size of the cave. There were huge formations of calcified stalagmites and stalagtites. All of the rock inside the cave was limestone. In fact, the whole mountain range was limestone.

Inside the cave, the temperature was cooler than it was outside. Of course, in the winter, the reverse was true.

Ramiro told them about the different formations, and the locals had even conjured up names for some of them, such as La Ballena. He explained that the formations were entirely protected now, and for that reason, the iron gate had been installed to keep vandals from entering.

Next, he took them deeper into the cave by leading them down a steep sloping hillside for at least 200 meters and arriving on the floor of another huge room. There were more formations, and in a couple of places there were some small ponds. Electricity had been supplied to the cave all the way from Bustamante, and as they proceeded, he turned on more lights.

They crossed the second large room, and they passed through a very narrow passageway which took them to another large room. The pathway was now treacherous and slippery, and they carefully made their way down it to the floor of that room. It was not as large as the previous two rooms but still considerably large.

Ramiro took them to the edge of that room and showed them a dropoff, telling them that cave explorers had gone on much further. This was as far as the lights went and was the limit to how far the tours were taken. He told them that cave exploration teams had come from all over the world, but still no one had ever reached the end of these caves. It remained a mystery just how far back the caves of Bustamante really went.

An hour had passed since they had entered, and Ramiro announced that it was time to return to the entrance at the top. They crossed the room, climbed the treacherous trail, passed through the narrow opening, locally called El Bujero, and they returned via the same route by which they had entered. Dust flew up in the air as they climbed the steep, sloping hillside to arrive at the first room. They crossed it and made the final ascent to the entrance where Ramiro opened up the iron gate and let them out.

By now, it was 4 PM, and he decided to close up the entrance for the day and walk with them back down to the cono.

"Man, I was really impressed with the size of that cave," Chispo told everyone.

"I've never seen a cave that big," said Andrew. He next told Ramiro in Spanish.

"Sí, es bien grande," Ramiro responded, agreeing that it was huge.

"Did you pick up any signs of the device?" Chris asked Rinto, Fraxino, and Chispo.

"None at all," Rinto answered. "I think it's either further up these mountains, or some or all of it could be somewhere on the next range over."

"But we didn't detect anything when we were over there checking out that landing spot," Chris pointed out.

"I know, but it's likely very subtle," said Rinto.

"We probably weren't paying attention in the right way," Fraxino explained.

"Yes, I guess that could be true," Chris admitted.

They descended on the same trail they had used to come up, and they arrived at the cono with Ramiro shortly after 4:30 PM. He saw the vehicle-craft and stared at it with surprise.

"¿Qué es? ¿Es su carro?" he asked, wanting to know if that was their car.

Chispo explained to Ramiro that it was a futuristic prototype vehicle. Chispo spoke Spanish very well for someone who had suddenly learned it only a few hours ago.

"Es un buen carro," Ramiro commented, saying that it was a good car. He asked them if they would give him a lift back to Bustamante. Rinto and Fraxino consented, and he loaded his bicycle into their vehicle-craft and rode back to town with them. Chispo did the driving and basically let the vehicle coast down the long hill.

Ramiro told them that his father-in-law, Daniel Mata, was very interested in the paintings and that he lived just up the street from him. He offered to introduce them to him, and they accepted his offer.

As they rounded the curve and entered town, Ramiro directed Chispo and said for him to turn left a few blocks up the street. They soon pulled up beside Daniel's house where Chispo parked, and they all stepped outside.

The backyard was unique in that it was set up like a rock garden. Among them were various Yuccas, Cactus plants, and Siempre Vivas. Some of the plants were from the desert valley, and others were from the local mountains.

"Daniel," Ramiro called out.

"Sí," he responded from the backyard. He made his appearance and came forward. "¿Cómo te va, Ramiro?" said Daniel, asking Ramiro how it was going. Then he saw the vehicle-craft and expressed surprise.

Ramiro introduced everyone. Daniel already recognized Roel and Rudy, and he greeted them, followed by greeting the seven others. Ramiro explained that these seven Americans had come to see the ancient paintings and the mountains.

Daniel responded with interest and told them that he had visited the paintings several times. He felt certain that they were very ancient and contained hidden meaning. He mentioned that the style of the depictions was very unique, and he talked about them for some fifteen minutes.

Daniel's profession involved going regularly to the mountains to harvest herbs and medicinal plants for selling to the town's people. At times, he would go and cut Palm leaves for use in weaving chair bottoms and backs.

They enjoyed talking to him. Once they were finished, Daniel wished them well. Ramiro did the same, and he walked to his house down the street.

The rest of them climbed back into the vehicle-craft. Now, Roel and Rudy directed Chispo, and they returned to their home. He parked beside the house on a side street.

Everyone got out of the vehicle and walked into the house. María was in the kitchen making lots and lots of flour tortillas to sell. They were now spread out all over the kitchen table and the counters. Roel and Rudy helped themselves to a few of them and offered some to the others. They were still hot, and they were good. Later, she would package them, ten inside each plastic bag, and carry them to local vendors.

They placed their daypacks inside the living room/bedroom. Nora and Idalia were away, playing with other children up the street. Roel and Rudy lay down on one of the beds to relax, and they chatted and visited with their new friends. Some of them took seats around the room, and others sat on the edges of the beds.

"¿Entonces, qué hacemos?" Roel said to everyone, asking what they wanted to do.

Andrew translated to everyone, and they started talking in English with each other.

"Well, dudes, I know we need to go up in the mountains and locate that device," Chispo began.

"I know, but there's no huge hurry," Rinto told him.

"That's right," Chris agreed. "Let's get a feel of this place and see if we can pick up any subtle hints from the people."

"Good idea, Chris," said Andrew.

"At the same time," Robert suggested, "we can go hiking up in the mountains and explore the slopes. Roel and Rudy can come with us."

"That'll work," said Steven. "If we pick up any strange feelings, or if something weird happens, then we'll know we're onto something."

"And we'll take it from there," Fraxino added.

Next, Robert told Roel and Rudy what they wanted to do, leaving out the part about searching for the device in the mountains. "Vamos a ir a las montañas para andar y acampar. ¿Nos acompañan?" saying they were going hiking and camping in the mountains and asking Roel and Rudy if they would accompany them.

"Sí," Roel and Rudy both answered, saying yes. Next, they asked them when they wanted to go, and they decided to go the next day. Roel went into the kitchen and asked his mother if that would be okay with her if they could go.

"Pues, sí. Vayan," she told him, giving consent to go. Next, she told him that supper would be ready in a couple of hours, and she asked him to pick up some chicken meat and some corn tortillas at the Cantu's store in the plaza. She handed him some money.

Roel walked back through the front room. "Tengo un mandado. Ahorita vengo," he told everyone, saying he had an errand and would be back soon. He told them to visit with Rudy until he would return, and he took his bicycle and left.

Rudy was quickly taking a liking to his new friends. His face showed a look of sincere friendship. In some ways, it was as if he already knew them and understood them and their reasons for being here. Robert and Chispo felt the sense of familiarity more so than the others.

Rudy asked them if he could also join them on all their adventures and be their guide alongside Roel. That was fine with all of them, and they quickly gave their consent. They talked about various things including what normal day activities are in Mexico and how they go about their way of life. He told them that he and Roel are presently in the prepa, the Mexican equivalent of high school, and that they go to school by bus to Sabinas Hidalgo. Presently, they were out for summer vacation.

Roel soon returned with a sack of groceries. He parked his bicycle in front of the house by leaning it onto the sidewalk. He walked inside and took the food to his mother.

"¿Mamá, está bien si ellos se quedan con nosotros?" Roel said to his mother, asking if it would be all right if his new friends could stay with them.

She said that would be fine, except that there were so many. She suggested to her son that maybe one of his friends could keep some of them.

Roel agreed to that. "Déjame hablar con unos amigos," telling his mother he would speak to some of his friends. He walked into the room where Rudy and everyone were talking. "Mamá dice que algunos pueden quedar aquí. Vamos a mis amigos para pedir permiso por lo demás de ustedes," he told them, saying that his mother said some of them could stay with them and for them to accompany Roel to talk to his friends so he could ask permission about the rest of them staying with one of his friends. All nine of them walked out of the house.

"Regresamos mañana," Roel called into the house, jokingly telling his mother they would return tomorrow.

"Roel!" his mother called back to him, knowing he was just kidding.

They all walked two blocks down the street and made a right turn at a corner stationery shop. Some kids were playing in the street. They had marked off a rectangular grid on the pavement, and they were playing volleyball. A little ways up the street, they came to the house where Roel's friend Pegaso lived. He was in the driveway at the moment and saw Roel and Rudy approaching with their friends. He appeared to have a friendly face and greeted Roel and Rudy in a friendly manner. They introduced Pegaso to their new friends, and all of them shook hands.

Although Steven felt somewhat nervous, he knew that the disturbing dream he had was nothing more than that . . . a dream. It was probably just a manifestation of the concerns and worries that Orolizo had for his soul link, who they now believed to be Pegaso. Steven had telepathically tuned in to that when he had spent the other night at Orolizo's house. Besides, even if the dream were to come true, Steven had his friends to protect him, and in addition to that, Steven was a moderately strong individual and probably wouldn't have a great deal of trouble defending himself if it were to become necessary. As all of these thoughts ran through his mind, he put himself at ease and was now self-confident about meeting Pegaso.

Pegaso's parents emerged from the house and met everyone. They invited them over to their patio under two decent size Pecan trees. In addition to his parents, Pegaso had two sisters, one of them 15 and the other one 14. They also emerged from the house, and he introduced them. Andrew, Steven, and Chispo noticed their beauty, especially the tall, slender one who was age 15. Her name was Lumita, and her younger sister was called Mena.

Pegaso briefly explained to his parents who everyone was, that he had briefly seen them early this afternoon, and that Roel and now Rudy were serving as their guides.

"Su ovni es lo unico. ¿De dónde vienen?" Pegaso said to Roel, commenting that their spacecraft was unique and asking where they came from.

"Tres vienen de otro mundo," Roel casually announced, telling him that three of them are from another world.

"Sí verdad. ¿Dónde?" Pegaso responded with interest, asking Roel if that was really true and from where they came.

"Zotola en la estrella, Al Nitak," he answered, saying Zotola in the star Al Nitak.

"Roel, no sé si está bien para decir eso," Robert said, telling Roel that he didn't know if it was wise to tell that.

"Está bien, Roberto. Pegaso es muy amigo," Roel responded, saying that it was okay because Pegaso was a good friend.

That sounded fair enough to them, but they reminded Roel not to tell the real reason to everyone for their own protection.

"A mí me interesan mucho las pinturas, ovnis, y todo eso," said Pegaso, telling everyone that the ancient paintings, spacecrafts, and other related subjects interested him very much.

They got to talking and visited with each other for over an hour. Lumita and Mena were fairly quiet, and they soon walked back into the house, leaving Pegaso and his parents to talk with them. As they visited, his mother was cooking beans in a large clay pot over a fire. Everyone, including Steven, found Pegaso and his parents to be very friendly with a willingness to communicate. They quickly put themselves at ease and enjoyed the visit.

Pegaso was a few years older than Roel and Rudy, and he had already finished the prepa. He was in the process of registering at the University of Monterrey where he would enter later this year. He was an intelligent young fellow with varied interests.

As they were talking, Chispo noticed a small metal sign above their front door. He started laughing in amazement.

"Chispo, what is it?" Rinto asked him.

"Dudes, look at what that sign says. We've already found him." He pointed toward it.

The sign read: *Bienvenidos a la casa, Orolizo-Ziscaya.*

"Well, I will say!" Robert remarked.

"Amazing!" Andrew commented.

"Huh! I'm just not believing this," Steven came around to say.

They asked Pegaso if that was his last name, and he verified that it was. His father's last name was Orolizo, and his mother's maiden name was Ziscaya.

"Dudes, that is just amazing!" Chispo commented with enthusiasm. "I know Steven identified him from his dream, but this is definite proof!"

"I'll say," Chris agreed.

"¿Qué, qué pasó?" Pegaso asked them, wanting to know what they were so surprised about. Chispo casually told him in Spanish that the name Orolizo surprised him because he actually knew somebody back home with that same name. Pegaso found that interesting and commented that it was a coincidence.

Roel and Rudy announced that it was time to return to their home as supper would now be ready. Roel then made his request to the Orolizo family if it would be all right for some of them to stay here.

"Pues sí. Está bien. Ya sabes, aquí estamos," Mr. Orolizo answered, saying that would be fine and that Roel already knew that they were right here, ready to offer hospitality.

Chispo felt a good connection of friendship with Pegaso, and he decided to stay with Pegaso's family. Steven, by now, had totally dismissed the disturbing dream and now felt at ease with Pegaso, seeing how genuine and friendly he actually was. Plus, he liked the looks of Lumita, and this would give him a chance to get to know her. Since Chispo now knew Spanish, thanks to Rudy, there would be no language barrier. Chris decided to join Steven and Chispo and also stayed with Pegaso.

"Bueno, gracias. Ya nos vamos," Roel announced, saying thanks and saying that they would leave now.

For the moment, Chispo, Chris, and Steven accompanied the others, and they walked back to Roel and Rudy's house to retrieve their backpacks from the vehicle-craft.

"¿Vamos a Villaldama esta noche?" Rudy brought up, asking them if they would like to go to Villaldama in the vehicle-craft to cruise the town. Villaldama was a nearby small town on the way to Sabinas Hidalgo. Everyone agreed to it, and they made plans to go.

They reached Roel and Rudy's house and entered. Roel told his mother that three of them would be staying at Pegaso's house. That was fine with her, but at the same time, she offered a clear invitation to all of them to eat supper with them. So, they stayed for supper.

She had prepared chicken, french fries, corn tortillas, and refried beans for everyone. There were also plenty of flour tortillas. All of them enjoyed the food, as they were hungry, following their afternoon activities.

It was shortly after 8 PM, and the sun had already disappeared behind the mountain range. In another hour, it would become dark.

After they ate, Roel and Rudy cleaned up and changed into some clean clothes for the evening. Andrew, Robert, Rinto, and Fraxino brought their backpacks in from the vehicle-craft. Then all of them left the house and boarded the vehicle-craft. Rinto drove. First, they went to Pegaso's house. He came outside to meet them as they pulled up. Chispo, Chris, and Steven got out of the vehicle-craft with their backpacks and took them into the house. Pegaso went inside with them and showed them where they would be sleeping. He was glad to have them as guests in his home. Once they were situated, they went back outside and boarded the vehicle-craft with the others.

"Que elegante es este vehículo," Pegaso commented as he looked over the inside, saying how elegant it was. "¿Vamos por Alvaro?" Pegaso now asked Roel, requesting that they go to Alvaro's house and pick him up.

"Sí," Roel answered, saying yes.

Alvaro was a good friend to Pegaso and also to Roel. He was Pegaso's sidekick, as they would soon realize. Alvaro and Pegaso did many evening activities together, and it made no difference that the two of them greatly varied in size with respect to each other.

Rinto drove them back to Calle Gral. Naranjo and turned right. Alvaro lived a little ways further down the street. They pulled up in front of his house.

"Pítale," Roel said, asking Rinto to blow his horn to signal to Alvaro. Rinto pressed a button with the heel of his foot, and the vehicle-craft's horn sounded. It was the first time Robert and his friends had heard it used, and it sounded very unique. "¿En dónde pitaste?" Roel asked Rinto with interest, wanting to know how Rinto blew the horn. Chispo answered for Rinto and told Roel.

By this time, Alvaro emerged from his house. He told them to wait a couple of minutes while he re-entered the house and quickly got ready. Then he emerged. He had changed into some clean clothes.

Roel gave directions, and Rinto drove a couple of blocks back over to Calle Mier, turned right, and they drove out of town. There were now eleven of them total, and it was a tight fit with all of them crammed inside. Nevertheless, it made no difference to them, as it was a common occurrence in Mexico for friends to pile into a vehicle together and go cruising.

It was becoming dark. As they exited Bustamante, they noticed that the narrow two-lane road was lined by plenty of Pecan trees and large estates. Rinto drove them for five kilometers to the main highway, crossing the bumpy railroad tracks just before reaching the intersection. He turned right and drove them for six kilometers to Villaldama.

Chispo inserted a holodisk into their on-board holodisk player and surprised their new Mexican friends with the pop songs done by *The Hydragyros* from Zantaayer. They found the music to be likable enough and right amusing, and Rudy also felt an uncanny sense of familiarity with the songs, even though he had never heard them before.

When they reached a Pemex gasoline station, Rinto turned left, and he drove them down a two-lane road which wound its way into Villaldama, crossing a small dry riverbed on a low concrete bridge, and entering the town center at the plaza. They circled the plaza several times while Roel, Rudy, Alvaro and Pegaso waved at friends of theirs and whistled at some of the girls they saw seated on the benches around the plaza. There were several young fellows courting their girlfriends, and they could be seen walking together on the sidewalks.

Next, Roel directed Rinto to drive to the other plaza a few blocks further east. He drove them to it and also circled several times while Roel, Rudy, Alvaro and Pegaso waved and whistled at more friends. Every now and then, Roel requested that Rinto blow the horn, which he did. Everyone laughed at the reactions and looks they received from their friends in the plaza.

Then Roel requested that Rinto park on the street side so they could all get out and walk. He did so, and all eleven of them walked into the plaza where they chatted with some of their friends. Needless to say, many of them wanted to know about the unique vehicle, and Chispo did the explaining, saying that it was an American futuristic prototype vehicle.

Around two blocks to the north of them, they could hear music coming from a building. Roel suggested they go check it out, and they walked over there. They were having a dance at the social center, as they discovered, and there were lots of teenagers inside, dancing to the disco music. Blue and purple lights were flashing on and off with strobe lights, and the music was quite loud. Since they were charging admission, they decided not to enter. Roel said it was best to save their money and wait until the Saturday night dance in Bustamante.

It was unusual that Villaldama would have a dance on a weeknight, but sometimes they did. In Bustamante, as they would later find out, it was a long standing tradition to have a dance every Saturday night from 9 PM to 2 AM without exception. During vacation periods, they would have more than one a week.

They walked back to the plaza where Roel, Rudy, Alvaro and Pegaso visited with more friends, including some girls, for half an hour. Then they returned to the vehicle-craft. Fraxino drove them back to Bustamante, but not before Roel and his friends requested that they circle the first plaza several more times.

On the way back, Chris said, "You know, I just realized the police never gave us any trouble."

"Oh, yeah. That's true," Robert realized and responded. Next, he asked Roel in Spanish how they got away with that, and Roel answered that Jorge had also told him that he would notify the other police stations in the district not to be alarmed if they see a weird vehicle-craft for the next few weeks. That was good to hear.

They arrived at 10 PM, and Fraxino pulled up in front of Pegaso's house, where Chispo, Chris, and Steven got out with Pegaso. Everyone had an enjoyable evening.

"See you all tomorrow, dudes," Chispo told them.

The four of them entered Pegaso's house for the night.

Fraxino now drove the rest of them the 2½ blocks to Roel and Rudy's house.

He parked on the street side, and they stepped out of the vehicle-craft and entered the house. María was inside, and Nora and Idalia were now with her. Roel and Rudy made some arrangements for Andrew, Robert, Rinto and Fraxino, and they placed their bedrolls on the floor in the same room where Roel and Rudy slept.

It was too hot to use sleeping bags. In fact, it was almost too hot to sleep, as they quickly realized. Since they were in an adobe house, its thick walls served to keep the daytime heat out, but at night, the opposite was true. The walls kept the heat inside, and the house felt somewhat like an oven. Each night in the summer, Roel and Rudy's family would set up fans so they could sleep more comfortably in the night. The richer people had swamp coolers and air conditioners.

At around 1 AM, María's husband came in from his nighttime social activities of playing cards and pool at one of the bars, locally called cantinas. His name was Antonio, and several years ago, he had suffered an accident on the job when he had fallen from a ladder and hurt his shoulder and back. For his disability, he was unable to work, and he lived on disability income from the government. Its pay was not as good as the income he used to receive, and as a result, María, Roel, and Rudy had to start working to help complete payments. They led a difficult lifestyle, having to work hard, but at the same time, they were good people with kind hospitality.

Morning came with sunrise at 6 AM. It was Friday, July 12. An hour later, the family began to stir. María and Idalia were the first ones up, and they entered the kitchen. María cooked some beans and french fries, and she warmed up some corn tortillas.

Roel and Rudy soon got up, along with Andrew, Robert, Rinto, and Fraxino. They packed up their bedrolls and got their backpacks ready for the overnight camping trip in the mountains. Roel and Rudy only had daypacks, so they loaded them with food and plenty of water. Andrew and Robert had just enough food left for two days. Rinto and Fraxino had plenty.

Rudy suddenly realized that he had not gotten permission from Felipe to get off work so he could accompany them and be their guide alongside Roel for their stay in Mexico. He quickly left by bicycle to go talk to Felipe. Fifteen minutes later, he returned and said everything was fine, that Felipe had granted him permission without any problem.

María served them some breakfast. Roel and Rudy took notice of Robert's Kellogg's Sultana Bran, and they couldn't resist wanting some of this unique cereal. Despite the fact that Robert's food supply was running low, he just couldn't turn Roel and Rudy down, with the irresistible look on their faces, as they kindly requested a bowl of Sultana Bran each. They both served themselves and began eating. What a status symbol it was for them to be eating exotic cereal from Australia for breakfast!

As they loaded up the vehicle-craft to leave, Antonio was still asleep, and Nora was just getting up. María wished them all well, told them to be careful, to behave themselves, and she saw them off. Rinto drove them over to Pegaso's house. They were still asleep, except for Mrs. Orolizo who saw them pull up. She came outside to greet them, and she asked them to come inside and wait in the living room for the others, which they did.

"Pegaso," she called out to wake him up.

While they waited in the living room, she rolled out flour tortillas with a wooden rolling pin and talked to them about their stay so far and how they liked Mexico.

Pegaso soon emerged from his bedroom and saw them. "Buenos días," he told them. They returned the greeting.

"Buenos días, hijo. ¿Cómo amaneciste?" his mother said to him, greeting him and asking him how he got up this morning.

"Bien," he answered, saying fine. He returned to his bedroom.

Chispo emerged from the bedroom, having just waked up. "Hey, what's going on, dudes?" he asked everyone. "Man, I gave Orolizo's quartz crystal sphere to Pegaso last night. He was glad to get it . . . said he'd actually seen it clearly in a dream a year ago. He was really surprised to see it in real life."

"Then he's definitely Orolizo's soul link," said Robert.

"Without a doubt, man," Chispo stated.

"What about Orolizo's letter?" Andrew asked.

"I've still got it," Chispo answered. "I'll give that to him the day we leave Mexico."

Chris and Steven emerged, saw everyone, and immediately returned to Pegaso's bedroom to pack their bedrolls and their backpacks. Chispo also now returned to the bedroom and got his backpack ready for the camping trip.

Pegaso soon entered the kitchen, quickly ate some tortillas for breakfast, and rushed out of the house. He took his family's pickup truck and left to join his father who he was working for this summer. Mr. Orolizo worked as a contractor, selling concrete blocks, rocks, and cement supplies for building, and he usually made a practice of getting up very early and starting his work at the crack of dawn.

Pegaso was unable to accompany them into the mountains because he had to help his father every day. Though he would never admit it, hiking and camping in the mountains were not of interest to him, and while he would only have said as an excuse that he had to work for his father, the truth was that he just didn't want to go into the mountains. He didn't like to walk much.

Alvaro would have been more likely to go, but he had to work for his father on his ranch. At the same time, however, Alvaro wouldn't have gone into the mountains unless his sidekick, Pegaso, also went, which therefore meant that the answer was always no. All of this Mrs. Orolizo explained to them as they were waiting for Chispo, Chris, and Steven to get ready.

This made them suddenly realize how lucky they were to have Roel and Rudy so readily available to be their guides and to accompany them into the mountains, without placing an obstacle that one or more of their possible sidekicks would also have had to come for them to accompany them. The truth was that Roel and Rudy didn't have any sidekicks, and they felt free to accompany their new friends as they pleased, and that definitely included a hiking and camping trip into the mountains. Further, there were only a few people in Bustamante who, like Roel and Rudy, would have gone into the mountains to camp at all.

By now, Chispo, Chris, and Steven were ready. They carried their backpacks out of the bedroom, took them to the vehicle-craft, and placed them inside. Pegaso's mother gave them some breakfast, and they left. She wished them well and saw them off.

Rinto drove the nine of them to the cono at the road's end, five kilometers away. He parked by the building in the same place as yesterday. All of them took their backpacks out of the vehicle.

Then he and Fraxino took their briefcase out of one of the inside compartments of the craft and opened it up. Rinto took the piece of Purple Rainbow Fluorite with him, and Fraxino took a piece of uncut and unbroken clear quartz crystal out of the array. Next, they put the briefcase back in its compartment inside the craft.

Roel and Rudy were curious as to what they were doing, and Chispo casually covered up the truth by telling them that Rinto and his brother were gurus and liked to conduct scientific experiments.

They closed the doors to the vehicle-craft, put on their backpacks, and began the climb along the same route they had taken to the caves yesterday.

CHAPTER 9

THE SEARCH IN THE MOUNTAINS

Since it was only 8:30 AM, the temperature was still moderate. As they ascended along the trail, the mountain ridge to their left blocked the sunlight and gave them shade. After an hour, they passed by the entrance to the cave.

They continued as the trail ran along the ridge horizontally for 200 meters and then made a right turn. Now they ascended steeply and passed by plenty of Palm trees, Oaks, Lechuguilla, and other plants. The route was partially forested with low scrub-like trees, many of them being a version of White Oak or Chestnut Oak.

The trail was partially overgrown by summer weeds, and plenty of branches stuck out into the trail from either side. Some of them were thorny and would cling to their clothing as they passed by. They briefly passed one small open meadow on the right. It was full of Lechuguilla plants. Then they re-entered more scrubland Oak forest until they came to another clearing with plenty of grass, Lechuguilla, and Zotól plants.

They crossed a bed of exposed limestone and had clear views of the mountain slopes ahead of them, including their cliffs and steep dropoffs. The Lion's Head Mountain sat at the top above it all. To their right they could see Bustamante and the valley well below them.

From here, the trail veered left and briefly descended and then went along fairly level as it hugged the side of a cliff on its left for several hundred meters. In some places, the cliff towered above them, and the trail was very narrow with a sharp dropoff to the right. They had to watch their step very carefully. One wrong move could have sent them below, possibly into a bed of Lechuguilla plants.

"Golly, this is narrow!" Steven declared in one of the narrowest parts.

"Yes, I'll say," Chris agreed.

"What time is it?" Andrew asked.

Robert checked his watch. "It's eleven o'clock."

"We've made pretty good time," Rinto said to everyone. "Here, let's rest in this wide spot of the trail coming up."

They carefully crossed the treacherous, narrow section and came to a ledge that was two meters wide and tucked into the base of a tall cliff above them. They plopped down their backpacks and took a rest on the widest part. As they looked around them, they could see cliffs and ledges towering way above them. Palm trees and other plants could be seen growing on some of those ledges.

One cliff wall was actually separated from the main cliff face with a deep and narrow crevice between them. It sat on the left side of the main ridge which descended all the way to the foot of the mountain by the cono. Accessing this separate, long and narrow table of rock would have been most difficult and would have required technical climbing gear. Its walls were at least 50 meters high on all sides. They marvelled at its immensity as they stared at it, way above them.

Roel and Rudy announced that they were hungry. They took out of their daypacks some homemade flour tortilla burritos and ate them. Everyone else suddenly felt hungry and decided to eat some lunch also.

The forest in this area was a little thicker than what they had just come through. The trees were taller and straighter, and they began to see some Red Oaks in addition to the numerous other Oak shrubs they had seen. Birds flew from tree to tree and made their calls, the most common bird being the blue Stellar Jay.

After lunch, they packed up everything and continued along the trail as it hugged the side of the cliff for several hundred more meters. Roel and Rudy pointed out Flor de Peña (*Selaginella pallescens*) to everyone. It was a moss-like, ground dwelling plant that grew in clumps at the base of rock outcroppings. Every time it rained, their leaves would quickly turn green and come to life. The locals used this type of plant for decorating the nativity scene under their Christmas trees.

In one section, they also came upon a section of Siempre Viva plants (*Echeveria secunda*), a turquoise-blue type of live-forever plant with its succulent leaves arranged like a rose flower. Each spring, they would send up several stalks, each containing numerous small, reddish-yellow blooms. Most of the Siempre Vivas grew in the highest reaches of the mountains, and they were mostly seen growing out of cracks in the rocks along the tops of the ridges.

As they walked along, they had some good views of the tall cliffs in the distance to their right across the canyon. Roel felt compelled to sing outloud, singing, "Quiero que sepas mi vida . . ." Next, he and Rudy shouted phrases and listened to their echos. Chispo followed, along with everyone else after that. The numerous cliffs in the distance reflected their sounds at different times, causing them to hear each echo several times.

The trail finally left the cliff wall, veered to the right, and briefly descended into a forested gully. Now the forest became thicker with more varieties of trees. In addition to Oaks, there were Maples, Ashes, Hickories, and a few Cherry trees.

They reached the dry creekbed and now made their way uphill. The going became steeper, and the trail seemed nonexistent, but at least the summer weeds were not so prevalent with the forest floor being heavily shaded by the numerous trees above them. There were plenty of large, moss-covered boulders throughout the creekbed, and they maneuvered themselves around them and over them as they followed the gully upstream.

Despite the shade, there were areas where Lechuguilla plants grew, mostly on the tops of large boulders. In addition to moss, many of the boulders and rock walls on either side of them had another version of live-forever plant growing on them.

They were well above the valley now, and since they were in the shaded gully, the heat of the day never reached them. In fact, it felt moderately moist and cool. At this time of year, temperatures in the valley reached as high as 43° Celsius, but up where they were, it was a pleasant 24°.

They came to a fork in the stream bed, and they decided to take a left. For five more minutes, they ascended in the same manner until they came upon what appeared to be an impassable, steep crevice above them. On either side of them, there were rock walls which were more impassable.

"Oh my goodness!" Steven declared. "How do we get by this crevice?"

"I don't know," said Robert. "¿Cómo le hacemos, Roel?" Robert said to Roel, asking him how they would be able to climb it.

"Pues, escálala," he answered, saying to scale it by rock climbing.

"Sí, mira, a la derecha se puede," Rudy now told them, indicating to them and saying that on the right hand side of the crevice, it was possible to climb it.

"I don't know, man," Chispo said to everyone.

Before they knew it, Roel started up the crevice with such agility, that it appeared like it could be done with the greatest of ease. Rudy followed. In less than a minute, both of them had climbed it and were waiting for the others.

"Ven. No hay problema," said Roel, telling them to come on up, that there was no problem.

"Well, I don't know," said Chris, hesitatingly.

Several of them balked. Chispo, quite by chance, was carrying a rope with him, and he suddenly remembered that he had it. He set down his backpack, dug out the rope, and threw it up to Roel and Rudy who secured it to a tree at the top of the crevice. One by one, they climbed up through the narrow crevice with the help of Chispo's rope, and they joined Roel and Rudy.

"Whew, we got by that obstacle!" Andrew declared.

"Chispo, that was good thinking, bringing that rope," Robert said to him after they had reached the top.

"Yeah, I figured we would need it somewhere. So, I threw it in at the last minute."

"I'm glad you did," Chris told him.

"We'll leave the rope here," said Chispo. "I'd say we'll need it on the way back."

Once they were all at the top of the crevice, they continued climbing the gully. The terrain continued to be steep, and there were plenty of boulders to negotiate. Some of the trees had trunks up to half a meter in diameter.

After fifteen more minutes, they were approaching the top of the gully. The forest opened up with the trees being smaller, and it became a little brighter. They reached a ridge on their left and followed it uphill through a pure stand of scrub Oaks. Along the way were various Yuccas, including Lechuguilla and a mountain version of Maguey. There were a few specimens in full bloom with stalks up to eight meters high.

As they continued ascending, they reached a large, open grassy meadow, and they were afforded views of the whole valley behind them and of the towering ridge of the mountain range still ahead of them. The trail was barely discernible as they now more gradually ascended through the meadow, later entering more highland Oak forests. There was another ridge to follow uphill, and then they reached a mountain meadow with plenty of summer wildflowers in bloom. There were also plenty of Prickly Pear Cactus (Nopal) and Lechuguilla.

They turned left and followed the trail into a mountain forest of Oaks and Hickories with the forest floor containing the odd Fan Palm tree and other shrubs. All of them decided to take off their backpacks and rest for a while.

Fifteen minutes later, they continued. They climbed a steep, rocky slope and followed a small gully uphill. Soon they turned right and made their way through an Oak and Hickory forest which was situated along the eastern face of the main ridge near the top of the mountain.

Along the way, they emerged from the forest for a short while and walked along a table of limestone bedrock. There were plenty of Lechuguilla and Nopal plants to have to negotiate. Bustamante could be seen way below them.

They re-entered the forest 100 meters later, and for the next 20 minutes, the trail meandered its way through a pure stand of fine Oaks and Hickories. Most of the route was easy going as the trail followed one of numerous bear paths along the forest floor which gently sloped downhill from the left to the right.

They made a brief descent and suddenly emerged onto a grassy saddle. A cool breeze was blowing from the northwest. The views were excellent, and for the first time, they were afforded some views of the desert valley to the west. They turned left and walked through the grassy meadow, laden with Lechuguilla plants and the occasional Maguey, and they soon reached the top of an immense cliff. They looked below them and out into the desert valley beyond.

"Wow, dudes!" Chispo remarked, somewhat laughing. "That is some massive dropoff!"

"I'm telling you," Steven agreed.

It must have been 300 meters to the bottom of the chasm directly below them.

Roel and Rudy were awe inspired by the dropoff, and Rudy didn't want to step too close for fear of possibly being blown off by the light breeze. He wasn't the only one who felt that way.

"I surely wouldn't want to fall off that cliff," Robert commented.

"Me neither," Chris agreed.

"There's the double mesa where we saw the paintings," said Rinto as he pointed to it in the middle of the desert valley. They could see different roads criss crossing the valley and a few certain sections of land that looked different, like they were being grazed or tilled. Directly beyond the double mesa sat the next range of mountains, and they could see the flat-topped peak they had briefly visited the other day in Rinto and Fraxino's craft.

As they looked around them, they could see the main ridge top sloping uphill to their south. To the north, they could see a couple of knolls on the ridge with the top of the Lion's Head Mountain beyond them. Further in the distance were a couple of other mountains, one of them called Pico Candela. It was the tallest mountain in the district at 1,920 meters, standing 60 meters taller than the Lion's Head.

"Dudes, let's set up camp here in this grassy saddle," Fraxino suggested to everyone.

"Yes, I'm for that," Robert agreed. "Let's camp where we can see both sides of the mountain."

"Good idea," said Steven.

They walked back over to the central area of the meadow, set down their backpacks, and chose some locations for their tents where there were no spikes of Lechuguilla and Maguey plants to bother them. Since Roel and Rudy had no tents, it was decided that they would pile in and share tent space with the others.

It was 2 PM when they had the three tents set up. Rinto and Fraxino told everyone that they wanted to go to the ridge top south of them to do some investigating and scanning of the area to see if they could pick up any signs or clues of the mysterious device. Roel and Rudy still had not been told about the device nor about the true reason the seven of them were in Mexico, and since neither Roel nor Rudy knew English, the seven of them could freely discuss it.

Chris decided to stay at the campsite, as he was quite tired after the long climb. They were now at 1,600 meters in elevation, nearly 1,200 meters higher than Bustamante.

The rest of them put on their daypacks, re-entered the Oak and Hickory forest and soon veered right, leaving the bear path as they climbed uphill. After having to push numerous tree branches aside so they could make their way, they came to the grassy ridge top. For the first few minutes, they continued to pass scrub Oaks. Then the ridge became steeper, and they were soon battling shrubs and bushes which made the going more difficult. In places, there were Lechuguilla and Nopal plants, and even though they watched their step, they occasionally got poked by their spikes and spines.

As the ridge further steepened, they climbed exposed limestone rock faces and had to carefully cross Lechuguilla laden gaps and spaces between rock boulders. In some places, they had to be very careful in their rock climbing because some of the limestone was loose, and rocks and footholds could easily have come off.

They started seeing Siempre Viva plants growing on small ledges and growing out of cracks in the rock faces. A few specimens were still in full bloom, even though most of them had bloomed in April or May.

Finally, the steep grade lessened, and they soon found themselves on a flat table of limestone with numerous small crevices through it. The surface of the bedrock was not smooth. It had many lumps and showed that it had been worn down by wind and rain erosion. Cypress shrubs, some the size of small trees, could be seen here and there along the narrow ridge. They were now at 1,800 meters in elevation.

The going was easier as they made their way south along the ridge. They descended slightly and had to sometimes pick their way around large Cypress shrubs and scrub Oak bushes. There were gaps in the otherwise continuous run of bedrock, and again there were plenty of Lechuguilla plants occupying those spaces.

The views were magnificent. They could see the whole desert valley with its various ridges of mountains running in its northern section. The double mesa could be seen and looked like nothing more than a couple of small mounds way below them. Bustamante in the other valley to the east of them now appeared very small. The road leading to it from the cono could be seen, and the whole valley appeared so far below them that they felt like they were viewing it all from an airplane.

To the south, they could see nearly to Monterrey, and there were numerous mountain ranges that were visible in the distance. One ridge not too distant had numerous Pine trees dotting its slope, and to their west, they saw another grove of Pines growing on the slopes below them near the large chasm.

"These views are equally as good as the ones we saw on Mt. Timpanogos," said Robert.

"Yes, you're right. They are," Andrew agreed.

"Where's that?" Rinto wanted to know.

"That's where we were right before we came to Antarctica and met you guys," Andrew replied.

"Oh, yeah," Rinto recalled. "Didn't you say that was in Utah?"

"That's right," said Andrew.

Both Roel and Rudy were relieved to make it to the top with everyone else. It was their first time up here also, and they were impressed by the views around them.

Further along the ridge, there was a clump of two large Cypress shrubs which attracted Rinto and Fraxino's attention. They decided to go over to them and see what was there.

As they approached the trees, they had to veer to the right and descend slightly. Then they climbed their way back up to the ridge top and reached the two trees. They occupied the whole width of the ridge, and the only way for one to have advanced further along the ridge would have been to go right through the large clump and under their numerous branches.

All of them gathered under the two trees, and the view to the north, framed by the Cypress branches, was spectacular. They could see the Lion's Head Mountain and at least three other mountains beyond that, and both valleys on the east and west sides of the mountain range were clearly visible. There was not a cloud in the sky, and the air was unusually clear with no haze.

"Okay, let's see what I can determine here," Rinto announced as he took the piece of Purple Rainbow Fluorite out of his daypack. Fraxino then took his piece of clear quartz crystal out of his daypack, and both of them began to slowly scan the whole region, each by holding his crystal in his outstretched hand. The others observed.

"What is it you're actually doing?" Robert wanted to know.

"I'm scanning the whole mountain range for variations in energy fields," Rinto explained. "I'm going to see if I can detect concentrations of energy. If the transmitter device is a large piece of crystal, like I think it is, and knowing the Atlantean society, that's almost certainly what it would have to be, then from this vantage point, I'll be able to sense a change in energy as I point this in the direction where it is. Are you picking up anything, Fraxino?"

"No, not yet," he told his brother as he slowly turned around with his right arm outstretched. "Oh wait . . . There! Did you sense that?" he enthusiastically asked.

"No, where?" Rinto asked him.

"Down there, due east of here," and Fraxino indicated.

Rinto pointed his piece of Fluorite in that direction. "Oh, yeah. I do feel a slight tingling now, but very faint. Here, hand me your piece of quartz. It's probably better tuned to it." Fraxino handed it to him, and Rinto pointed it due east. "Wow, that is a strong pulse! This quartz piece must be very directional or selective in picking up the right frequencies."

"Dudes, let me check it out," Chispo requested. Rinto handed him the piece of quartz, and Chispo proceeded to scan the region toward the east. He also felt the strong pulse. "Man, it looks like it's coming from that group of cliffs down the mountain from us. I believe we passed right by them this morning."

"Do you think it might be that free standing narrow wall of rock we all looked at during lunch?" Steven asked them.

"That's possible, man," Chispo replied. "It's a hard to reach spot."

"That wall is nearly inaccessible," Rinto agreed, "and that would be a suitable spot for them to have placed it."

"And the outer side of it faces straight toward Bustamante," Fraxino pointed out.

"That's a good point," said Rinto.

"Tom did say that the residents living nearest the mysterious device are the most affected," Chispo recalled. "And according to what Orolizo told us . . ."

While Rinto, Fraxino, and Chispo got carried away theorizing about the mysterious device and its possible location, Andrew, Robert, Steven, Roel, and Rudy left the double Cypress clump and explored the area. They walked to other Cypress shrubs and hopped over gaps in the limestone ridge bedrock.

Suddenly, Roel was compelled by instinct to look down a crack that was barely wide enough to put his arm between. He crouched down and plunged his hand and arm down the crack, and seemingly with the greatest of ease, he pulled up a flat, rectangular piece of bronze the size of his hand. "Chispo, ven aca," he called out to Chispo, telling him to come over. Roel held up the piece to show everyone.

"¿Qué tienes?" Chispo asked him with enthusiasm, wanting to know what he had in his hand.

"Una placa de metal," Roel answered, saying that it was a metal plate.

"¿De veras?" Chispo responded, asking if that was really so. He walked over to Roel, who was on the western slopes of the ridge and a little ways downhill from the ridge top.

Rinto and Fraxino put their two crystals in their daypacks, and they emerged from the Cypresses. Everyone else also came over to Roel. Chispo was the first one to arrive, and Roel handed him the piece. As Chispo brushed off some loose dirt and stared at it, he started laughing.

"What is it, Chispo?" Robert asked as he arrived.

"Dudes, this is amazing! It's a bronze plaque with a bunch of Atlantean hieroglyphic script." Chispo stared at it some more and proceeded to read it. "Oh cool! It's a memorial marker to the leader of their group . . . those who stayed behind and settled this region when the rest of their group went starbound. It even has a depiction of a mountain with a beam or ray taking off from it, just like what we saw on those ancient paintings on the mesa cliffs."

"Really? Let's see it," Rinto requested. Chispo handed it to him. "Wow! This is a really good find." Rinto stared at some more of the inscriptions below the mountain depiction. "In memory of Bocaleo, a fine leader and an intelligent, perceptive man. He will be missed. May he go well in his return journey."

"Huh! How interesting," Steven commented.

"In his return journey. What does that mean?" Andrew wanted to know.

"On our world," Chispo explained, "we believe that when a person dies, his soul then returns to its place of origin, or you might say, its real home."

"Sometimes it may be our world," Rinto added, "or it could be an alien world, sometimes a non-human world."

"That's right," said Fraxino. "Souls come from anywhere in the universe."

"¿Roel, cómo encontraste esta placa?" Robert asked Roel, wanting to know how he found the bronze metal plate.

"Mi cerebro me dijo," he answered, saying that his mind simply told him.

"Roel es así," Rudy told him, explaining that Roel is like that. Then Rudy explained that whenever they lose items around the house, they just ask Roel where they are, and he can almost always find them right away.

"You mean Roel can find lost items, just like that?" Robert asked everyone.

"Oh yeah, man. That's known as obeying your instincts," Chispo commented. "They can serve a person well."

"Chispo, did you say the man's name was Bocaleo?" Andrew asked.

"That's right, and he was their leader."

"¿Roel, no me dijiste que esta región se llamaba Boca de Leones?" Andrew now asked Roel, checking to see if he had indeed said that the whole region used to be called Boca de Leones.

"Sí," answering yes.

"Pretty good coincidence," Andrew remarked. "His name probably brought about the origin of that name, Boca de Leones, likely long before it came to be called that."

"Hmm . . . I'd say you're right," Robert agreed.

"Many times, the origin of names goes back further than you realize," Rinto told everyone.

"Words have all kinds of origins," said Andrew.

"I know. It's amazing sometimes!" Steven declared.

"You know, I just got to thinking about something," Robert brought up. "Boca de Leones means mouth of the lions, and that title implies that there is danger. If the people living near these mountains are really the most affected, being more violent and aggressive, then that's a very fitting title for this region."

Chispo was the first one to respond. "Far out, man! Sometimes the hidden meaning of words really does surprise me."

"So, what did you determine while we were looking around?" Steven asked Rinto, Fraxino, and Chispo.

"We think the transmitter is somewhere in the vicinity of that narrow wall of rock we saw on the way up here," Rinto answered. "We're not sure yet. I need to get another directional reading, likely from atop the Lion's Head Mountain over there, and with both readings, we'll be able to pinpoint its location."

"Why don't we get a second reading, like from the place we ate lunch?" Steven suggested.

"We can," Rinto admitted, "but still, I need a more distant reading so I can record the broader sense of information from the whole region into this Purple Rainbow Fluorite, and the Lion's Head Mountain looks like a good location for that."

"What we're thinking we're going to need to do is go back home for several days," Fraxino informed them, "use the data we will have collected, and grow some certain crystals, engineering them for the specific task of switching off that device."

"I have a better idea," said Andrew, smiling. "Let's find the device, pick it up, and take it to Tom for the Galactic Federation to destroy."

"No, man, we can't be so straightforward with this," Chispo told him. "That could be very dangerous."

"That's right," said Fraxino. "There's no telling how much intelligence has been grown into that crystal. The Atlantean society was a whiz when it came to growing crystals. If we were to take the crystal with us like Andrew suggested, it could tamper with our controls and ruin them, causing us to be stuck."

"That's why we're being very careful and detecting it from a safe distance," Rinto explained. "This Purple Rainbow Fluorite and the quartz crystal that Fraxino is carrying are both recording information pertinent to the mysterious device. When we return home to grow the appropriate crystals, these two crystals, through their own intelligence, will transfer the necessary data into them, such that they will learn and figure out how to switch off the device after we return here with what we will have engineered and grown."

"Yes, I will admit that it's very wise to act carefully," said Andrew.

It had been two hours since they had left their campsite, and the time was now 4 PM.

"Are we ready to return to the campsite?" Robert asked everyone.

"Yeah, let's go," said Rinto. "I'm starting to get hungry."

"What about the bronze plaque?" Robert asked. "Is it better to leave it here or take it with us?"

"Well, Roel found it," Rinto pointed out. "It's up to him if he wants to souvenir it or leave it here."

"¿Roel, qué vas a hacer con la placa?" Robert said to Roel, asking him what he was going to do with the plaque.

"Me la voy a llevar," he answered, saying he was going to carry it with him. Further, he said that since it had some historical value, he was going to treasure it as a keepsake.

They started walking back, making their way north along the ridge of bedrock.

"¿En serio, qué es lo que están planeando?" Rudy asked Robert, wanting to know what they were really up to.

"Espérame. Déjame ver," Robert replied, asking Rudy to wait while he would check and see. "Chispo, do you think it's okay if we go ahead and tell Roel and Rudy what we are really here in Mexico for?"

"Sure, man, I don't see why not," Chispo consented. "Roel and Rudy come across to me as kind, honest dudes. Rinto, Fraxino, what do you say? Do we tell them?"

"I believe that will be all right," Rinto approved. "We don't want to tell very many people, but since they are our guides, and since they now know we're up to something extra, we'll tell them."

For the next 15 minutes, Chispo related the whole story to Roel and Rudy, and at the same time, he requested that they not tell other people, at least until the end of their stay in Mexico. Roel, even though he was intelligent, reacted with surprise and also with disbelief at some of what Chispo said, but Rudy understood and related to all of it, almost as if it were second nature to him.

As they would later find out, Roel was a person of different ideas. His main interest in this whole mission was to have the status symbol of serving as their guide while they were in Mexico. It gave him something to talk about with his friends in Bustamante and Villaldama. While Roel was their friend on one level, he was also using them to fulfill his desire and reality of being their guide. Still, through Roel's complex ways of understanding, he was enjoying his time with them, and they would come to realize that Roel understood life and the value of friendship better than most people in Mexico.

Rudy also enjoyed the company of his new friends and enjoyed serving as their guide. Also, he had a sense of familiarity to some of them, and it seemed as if they had always known him.

By now, they were descending the steepest part of the ridge, carefully picking their way over boulders, exposed rock faces, and Lechuguilla. They re-entered the highland Oak and Hickory forest and then emerged onto the grassy saddle once again. Chris was inside one of the tents, and he had been taking a nap.

"Oh, hey. How was it up there?" he asked them as they arrived.

"Man, we think we know where the transmitter is," Chispo informed him, "and Roel here found a really neat bronze plaque in a rock crevice."

"Oh really?" Chris responded.

"Roel, enséñale la placa para que la vea," Chispo said to Roel, asking him to show Chris his bronze plaque. Roel took it out of his daypack, and he handed it to him.

"Oh neat!" Chris exclaimed as he looked at the writing on it. Then he saw the depiction on it. "Wait, isn't that one of the depictions we saw on the mesa sidewalls?"

"It is, man," Chispo verified. "This plaque is a memorial marker to the leader of the first settlers, and his name, as best can be translated, was Bocaleo."

"Huh! That sounds sort of like the name this whole region used to be called."

"Exactly, man," said Chispo. "We're speculating the origin of that name came from the dude mentioned on this plaque."

They told Chris what they realized about the meaning of the name, Boca de Leones, that it implied there was danger, and they also told him what they had found out about the transmitter device and how they planned to go about locating it and eliminating it. Chris found it interesting and agreed that it would be wise to pinpoint it and eliminate it in very careful ways, from a safe distance.

Other people had occasionally camped in this grassy saddle, and there was a small fire pit on the eastern side around 50 meters from them. Roel and Rudy decided to light a fire so they could warm up their burritos and extra tortillas. They entered the forest and gathered fallen logs and twigs. A few minutes later, they returned, each with an armful of wood, and they built and lit a fire. In a short while, they had a roaring blaze, and they started roasting their burritos and tortillas over the flames. Everyone else came over and also prepared supper.

It would be three more hours before dark. After they ate, some of them walked back over to the cliff top and looked at the desert valley beyond them. They explored the local area and walked over to the first knoll north of them.

As evening arrived, the temperature became cooler, and they put on their jackets. They gathered around the fire and chatted with each other.

"You know, that name, Boca de Leones, interests me even more as I think about it," Robert brought up.

"I know. It does imply some sort of danger," Andrew commented. "¿Cómo peligroso es Bustamante en comparación a otros pueblos?" Andrew asked Roel and Rudy, wanting to know how dangerous Bustamante was in comparison to other towns.

"Pues, es tranquilo, pero a veces, hay bastante peligro," Roel answered, saying that it was tranquil, but at times there was a considerable amount of danger. He and Rudy explained that during the past 300 years, there had been dangerous upheavals where many of the residents had run for their lives and hidden in the mountains for days. More recently, the people have, at times, had fights among themselves, and they pointed out an interesting fact that there was more personal fighting per capita in Bustamante than for the other towns in the district, that is, the towns further from the mountains. Roel and Rudy explained that people over in Sabinas Hidalgo have sometimes labeled the people of Bustamante as being peleoneros (fighters) and they suspect the reason for this was that Bustamante simply lacked modern culture.

With the information now having been told to Roel and Rudy about the mysterious transmitter device, it now seemed possible and made sense to them that maybe Bustamante wasn't behind the times after all. The true, underlying reason for the tension, violence, and aggression among some of Bustamante's residents was due to the subtle effects of the device. They now speculated it was likely transmitting vibrational frequencies which happened to coincide with the negative vibrational frequencies people transmit when they are angry, and as a result, since these vibrations were constantly existent near the mountains, certain people were affected by them, and their negative side would sometimes mysteriously awaken.

Roel and Rudy related an actual account of a gringo woman and her husband who had come to stay in Bustamante one winter a few years ago. She was a retired school teacher and had the reputation of being a kind and compassionate person back in her home town, so they said. She had made use of a long time friend of hers. He had been one of her former students. He helped her bring tools and equipment to her relatives, a favor for which she was grateful . . . for a while.

No more than she had stayed in town a week than she started making false accusations about some of the natives. She became verbally aggressive and vicious with some of them, as well. In addition to that, she suddenly and mysteriously rejected her former student friend who had also decided to stay in town to visit and enjoy the friends he had made from previous trips. She accused him of stealing some of the equipment he had brought. She also spread malicious rumors about him around town, causing some of his friends to turn against him. He was hurt by her rejection and literally baffled by the weirdness of it all. As a result, he felt uneasy and returned home to the United States.

Later on, she actually got into some fights and ended up getting killed, as some of them got angry and freaked out. Her husband who had come with her was shocked by such activity. He was scared to death, and he immediately loaded his truck and fled town. The police later caught the murderers and put them in jail, but it was too late because she had already lost her life.

"Dudes, that's wild!" Chispo commented. "At the same time, I have heard that for Earth humans, if you stir up energies the wrong way, they can sometimes go haywire and bring about serious repercussions with disastrous results."

"And the mysterious transmitter device is obviously facilitating that process near these mountains," Rinto added.

"I agree, man," Fraxino responded. "That case story Roel and Rudy have told us sounds just like what we suspected was happening. Tragedies like that one are more likely to occur in Bustamante than elsewhere because the people, without realizing it, are resonating to the negative vibrational frequencies transmitted by the device."

"Actually, what could be going on," Chris speculated, "is that various people have negativity within them, and when they come to visit Bustamante, the existing negative vibrational frequencies sort of trigger them to awaken in those certain people. You might compare it to a catalyst."

"But not everyone is affected," Steven pointed out.

"That's right," Chispo agreed. "Not everybody has the same natural frequency of vibration, and those whose vibrations most closely match that of the device, even though they may have been brought up as good people with proper training and background, are caused to resonate with the device without realizing they are doing so. What is noticeable is their sudden change of behavior for the worse."

"None of us has been affected," said Steven.

"We don't have frequencies that match it," Chispo explained. "Therefore, we're immune to it."

"The same is true for most of Bustamante's residents," Fraxino added. "They have natural frequency immunity."

"Natural frequency immunity," Steven repeated. "I find that an amusing description."

Roel and Rudy went on to explain that over the years, they had noticed that certain people were prone to thinking badly, well actually, erroneously. They would get their facts mixed up and the gossip would spread like wildfire. Through the gossip, they had heard that the gringo woman had been falsely accusing people of doing things they didn't do, and she had resorted to defaming certain individuals in the town, people who had a good reputation. As a result, they stirred up a ruckus, and they eliminated her.

"I don't know for sure, man," Chispo speculated, "but it sounds like the woman was definitely affected by the transmitter device, and the negative vibrations strongly resonated with her natural frequency, causing her to harbor and create negative thoughts and false interpretations of the actual truth."

"It sounds like they were resonating so strongly in that individual," said Rinto, "that she was becoming mentally blinded from the actual truth."

"Yes, very. I agree," Fraxino responded. "What a wicked shame!"

"I know," Andrew agreed. "That's too bad."

"Well, she was a school teacher according to what Roel and Rudy told us," Robert pointed out. "Why didn't she put forth an example like one?"

"Yeah, really," Chris responded.

"It's like Rinto said," Chispo reminded them. "She became blinded from the actual truth."

"It overtook her mind and prevented her from being reasonable," Rinto added.

Roel and Rudy next related a weird story about how Bustamante's residents can suddenly freak out and be totally unreasonable. That former student friend of the retired American school teacher had stayed with her relatives the first time he had come. It was during the Christmas holidays, and while he was staying with them, he helped them with some of their chores and with their work. Each day he went to change into his old work clothes in the back room of their house. One day, he went to the room and changed clothes as usual, and the mother of family angrily entered and scolded him for changing clothes. When he asked her why she was angry, she picked up a garden hoe to attack him with it! He defended himself, and then her three daughters came to the scene and got in on it. Suddenly, one of the daughters went hysterical and took off to the police station to complain that he lacked respect for her mother and to have him removed! He was absolutely shocked at such unreasonable behavior, and he took his things and left. He spent the remainder of his stay in Bustamante with some new friends of his.

They had never told him the real reason why they had run him off. It was half a year later when he had returned to Bustamante to stay again with his new friends that they informed him that the room where he had changed clothes happened to be the same room that had the Christmas tree and nativity scene. In Mexican culture, changing clothes in that room was extremely disrespectful.

"Golly! That's terrible!" Andrew declared.

"You mean they ran him off for *that*?" Chispo asked with genuine concern. "That's insane!"

"I mean, it's not like the guy changed clothes outdoors in front of everybody," Rinto remarked.

"I know, man," Chispo agreed. "You just don't run somebody off for going into a room and changing clothes."

"Yeah, I know," Robert agreed. "After all, the fellow did it to help them out with their work."

"I can't believe they were so unreasonable!" Chris declared.

"Yeah, really," Robert agreed. "What an angry bunch of hornets!"

"What did the police do to the guy?" Steven wanted to know.

Robert translated the question to Roel and Rudy, and they said the police, realizing how hysterical the woman was, only mandated him to take his things and leave their premises, which he gladly did right away. Roel and Rudy said they actually knew the fellow and said they had last seen him several months ago. Despite the bad luck he had experienced with that family and then later the rejection from his former teacher, he decided to still continue coming to Bustamante to enjoy his new friends.

"That much is good to hear," Rinto commented.

"Dudes, that is *weird*!" Fraxino declared. "I'm convinced the transmitter device caused that."

"Even still," Robert pointed out, "they don't have an excuse to have run that fellow off."

"There's something I just got to wondering," Chris brought up, changing the subject.

"Yes, what?" said Rinto.

"I wonder if there's any hidden meaning in the name Bustamante."

"Hmm . . . Let's see," said Andrew as he thought.

"Well, the first four letters spell the word *bust*," Robert pointed out. "That's a negative, fighting term."

"Good gracious, you're right!" Steven exclaimed.

"Yes, but on the other hand, if you look at the next four letters," Andrew pointed out, "they spell the word *aman*, which is the Spanish word for, *They love*. The last two letters spell out the Spanish word *te*, which means, *you*. So, in sort of an indirect way the last six letters say, *They love you*."

"But then when you think they love you in that town," Chris cleverly added, "their love gets busted up, that is, destroyed by the negative vibrations that come out in some of the people."

"You got it, dude," Fraxino stated.

"Far out!" Chispo declared with a surprised look on his face. "Dudes, whoever gave that town the name Bustamante acted according to subconscious higher motives and didn't even realize it."

"Golly, that's amazing!" Robert declared as he realized the interpretation of that name.

"Sometimes, I just can't believe what we're discovering and figuring out!" Steven commented.

They continued to sit around the fire and relate stories to each other, discuss the culture, and speculate on things. Darkness arrived around 9 PM.

Roel and Rudy informed them that at night it was said that animals, including coyotes and bears, would roam the ridges, but with the fire going, they would stay away. Even still, Robert and his friends knew that without a fire, the animals would still have kept their distance, but in Mexico, it was engrained into their tradition that when people camp, they have a campfire.

They got to talking about the house they were living in, and Roel and Rudy informed them that Mr. Cantu who runs the store at the plaza owns their house and rents it to them. The Cantus had recently put the house up for sale for U.S. $8,000. Roel and Rudy were worried that their family might have to vacate the house at any moment. Further, there were very few suitable houses available for rent in Bustamante. Since their father was on government disability, he didn't have enough money to buy the house so he and his family could stay there, and since wages were so low in Mexico, it would literally take them years to save enough money to buy it.

The stars came out, and they could be seen very clearly in the night sky. They could also see the lights of Bustamante at the foot of the mountain, and further in the distance to the right, they could see Villaldama. The headlights of trucks and cars could be seen moving in a straight line along the distant north/south highway connecting Anahuac to Monterrey. Way in the distance to the north, they could see the lights of the town of Lampazos, 50 kilometers away.

An hour after dark, they let the fire die down, and they moved to their tents to sleep for the night. While they were lying inside the tents and drifting off to sleep, Roel and Rudy related to them a story from their native homeland.

They were not originally from Bustamante, even though they had lived there for the past eight years. Before they moved to Bustamante, they lived on a beautiful remote ranch located in the middle of the Mexican highlands in the state of Zacatecas. There were no native trees, except for the Palma Real trees, a close relative of the Joshua Tree, and also the large Nopal plants (*Opuntia lindheimeri*) which in Zacatecas, grew to the size of small trees. In the past, Eucalyptus trees had been brought in from Australia, and they could be seen in the town of San Miguel a few kilometers from their ranch.

Roel and Rudy said they and their parents used to live with their grandparents on a large estate ranch situated at least a kilometer off the road. The terrain was beautiful, and their father and grandfather used to farm it by growing various beans and running goats and cattle. It was hard work, but it was a peaceful and tranquil lifestyle.

Fifteen kilometers away was Pinos, a small town the size of Bustamante, and it was situated on the southwestern slopes of a dry, treeless mountain towering above the surrounding plains. They used to go there for supplies and ride with their grandfather in his pickup truck. Each time he went, he would take his cylindrical shaped LP gas tank and have it filled. In town, he would buy them toys and give them treats, and they used to go visit their relatives.

They lived in an adobe house built in the configuration of the letter U, and to go from one room to the next, you had to go outside since the rooms were not connected by interior doors. There was no electricity nor running water. They didn't even have telephone service. Nearby, there was a spring that seeped out of a small hillside, and their mother and grandmother spent a lot of time there, collecting water from a hand dug well and washing clothes. Their aunts and cousins would gather there and gossip about life as they washed their clothes on washing boards, after which they would hang them to dry on the spines of Nopal plants.

One of their aunts used to enjoy playing hide and seek with them, and they used to run up and down the narrow dirt lane and hide behind Nopal bushes. Those were good days for Roel and Rudy, and they had good memories of those times.

It was eight years ago that their father, Antonio, got offered a good position at a large chicken ranch ten kilometers outside of Bustamante, and he moved up there, taking his wife and children with him. Roel and Rudy longed for the days of their childhood, and they missed their homeland. They had not been back to Zacatecas since the time they had moved away from there.

They fell asleep for the night and slept comfortably with their tents on top of the thick grass below them. In the middle of the night, Roel thought he heard a bear roaming in the forest next to them. He got up to investigate and shined his flashlight into the woods. When he saw nothing, he was satisfied, re-entered the tent, and went back to sleep.

It was another clear morning, and the sun was shining on their tents right at the crack of dawn. Everyone began to wake up. Roel and Rudy weren't so accustomed to hiking in the mountains, and their legs felt a little sore. They packed up their bedrolls and took down their tents. After they had some breakfast, they loaded their backpacks and left.

They had not seen water anywhere in these mountains. All of the streams in this part of the range were usually dry, and the only time they ran was after a heavy rain. Luckily, they had each brought several liters of water with them, and they were going to need all of it.

It was 8 AM when they left the grassy saddle. They returned to the cono via the same route they had ascended yesterday. As they walked through the highland forest, the morning sunlight filtered through the Oaks and Hickories to the forest floor. In half an hour, they were through the forest and began the long descent along the ridge, later turning left and following the gully down the mountain.

After they had descended the steep crevice, Roel untied the rope and threw it down to Chispo, and he carefully climbed down the crevice. They carefully made their way down the steep gully and later came to the trail beside the cliff. It was now 10 AM.

Again, they rested where they had eaten lunch yesterday. They called out and shouted words and listened to their echos, still finding the multiple echos rather amusing.

"Let's go up to the narrow wall of rock above us," Robert proposed, "and see if we can find that crystal device."

"I don't know," said Rinto with caution. "Let's wait until we've taken a second reading from atop the Lion's Head Mountain. Besides, I'm pretty tired."

"What's it going to hurt if we go on up there?" Robert wanted to know.

"Dudes, that device may detect our presence," Fraxino told them. "We don't want it to know we're up to something until we're ready for it to know."

"Once we further pinpoint its location," Rinto explained, "we won't have to spend so much time and effort combing and searching the slopes, cliffs, and ledges, We'll be able to go right to its location."

"Right now, we're not totally sure that's where it is," Chispo added.

"Okay, I see your point," Robert admitted. "That's a good idea."

"¿Qué dijeron?" Rudy asked them, wanting to know what they had just talked about.

Robert told Rudy and Roel that they were talking about the device and how to go about locating it.

After resting, they continued the descent and passed by the cave entrance an hour later. There were several people waiting outside while the rest of their group was still inside on the tour. Roel knew a couple of them, and he chatted with them for a few minutes. He told them that he and his brother were serving as guides for the seven of them during their stay in Mexico and that they had camped in the mountains overnight. Then Roel shook hands with them, and they said, "Nos vemos."

They descended 40 more minutes and arrived at the cono near noon. The weather was now hot. Rinto opened up the doors of the vehicle-craft, and they climbed in. In fifteen minutes, they were back in Bustamante, and they first went to Pegaso's house where Chispo, Chris, and Steven got out. Rinto drove the rest of them to Roel and Rudy's house, and he parked on the streetside.

María was at home and came outside to greet them. She was relieved to see them back home again safely. Nora and Idalia came outside. They were playing with some other children, and Nora had a jump rope in her hand. They briefly greeted everyone and then ran over to a neighbor's house. María invited them inside to eat. They took their backpacks out of the vehicle and entered the house. She had pretty much the same type of food prepared as the other day. They were hungry after their long descent all morning, and they ate well.

Roel and Rudy told their mother that they went all the way up to the Cypress ridge, stood on the edge of a huge cliff, suffered through 90 km/h winds, that they had camped in a grassy saddle, thought they heard a bear in the night, and had suffered from thirst all the way back this morning. They described the trail by the cliff as being extremely narrow and dangerous, and they basically exaggerated all points of their trip to make their efforts sound more impressive. At the same time, Roel especially enjoyed stretching the truth because he liked seeing his mother's worried reaction. When she threatened never to let Roel and Rudy accompany them into the mountains again, they immediately toned down their story and admitted that they had been exaggerating. She suddenly felt relieved, and she gave her sons a playful but weird look for the way they had related their story to her.

Then Roel revealed the plaque he had found on the Cypress ridge, and he showed it to his mother. She was most impressed and inspected it with enthusiasm and interest. She advised him to keep it in a safe place so no one would do any harm to it, namely his sisters and their friends.

Once they finished lunch, they entered the living room/bedroom to lie down and rest. Roel turned on the stereo and listened to local music on one of the local radio stations. Andrew, Robert, Rudy, Rinto, and Fraxino were also feeling exhausted and decided to lie down and relax on the spare beds. They drifted off to sleep.

CHAPTER 10

HIDDEN DANGER

An hour later, María came to them and awakened them. "Roel, levántate. Te habla Pegaso," she said to Roel, telling him that his friend Pegaso had arrived and wanted to talk to him.

He soon got up off the bed and stepped outside to talk to Pegaso on the street. Roel greeted him by shaking hands in a playful manner. Chispo, Chris, and Steven had also come with Pegaso.

"¿Cómo te fue?" Pegaso asked Roel, wanting to know how their camping trip went.

"Muy bien . . ." Roel began, saying that it went very well, and he proceeded to tell Pegaso some exaggerated accounts of the truth. He thoroughly enjoyed seeing the impressed and surprised look on Pegaso's face. Chispo began to correct the exaggeration, but then he realized that Roel was playing.

"¿Vamos al molino?" Pegaso offered, inviting Roel and everyone to the swimming pool.

"Sí," Roel answered, saying yes. He asked Pegaso and the others inside. Rudy got up along with the four others, and they all put on some shorts to go swimming. María handed them some towels, and they left the house. Roel requested that Rinto drive them to the molino, but Rinto said that since it was only a few blocks, they would walk.

The molino was situated on the northwest side of town on Calle Mier. They had passed by it on the left the very first time they had entered Bustamante when they had come in from the canyon. They walked in the gate, and there was a lady at the ticket counter charging a small admission. Everyone paid and entered.

All of it was outdoors, and there were numerous swimming pools of various sizes. Lots of people were gathered here today. Many of them were swimming, and some of them were having picnics. Some of the Pecan trees were quite large with trunks up to one meter in diameter. They offered a lot of shade to what would otherwise have been a very hot and sunny place in the middle of the summer.

They walked through the grounds to the largest pool. Roel and Rudy saw several of their friends, and they introduced their new friends to them. Two of them were Hector and Pablo Cizneros. They were also friends with Pegaso and lived down the street from him. Hector was a big fellow, slightly larger than Pegaso, and his brother Pablo was not as tall. They were friendly, and they chatted with Andrew, Robert, and Chispo for several minutes. Hector, like Pegaso, would be entering university in Monterrey later this year. Pablo was Rudy's age, and he was attending the prepa in Sabinas Hidalgo.

Roel asked them what they would be doing tomorrow, and they said they weren't doing anything. They got to talking about Monterrey, and then Roel looked at Chispo and said, "¿Vamos a Monterrey mañana?" asking if they could all go to Monterrey tomorrow.

Chispo talked it over with Rinto and Fraxino. Roel explained what they had in mind, touring the Macroplaza of Monterrey, visiting the central flea markets, and walking to different shops including record stores. They also mentioned an amusement park. All of that sounded appealing to them, and they said sure.

Hector and Pablo said, "Nos vemos," (See you later) to everyone and walked to another area of the molino to visit with other friends.

Roel and Rudy and the others jumped in the pool and began to play vigorously: splashing water on each other, laughing, racing each other, and having a good time. Later, they got out of the pool and sat on the concrete railing by the sidewalk under one of the large Pecan trees. Some of their friends came over, and they visited with them.

Robert decided to walk off by himself to a different pool while the others rested. This one had some waterfalls entering it from a trough, and there was a diving board as well. He dove in and swam around. There were some others in the pool, and before he totally realized it, he recognized a fellow who looked familiar and instinctively shook hands with him. Then they both looked at each other and realized they didn't know each other after all. They were somewhat taken aback.

Then Robert remembered he had seen him riding his bicycle in the street near the corner where Roel had stepped out of the vehicle-craft to talk to Alvaro and Pegaso, the first day they were in Bustamante. Robert mentioned that to the fellow, and he remembered having seen them.

"Ustedes son los gringos que vienen en el vehículo futuristico. ¿Verdad?" he said to Robert, asking if they were the Americans that came in the futuristic vehicle.

Robert told him that was true, and they got to talking. They introduced themselves to each other. His name was Victor, and he lived on the same street corner where they had pulled up that day when Roel chatted with Alvaro and Pegaso. He was age 14 and had finished his last year of secundaria school. He would be entering the prepa in Sabinas Hidalgo this fall. He told Robert that he bicycles around a lot and that he had seen the vehicle-craft parked by the cono yesterday.

Robert and Victor talked about Roel, Rudy, Alvaro and Pegaso, and Victor said what he thought about them. "Sí, Roel, Rudy, y Alvaro me caen bien, pero ten mucho cuidado con Pegaso. Se enoja muy fácil y de volada," Victor told Robert, saying that Roel, Rudy, and Alvaro came across to him as good fellows but to be very careful with Pegaso because he gets angry very easily and in a hurry.

Robert asked Victor why, and he explained that Pegaso appears friendly, but there are times when he has spells and is emotionally uncontrollable, quite dangerous at times. He said that Pegaso's father has had to catch him and constrain him on various occasions. This was disturbing to Robert but came as no surprise since he knew that Pegaso was Orolizo's soul link.

At that moment, some of Victor's friends called him. He turned to answer them and left.

Robert returned to the others who were still sitting on the concrete railing and relaxing. He told Chispo he needed to talk to him alone, and both of them briefly left the others and walked over to another Pecan tree to chat. Robert told him he just met one of Pegaso's neighbors, and he related to Chispo what Victor had just told him. Chispo reacted with concern, but at the same time, he was not very surprised, based on what Orolizo had earlier told him.

"I just wanted to tell you for what it's worth," Robert concluded.

"Thanks, man," Chispo said to him.

"You're welcome."

"We'll take precautions," Chispo assured him. "Let's keep this to ourselves. Just between you and me, I can overpower Pegaso if he suddenly gets out of hand, and I'll make sure and protect Chris and Steven if it becomes necessary."

"Good."

They returned to the others, and all of them took one more swim in the pool. Then they walked back to Roel and Rudy's house. Chispo, Chris, and Steven returned to Pegaso's house with him.

It was now 7 PM, and María served them supper. It was Saturday night, and Bustamante was having a dance, as always, in the social center building next to the school down the street. Roel never missed a dance, unless he happened to be deathly ill, and the chances of that happening were remote. It was a major social event which Roel thoroughly enjoyed, and it was, as they call it in Spanish, his vicio, which meant his vice or addiction. In fact, the dances meant so much to Roel that he felt he would literally die if he were to miss one.

Rudy, on the other hand, was more moderate. He went to most of the dances, but not all of them. Since he had his new friends staying with him, he would just as soon have missed tonight's dance, but he didn't.

Roel invited them to come, and Fraxino showed some interest. Rinto was not very interested, and neither were Andrew and Robert. However, the idea of meeting some pretty young ladies stirred up their interest enough that they decided to go, if nothing else to peep in and see what the dance was like.

They finished supper, and they showered and cleaned up. Roel and Rudy put on some evening clothes which consisted of a clean collared shirt, new pants, and some black shiny boots, a typical Mexican attire. When they were all ready, they walked to Pegaso's house. He also had invited Chispo, Chris, and Steven to come with him to the dance. By the time they arrived, they were just leaving the house, ready to go. All ten of them began to walk down a narrow dirt lane parallel to Calle Gral. Naranjo and one block over from it.

It was now 8:30 PM, half an hour before the dance would begin. Each week, they would hang a banner flag by the building announcing which group might perform. If there was no group, then they would play records and tapes of various songs.

"Man, you're not going to believe this one," Chispo enthusiastically brought up as they were walking. "Steven decided to call home to let his family know he was fine and was having a good trip. He had his family return his call, and he gave them the number to call back. Dudes, Pegaso's phone number is the same as mine!"

"You're kidding!" Robert remarked. "You mean 60375?"

"Exactly, man," Chispo confirmed. "I was really stunned! Do you realize the chances of a coincidence like that happening?"

"Something like one in 100,000," Robert answered.

"That's right," said Chispo.

"Well, I will say!" Robert declared. "That is amazing. Well, you know what I told you back when I met you about that message that Morris heard about '60375 . . . Go meet him,' don't you?"

"Right," said Chispo.

"Well, we met and all that," Robert told him, "but I didn't think there would be a second one."

"I didn't either, man," Chispo admitted. "This really surprised me."

"Chispo," said Chris, "you know how you had told us the crystals that you and Robert exchanged probably communicated and set up that coincidence?"

"Yes."

"Well, it could be," Chris went on, "that Orolizo's quartz crystal ball he sent with you had something to do with setting up this phone number coincidence."

"So, you're saying our phone numbers were set up to be the same as an extra means of verification that Pegaso is Orolizo's soul link?"

"Right," Chris answered. "Even though you had enough verification already, this ensures it even further."

"That's good thinking, Chris," said Chispo.

"Chispo," said Robert, "I don't think this coincidence was meant for me so much as for you."

"I agree, man, but even still," Chispo pointed out, "what Morris heard about 'Go meet him' is valid for Pegaso too. He and I were obviously meant to meet, but you've met him also."

"Yes, that's true," Robert admitted.

"It looks like somebody or something wanted to make very sure you and Pegaso would meet," Andrew told Chispo.

The others had been listening to their conversation, and they now arrived at the playground next to the social center building. The sound of the disco music was booming, and the building's windows were rattling.

Alvaro had just arrived, and he came over to them. They shook hands, and they told him how everything went in the mountains. Roel and Rudy related their experiences, and they really exaggerated the story this time. They had the hair on Alvaro's arms standing on end. Then he gave Roel and Rudy a look of, *I know you're only joking*, and they all burst out laughing.

They walked to the entrance of the building. Three policemen were guarding the area to keep people from having fights. Admission was 450 pesos, around U.S. $1.50. They were just starting.

"I don't know," said Robert. "It's just too loud for me."

"Aw, come on," Fraxino urged.

"I agree with Robert," Rinto told them. "It's just too loud."

"Loud noises get to me too, man," Chispo admitted. "Let's walk over to the plaza."

At about this time, Lumita and Mena, Pegaso's sisters, arrived with some female friends of theirs. They had on some pretty dresses, and they entered the dance. They briefly said hi to them as they entered.

Roel and Pegaso definitely entered the dance. Andrew, Chris, Fraxino, and Steven also entered. Rudy and Alvaro decided to accompany Robert, Rinto, and Chispo to the plaza, and they left the social center. Rudy and Alvaro's boots clearly made knocking sounds with the pavement as they walked along. Alvaro had on a large sombrero.

In a few minutes, they rounded the corner and entered the plaza, passing by the church on the way. Rudy and Alvaro each crossed himself in front of his chest with his right hand. As they would soon realize, it was a Mexican custom to cross oneself when passing in front of a church whether on foot, on horseback, on a bicycle, or in a car.

Numerous people were seated on benches in the plaza, and they were socializing. Robert saw Victor talking to four other fellows. At the same time, Rudy and Alvaro saw some other friends of theirs and walked over to them.

"Chispo, there's Victor, the guy I was telling you about this afternoon," Robert told Chispo and pointing to Victor.

"Robert, ven," Victor called out, inviting him over.

Robert, Chispo, and Rinto walked over to them. Victor introduced them to his friends: Alberto, Juan Angel, Julian, and Luis. They asked them how they liked Bustamante, and Chispo answered that he enjoyed it. At Victor's request, they got to talking about the mountains, and Chispo related the whole story. Though not as extreme as Roel's version of the story, Chispo did exaggerate it to some degree, enough to make it sound exciting.

"¿Y las muchachas?" Luis brought up with a smile on his face, asking Chispo and his friends what they thought of the girls in town.

"Sí, son bonitas," Chispo answered, saying that they were pretty.

Luis next asked them what they thought of Pegaso's sisters.

"¿Quién, Lumita y Mena?" Chispo said, asking if they were talking about Lumita and Mena.

"Sí," answering yes.

"Pues, Lumita es bonita, y me gustaría por una novia, si yo quisiera," Chispo casually told him, saying that Lumita was pretty and would please him for a girlfriend, if he wanted one.

"Ah, cuñados . . . tú y Pegaso," Luis declared with a smile, joking with Chispo that he and Pegaso could be brothers-in-law.

"A lo mejor sí, pero quien sabe," Chispo admitted, saying that maybe so, but who knows.

Luis gave out a good laugh. Julian laughed heartily while Victor did the same.

Alberto and Juan Angel joined in, and soon everyone was laughing.

For the next half hour, they talked about various subjects of culture and travel. Luis and Victor were very inquisitive about their special vehicle-craft, and they asked for a ride in it. Chispo asked Rinto if that would be all right.

"Yes, that's fine," Rinto consented. "What about right now?"

Chispo told them, and they eagerly got up from the benches they were sitting on, ready to go. Robert walked over to Rudy and Alvaro and said they were going to walk back to the house for the vehicle-craft to give Victor and his friends a ride around town.

Rudy and Alvaro decided to remain in the plaza to continue chatting with other friends. Rinto, Chispo, Robert, Victor and his friends left the plaza and walked to Roel and Rudy's house where the vehicle-craft was parked. In ten minutes, they got there. Rinto opened up the doors, and all eight of them climbed in.

"¿Qué te parece, Victor?" Robert said to Victor, asking him what he thought of the vehicle.

"Con madre," he answered, saying that it was really cool and far out.

"Está bien padre este ovni, Mr. Robert," Luis told Robert, commenting how unique the spacecraft was.

"Sí, verdad," Robert agreed, saying that was true.

"Vamos a dar una vuelta, ya," Alberto eagerly urged, already wanting to cruise around town in the vehicle-craft.

Chispo did the driving. He started the engine and drove them to the western edge of town near the foot of the mountains. Then he drove them down a street called Independencia, and they pulled into the plaza. At their request, Chispo drove around the plaza several times, and they called out and whistled to other friends who saw them passing by. By now, most people in Bustamante knew about Rinto and Fraxino's unique vehicle, and they didn't give them such weird looks of surprise anymore.

Next, he drove them over to the school a couple of blocks away, and they also cruised by the social center building. Luis and Julian whistled to several of their friends. They went over to Calle Mier, the main street through Bustamante, and they cruised it a couple of times. Then Chispo returned them to the plaza.

"Gracias," Victor told Chispo, saying thanks.

"Hasta luego," Julian told Chispo, Rinto, and Robert.

"Nos vemos," said Luis.

"Que les vaya bien," Alberto and Juan Angel both told them, wishing them well.

The five of them stepped out of the vehicle-craft and returned to the benches in the central part of the plaza.

"Where are Rudy and Alvaro?" Robert asked Chispo and Rinto.

Rinto quickly scanned the plaza. "I don't see them. What about you, Chispo? Do you see them?"

"No, man. I don't see them either."

"They probably entered the dance," Robert mentioned.

"I don't know about you all," Chispo announced, "but I'm ready to hit the sack, as they call it."

"Me too," Robert agreed. "I'm tired."

Chispo drove them back to Roel and Rudy's house and parked beside the house. Chispo walked back to Pegaso's house while Robert and Rinto walked into Roel and Rudy's house.

María and her daughters were already sleeping. All of the lights were turned off, and the living room/bedroom had several fans running. Robert and Rinto were very quiet as they placed their bedrolls on the floor by Roel and Rudy's bed, and they went to sleep for the night. At 2:30 AM, Roel, Rudy, Andrew, and Fraxino entered, turned on the lights, and entered the kitchen to eat a snack. After a few minutes, they entered the living room/bedroom and went to sleep for the night.

Everyone except Robert and Rinto slept late. It was 10 AM before Roel and Rudy woke up. Their legs were sore after all their activity in the mountains, and in addition to that, the dance. Andrew and Fraxino slept later. Robert and Rinto had gotten up at the same time as María, and she had fixed some breakfast for everyone. She had gone to a neighbor's to house clean for the day, and she had taken her daughters with her. Though she usually rested on Sundays, she needed the extra money and decided to work today. Her husband, Antonio, had come in during the night, and he was still sound asleep.

Roel and Rudy began to stir, and Robert and Andrew talked with them as they woke up.

"¿Vamos a ir a Monterrey con Hector y Pablo?" Roel proposed, inviting everyone to go to Monterrey with Hector and Pablo for the day.

They got out of bed, and everyone began to get ready to go. After eating some breakfast, they left the house and climbed into the vehicle-craft. Rinto drove them to Pegaso's house. Both Mr. and Mrs. Orolizo were in the kitchen when they arrived.

"Buenos días. Pásen," Pegaso's mother told them, greeting them and welcoming them inside.

They entered. Mr. Orolizo offered them some breakfast, but they declined since they had just eaten. Chispo, Chris, and Steven were just getting up, and they came into the kitchen.

"What's going on, dudes?" Chispo said to them.

"Ready to go to Monterrey with us for the day?" Rinto offered.

"Yeah, sure," Chispo answered.

They went back to Pegaso's bedroom and got ready. A few minutes later, they returned to the kitchen and ate some flour tortillas with beans.

"Where's Pegaso?" Robert wanted to know.

"He's still in bed," Steven answered.

"Doesn't he want to come with us?" Robert asked with concern.

"No, man, he doesn't," Chispo flatly answered. "I asked him three times."

"Well, okay," said Robert. Suddenly, he felt a strange feeling, but he kept it to himself.

All of them left the kitchen and said goodbye to Mr. and Mrs. Orolizo for the day. They climbed into the vehicle-craft, and Rinto drove them down the street to Hector and Pablo's house. Roel stepped down, went to their side door, and knocked on it. Their mother came to the door and spoke to Roel a couple of minutes.

Chispo had a look of surprise on his face as he looked at Mrs. Cizneros. "Dudes, she looks just like my mom!"

"Hmm . . .You're right. She does," Robert agreed, as he recalled in his mind what Vironga Colancha looked like.

"Hey Chispo, maybe this is your mother's soul link," Rinto jokingly told him with a smile.

"Yeah, right," Chispo responded with a playful smirk on his face, and they laughed about it.

Roel re-entered the vehicle-craft. "Dice que ya se fueron. No se encuentran," he informed them, saying she said that Hector and Pablo had already gone and were not at home.

"That's strange," Andrew commented to everyone. "Didn't they say they were going to go to Monterrey with us today?"

"That's the way I heard it," Robert answered.

Roel and Rudy said that Sabinas Hidalgo was equally as good and proposed that they go there instead. That sounded like a good idea. Rinto drove them to Calle Mier where they turned right and left Bustamante.

It was nearly noon, and the weather was hot and sunny, a nice summer day. Chispo popped a holodisk into the player, and they listened to music while going down the road.

Fifteen minutes later, they were in central Villaldama, and there was a flea market set up on the south side of the plaza. Rinto pulled over and parked just beyond it, and all of them got out, walked back to the plaza, and looked it over. There were several fruit and vegetable stands with plenty of farm produce. Another table had different herbs for sale. Other tables had cassette tapes for sale and other knick knacks.

Roel and Rudy looked at the selection of the cassettes and had the man at the counter play a few of them. Rudy bought one of them. Several of them bought fruit at the fruit stand. After looking around the stands a few more minutes, they walked back to the vehicle-craft.

Chispo now drove them, and they left Villaldama on the street heading east, passing by the other plaza on the way. When they rounded a curve to the left, they entered the countryside. There were a few farms here and there, but much of the land was untilled and had plenty of Mesquite shrubs. The narrow two-lane highway was somewhat bumpy, and there were curves.

"¿Qué grupo compraste?" Robert asked Rudy, wanting to know what group was on the cassette tape he purchased.

"Los Chamos, Tú Como Yo," Rudy answered, saying the group was called Chamos, and the album title was called, Tú Como Yo.

"Dudes, I don't know about you all," Chispo brought up, "but something's not quite right with Pegaso."

"I know," Chris agreed. "Why didn't he want to come with us?"

"It's like I offended him, man," said Chispo, "but I can't imagine how."

"I did get a strange feeling in Pegaso's house this morning," Robert admitted.

"¿Roel, qué pasó con Pegaso?" Chispo asked Roel, wanting to know what happened to Pegaso.

"Pues, no sé. Pegaso es así. No le hagas caso. Déjalo," Roel answered, saying he didn't know, except that Pegaso is moody, and for Chispo to overlook it and not make a cause of it.

Halfway to Sabinas Hidalgo, the highway entered some hills and followed the winding course of a dry river, crossing it several times on concrete low-water bridges. In some places, the road was dangerously narrow with plenty of curves, some of them sharp. They crossed one last concrete bridge and entered the outskirts of the large town.

Over the next three kilometers, they passed by lots of houses on both sides of the road, a Pemex gasoline station on the left, and more houses and businesses. Roel said for Chispo to turn right. He did so, and they arrived at the central plaza of Sabinas Hidalgo. There were trees, flowers, and park benches within the square, and on the outside of it were government buildings and places of business. Everything here was closed on Sunday, so they left the plaza, and Chispo drove them to the national highway a little further east.

There were several turns to make on the way, and then they arrived at the main north/south highway on a curve by a Pemex station. Roel directed Chispo to turn left. He drove them a few blocks north and pulled over on the roadside and parked, according to Roel's instructions. There were several shops of various types, including a couple of record stores and some restaurants.

Needless to say, they were getting some strange looks from some of the people, wanting to know what strange sort of vehicle they were riding in. Some of them came up to them and made comments and asked them about it. Chispo gave the usual story to all of them, saying it was an American futuristic prototype vehicle.

All of them got out of the vehicle-craft and walked up and down the street, checking to see what Sabinas Hidalgo's shops and restaurants had to offer. Roel and Rudy pointed to a restaurant that specialized in tacos, and they entered to eat some lunch. It was a decent restaurant on one of the street corners, and they served good tacos at a cheap price. As a courtesy to Roel and Rudy for being their friends and guides in Mexico, Robert and the others bought them their meals.

After lunch, they browsed the record and tape stores, and also had a look at some of the radios, stereos and speakers for sale.

Roel also browsed some of the clothing and shoe stores, looking at possible shirts and pants to wear at future dances. He looked at the various boots as well. To Roel, appearance was very important, and he always wanted to wear the clothing of the latest styles to look impressive for the girls each Saturday night. Many girls in Mexico were very critical of a guy's attire when he didn't meet the latest fashions.

For Rudy, on the other hand, appearance and latest fashions were not much of a concern. While he also went to the dances, he reasoned that the more genuine girls would not make a fuss over clothing styles. He would just look normal, and the right girls would like him anyway.

They returned to the vehicle-craft, and Roel and Rudy directed Chispo to drive them to the flea market on the north side of town. When they arrived, they found a lot of people there. They had trouble finding a parking spot but finally did find one a couple of blocks away. All of them got out and walked into the flea market grounds. There were numerous rows of stalls, and a little of everything was for sale. On the left side of the flea market, they were selling lots of fruits and vegetables. It was set up similarly to Villaldama's flea market but much larger.

They did a couple more errands, including a stop at a large supermarket called Garza Morton. Andrew, Chris, Robert, and Steven found the prices so reasonable that they decided to stock up on a few days of food now, instead of transporting themselves to Devonport, Tasmania's Coles New World and Roelf Vos supermarkets for their next supply.

Before they left Sabinas Hidalgo, Roel and Rudy had Chispo drive them over to their aunt and uncle's house on the northwest side of town. They visited for an hour, and they enjoyed meeting Roel and Rudy's new friends.

By now, it was late afternoon, and they decided to return to Bustamante. On their way back to the highway to leave town, they passed by the prepa school where Roel and Rudy attend. It was on the western edge of town, and it was a modern facility that took in students from the whole region.

Next, they took some back streets and later intersected the highway on the western outskirts of town. Chispo turned right, and they began their trip back to Bustamante.

"Ah, la Turbina," Roel suddenly recalled as he saw the sign on the left for a scenic waterfall. He suggested they turn left and drive in there to see it.

Chispo turned, and they soon arrived at the river's edge. There were some scenic waterfalls across the river, and they were pouring over a low cliff. Baldcypress trees lined the river on both sides. After exploring the area for a while, they climbed back into the vehicle-craft, and Rinto now drove them back to Bustamante. While they were on the way back, they talked.

"¿Entonces, qué hacemos mañana?" Roel asked them, wanting to know what they would do tomorrow.

Chispo explained that they needed to go into the mountains again to get a second reading on the transmitter device and that taking the reading from atop the Lion's Head Mountain would be a good spot.

"Acampamos o vamos por el día?" Rudy asked, wanting to know if they were going to camp or just go for the day.

"Creo que por el día es suficiente," Chispo answered, saying he believed that going for the day would be sufficient.

They discussed the subject and made plans to set out from Bustamante at the crack of dawn. They would hike up the righthand ridge to access the main ridge above, turn left, and reach the summit. Roel informed them that people can do it in a day, but it's a long day. It was decided that they would go to bed early and be well rested for tomorrow.

Robert, well actually, all seven of them were feeling sincere appreciation for their new friends here in Mexico, especially for Roel and Rudy, their trusted friends and guides. How great it was for Roel and Rudy's family and the Orolizo family to simply take them in like family and offer them kind hospitality. Bustamante's residents came across as genuine and friendly, every bit equally as friendly and hospitable as the residents of other star systems they had already visited earlier this summer. They felt an overwhelming feeling of true friendship.

What Tom had said about the mysterious transmitter device having adverse effects upon Bustamante's residents did not seem to hold true to them. They knew they were among true friends, and though the retired American school teacher had met with tragedy some years earlier in Bustamante, they realized that it was mostly her fault for allowing the device's negative vibrations to take her over. In fact, they didn't sense any danger at all.

They entered Villaldama, and Roel and Rudy requested that Rinto cruise around the plaza several times. Occasionally, at their request, Rinto blew the horn as they passed by certain people they knew. They took great delight in watching their reactions, and they sometimes burst out laughing at their weird stares.

Next, they returned to Bustamante, arriving shortly before 7 PM. Rinto first drove them to Pegaso's house where Chispo, Chris, and Steven got off. They walked into the house.

Rinto drove the rest of them to Roel and Rudy's house where he parked. They all got out and walked inside. María had been home for some time, and she had supper ready for everyone. Roel and Rudy walked into the kitchen first and told their mother how things went.

"Andamos todo el día. Estuvo bien," Roel told her, saying they ran around together all day long and that they had a good time.

"Sí, y pasamos por el mercado de pulga," Rudy added, saying that they went to the flea market.

They continued relating the day's events while the others came into the kitchen to eat. María served them a stew of meat and vegetables along with tortillas.

Halfway through the meal, Nora and Idalia came home from playing with their neighbor friends. They were noisy as they laughed and played with each other in the kitchen, and María served them and told them to quiet down and eat.

Suddenly, when they were nearly finished with supper, Chispo walked into the front room through the front door. He had his backpack on, and he plopped it on the floor. Chris and Steven were right behind him, also with their backpacks, and they entered.

Rudy went to see who had so suddenly entered. "¡Chispo! ¿Qué pasó, hombre?" Rudy asked him with concern, wanting to know what happened to him.

Chispo's face showed a look of nervous anger and fright at the same time, and Rudy could immediately tell that something was very wrong. "¡Pegaso me atacó!" he told Rudy, saying that Pegaso attacked him.

By this time, everyone else had also come into the room. María looked at the three of them with a worried, concerned look on her face.

"Man, that Pegaso is crazy!" Chispo declared, ranting and raving. "The dude suddenly attacked me! I mean he was . . ."

"Chispo, calm yourself down," Rinto broke in and told him. "Tell us what happened."

Rudy pulled up a rocking chair and offered it to him. Chispo took a seat, and he started to put himself at ease as best as he could.

"Man, we're staying over here," Chispo told them. "I'm not going back into the mouth of the lions at Pegaso's house."

"Dude, we'll work that out in a minute," Fraxino told him. "Just calm yourself down first."

Steven decided to say something. "Guys, do you remember that disturbing dream I had the other night when I stayed with Orolizo and Lumela?"

"Yes," Robert answered.

"Well, it was basically like that, except Chispo was attacked instead of me."

"Why in the world did Pegaso attack you, Chispo?" Robert asked with genuine concern.

By this time, Chispo was calm enough to speak more reasonably, and he began to relate the whole event in English. Andrew and Robert translated it into Spanish as he talked.

"Dudes, I didn't have that uneasy feeling for nothing this morning," he began. "I'm telling you, no more than Chris and Steven and I entered Pegaso's bedroom than the trouble began. Pegaso was watching a videotape on television. Before we could even say hi to him, he got up from his chair and angrily grabbed me by my shirt and said, '¿Qué dijiste sobre mi hermana? Díme la verdad. ¡Eh!' That translates to, What did you say about my sister? Tell me the truth. Eh! I quickly threw his hands off of me, and he repeated the question, this time jabbing me in the ribs.

"I flung his hand off and yelled at him, saying, 'Watch it, dude!' He didn't take my warning, and he repeated the same question again, this time jabbing me in my neck and sending me reeling across the room! Before I could get back up, he began to rush toward me to further attack me, but at that moment Steven managed to catch him from behind and constrain him by wrapping his arms around him with all his might. Before Steven knew it, Pegaso freed himself up and flung him off, sending Steven crashing against the wardrobe.

"He started back at me again. The look in his eyes said he wanted to kill me. Dudes, I'm sorry, but I lost my temper! I slammed him a hard blow in the stomach which doubled him over with pain. Then I pinched him on the left shoulder and made him unconscious."

"Chispo, you socked him one in the stomach?" Andrew asked with a look of surprise.

"Man, the guy was going to kill me!" Chispo exclaimed. "That was it when he jabbed me in the neck and knocked me across the room. Once a person does that to me, anything goes!"

"Well, then that was justified what you did," Andrew agreed.

"What happened next?" Robert wanted to know.

"His father came into the bedroom, wanting to know what happened," Chispo told them. "He had been in the kitchen, and he heard us getting knocked around. He was shocked to see his son on the floor, lying unconscious, and he started to react with anger. I quickly explained that his son had viciously attacked me and that I had to defend myself. He already knew his son's hot temper, and he immediately saw reason and was apologetic to us. At the same time, he was embarrassed for his son's unreasonable, angry attack. He and I picked Pegaso up and laid him on his bed.

"Next, we walked into the kitchen," Chispo continued, "and we talked a few minutes with his father. Pegaso's mom walked in at that moment from visiting some neighbors. She was shocked when we told her what happened, and she showed sadness and started crying. I handed him the note that Orolizo had sent with me, explained it to him, and asked him to give it to Pegaso after we leave Mexico. I said I'd come by later to translate it to Spanish for him."

"Mr. Orolizo escorted us to the bedroom," Steven now told them. "We collected our backpacks, our things, and we left."

"Golly! That's terrible!" Robert declared. "I had just this afternoon thought how nice it was to have friends down here, and I felt sincere appreciation for them."

"I did too," Steven admitted.

"Dude, that's really crazy that Pegaso got so angry because of your kind comment about his sister," Fraxino remarked.

"To get mad over that, he's got problems," Rinto stated.

"I know, man," Chispo agreed. "We had all put ourselves at ease about Pegaso."

"All of us, including me, let our guards down," Steven admitted, "and we got bitten."

"Well, Steven," Andrew pointed out, "you didn't have that disturbing dream about Orolizo's soul link for nothing."

"I know," Steven admitted. "I didn't take it seriously enough."

"None of us did," Chispo admitted. "Dudes, I tell you, that Pegaso was a tiger by the tail! I'm still shaken up!"

"I know," Andrew said to Chispo. "Well, at least you're safe now."

"Chispo, I think you did the right thing, slamming him a blow in the stomach," Robert told him.

"I agree, man. It was either that or get killed by him!"

"I just can't believe he got so angry over a kind comment you made about his sister," Rinto said to Chispo.

"Back on our world, we take comments like that as a compliment," Chispo informed them.

"Yeah, really," Robert agreed. "That's the way it's supposed to be here on Earth."

"One of Pegaso's neighbors came by right after it happened . . ." Chris began.

"Right, Pegaso's neighbor, Victor, who we talked to in the plaza last night, came by," said Chispo, continuing for Chris. "He had heard us yelling all the way down at the corner of the street where he lives, and he rushed over to be sure we were okay."

"That was nice of him," said Robert.

"It was, man," Chispo agreed. "He talked to us as we left and told me I didn't do anything wrong. 'Tú tienes razón,' he told me, saying that I was right."

"Evidently, Pegaso is very jealous, and he's very protective of his sisters," Andrew commented.

"Well, he doesn't own them," Chispo stated.

"That's true," Andrew agreed, "but in Latin American culture, the older brothers traditionally look out for their sisters."

"Dude, the girl is already 15 years old!" Chispo insisted. "Can't guys look at girls and make compliments about them?"

"Oh, well then you're right," Andrew admitted. "Once a girl reaches 15, guys can look at her and take her out on dates."

"That's what I thought," said Chispo. "I mean, Pegaso treated me like I had made sexual advances at her, and I certainly never did that!"

Roel and Rudy had been listening to the conversation, and Robert and Andrew had been translating the best they could. Chispo now told them in Spanish and ran through the whole story again, clarifying details that were missed. Roel and Rudy were shocked that Pegaso had been so rash and violent over such a small thing. Roel was more surprised than Rudy. Pegaso was Roel's good friend, and he had never seen Pegaso act that way. Though he had heard rumors about Pegaso's violent side from people like Victor, he hadn't believed them . . . until now. It really disturbed Roel, and he felt somewhat afraid.

Evidently, Victor was a very perceptive, intelligent fellow, and he carried a reputation of being able to say the right things at the right time to give people warnings.

"How in the world did Pegaso find out what I said?" Chispo wanted to know.

"Do you think Victor or one of his friends told him last night?" Rinto asked everyone.

"I don't think it was Victor," said Chispo.

Andrew asked Roel and Rudy in Spanish if they knew anything about who told Pegaso.

Rudy came forth and answered. "Alvaro y yo te oímos en la plaza anoche. Fue Alvaro. No dije nada a nadie, pero Alvaro sí, le dijo," saying that he and Alvaro heard Chispo telling Victor and his friends in the plaza last night. Rudy said that he didn't tell anyone, but Alvaro did, being Pegaso's side kick and best friend.

"Why that little squirt!" Chispo angrily shouted. Then he suddenly calmed down, realizing that Alvaro had unknowingly done them all a favor, serving as a catalyst to bring out Pegaso's true, underlying, dangerous and vicious side. It was not Chispo's choice to have fair weather friends like Pegaso, so he was glad to find out the truth about him.

Roel and Rudy asked their mother if Chispo, Chris, and Steven could also stay in their house.

María, feeling sorry for them, said, "Pues, sí. ¿Cómo no?" giving consent.

There was plenty of floor space in their spare catch-all room next to the kitchen. The three of them thanked her and carried their backpacks into the room and spread out their bedrolls.

They continued to talk about the incident. Chispo was so upset at Pegaso's vicious turn against him that he didn't want to see his ugly face ever again. He would definitely relate this story to his friend Orolizo on his next visit to the Atascosa people. What hurt Chispo the most was that he had been tricked. He had given Pegaso his true friendship. Temporary, short term friendships were just not a usual practice in his homeland of Zotola. Back on their world, people made a practice of having true, lasting friendships.

Rinto and Fraxino, out of their concern for what happened, decided to go to Pegaso's house to be sure he was okay. Roel accompanied them, and so did Andrew to serve as a translator, and they hoped they could talk to Pegaso and see if they could fix things up.

Rudy stayed home and continued talking with Chispo about the bad incident. He showed genuine concern and had a true understanding of human character as he reasonably explained the culture differences to Chispo in a matter-of-fact manner. Rudy assured Chispo that he and Roel were his true friends, and he expressed his appreciation of the seven of them and that he and Roel were enjoying being their guides. Chispo, along with the others, were coming to realize that Rudy had a lot of the same characteristics and mannerisms as a Zotolan. To Chispo, in many ways, it seemed like Rudy's spirit was from there.

Meanwhile, Rinto, Fraxino, Andrew, and Roel had walked over to Pegaso's house. When they arrived, they knocked on the side door that entered the kitchen. Pegaso was talking with his parents at the table, and they were having a serious discussion.

"Pero dijo que mi hermana le gustaría por una novia!" Pegaso exclaimed to his parents, saying that Chispo said that his sister would please him for a girlfriend.

"Sí, mi hijo, pero Lumita ya tiene 15 años. Déjalo. Ellos ya no están aquí," his father said, reminding his son that Lumita was already 15. He told Pegaso to leave it alone because Chispo, Chris, and Steven were no longer staying with them.

Pegaso's mother saw Roel and his friends at the door. "Pásen," she said to them, asking them to come inside.

"Venimos para arreglar," Roel calmly told her, saying they had come to fix things up.

Pegaso was still angry, and he immediately started telling Roel the whole story.

After a couple of minutes, Roel responded and said, "Pues, Pegaso, ya sabes que es malo usar la violencia. Chispo no es de aquí," reminding Pegaso that it was bad to use violence and that Chispo was not from here.

Pegaso didn't quite know how to answer Roel. He was at a loss for words because Roel's comment embarrassed him.

With Andrew serving as a translator, Rinto and Fraxino explained that where they come from, people value their friendships, and they keep their friends for life. They talk through possible problems, but they never cancel their friendships over them. Also, they pointed out that Chispo had been Pegaso's true friend, brief as it was, and he would never have done anything intentional to have destroyed the friendship. It had never crossed Chispo's mind that making a nice comment about Pegaso's sister would be taken with offense, let alone come anywhere near this disastrous an outcome!

Pegaso thought about it. Though he would never admit it, he had a sense of pride to uphold in himself, and there was just no way he was going to humble himself and admit that he had made a major mistake, let alone apologize.

"Pídele disculpas, ya," Roel insisted to Pegaso, telling him to go to Chispo and ask his forgiveness.

Pegaso firmed up his face. "No," he flatly and stubbornly answered.

"Bueno, ya no me siento agusto contigo. Me diste verguenza. Chispo era tu amigo," said Roel, telling Pegaso he no longer felt at ease with him, that he was ashamed of him, and that Chispo used to be his friend.

"¡Véte, ya!" Pegaso angrily blurted out, ordering Roel to leave.

Without saying another word, Roel, Andrew, Rinto, and Fraxino got up from the table. Pegaso got up and walked back to his bedroom.

"¡Pídele disculpas!" his father shouted, ordering him to go to Chispo and ask his forgiveness.

"¡No!" Pegaso defiantly shouted back.

"¡Pegaso!" his mother shouted.

"Ya no me hables," he said to his mother, telling her not to speak to him. He entered his bedroom and slammed the door.

She walked back to his bedroom and shouted to him through the door. "Ten respeto por tu papá y por tus amigos!" saying for him to have respect for his father and for his friends.

"Vámonos. Ya no razona," Roel told Andrew, Rinto, and Fraxino, saying it was time to go and that Pegaso already didn't know how to reason.

The four of them left Pegaso's house and returned to Roel and Rudy's house. Rudy and Chispo were still talking about Pegaso.

"Está loco. Ya no me cae. Es muy orgulloso," Roel said to Chispo as they walked in, informing him that Pegaso was crazy, that he was no longer Roel's friend, and that he was too proud to come and ask forgiveness.

"¡Que tonto!" Chispo commented, saying how crazy. He thanked Roel and Rudy for being his friends and for making an effort to fix the problem.

Since they would be leaving early in the morning, they decided to go to bed early to be well rested for the long day tomorrow. All of them slept well, except for Chispo and Steven who were left somewhat shell shocked and nervous. They sometimes shuddered in their sleep. In time, the shock of their dangerous experience would wear off.

CHAPTER 11

THE LION'S HEAD

At 5:30 AM, Roel and Rudy got up, along with some of the others. It was still dark outside. They packed their daypacks with lunches, extra food, water, and extra clothing.

Rinto and Fraxino went out to the vehicle-craft and sorted through the crystal array in their briefcase. In addition to taking the Purple Rainbow Fluorite and the clear quartz uncut crystal, Rinto also took a long, narrow green crystal in hopes that it would help them further pinpoint the transmitter device's location. With that done, they closed the briefcase, placed it back in its compartment inside the craft, closed the doors, and walked back into the house.

Roel and Rudy were busy getting their food together. Andrew, Chris, and Robert were doing the same. Chispo and Steven were still not up. They had trouble getting to sleep last night, and they felt drained this morning. María had gotten up to help them all get ready, and she brought Chispo and Steven a type of herbal drink to help them feel more awake. Even still, they found it difficult to wake up.

Finally, not long after 6 AM, all nine of them left the house. Chispo and Steven finished waking up while walking the first few blocks down the street leaving town.

They walked due west on Calle Gral. Naranjo heading in the direction of the mountains. The sun was just breaking the horizon, and darkness faded. It remained clear all day. They soon crossed the most westerly street, and Calle Gral. Naranjo narrowed into a one-lane road and wound its way through scrubland of Mesquite, Maguey, Cactus, and Nopal plants. Goats and cattle could be seen and heard as they were roaming and grazing.

The lane took them around the righthand side of a small hill. They continued as the lane narrowed even more and became a footpath which wound its way through the same sort of terrain. They began to ascend as the path entered the lower section of the mountain canyon.

Suddenly, Roel and Rudy indicated for them to turn left on an almost undiscernible path which went up to the first saddle of the righthand ridge. The ascent was steep and sometimes treacherous, and after half an hour, they reached the low saddle. They decided to take a quick rest.

"Whew!" Steven declared. "That section was sort of steep."

"And we've only just begun," Chris added.

They saw the towering ridge rising above them. It seemed massive, but at the same time, it looked easy enough. All they needed to do was follow the backbone of the ridge, and they would arrive in short order.

"Man, am I glad to be out of Pegaso's house!" Chispo told everyone with a sense of relief.

"I'll bet you are," Robert responded.

"I'm glad we're all staying in the same location now," said Chris.

"I know, man," Chispo agreed. "It's safer for all of us."

"I heard that," Andrew responded.

"It was midnight before I could finally get to sleep," Steven admitted.

"I hear you, man," said Chispo. "I must have been awake that long, too. I was too nervous to get to sleep sooner."

"Well, we're all okay now," Robert assured everyone.

They continued ascending, and they basically followed the narrow and sometimes dangerous righthand ridge for a number of hours. It was rough going. The footpath soon faded entirely, and they were bashing through scrub bushes, climbing steep rock faces in places, and at the same time dodging Lechuguilla, Nopal, and Zotól plants throughout. Some of them felt like turning back, but the sight of the Lion's Head Mountain gave them enough incentive to keep on going.

Roel and Rudy were climbing the ridge with apparent ease, even though they had never been up the Lion's Head before. Despite the fact that they had done very little hiking in the mountains, they were naturally good at it, and they had the stamina of people who would go every week.

The going became especially narrow and steep, and they had to make their way up jagged rock faces, which in some places required helping hands to push and pull each other up. Along this same stretch, they could see the canyon between the left and right ridges, and it was a sheer dropoff into the canyon from where they were.

Afterwards, the going became slightly easier. The ridge widened. They made their way through another saddle, passing by a trail intersection on the right. Up here the trees were now larger. Most of them were Oaks, and the ground was now covered with grass, interspersed with Maguey and Lechuguilla plants.

Evidently, the trail they intersected was an alternate route to the summit from the canyon on their right, and the rest of the ascent was now easier as it followed this somewhat discernible path into a highland forest of decent size Oak trees and some Ash trees. There was another trail that went horizontally to the left, but they continued straight ahead and ascended the forested hillside. At the upper end of the highland forest, they reached the main north/south ridge with a final scramble up a sloping rock face, simultaneously battling scrub bushes and Lechuguilla plants.

Suddenly, on the ridge, they were afforded excellent views of the desert valley to the west of them. All of them were glad to have made it. Behind them, now that they were above the highland Oak and Ash forest, they could see Bustamante way below them. They were now more than 1,600 meters in elevation, almost as high as they were the other day on the Cypress ridge.

Roel and Rudy led the way as they turned left and followed the main ridge for at least a kilometer. It was narrow, less than the width of the Cypress ridge to their south. For the first section, the ridge was entirely horizontal, and they walked along feeling like they were on top of it all, having views way below them on both their right and left sides.

Soon enough, they were ascending again, and they followed the ridge as it became considerably steep. They scrambled up a few rock faces, battling shrubs and Lechuguilla plants again. At least the temperature was moderate at this altitude. They knew it was another hot day as usual in both valleys below them.

The steep grade lessened, and they soon found themselves on a long and fairly wide flat table of limestone bedrock with the same features as the limestone at the Cypress ridge. In fact, there were a few Cypress shrubs growing in selected areas on this table as well. Various Yuccas, most of them Lechuguilla plants, were growing up here, along with Zotól plants and other bushes.

It was now 1 PM. They had made the ascent in six hours. All of them were hungry, and they decided to have lunch at the summit and enjoy the views. They could see far and wide in all directions. The skies had remained clear and blue with almost no haze. To their south, the main ridge of the mountains continued, but to descend to it would have required ropes and climbing gear because the south face of the Lion's Head was a sheer cliff that was some 70 meters in height. The two knolls and the saddle beyond them where they had camped were clearly visible with the Cypress ridge beyond that.

Here on the summit, there was an orange banner flag mounted on a metal pole and supported by wires. It was in poor condition, having endured the wind, rain, and sunshine for years. There was also a small log book inside a plastic box. Each one of them signed it and wrote about the journey up from the town this morning.

While they were eating lunch, Chispo talked for several minutes with Roel and Rudy about different things. He had really become fluent in Spanish.

"Chispo, I still can't get over it that you learned Spanish in a heartbeat," Robert commented.

"It surprised me too, man," Chispo admitted.

"It must be nice," Rinto told him. "The rest of us have to learn it the hard way."

"Well, maybe your mind will pick it up, too," Chispo responded in a reassuring manner.

"I'm not really worried about it," said Rinto. "With you around, we have someone who can translate directly from Artenian to Spanish."

"Speaking of picking up languages off the minds of people," said Robert, "I notice it's a lot easier for me to speak Spanish with the people here in Mexico than it is to speak Spanish to English-speaking Americans back at home."

"Yes, I know what you mean," said Andrew. "It's easier for me, too. Here, I remember the words a lot more easily."

"Yes, that's right," Robert agreed. "I do too."

"In a subtle way," Chris told Andrew and Robert, "you're probably picking up some of the Spanish from the minds of the people here."

"I'd say you're right," Robert agreed.

"Yes, but nothing to the extent that Chispo suddenly picked it up," Andrew pointed out.

"Nor to the extent that my father picked up English from you all," Rinto added.

"Dudes, I will admit not many of us have that ability," said Chispo.

"Oye," Roel suddenly called out, telling everyone to listen.

"¿Qué pasó?" Rudy said to Roel, asking him what happened.

"Mi cerebro me dice que Pegaso y otro amigo mío, Beto, están planeando una venganza," Roel informed them, saying that his mind was telling him that Pegaso and another friend of his, Beto, were planning to get revenge.

Roel didn't realize it, but he had considerable telepathic abilities that were more advanced than most Mexicans. In his mind, he could see the image of Pegaso and a friend of his, Beto, talking over plans at Beto's house. He even heard part of the conversation. ". . . y podemos echar un cuete . . ." (. . . and we can throw a firecracker . . .) It was considerably disturbing to Roel. He had thought Pegaso was his friend, and now he had just telepathically viewed his plan of betrayal. Beto was also Roel's friend, even though he hadn't yet introduced his new friends to him, but now he thought differently.

"¿Qué van a hacer?" Chispo asked Roel, wanting to know what Pegaso and his friend were planning.

"¡Pegaso está loco!" Roel exclaimed, saying Pegaso was crazy. "¿Por qué no puede admitir que estuvo mal lo que hizo?" wanting to know why Pegaso couldn't admit that it was wrong what he did to Chispo.

"Diga lo que van a hacer," Rudy told his brother, asking him to say what Pegaso and his friend were going to do.

Roel told them all he heard was something about a firecracker, but he was almost 100% certain that they were talking over plans to take revenge on Chispo for having defended himself by socking Pegaso in the stomach. Chispo reacted with surprise, and Roel explained to Chispo that since he was in Pegaso's home, he was supposed to have endured any type of abuse that Pegaso would have delivered. Hitting Pegaso in his own home for whatever reason was considered very wrong in Pegaso's view, even though Roel didn't agree with it. Further, in Mexico, many people are very vengeful, and they never forget the bad. They hold grudges for years. He warned Chispo that they might do some vandalism to the vehicle-craft, like knife the tires or throw a homemade petroleum bomb under it. Chispo translated what Roel said and told Rinto and Fraxino.

"Dudes, they're not touching our cruiser craft!" Fraxino firmly stated with confidence. "We've armed our craft with crystallized protection."

"Smart move," Chispo told them. "I didn't realize you had done that."

"Yes, we installed that protection before we first came to planet Earth," Rinto informed them.

"We programed our on-board controls crystal to instinctively cause would-be vandals to lose interest and leave the craft alone," Fraxino explained. "The more intentful ones become afraid and are caused to abandon their devious plans and walk away."

"That's good to hear," said Steven.

"That's right," said Rinto. "We can't afford any harm to our craft this far from home, but just for added protection . . ." He got up from where he was sitting and dug out of his daypack the piece of Purple Rainbow Fluorite. Next, he placed it on his forehead above and between his eyes, and he faced toward Bustamante, appearing to concentrate. "There, that will take care of it."

"What did you just do?" Chris asked Rinto.

"I just sent a telepathic message to our on-board controls crystal that danger to the craft is imminent, and I gave it a boost of protection with this piece of Fluorite . . . Yep, confirmation, message received."

"What?" Chris asked.

"Our on-board controls crystal just telepathically confirmed reception of my warning message, and it's taking appropriate protection measures," Rinto answered.

"That's good," said Chris.

Chispo translated to Roel and Rudy and told them what Rinto and Fraxino said and that Rinto telepathically sent a boost of protection to the vehicle-craft.

"Right, Fraxino," Rinto announced. "Let's get the region scanned into our crystals and see what we can find out."

"Right on, dude!" Fraxino enthusiastically responded. He took the quartz crystal out of his daypack. Holding the crystal in his right hand with his arm outstretched, he began to slowly scan the horizon from left to right, covering the area toward the south where he suspected the device was located.

Rinto started to do the same with the Purple Rainbow Fluorite. Then he set it down and took the long, narrow green crystal out of his daypack.

"What type of crystal is that green one?" Robert wanted to know. "It doesn't quite look like Fluorite."

"No, it's not Fluorite," Rinto answered. "On our world, we call it Kanágran. I don't think any of this type of crystal occurs on planet Earth."

"Really?"

"That's right," Chispo now answered. "Man, it's even rare on our world. It's specifically used as a directional locator."

"Are you getting any readings?" Rinto asked his brother.

Fraxino was still scanning the region. "Not yet . . . Wait! There it is, right over there on the free standing wall, just where we already suspected."

"Really?" Rinto responded with interest. He aimed the Purple Rainbow Fluorite in the same direction and could feel the slight increase and variation in the energy field. "Yes, you're right. Let's see what I detect with the green piece of Kanágran." He slowly pointed it toward the free standing rock wall in the distance. "Cool! I definitely feel that one, and it's a strong force!"

"It's right where we thought, isn't it," Fraxino confidently said to his brother.

"Yep, right on the mark," Rinto confirmed. "It's on this side of that free standing rock wall about halfway down and perched on a ledge. The wall faces right toward Bustamante."

"Then no wonder people like Pegaso are acting so volatile," Chispo remarked.

"That's almost certainly why," Rinto confidently commented. "Okay, we found it. That was easy enough. I'll just let this Fluorite absorb the necessary coordinate information, and we'll be ready to head back down to Bustamante." He pointed the green Kanágran right at the location and held the Purple Rainbow Fluorite behind it to receive the data. Then he carefully placed the two crystals back in his daypack. Fraxino did the same with his quartz crystal.

"Dudes, let's make tracks and head back down the mountain," Fraxino eagerly announced.

Everyone was just finishing lunch. They put their lunch sacks into their packs and got ready to leave. It was a little bit after 1:30 PM.

Suddenly, on the western side of the summit, they heard a whirring sound. Immediately, they turned to see what it was. A pink glow came into existence, and a person materialized.

"¡Caramba!" Roel exclaimed as he jumped back with surprise.

"Morris!" Robert exclaimed.

"¡Caray! Es un brujo," Rudy remarked, expressing surprise at seeing what he thought was a magician.

"It's Morris!" Steven remarked, mouth dropped open.

"¿Qué fue? ¿Quién es?" Roel asked, wanting to know what just happened and who had just appeared out of thin air.

It was the first time Roel and Rudy had seen such a transport precedure, and they were startled out of their wits. Robert explained to them that Morris was a friend of theirs, was with their group earlier this summer, and that he had arrived here by a form of teleportation.

"What's up, dude," Fraxino greeted Morris.

"What's up?" Chris asked.

"How's it going, Morris?" Rinto asked. "What a surprise to see you suddenly show up here."

"I'd say all of you are surprised," Morris commented. "How are things?"

"Pretty good," Andrew replied.

"Morris, meet our new friends," said Robert as he introduced them. "This is Chispo."

"What's up, Morris?" he said, greeting him, and they shook hands.

"So, you're Rinto and Fraxino's neighbor and good friend," Morris said to him. "Nice to meet you, Chispo."

"Same here, man, and thanks for sending me that green Fluorite ball by way of Robert. I was *really* impressed by it."

"Oh, that's all right," said Morris. "I'm glad you like it."

"Morris, these are our new Mexican friends and guides, Roel and Rudy," said Robert, introducing them.

"Hello, Roel and Rudy. Nice to meet you."

"Buenas tardes," Roel calmly said, greeting Morris, and shaking hands with him.

"Mucho gusto en conocerte," Rudy said, telling Morris he was pleased to meet him. They also shook hands.

"So, how's your dolphin research coming along?" Rinto wanted to know.

"Very well," Morris answered. "Dolphins are very interesting beings.

Delikadove, the world where they used to live, the one I've been visiting by the way, is a beautiful place. There is so much richness of color and activities one couldn't even dream of. Their communication skills are . . . Anyway, enough of that."

"How did you know where to find us?" Robert asked.

"As soon as Rinto pulled his green crystal out of his pack and aimed it at that wall," Morris explained, and he pointed directly at the distant, free standing rock cliff, "I could telepathically see all of you up here . . . beautiful spot, isn't it?"

"You saw us?" Rinto asked with surprise.

"Oh yes, I did, and I figured I'd better come right away so you can hopefully avoid the danger that awaits all of you."

Chills went down their backs.

"Dice que hay peligro," Chispo translated to Roel and Rudy, informing them that Morris said there was danger.

"¿Ves? Ya te dije," Roel responded, telling Chispo that's what he already told him.

"Danger? What sort of danger?" Robert wanted to know.

"I could see the image in my mind," Morris told everyone. "As we speak, there are two guys down there in that town who are plotting an evil act of revenge," and he pointed at Bustamante way below them.

"Pegaso and Beto?" Andrew asked.

"I don't know their names," Morris replied, "but you needed to be forewarned

about it. If I were you all, I would accomplish your mission and leave as soon as possible. Don't linger around. The transmitter crystals know of your presence, and they're likely to play games with you all, namely stirring up negative vibrations and energies in that town you're staying in."

"We're being as careful as we can," Rinto assured Morris. "We want to be successful at switching off that device. Wait, are there more than one of them? You said *transmitter crystals.*"

"I did indeed," Morris confirmed. "You need to investigate that range of mountains over there," and he pointed to the range west of them on the other side of the double mesa.

"Oh," Rinto responded, showing a look of admitting he had overlooked that possibility.

"I had a feeling you all were about to overlook those mountains," said Morris. "That's what the transmitter crystals wanted you to do, to make you think this project would be a piece of cake. There's a duplicate sitting over there on that second peak," and he indicated. "It serves as a booster and works in conjunction with the other one so the overall force is stronger. Two of them were placed in this region so their combined forces would successfully boom the blocking forcefield to the Orion Belt."

"We went over there our first day to Mexico," Robert told him.

"And you didn't find it, did you?" Morris responded.

"No."

"It didn't make its presence known," Morris pointed out. "Those Atlantean transmitter crystals were grown with an appalling amount of intelligence instilled within them. Go back over there and search. Take that fellow with you." He pointed straight at Roel. "His locator instincts are very good. He will find it straight away."

"How did you know Roel was good at locating things?" Steven asked.

"I can tell a lot by looking at a person," Morris replied. "The important thing to remember is to keep an open mind. Look at all possibilities. It will save you a lot of trouble in this mission of yours. It's fine to be confident, but don't go overboard about it. All nine of you were caused to be brought together for specific reasons, and I wouldn't have stepped in like this, but since the federation needs those transmitters crystals eliminated and since your safety is at stake, I decided to come and tell you myself."

"Yes, well thanks for coming," said Robert.

"Morris, can you tell us the real reason you couldn't come with us to the Orion Belt?" Andrew wanted to know.

"You're fishing, Andrew," Morris told him with a smile. "That I will tell at the appropriate time. Also, there is a link to a parallel universe. Robert is a central . . . No, I better not tell . . . not until later. Right, enough already. That will be all for now."

"What, you're leaving already?" Rinto asked.

"Morris, wait," Robert called out. "You just met Chispo. I thought you had earlier told us you weren't supposed to."

"That's right. I wasn't, but Chispo now has the green Fluorite ball, and I have already done considerable dolphin research. Yes, the dolphins await me. Their land counterparts, the dolphs, are right in the middle of an important project, and I said I'd only be away from there for a few minutes so I could come help my human friends and guide them in the right direction. All the best."

"So long, Morris," said Robert.

"Que te vaya bien, brujo," Rudy told him, wishing the magician well.

Morris placed his hands on either side of himself. The pink glow overcame him, along with the sound of whirring wind, and he disappeared, followed by the fading away of the pink glow and the whirring wind.

"Golly! What a surprise that was!" Robert exclaimed, somewhat stunned.

"Next time you see him, tell him I said thanks," Rinto sincerely told Robert. "Fraxino, pull your quartz crystal back out of your daypack. Let's scan the whole 360° this time."

They took out their crystals and scanned the scenery the whole way around them.

"There it is, dude," Fraxino admitted, "right on that second peak, the same one we had already landed on."

"Rinto pointed his piece of Kanágran toward the range. "Wow! It's almost as strong as the original one." Again, he recorded the data by using the Kanágran in conjunction with the Purple Rainbow Fluorite.

"Man, that was so lucky that Morris showed up," Chispo told Rinto and Fraxino.

"You're not kidding," Rinto agreed. "Any more variations, Fraxino?"

"None that I can find. And you?"

"I believe that's all," Rinto announced. "Let's go."

It was approaching 2 PM, and if they wanted to return to Bustamante by dark, they knew they had better not linger any longer. Rinto and Fraxino put their crystals back in their daypacks, and all of them began the long hike back down the mountain to Bustamante.

"That Morris comes across to me as a very perceptive individual," Chispo remarked.

"He is," Robert verified. "It's like Tom told us. He knows a lot more than he lets on."

"¿Cómo te cayó Morris?" Robert said to Rudy, asking him what he thought of Morris.

"Es un brujo," he answered, saying that Morris was a magician.

Roel answered likewise, and he asked why Morris had pointed at him. Robert explained that Morris recommended that Roel accompany them to the second peak on the other mountain range west of here so he could help them find the duplicate crystal transmitter device.

"Man, I can't believe he just shows up like that," Fraxino remarked, "knows exactly where the device is, and then immediately points out that we overlooked a duplicate."

"I know," Rinto told his brother. "That Morris must know a lot. Here we search for days, and he pops in here and already knows the answer. No matter what, I appreciate it."

"Chispo," Andrew brought up, changing the subject, "wasn't that quartz crystal ball you gave Pegaso supposed to help him and dissipate any angry feelings and energies?"

"Yes, it was, only I don't think it's had enough time to influence him in that manner."

"Is it going to do any good now?" Andrew wanted to know.

"I hope so, in the long run," Chispo answered.

"You don't think Pegaso and that Beto guy are really going to do anything to us, do you?" Chris asked everyone.

"No, I don't think so," Rinto replied, "now that I've given our craft a boost of protection."

"We don't have any need to worry about it," Fraxino reassured everyone.

"I don't know, man," Chispo reminded Fraxino. "Morris didn't show up for no reason."

They reached the north end of the flat table of bedrock, and they began the steep descent, following the narrow ridge. They descended to the horizontal portion of the ridge and continued further north. Right before they reached a point where the ridge would drop again, they turned right and immediately entered the Oak and Ash forest, descended through it, and over the next six hours, made their way back to Bustamante along the same route they had used this morning.

Some of the descent was difficult. Dodging Lechuguilla and Nopal plants was sometimes a delicate maneuver. Some of them slipped and fell a few times, occasionally getting poked by a thorn or a Lechuguilla spike. Luckily, they made it back to Bustamante without any serious mishaps, and they walked into the edge of town at 8 PM. The sun had already set behind the mountains, and it would become dark in less than an hour.

They reached Roel and Rudy's house and were relieved to see the vehicle-craft still parked there and unharmed. Nora and Idalia were out front playing in the street, and they greeted them, asking how their trip went.

They entered the house. María was relieved to see them. "Estuve con pendiente por ustedes," she told them, saying she was worried about them. She had some supper ready, and everyone entered the kitchen to eat.

Afterwards, Roel went into the front room and turned on the stereo to listen to local Mexican music. Rudy and the rest of them also entered, and they relaxed, some of them in chairs and the others on the beds. They felt tired after their long hike, and it felt good to relax.

Antonio, María's husband, walked in, followed by Nora and Idalia. "Buenas tardes. ¿Qué onda, chavos?" he said to everyone, greeting them and asking them how it was going.

"Fuimos hasta la Cabeza de León," Roel answered, saying they went to the Lion's Head.

"¿Fueron? Que bueno," Antonio responded, saying that was good.

Roel and Rudy told him all about it, and he was impressed by all they had done. Though Antonio was generally quiet, he was a good man who was kind and understanding. He knew his sons were good and reasonable, and he let them have a decent amount of freedom. At the same time, he had been a good teacher to them as they were growing up and had instilled in them a sense of ethics and courtesy. He walked into the kitchen, and María served him some supper.

A few minutes later, someone called from outside on the sidewalk. Roel got up from sitting by the stereo and went to answer the door. It was his neighbor, Sergio. His two brothers, Luis Beto, and Santos, were with him.

"¿Cómo están? Pásen," Roel told them, greeting them and inviting them inside.

"Ah sí, tienes muchas visitas," Sergio commented with a smile, saying that Roel had many visitors.

Sergio and his two brothers took seats on the edge of the beds, and for the next half hour, they visited with everyone. They had been curious to meet the seven Americans in the "futuristic prototype vehicle." They chatted about their hike up the Lion's Head Mountain and also about their campout in the mountains the other night. No one mentioned the real reason the seven of them had come to Bustamante, nor did they reveal the fact that Rinto, Fraxino, and Chispo were from Al Nitak.

"Bueno, mucho gusto," Sergio told them, wrapping up the conversation and saying it was nice meeting them.

Roel, Rudy, and the rest of them wished Sergio and his brothers well. They walked back outside and returned to their house up the street.

Darkness had now arrived. Everyone decided to go to bed for the night. Chispo and Steven were especially tired, not having had sufficient sleep the night before. They spread out their bedrolls, and soon after lying down, they fell fast asleep. The rest of Roel and Rudy's family soon followed.

An hour later, at 11 PM, everyone was suddenly awakened by a most disturbing POW!! It had come from the kitchen.

"¡Dios mío!" María exclaimed.

"¿Qué fue?" Roel asked everyone, wanting to know what that was.

Everyone else made immediate comments, and Antonio walked into the kitchen to investigate. Roel and Rudy soon followed. María also entered. They were considerably startled. Nora and Idalia started crying in reaction to the terribly disturbing noise they had just heard.

There on the floor lay a gray-silver cardboard wrapper, the remains of a large firecracker! The room also had a sharp odor of exploded gun powder. The kitchen window had been slid open and the firecracker thrown in. Unfortunately, the window had not been locked since the lock had broken some months earlier. The culprit had long gone.

Rinto, Fraxino, and Chispo, who were also startled, felt a sharp sense of worry that a bomb had been thrown under the vehicle-craft. As soon as that thought crossed their minds, they raced outside to investigate. Fortunately, no one had touched it, and they were relieved.

"Man, am I glad you gave our craft a boost of protection," Fraxino told his brother.

"You're not kidding," Rinto responded.

Rudy came outside. "¿Está bien su vehículo?" he said to them, asking if their vehicle-craft was all right.

Meanwhile, Roel was inside the kitchen with the others. He told his parents he suspected his former friends, Pegaso and Beto, did it.

"Pues, les llevamos a la policía," María firmly declared, suggesting they go to the police and report them.

"No, déjalo. Son jugetones," said Antonio, urging his wife to leave it, that they were just playing a prank.

"Para mí, no," María disagreed, saying she was taking this seriously. Immediately, she threw on a shawl to cover her night gown, put some shoes on, and left the house to walk to the police station by the plaza a kilometer away.

Seeing his mother leaving, Roel then went to his bedside, threw on some long pants over his shorts, put his shoes on, and left. "¡Mamá, espérame!" he called out to her, asking her to wait up as he ran down the street to catch up with her. Roel could tell that his mother was hopping mad, and nothing was going to stop her from reporting those culprits. For her own safety, he accompanied her since he didn't want her walking all that way by herself at night. Meanwhile, Antonio guarded the house. María would have gone to the Orolizo's house to use the phone to call the police station, but since Pegaso was a suspect, she knew that was not an option. The safest method was to have the police round up Pegaso and Beto for questioning.

As soon as María and Roel arrived and reported what happened, the police took immediate action. They sent out a bulletin by CB radio to every one of their vehicles on duty, and in minutes, they located Pegaso and Beto taking cover under a Mesquite shrub on the banks of the dry river. Twenty minutes after the firecracker had been thrown in the kitchen, the police pulled up in front of Roel and Rudy's house with two of their Dodge pickup trucks. One was carrying Pegaso and Beto, and the other was carrying Roel and his mother.

Both Pegaso and Beto had faces showing pride and resentment. They were quite defensive as the policeman, Jorge, questioned them if they were behind it. Rudy brilliantly thought to check the ground by the kitchen window for shoe and boot prints, upon which Jorge checked Beto's boots and Pegaso's tennis shoes. Sure enough, their bottoms matched the prints that had been made on the soil. They were caught.

"Yo no fui," Beto insisted, denying he did it. Pegaso made a similar comment.

"Pues, aquí están sus huellas," Jorge told them, pointing out that their boot and shoe prints matched the prints on the soil.

"¿Por qué, Pegaso y Beto? Yo pensaba que eran mis amigos," Roel told Pegaso and Beto, asking them why they did it and that he thought they were his friends.

Beto gave Roel a look of denial, but Pegaso gave Roel an angry stare with the implication that he intended to come back and kill him. Roel read the look on Pegaso's face and immediately told Jorge what he suspected Pegaso might do.

Suddenly, Pegaso started struggling with all his might in an effort to escape. Beto saw the opportunity and took off running down the street. While Jorge and Roel managed to constrain Pegaso, the other policeman, Juan, took off running after Beto. Juan was the quickest policeman on the force, and it was fortunate that he was one of the policemen on duty at this hour. Even though Beto was quick, Juan caught him in half a block and brought him back.

Next, they handcuffed Pegaso and Beto, loaded them into one of the police trucks, and took them to the station to be charged. María and Roel returned to the station with the other policeman, and they filled out some forms, charging them and swearing out a warrant for their arrest. Pegaso and Beto were each charged a fine of 5,000 pesos, and they were sentenced to three days in the local jail. Beto was charged with throwing the firecracker, and Pegaso was charged as the instigator and accomplice.

By the time all that was taken care of, including the police contacting Beto's and Pegaso's parents and talking to them, it was well after midnight. Juan returned María and Roel back to their house. Everyone else had already gone to sleep, and Roel and his mother soon did the same.

Robert and his friends were beginning to wonder if Mexico was really a safe place to visit. At least they wouldn't have any more trouble from Pegaso and Beto since they would be spending the next three days behind bars.

Morning arrived with nice and sunny weather. It was Tuesday, July 16. Everyone slept late, and it was 9 AM before any of them began to stir.

As everyone was getting up, Roel and Rudy suggested to all of them that the safest thing for them to do would be to leave town today. They explained that Pegaso's friends and Beto's friends were bound to find out, and then the whole town would find out. Some of their friends might be coming to get some sort of revenge. Roel and Rudy felt afraid for their own safety because they felt like some of the town's people might start freaking out in reaction to the gossip that might spread. They didn't want to take any chances, and they hadn't forgotten the tragedy that occurred several years ago with the retired American school teacher.

"Para que vayamos, ya. ¿Nos llevan con ustedes?" Roel said to them, suggesting that they all leave town and requesting that they take them with them.

"Sí, seguimos siendo sus guías," Rudy added, saying that he and Roel would continue to be their guides.

They talked it over some more while they were eating some breakfast, and it was decided that all nine of them would pack and leave this morning, drive out of town heading northwest on the gravel road to the Ojo del Agua, and enter the desert valley. They would investigate the other mountain range and then travel back to Al Nitak, taking Roel and Rudy with them.

After explaining the situation to María, she was in agreement with them that the best thing for them to do would be to leave and go camping for several days. Roel and Rudy left out the part about their accompanying them back to Al Nitak.

As far as María knew, all seven of them were American tourists in some futuristic vehicle. She had never been told that Chispo, Rinto, and Fraxino were extraterrestrials. She helped Roel and Rudy get packed, and she loaded them with several days of food.

Suddenly, an idea occurred to her. Instead of their going camping, perhaps they could carry her sons to Zacatecas to visit their grandparents, let things cool off, and then return to Bustamante. Chispo translated to Rinto and Fraxino what she had requested, and they talked it over.

"Well, what do you think, guys?" Chispo asked them, wanting to know what they thought about María's idea.

"I don't know," Rinto replied, doubtful. "Our craft is extraterrestrial. What are they going to say about us on the highways we use to get there? We would have to go through Monterrey and Saltillo."

Chispo explained Rinto's concern to Roel, and he explained that the police here in Bustamante could issue a travel permit valid anywhere in Mexico.

That was good to hear, but Fraxino hit upon a better idea. "Dudes, let's fly down there," he suggested.

"I know, but once we land in Zacatecas, we're still going to need a permit," Rinto pointed out. "Besides, where are we going to get hydrogen fuel? I'm sure Pemex doesn't sell it."

"They do have butane gas," Robert mentioned.

"That will probably work, but I'm still wary," said Rinto. "That Richmond engine has always run on hydrogen. Fraxino and I have never run any butane gas through it, not even when we took Chispo to Tennessee last year. I mean, it would probably work. Fraxino, how much fuel do we have left?"

"Half a tank," Fraxino answered.

"Well, I kind of want to investigate those other mountains and then head right back to Zotola," Rinto told everyone.

"Look man, Roel and Rudy have been invaluable guides to us here in Mexico," Chispo pointed out. "The least we can do is run them by Zacatecas to visit their family. They haven't been there in eight years."

"All right. That's cool," Rinto consented.

Andrew, Chris, Robert, and Steven were not really concerned either way. Even though the main objective of their mission was to successfully switch off the transmitter crystals, a side trip to Zacatecas sounded fine to them.

They got cleaned up. Then they packed their backpacks and loaded them into the vehicle-craft. Roel and Rudy packed an old suitcase with extra clothing and carried it to the vehicle. They also took a road atlas with them. By late morning, everyone was ready. María wished them a safe journey. She handed them a letter she had written to her parents during the past hour, and she asked them to take it to them. They said goodbye to her she saw them off. Nora and Idalia had been playing with some neighbors up the street, and they ran over to say goodbye.

With all nine of them loaded, Chispo drove them to the police station where they parked. Roel led Chispo, Rinto, and Fraxino into the small building and explained to the comandante that they needed a travel permit for the vehicle-craft. The comandante walked over to the back of one of the government buildings of the presidencia to get the form, and he returned with it ten minutes later. He had Roel, Rinto, Fraxino, and Chispo sign it, list where they were going, and then the comandante stamped it with a red ink stamp. That was all there was to it. They were now legal to travel anywhere in Mexico.

They got back into the vehicle-craft. "Ya está listo, todo," said Roel, telling them that everything was all taken care of, and that they were ready to go.

Chispo continued being the driver, and Roel directed him over to the main street, Calle Mier. They turned left and drove out of town, passing by the molino on the right.

The pavement soon ended, and the road narrowed to a one-lane rough gravel road. For the next ten kilometers, they followed the winding road through scrubland and then through beautiful forested sections alongside the river until they arrived at the Ojo del Agua on their right.

Roel and Rudy hadn't been here for some years. So, Chispo pulled over and parked while some of them took a swim. While they did so, Chispo, Rinto, and Fraxino stayed in the vehicle and talked over plans. After half an hour, those who had been swimming dried off and climbed back into the vehicle-craft.

Rinto now drove. They left the Ojo del Agua and ascended the rough, one-lane road, leaving the canyon and entering the desert valley on the western side of the mountain range.

"All right, dudes," Rinto announced with enthusiasm. "We're airborne!" He pulled back the lever, and they left the ground.

"¡Caramba!" Roel exclaimed.

"¡Caray!" Rudy remarked.

Neither one of them had yet been in the craft when it was flying, until now. They were taken by surprise, even though they figured that's what they would be doing in order to access the mountains and then travel to Zacatecas.

Without making a sound, Rinto steered the craft, and it quickly accelerated and flew them in a matter of minutes to the double mesa some ten kilometers to their south. Roel and Rudy requested a quick look at the mesa sidewall paintings, and Rinto consented. He approached the mesa and slowed the craft. Then he carefully maneuvered the craft and hovered near the walls of the cliff and slowly moved alongside them, giving Roel and Rudy a view of them through the windows. They were impressed, and Roel had a strong feeling that Atlantis was indeed connected to these drawings, and in addition to that, the planet Mars.

After spending some ten minutes viewing the paintings from their hovering craft, Rinto flew them up to the second peak of the mountain range west of them, and he gently touched down on the flat table of limestone bedrock at its summit.

"This is where Morris told us the second transmitter crystal is, right?" Rinto asked everyone.

"This is the place, man," Chispo answered.

"Okay, let's go to searching and see what we can turn up," Rinto announced.

He reached into a different inside compartment and took out a piece of translucent red crystal which he intended to use to record information upon locating the device.

Each one of them went in different directions, searching for the crystal transmitter. They peeped over the edges of the cliff walls on all sides of this flat limestone bedrock summit.

Roel casually walked to the southern end of the flat summit and peeped over the edge of the cliff. "¡Ya!" he shouted, announcing he had already located it! Thirty meters below him, sitting on a ledge and surrounded by Lechuguilla plants was the large piece of greenish-yellow crystal. It was around one meter in diameter.

"Well, I will say!" Robert remarked, being in a different location.

"Just like Morris said," Andrew commented.

All of them came over to where Roel was standing.

"¿Ya lo encontraste?" Andrew said to Roel, asking him if he already found the crystal transmitter.

"Sí," answering yes.

"Bien hecho, hombre," Chispo praised Roel, saying he had done well.

Chispo was the first one to peer over the edge. "Wow, dudes! It's a dodecahedron!"

"Cool!" Fraxino remarked. He peered over the edge. "Radical, dudes!" he exclaimed.

"Wait up. Let me get my rope," Chispo told everyone.

"No, that's okay," Rinto told him. "I can record what we need from right here." Standing on the edge of the cliff, Rinto took the piece of red crystal out of his pocket and outstretched his arm, holding the crystal directly above the large dodecahedron 30 meters below. He turned the piece of red crystal through different angles over a period of three minutes. "There. That's got it."

"That's all for here, then?" Steven asked.

"Yep, that takes care of it for here," Rinto answered. "Now, we're going to need to do the same for the original one."

"I thought you said it would be dangerous to do that," Chris brought up.

"Oh, yeah. That is a possibility," Rinto admitted, recalling what they had earlier talked about.

"No, I think it's safe," Fraxino assured his brother. "Besides, we have to obtain the necessary close range data from both of them to take that information back home with us."

"That's one reason they're using that red crystal," Chispo explained to the others. "They're going to store that crystal inside a separate, protected compartment so it doesn't contaminate the distance data we've already recorded into the other crystals."

They boarded the craft. Rinto left the ground and flew them over to the other range of mountains. He brought it in for a landing and touched down at the grassy saddle where they had camped the other night.

"Okay, how do we want to do this?" Rinto asked everyone.

"Let's leave the briefcase here with some of us staying behind to guard it," Chispo suggested. "The rest of you can fly over there to the free standing cliff wall and locate it. I'll stay here."

"Who else wants to stay here?" Rinto asked.

"I will," said Chris.

Robert and Rudy also decided to stay, and the rest of them flew away in the craft as it left the ground and swiftly accelerated, veered right, and disappeared from sight behind the Oak and Hickory forest. For the next 30 minutes, they remained there in the grassy saddle and kept the briefcase with them.

Meanwhile, Rinto, Fraxino, Andrew, Steven, and Roel cruised along the ridge and then descended to the area where the free standing narrow cliff was separated from the main ridge. It was only five meters wide, and it had scrub Oaks, Palms, and Lechuguilla plants growing on its top. With difficulty, Rinto carefully guided the craft to gently touch down.

They walked around and explored the unique area on top of this narrow wall, and they peeped over the outer edge toward Bustamante in places. In five minutes, Roel located the crystal transmitter. Like the one they had just found on the other mountain range west of them, this one was 30 meters below the top of the cliff and perched on a ledge that was full of Lechuguilla plants. Again, it was a dodecahedron, and it was a perfect match in color and size.

Rinto took a different piece of red crystal and recorded the data in a similar manner as he had for the other one. With that done, he placed the crystal in the special compartment with the other red crystal. They climbed back into the craft, left the site, cruised back up to the main ridge, and touched down in the grassy saddle once again. By now, it was two o'clock in the afternoon.

The others climbed back in, and they took off flying again. Rinto caused the craft to swiftly accelerate in a horizontal direction. In almost no time, they were clearing the top of the 300-meter cliff above the large chasm on the western side of the saddle. Next, the craft further accelerated and veered to the left, and they cruised south through the desert valley at an air speed of 500 km/h.

Fraxino put a holodisk into the player and they listened to more Zotolan pop music.

"Zacatecas, here we come!" Rinto declared.

CHAPTER 12

ZACATECAS

According to what Roel and Rudy had told everyone, their grandparents lived on a ranch some 15 kilometers southwest of Pinos, Zacatecas, which was around 700 kilometers south of Bustamante.

"Okay, let's check out the road atlas," said Fraxino.

Chispo translated to Roel and Rudy, and Rudy dug it out of their suitcase and handed it to Fraxino. As they were flying along, Rinto inspected the appropriate maps.

"So, Pinos is around 100 kilometers southeast of the city of Zacatecas," Rinto commented. "Okay, we'll pick up altitude, dodge Monterrey and Saltillo, and cruise on to Zacatecas, veer left before getting there, and cruise over to Pinos. Wow, the terrain between Saltillo and Zacatecas looks desolate, according to this map!"

In minutes, they came to the southern end of the desert valley. Monterrey could be seen in the distance southeast of them. Rinto picked up considerable altitude, veered right, and flew over the tops of the mountains between Monterrey and Saltillo. Some of the peaks were more than 3,000 meters in altitude. Saltillo was soon visible to their right and situated at the base of several mountains.

Further south, they could see the highway far below them winding its way by a town called Concepción del Oro at the southern foothills of the mountains. At this point, they cleared the mountains and were now flying over a huge expanse of desert stretching out to the horizon.

"Dude, this looks like back home in Zotola," Fraxino commented.

"I know. That's what I was just thinking," Robert agreed.

"Lower the altitude of the craft, Rinto," Chispo requested. "Let's check this out, man."

Rinto did as Chispo suggested. Everyone was struck with surprise to see the countryside look so similar to the scenery of the desert valley south of Zantaayer between the Ciruclar and Placatera mountain ranges. Rinto decided to touch down on the two-lane highway and drive a few kilometers, seeing there was so little traffic.

In minutes, he made contact with the road's surface, cruising at a speed of 100 km/h. He started the engine, moved the transmission lever from neutral to fifth gear, and engaged the clutch. Even the plantlife looked similar with scrub bushes and Cactus shrubs here and there. The only noticeable difference was the color of the sky, being a deep blue here instead of the turquoise blue back on their home world of Artenia.

"In a way, I feel like we're back home, cruising one of our highways," Rinto told everyone.

"Let's pull over and eat some lunch," Fraxino requested. "There's a turnout just ahead."

He slowed down and pulled the vehicle-craft over, parking on the wide dirt turnout. Everyone stepped out into the moderately hot, sunny 35° Celsius weather, and they dug some food out of their backpacks. Roel and Rudy ate what their mother had sent with them. Occasionally, a car or truck would pass by on the highway, but no one stopped to bother them.

The ground all around them was flat and desolate, and there were plenty of Mesquite shrubs and Yuccas, a few Palma Real trees, and some weird looking sizeable Cactus trees and shrubs. Robert went over to look at one of them. It looked similar to something he had seen on Sirius B earlier this summer, and memories came back to him about the city of Ahntraytitral and the tour they had taken with the homestay families Tom had set them up with.

After half an hour, they finished lunch and climbed back into the vehicle-craft. Rinto continued to drive, and he proceeded south on the straight and narrow two-lane highway to Zacatecas. As far as the eye could see, the highway continued flat and straight ahead to the horizon.

He pulled back the lever, and they left the highway's surface. The craft swiftly accelerated, and they gained altitude, attaining 8,000 meters with a cruising speed of 800 km/h.

In less than an hour, they were cruising by the city of Zacatecas on their right. Rinto slowed the speed of the craft, and ten minutes later, they were 100 kilometers southeast of Zacatecas and were now approaching the town of Pinos. It was visible below them and situated on the southwestern slopes of a dry and treeless mountain. Rinto brought the craft in for a landing and touched down on the highway a few kilometers north of Pinos.

It had been a such a long time since Roel and Rudy had been there. They were just children the last time they had come, eight years ago. They were doing their best to remember the layout of the town. They knew they had an uncle named Antonio who lived in the lower end of town.

It was 4 PM when Rinto drove them into Pinos. There were small businesses on both sides of the road and a Pemex station on the left, the only fuel station in town. They crossed a bridge, and the road narrowed as they entered the central district with streets lined by She-Oak trees, Eucalypts, and tall narrow Cypress trees.

Some of the people, needless to say, were giving them some weird looks because of their unusual looking vehicle-craft. By now, they had become accustomed to such gazes and stares from the people.

They entered the town center at the plaza with a cathedral on their right on the downhill side. Large Cypress trees grew in the plaza's interior grounds, and park benches lined its perimeter. The whole plaza, actually the whole town, was perched on a sloping hillside with the bottom of Pinos at the foot of the mountain where it touched the desert plains.

The whole region was at a high altitude, more than 2,500 meters. Most of Zacatecas sat on the high desert plains in central Mexico, and not far to the west of them was the continental divide. As a result, the temperature was a pleasant 30° Celsius. The skies were perfectly clear at this time of year, the same as in Bustamante.

Rinto parked the vehicle-craft by a place of business on the streetside, and everyone stepped outside and walked around the plaza to look around. Roel asked certain people if they knew his uncle, Antonio, and if they knew where he lived. It wasn't long before he found someone who knew him, and he gave Roel directions.

After looking around the plaza some more, they returned to the vehicle-craft. Chispo now drove. Roel directed him to take the narrow street by the cathedral, and he drove them down the somewhat steep street to the lower part of town. When they neared their uncle's house, Roel and Rudy recognized it. Chispo parked on the streetside while Roel went to the door and knocked.

His uncle ran a motorcycle mechanic's garage, and one of his workers was testing out a motorcycle at the moment. Antonio, who was in his house beside his garage, came to the door and opened it. A look of surprise crossed his face as he looked at Roel. He realized he was looking at someone familiar, but he couldn't place him. Roel greeted him and explained that he and some friends had come down from Bustamante.

"Ah, sí, mi sobrino. ¿Cómo estás?" Antonio greeted him, recognizing him as his nephew and asking how he was doing. "Pasa con tus amigos," he said to Roel, telling him to bring his friends and come in.

Roel motioned all of them to enter. Everyone got out of the vehicle-craft and walked inside.

Antonio pulled up some chairs for them to have seats. He called for his wife to come forward from the back of the house where she was doing some washing. Her name was Eustolia. Both of them greeted Roel and his brother, followed by everyone else.

They talked for a while. Roel did most of the talking as he explained that this group of Americans had arrived last week in Bustamante. They were driving a futuristic prototype vehicle and had come for purposes of doing research in the mountains. Roel said he and Rudy had become their guides and that they were enjoying their new friends. They had been cruising the towns in the region near Bustamante, and they had been hiking and camping in the mountains. Roel also admitted that he and Rudy felt tired after their long hike up and down the Lion's Head Mountain, only yesterday.

Antonio's wife, Eustolia, soon returned to what she was doing in the back of the house. He now led them across the street to another building. It belonged to his brother-in-law. He opened the door to the front room, and there were several double beds inside, enough to sleep all nine of them. Antonio told them they were welcome to sleep here during their stay in Pinos.

With that, he left them to it and said for them to come over within the hour to eat supper with them, and he walked back across the street. Roel and Rudy started preparing the beds while the other seven took their backpacks out of the vehicle-craft and brought them inside the room.

The exhaustion had caught up with them after their long day yesterday, and the disturbing firecracker incident last night had not helped matters either. They lay down on the beds and relaxed. Some of them talked, and some of them fell asleep. Before they realized it, all of them had drifted off to sleep.

Knock! Knock! Antonio was at the door. An hour had already passed by. Rudy got up and opened the door.

"Ah, están dormiendo," said Antonio, commenting to all of them that they had taken a nap. "Para que vengan a comer," he said to them, inviting them to come eat.

Everyone finished waking up, and they all walked across the street to the house and entered. Antonio's wife had fixed a good supper of rice and beans with tortillas and hot sauce, and she served them at their kitchen table in the back of the house.

By now, Antonio and Eustolia's children had come home for the day. Their names were Joel and Malena, and they were around the same age as Roel and Rudy. They were both working different jobs at one of the markets up the hill in the town's central district.

While they were eating, Antonio informed Roel and Rudy that their grandparents were doing fine. His grandfather still came to town once a week for supplies and would usually stop by here. He caught them up on their other relatives and cousins. Many of them lived in the small village of San Miguel, which was on the road going to their grandparents' ranch.

They talked for some time as Antonio related to them different stories about Pinos. He told them that back several hundred years ago in the days when Pinos was founded, there used to be a grove of native Pine trees near where the central district is today. Their location on the southwestern slopes of the mountain overlooking the central Mexican highlands was attractive to the settlers at the time. As a result, some of them decided to make their home there. In more recent times, the climate had become somewhat drier. The native Pines were now gone, but in their place they had planted Cypress trees as ornamentals to decorate the streets.

Roel and Rudy were beginning to feel considerable soreness in their legs, 24 hours after having completed their hike up and down the Lion's Head Mountain. It became dark at 8:30 PM, and they didn't feel like staying up any longer. They weren't the only ones. All of them decided to go to bed early. They thanked Antonio and Eustolia for the supper, walked to the building across the street, and went to sleep. They slept comfortably all night long, knowing that no one here was going to toss them any firecrackers.

It became somewhat cool during the night, which was usual in Pinos since it was in the central Mexican highlands.

They were awakened around 7 AM to the sound of motorcycle engines being tested and run at Antonio's garage across the street.

He soon came over and knocked on the door, saying there was breakfast if they wanted it. All of them got up, and a few minutes later, they walked across the street. Eustolia had prepared beans with tortillas and french fries, not too different from the type of food that Roel and Rudy's mother had been serving them.

Antonio gave directions to Roel and Rudy about how to go to their grandparents' ranch. Then he went ahead and began work on repairing a motorcycle. The nine of them went back across the street and took out of their backpacks what they would need for the day, and then they boarded the vehicle-craft.

Chispo did the driving as Roel gave directions. In a short distance after leaving Antonio's house, they were at the edge of Pinos at the bottom of the mountain. Chispo turned left on the highway, and they proceeded for several kilometers, after which they turned left on a rough dirt road that took them to the village of San Miguel. They had to drive slowly, as no section of the road was smooth.

Though several of Roel and Rudy's uncles, aunts, and relatives lived in San Miguel, the first priority for them was to visit their grandparents who they had not seen for eight years. According to Roel's directions, Chispo drove them through San Miguel, and they proceeded for another two kilometers to the entrance of the ranch.

After turning, Chispo drove them for a kilometer down the narrow dirt lane. The scenery was truly beautiful here in the rural Mexican highlands of Zacatecas. Although the terrain was in one respect generally flat, there were some rolling hills. Further in the distance, they could see some small mountains clearly visible and standing above the terrain. No trees grew on them, but their colors of beige, brown, and red made them appear to stand out.

Like Roel and Rudy had told them, there were beautiful Palma Real trees here and there, along with some of the largest Nopal shrubs they had ever seen. Some of them were indeed the size of small trees. There were also some large Maguey plants, and some of them were in full bloom.

Chispo drove them down through a gully and up the other side, and they pulled up to the adobe ranch estate of Roel and Rudy's grandparents. There were many goats, a few dogs, and chickens that ran loose everywhere. Their grandfather, Arturo, heard them arrive, and he stepped outside. Their grandmother, whose name was Eliza, soon followed, making her appearance from within the u-shaped enclosure of the adobe buildings.

The whole house showed signs of age and was in much need of repair. All of the cement had fallen off the walls, exposing every one of the brown dirt adobe blocks. The roof was basically flat and was also made out of adobe blocks resting on top of numerous horizontal poles made out of Maguey bloom stalks.

Arturo and Eliza were completely taken by surprise, not knowing what to think of the strange vehicle-craft, and they gave them weird, questioning looks.

Roel and Rudy were the first ones to step out of the vehicle. "Abuelitos," Roel called out, saying grandparents.

"Son nuestros nietos," Arturo said to his wife, commenting that they were their grandchildren.

Eliza now recognized them, and she and Arturo walked over to them, glad to see them. They gave each other hugs, and they invited them and their seven friends to come inside. All of them got out of the vehicle-craft and walked inside, following Roel, Rudy, and their grandparents.

They talked about the fact that it had been a long time since they had seen them, and they commented that they were no longer children and were now grown up. Roel and Rudy explained to them about their seven American friends who showed up in Bustamante last week and that they had been serving as their guides in Mexico.

Roel handed his grandparents the letter María had written them. They read it with interest and laughed at some of María's comments about Roel, Rudy, Nora, and Idalia. They talked about life here at the ranch, and Roel and Rudy told them how things were going for them in Bustamante.

After visiting for a while, Arturo and Eliza took them over to a neighboring house so Roel and Rudy could also visit with their aunt Catalina. Arturo and Eliza also had a son, their oldest, who still lived on the ranch. His name was Miguel, and he had a son named Ramiro who was a year older than Roel. All of them were glad to see each other, and they talked about what they had been doing since they had last seen each other.

Soon Arturo, Miguel, and Ramiro had to go to the back of the farm to harvest beans for the rest of the day. They invited them to walk back there later to see their operation. Meanwhile, Eliza and Catalina took everyone to the spring. Roel and

Rudy laughed with their aunt as they reminisced about their childhood days when she used to play hide and seek with them among the Nopal bushes.

While Eliza and Catalina tended to some washing by the spring, Roel and Rudy took Chispo, Robert, Rinto, and the others on a tour through the Nopal bushes, and they went up and down the hillsides of the gully on the narrow, winding dirt lanes. They told them childhood stories of how they used to play with their cousin, Ramiro, and also with more cousins from San Miguel and Pinos. Those were fun days for Roel and Rudy, and they wished they had never left this place. It was great to be back in their homeland again.

They spent a couple of hours walking around and exploring the ranch. Then they walked to the back of the farm and found Arturo, his son, and grandson tending to a crop of beans. They chatted for a while, and then Roel and Rudy took them to another area where they used to run and play. The back of the farm had another gully which was a deep, dry creek bed. It had steep banks and dropoffs in some places.

Rudy showed them his favorite climbing tree, a large Nopal. He and Robert climbed up into the large shrub, being careful not to be stuck by the spines on the thick, succulent leaves. They waved to everyone below them in the gully where they were exploring. Afterwards they climbed back down and caught up with the others who were now on their way back to where Arturo, Miguel, and Ramiro were working.

They were nearly ready to return to the house for lunch. A few minutes later, they dropped what they were doing, and all of them walked the half kilometer back to the house. Arturo and Eliza had a small woods of Nopal trees on the east side of their house, and they walked through those woods on the way back. It felt really strange to be walking underneath those strange plants with their branches overhanging the multiple paths made by the goats that ran through there.

Eliza was in the kitchen preparing lunch. The LP gas tank was empty, so she was cooking over a fire. The kitchen was in the back portion of the u-shaped house, and access to it was through a low door. Actually, each room of the house was accessed through a low door from the outside. The kitchen walls were jet black from years of fireplace smoke and soot. There was no running water, nor was there a sink. Water was obtained from the spring down the lane. Also, there was no electricity. Another feature of the kitchen was that every ledge was occupied with brush, firewood, and twigs. Chickens entered and left as they pleased, and they were sometimes a nuisance the way they would walk in looking for food scraps and then leave in a fluster when Eliza would run them off.

She gathered up enough bowls and served them all lunch. Robert and his friends along with Roel and Rudy took seats on some of the dilapidated chairs in the kitchen. Others remained standing. Two of their dogs came up to the kitchen entrance, hoping to be thrown a few morsels of food.

They finished lunch, and Arturo announced that they were going back to work. They mentioned to Roel and Rudy where their other relatives lived in San Miguel and recommended they go by there before going back to Bustamante. With that,

Arturo, Miguel, and Ramiro said goodbye to them, wished them a safe journey back to Bustamante, and they returned to the back of the farm.

All of them thanked Eliza for the lunch. She wished Roel and Rudy well, told them it was great to see them, and said goodbye to them. Everyone walked to the vehicle-craft and climbed in. Fraxino did the driving. Catalina happened to come down the lane at this moment, and she walked over to them.

"Que les vaya bien," she said to Roel, Rudy and their friends, wishing them well.

With that, Fraxino started the engine, and he drove them back to the San Miguel Road. On the way, Rinto, Fraxino, and Chispo talked over plans and then talked with Roel and Rudy. They decided to spend tonight in Pinos and leave tomorrow to return to Al Nitak so Rinto and Fraxino could get started growing the necessary crystals to bring back to Mexico to use in switching off and eliminating the transmitter devices.

Fifteen minutes later, they were pulling into the village, and Fraxino pulled over on the roadside. All of them got out and walked from house to house with Roel and Rudy, and they soon located some of their relatives. Roel and Rudy's parents both came from large families of seven or eight children each, so they had numerous uncles, aunts, and cousins. For the rest of the afternoon, the seven of them accompanied Roel and Rudy as they visited various houses and chatted with numerous relatives.

In one of the houses, Roel and Rudy visited one of their uncle's families. There were four children in this family. One of the daughters, named Camila, was Roel's age. As they were visiting, Roel started looking at her. The two of them got to talking, and it wasn't long before they were unaware of the rest of the conversations going on between the other relatives. Roel soon found her quite literally attractive, and they connected very well as they visited and got to know each other. Meanwhile, Rudy took over and talked with his uncle and aunt while Roel and Camila continued talking to themselves.

This uncle brought up an offer that there was plenty of summer work to be done and wondered if Roel and/or Rudy would be interested. Rudy explained that he already had a job in Bustamante and that he was taking time away from that to be a guide for his new friends.

"Roel, te habla," Rudy said to Roel, getting his attention and telling him that his uncle was speaking to him.

Roel broke away from his conversation with Camila, and his uncle told him about the summer job offer. He would have declined, but since he had just met his pretty cousin, Camila, he pondered the possibility of taking the offer. He told him he would think it over. They all talked for a while longer. Roel thoroughly enjoyed meeting Camila. Feelings of excitement ran through him.

This was their last stop. They had been visiting numerous relatives in San Miguel all afternoon, and they decided to return to Pinos. On the way back, Roel was somewhat sullen. Robert and Chispo were the first ones to notice that, and they asked him what was the matter. He explained that he already missed his cousin, Camila. He had wanted to visit with her longer.

They arrived back in Pinos. Antonio and Eustolia fed them supper. They had enjoyed a unique and interesting day visiting numerous Mexican families.

During the evening, Antonio walked them up to the plaza. Several of the food stalls were open and were serving tacos, salads, and other foods. Music was being played from speakers at the top of the cathedral, and it could be heard throughout the streets. After having a good look around, they returned to where they were staying across the street from Antonio and went to sleep.

Upon waking up the next morning, Fraxino announced, "All right, dudes. We're cruising back to Zotola!"

"Right on, brother!" Rinto enthusiastically agreed.

It was now Thursday, July 18. They got up and loaded their backpacks into the vehicle-craft, after which they went across the street and ate breakfast with Antonio, Eustolia, and their family. As they were finishing, Antonio wished them well and started work.

"Aquí me quedo," Roel suddenly announced, saying that he was going to stay in Pinos.

"¿Cómo?" Robert asked in surprise, wanting to know what Roel meant by what he just said.

"Es Camila. ¿Verdad?" Chispo said, asking Roel if the real reason was Camila.

"Sí," answering yes.

"Pues, Roel, eres nuestro guía," said Robert, reminding Roel that he was their guide.

"¡No sé nada de eso!" Roel haughtily responded, claiming he didn't know anything about that.

Robert, Andrew, and Chispo who immediately understood him, felt taken aback. Rudy was also surprised at his brother's sudden announcement.

"Roel, tienes una obligación con nosotros," Rudy said to his brother, firmly telling him he had an obligation to be their guide.

"Pues, véte con ellos. A mí no me interesa. No tengo ganas de ir," Roel quickly responded, telling Rudy to go with them, and stating that being their guide no longer interested him, nor did it give him any benefit.

"¿Roel, qué pasó contigo?" Chispo asked Roel, wanting to know why he was acting that way.

"No quiero ir," he answered, flatly stating that he didn't want to go.

"Well, I will say!" Robert told everyone. "Why doesn't Roel want to come with us?"

For the next several minutes, they did their best to talk Roel into coming with them. Rudy also talked with him. No matter what they said, Roel stubbornly refused to go. His cousin Camila was on his mind, in addition to the summer job offer from his uncle.

The seven of them just couldn't believe it. They were beyond shocked. In a way, it was as if Roel was no longer their friend. Rudy then made it clear that he himself was going to continue to be their guide, with or without Roel, and if that was how Roel wanted it, then they would just leave him behind. Eustolia also had her input and explained to Roel that he needed to fulfill his obligation to be their guide alongside Rudy, but nothing she said was convincing enough. Roel was staying, and that was final.

Though he said nothing of it, the true reason he didn't want to continue being their guide was that he was afraid to return to Bustamante, even though the others were going to spend several days on Al Nitak before going back there. For Roel, it was too soon. He would wait at least a month before he would venture back there. He had not forgotten Pegaso's angry stare the other night when he and Beto were arrested.

Further, Roel could not help feeling internal resentment at Chispo because if he had just not made that complimentary statement about Pegaso's sister, Lumita, being pretty, the whole problem with Pegaso would never have occurred. In a way, due to the danger from Pegaso, he felt like he was being indirectly punished for having defended his new friend, Chispo. In some ways, he wished he hadn't. After all, he had known Pegaso much longer than Chispo. No matter what, Roel knew he had done the right thing because Pegaso had been very wrong.

Roel had now found two convenient excuses to stay in Pinos, and he was therefore able to cover up the truth by not even mentioning it. Roel was a very cunning individual, and he knew that continuing with the group by accompanying them to Al Nitak might have caused them to find out his true reasons.

"Pues, saca tus cosas de nuestra maleta, y quédate!" Rudy said to Roel with disgust, telling him to get his things out of their suitcase and just stay! That's exactly what Roel did.

Andrew and Robert talked with Roel and settled up with him about how much money to pay him for having been their guide. They paid him, wished him well, and said goodbye to him.

"Gracias. Que les vaya bien," Roel said to them, telling them thanks and wishing them well.

The rest of them, now eight of them, boarded the vehicle-craft. Antonio had gone up the street on an errand. Eustolia wished them well, and they thanked her for everything. Rinto did the driving, and he drove them away. Eustolia and Roel waved at them.

Deep down, it was sad for Roel to part with his friends, but because of his nature of having to deal with his internal conflicts about this whole problem, he was unable to bring himself to admit or show his sadness. Reacting haughtily and angrily at the last toward them had made it easier for him to tolerate his own emotional pain of having to part with them. He had done it for his own safety. There was no way he was going back to Bustamante any time soon. Though he had served as their guide initially to achieve a status symbol for himself, he now realized and was having to admit to himself that he had developed genuine feelings of friendship for them. Once the vehicle-craft was out of sight, the sadness came to him, and he teared up and cried. Eustolia comforted him, and they walked into the house.

Meanwhile, Rinto drove them down the hill and out of the south side of town. At least they still had Rudy as their guide. They had him to thank for that. He was more straightforward than his brother, Roel. Chispo and Robert had realized this fact early on. Besides, Rudy had a sense of adventure, enjoyed his new friends, and was curious to visit Chispo, Rinto, and Fraxino's homeland of Zotola.

Once they were a few kilometers south of Pinos, Rinto switched off the engine, pulled back the lever, and they left the ground. He caused the craft to swiftly accelerate, pressing them back in their seats, and they gained sufficient altitude.

"Zotola!" Rinto shouted with enthusiasm.

The forcefield accompanied by a faint green glow overtook them, and they felt themselves dematerializing.

CHAPTER 13

RETURN TO ZOTOLA

Before they fully realized what had happened, they were restored to normal and were now flying around 5,000 meters above a desert valley which to Rudy didn't appear very different from Mexico. While the seven of them were used to Rinto and Fraxino's version of teleportation, it was somewhat disorienting to Rudy.

"¿Qué pasó?" he asked, wanting to know what just happened. He looked out the window. "¡Caray! El cielo es mas verde," he said, expressing surprise and commenting that the sky was now more green.

It was only a short time after the crack of dawn in Zotola, and Al Nitak sat low in the horizon of the morning sky. At this time of day, there was more green to the sky than during the middle of the day.

They had made their appearance over the desert valley situated between the Ciruclar and Placatera Mountains south of Zantaayer. Rinto lowered the craft's altitude and brought it in for a landing on the two-lane highway, seeing there was so little traffic at this early hour.

They had used only a quarter tank of hydrogen fuel during their trip to Zacatecas: driving around Pinos, going to and from the ranch, and also that touch down landing on the highway between Concepción del Oro and Zacatecas.

Rinto drove them north along the highway. They crossed the Ciruclar mountain range, and as they made their winding descent through the forested mountain slopes into Zantaayer, Rudy was struck with a sense of familiarity which he couldn't pinpoint.

"He estado aquí. Casi estoy seguro," he told everyone, saying that he had been here before and that he was almost sure of it.

"¿Sí, verdad?" Robert responded, asking him if that was right.

Rudy answered yes and commented that the place was giving him goose bumps and that previously unknown memories were coming to him. Robert told the others what Rudy was experiencing, and Steven suggested it might be from a past life. Rinto and Chispo suggested that Rudy might have a soul link here in Zotola, and that since he was now here, he was experiencing new, previously unknown memories.

Rinto drove them through Zantaayer's central district and turned left. Ten minutes later, they were pulling into the Zapatero's driveway. They stepped out of the vehicle-craft and started unloading their backpacks and supplies.

"We're back home, dudes," Fraxino announced.

"Right on, brother!" Rinto agreed. "Here, let's unload these crystals and take them to our crystal base computer and analyze them."

Glecko heard the commotion and came outside. "Land sakes! You're back home, guys. How was it in Mexico?"

"We had a blast," Chispo answered.

"Yeah, literally," Rinto responded. "No, really, we had a good time."

"Did you find what you were looking for?" Glecko wanted to know.

"We did indeed, Dad," Fraxino answered. "We've located two crystal transmitters, and now we've come home to engineer and grow the appropriate crystals to switch them off and eliminate them."

"Nice going, sons," Glecko praised them.

"Thanks, Dad," said Fraxino. "We're going to get started analyzing the data we've collected, right now."

All of them were now carrying their backpacks into the Zapatero's house.

"Oh, you've brought someone else with you," Glecko commented when he noticed Rudy.

"This is Rudy," Chispo informed him. "He's our new friend from Mexico, and he was our guide the whole week we were there. He also has a brother, but he decided not to come with us."

They greeted each other and shook hands. Glecko soon found out that Rudy didn't speak English nor Artenian, but since Chispo, Andrew, and Robert knew Spanish, there was no problem with the language barrier.

They entered the house and set their backpacks in the front room.

"Sosta's not up yet. She'll be up soon," Glecko informed them. "Come on in and help yourselves to some breakfast."

For the next hour, they chatted with Glecko and told him all about Mexico and their adventures into the mountains above the town of Bustamante, their visit to the ancient paintings, the coincidences they discovered, and the two transmitter crystals they located. Glecko was impressed.

Chispo told the hair-raising story about Pegaso and the culture difference pertaining to saying compliments about the appearance of young women, the firecracker incident, and the arrest.

"Wow! You've really had some adventures," Glecko remarked.

"Man, I'm telling you," Chispo agreed.

"It's a good thing you have crystallized protection on your craft," Glecko told them. "There's no telling *what* they could have done to it."

They carried on talking for a while longer. Sosta came into the kitchen and was surprised to see everyone. They said hi to her, and Glecko filled her in on what the fellows had been doing in Mexico for the past week.

Meanwhile, Rinto and Fraxino took their briefcase of crystals they had used to collect the data and went to their crystal base computer. Everyone else soon came into the room. Rinto was just switching on the equipment, and he placed the Purple Rainbow Fluorite, the green piece of Kanágran, the clear quartz, and also the two pieces of red crystal on a table nearby.

"Okay, let's see what we've got here," said Rinto as he reached for the piece of Kanágran and placed it on the tray to analyze first.

Characters and hieroglyphs started showing up on the screen as the computer's crystal array and Ulexite central crystal started interpreting and translating the data. Upon Rinto's typed commands, the computer translated the text to English for everyone to read.

"Huh! What's this?" Rinto remarked.

"That's wild!" Chispo remarked as he started to read the text.

"It's something about renegades," Andrew commented.

"What are renegades?" Rinto wanted to know.

"People who rebel and go against the grain or norm of society," Andrew replied.

Rinto started to narrate the text. "In the days when the twin dual crystal transmitters were placed in the mountains, there was a ring leader scientist of the Atlantean renegade group who stayed behind on Earth. His name was Cobra Ressmahlo, and he was a trouble maker who had set into motion various living quantum energy systems which caused adverse effects and human conflicts in the society of Atlantis. He was known as the instigator of the renegade group, and through what he enacted, he will be remembered throughout the region in subtle and unrealized ways for many millennia to come."

"What's that supposed to mean?" Robert wanted to know.

"You've got me," Rinto admitted. "What did the computer give us that for? It's totally irrelevant!"

"I know, man," Fraxino agreed, "and what on Earth are living quantum energy systems?"

"And who in the world is Cobra Ressmahlo?" Chris wanted to know.

"I've never heard of him," said Steven.

"Chispo, hand me the index plate from our box of holographic plates," Rinto requested. Chispo walked over to the box, lifted off the lid, took out the appropriate plate, and handed it to him. "Thanks," Rinto said to him. "Maybe this will provide us with an answer." He took the piece of Kanágran off the tray and placed the holographic index plate on the same tray. Information soon showed up on the screen, followed by the English translation, and they looked through the selection. "Do any of you see anything relevant to what we just read?" he asked everyone. A few seconds passed by.

"Oh, wow! There it is, dude!" Fraxino exclaimed with enthusiasm. "Plate number 80 . . . *Living Quantum Energy Systems and Reality.*"

"Sure enough!" Rinto admitted with surprise. "Chispo, reach for plate number 80. I wonder why we didn't notice that one before?"

"Rinto, if I remember correctly," Chispo reminded him as he handed him the plate, "you were anxious to get away from here last week."

"Yeah, that's right," Rinto recalled, and he placed plate number 80 on the tray alongside the index plate. At first, hieroglyphs popped up on the screen, followed by the English translated version. He began to narrate.

"Research in science has led certain Atlantean top scientists to discover a most interesting life force, that of quantum energy systems. Once these reality dynamics are set in motion, these living energy patterns can endure for many thousands of years and control the destiny of events in undetected and unrealized ways. They are, quite literally, self-feeding energy systems with their own life force.

"Many Atlanteans have discovered that quantum reality machines or in other words, quantum energy systems are the root cause of many synchronicities in life, even though the energy systems may have been set into motion many thousands of years ago or even longer.

"They can be used in good and bad ways, and they can be placed as a non-physical enveloping shroud around any individual, usually without ever being detected. Depending on how they are installed, they can bring individuals good fortune, friendships, and protection, or they can bring bad luck, including mysterious loss of friendships.

"According to negotiations and agreements made by Atlantean society members, a number of these quantum energy systems will be created and set in motion shortly before the fleeing of some 65,000 residents to the star Al Nitak. They are to be created with good and positive intentions with programmed messages that will be intended for certain future individuals to discover at the appropriate times thousands of years from now.

"For future Earth societies and civilizations, the primary key to discovering the aspects of the Atlantean society will be through the realization by certain individuals of synchronicities that will bring certain people together to discover and unravel the subtle information that will be left behind. Living quantum energy systems intertwined with reality is a unique and subtle way of communication over great spans of time, and when its patterns are realized and understood, the phenomenal wealth of information they carry will be released."

"So, *that's* how synchronicities can work," Andrew commented. "Pretty interesting."

"Well, I will say!" Robert remarked. "I guess there was some relevance after all."

"That must be what happened to us," said Rinto.

"I know," Chris agreed. "We've definitely discovered and unraveled subtle information left behind, namely those ancient paintings."

"I was going to say the same thing," Robert responded.

"Yes, but what does this have to do with that dude named Cobra Ressmahlo?" Fraxino wanted to know.

"Well, we earlier read that he will be subconsciously remembered for many millennia to come," Andrew pointed out, "and in the region, likely where the dual crystal transmitters are located. Cobra Ressmahlo . . . Hmm . . . That sounds like the Spanish words, *Cobrar es malo*, which in English means, *To charge is bad*."

"Wait a minute. I believe I've got it," Chispo suddenly announced. "Whenever someone in Mexico charges someone else money, and if the person being charged happens to be vibrationally attuned subconsciously to the quantum energy system the dude enacted, he or she will subconsciously think of his name since he or she will automatically think of the Spanish word for charge, which is *cobrar*. Since Cobra Ressmahlo was a trouble making renegade, then through the time line, he would be remembered in a bad way, causing people to suddenly get angry when they are charged money."

"Chispo, where did you get that from?" Rinto wanted to know. "That wasn't written on the screen."

"I don't know, man," he admitted. "It just popped in my head."

"It is actually true that many people in Mexico get inordinately angry over being charged money," Andrew informed them. "¿Verdad que cobrar es un lío?" Andrew now said to Rudy, asking him if it was indeed true that charging someone money usually caused complications.

Rudy verified that was true and told everyone there was an old saying in Mexico that says, *If you want to lose a friend, charge him money.* He went on to inform them that many people in Bustamante have lost friendships over charging each other money, even though the amount of money may have been very small. For some people, charging them money sets off a trigger, releasing an angry response. He admitted that even his own brother, Roel, gets angry and unreasonable at being charged money.

"That is weird," Robert remarked. Suddenly, the *No fío porque cobrar es un lío* sign he had seen in the back of the Cantu's store came to mind, and he now realized why it was there.

"And the root source of the problem could have come from that guy's name," Steven speculated.

"Because he deviously set into motion a quantum energy system so he would be remembered in a subtle way," Rinto added.

"Well, I mean in our country, we charge each other money all the time, and we don't have weird problems like that," Steven pointed out.

"That's because most of us don't speak Spanish," said Andrew, "and as it turns out, the Spanish words, *Cobrar es malo*, match that guy's name."

"Dudes, it could be this irrelevant information popped up to tell us one of the reasons for such conflict in northern Mexico, especially in Bustamante," Chispo told them. "I mean this thing about Cobra Ressmahlo may be just one of many such quantum energy systems that were set in motion by devious individuals from the days of Atlantis."

"And the dual transmitter crystals are likely feeding those energies," Chris added.

"That's likely true," said Rinto. "Once we switch off and eliminate the crystal transmitters, the conflicts and anger may disappear."

"I hope so," said Robert.

"Well, at least the Atlanteans set a bunch of positive energy systems into motion before they came here," said Rinto, "according to what the text from this plate says."

"Something just came to mind," Robert brought up.

"What?" Chispo asked.

"Ever since I learned that Spanish word *cobrar*, I've always wondered why it was so similar to the word *cobra*, which is a type of poisonous snake. Way in the back of my mind the word *cobrar* has always had negative connotations."

"And that's because a cobra snake is generally considered to be bad, right?" Steven asked.

"That's right," Robert answered.

"Now we know the word *cobrar* may have come from that dude's name from the days of Atlantis," said Chispo.

"Sometimes, the origin of words goes back much further than we realize," Andrew mentioned.

"Who knows. The cobra snake may have indirectly gotten its title from the same ancient source," Chris speculated.

"Hey, look at that one," said Robert. "Plate number 97 . . . *Mysterious Rejections: Dreams vs. Reality*."

"Yeah, that looks interesting," Rinto commented.

"Robert, did you say number 97?" Chispo checked.

"Right," Robert answered.

Chispo reached into the box, found the appropriate plate, and handed it to Rinto who put it on the tray. In less than a minute, they were viewing its contents, and Rinto began to narrate the text.

"Mysterious rejections have long been a most curious and annoying aspect of Atlantean human society. Top psychoanalysts in their field have arrived at the most up-to-date theory so far presented for explaining the reasons of mysterious rejections.

"It is a known and chilling fact that certain people will one day reject one or more selected good friends for no apparent reason, even though the friendship may have been a very good one and a long one, in addition to the rejectees having always been kind and considerate.

"It has been determined that the certain individuals who perform the mysterious rejecting are acting according to what they believe to be reality, though in truth the reality is better than they believe. Some of them may likely have had disturbing dreams about the ones they reject. As a result, the rejecters become seemingly emotionally unstable and become laden with internal conflicts.

"Further, for a number of them, even though they never realize it, they have parallel world counterparts living in alternate realities. They may be entirely congenial in this world's reality of life, but in their alternate reality associations with each other, they could be in conflict and may have possibly fought with one another. These non-peaceful patterns have been known to filter into this reality for some of those certain individuals, causing them to mysteriously reject selected, truly good friends."

"I hear you, man," Chispo said to Rinto. "Pegaso is a prime example."

"Yes, we even know who his parallel world counterpart is," Andrew added.

"Orolizo of the Atascosa," said Robert.

"Didn't Roel and Rudy tell us that the retired American school teacher had rejected her former student friend who had helped her out?" Chispo asked Andrew and Robert.

"That's right," Andrew replied.

"Then this does make sense and somewhat explains why she so suddenly rejected him," said Chispo.

"That's true," Andrew agreed, "but she was also affected because she resonated very strongly to the vibrations of that transmitter device in the mountains."

"Wait, here's more," Rinto announced. He continued narrating.

"Sometimes the machine of time allows good friends to maintain their friendship for a limited time, according to destiny. Without warning, a friendship can come to an end very abruptly, always shocking the person being rejected.

"Some of the Atlantean society members are now blaming the above said unfortunate circumstances on the devious reality controlling experiments conducted by past top scientists over the past 2,500 years and by present-day ones as well. Upon the fleeing of most of the Atlantean society to Al Nitak, they will then be freed of all quantum reality programs that are presently running on planet Earth, many of which will likely continue to run their course for numerous thousands of years into the future. Since they were designed to carry the frequencies of vibration equal to the vibrations people carry when they are angry or under duress, their resonance will be amplified and will cause many adverse effects and future human problems of conflict."

"So *that's* why they wanted to be left in peace when they came here," Andrew realized.

"Now we finally have a decent explanation as to why they went to such trouble to put the block in place," said Robert.

"So, the devious scientists installed quantum reality programs that would cause adverse effects," Steven commented.

"Why would they even want to do such things?" Robert asked everyone.

"Well, they were devious," Rinto pointed out.

"Man, they were misguided," Chispo declared. "They were probably performing mood control experiments."

"Must have been," said Robert.

"If I were moving to a new world," said Andrew, "I'd want to block them, too."

"Yeah, really," Chris agreed. "Who wants adverse effects and human conflicts? I don't."

"Right, that takes care of this holographic plate," Rinto announced. "Let's see what these crystals now tell us. He took the plate off and placed the two red crystals on the tray.

Hieroglyphic text, coordinates, and diagrams soon popped up on the screen, followed by English text.

"Wow, man! This one has literature with it too," Fraxino remarked.

Rinto looked at the text. "It looks like we latched some data pertaining to the history of the transmitter crystals. The makers must have installed a historical data capsule within the two crystals."

"Really? Read it to us," Chispo requested.

Rinto began to narrate. "Ever since the mysterious disappearance of the green Fluorite peace keeping crystal from Atlantis over 2,500 years ago, there have been numerous problems caused by experiments conducted by top research scientists of our society. They have performed mood control experiments and have set into motion numerous quantum energy systems programmed to cause adverse effects many thousands of years into the future."

"Sounds like what we just talked about," Chispo mentioned.

"I know. Let me continue," said Rinto. "Many of these scientists were multi-faceted and were communicating on higher levels via telepathy and astral travel, and it was via these levels of reality that they were conducting their devious experiments. One of the experiments indirectly caused the devastating crustal displacement, ruining the Atlantean homeland by sliding it to the south pole. Something had to be done.

"Some of the top scientists were of decent mind and character, and they set out to design a way to block the devious scientists. Since the Atlantean society knew they would soon have to flee their homeland and go to the star Al Nitak, their good scientists grew a total of twelve dodecahedron transmitter crystals designed to emanate positive vibrations throughout planet Earth. They would endure for a period of 500 years, blocking telepathic communication and spiritual and astral travel to the star Al Nitak and its two neighboring stars for those who stayed behind. At the end of the 500-year period, they would switch themselves off.

"They were successful in growing the crystals, and they designed them in such a way that if any of the top scientists were to tamper with any one of them, it would automatically trigger itself to endure indefinitely, much longer than the agreed 500 years. Further, it would absorb the negative vibrations of the quantum reality programs existing and amplify them by feeding energy into them.

"This was an ingenious design which would successfully deter would-be devious scientists who stayed behind from tampering with any of the twelve transmitter crystals. At the same time, the transmitters would not feed energy into the quantum reality programs, so long as the top scientists would keep their hands off the twelve transmitter crystals. These dodecahedrons were strategically placed around the world, most of them hidden in mountains. The two main crystals were placed at the new latitude of 26.5° in the southern section of . . . North America.

"The 400 top scientists had the option of staying on Earth or going to Al Nitak with the rest of them, but on Al Nitak they would be constrained and would not have free reign to conduct their experiments. Therefore the Atlantean society pointed out the benefits of staying behind on Earth. They would have free reign to continue their lives as they would please, and they would be able to teach other primitive civilizations throughout the world, offering them technology and knowledge. They would be worshipped. As the thought of being worshipped appealed to them, they accepted the offer as a challenge and stayed behind on Earth.

"The Atlanteans did not want the devious scientists to go with them to their new world because they desired to be left in peace, wanting nothing to do with the quantum energy systems and programs that had been created and set in motion on Earth over the past 2,500 years. What they desired was peace, tranquility, and true friendships, and they knew they would have that by leaving all devious scientists behind on Earth.

"While the ones who stayed behind on Earth knew better than to tamper with the cleverly designed transmitter crystals, their descendants did not. 200 years after the Atlanteans fled to Al Nitak, a civilization living several hundred kilometers south of the two main transmitter crystals set out on an expedition to find the legendary crystals and switch them off in hopes that they could then travel to their ancestors' new home planet around the star Al Nitak.

"Much of the information and technology had been lost through the generations, and much of the past had fallen into oral legend. Once the expedition leaders found one of the two crystals and tampered with it, they quickly realized they had made a major mistake. The device immediately triggered itself to endure for an unregulated and indefinite period of time, in addition to now feeding energy into the existing quantum reality programs, causing them to be amplified. In desperation, they located the other crystal the next range over, hoping they could switch it off, but they met with failure.

"The Atlantean society had discussed the possiblity of installing these blocking transmitter devices on their new world around Al Nitak, but that would mean they would be blocked from the entire galaxy. Their desire was to block Earth, the Sol System, and its nearby neighboring stars from communicating with Al Nitak and the Orion Belt. The safest option was to install them on Earth, knowing that if the ones who stayed behind were to tamper with them, they would only be making things worse for themselves and would be strengthening the blocking force to last longer."

"Hmm . . . What an interesting story!" said Andrew.

"Wow, man!" Chispo remarked. "Those two red crystals recorded quite a wealth of data."

"They did, indeed," Rinto agreed.

"And all of that came out of those two red crystals?" Steven asked Rinto.

"That's right," he answered.

"So, the two transmitter crystals got tampered with by their descendants some 200 years later," Robert commented.

"Now we know why they're having such adverse effects," said Chispo. "The crystals are feeding energy into and amplifying the quantum energy systems and reality programs that were set up by devious Atlantean scientists."

"It's just amazing how long those programs can endure," Steven declared.

"I know," Robert agreed. "I had never even considered that such a thing was possible."

"So, afterwards," Fraxino speculated, "the expedition group must have gone to the double mesa and drawn those depictions to record their thoughts for future generations to interpret."

"That's likely so," said Andrew.

"Well, if that's all from these two crystals," Rinto announced, "let's see what the other crystals have to tell us." He replaced the red crystals with the piece of Purple Rainbow Fluorite. Information soon popped up on the screen.

"Hmm . . . looks like it's telling us the general vibrational nature for the region," said Andrew as he looked on at the text.

"Yep, it says there is indeed a lot of tension and unsettled thoughts circulating through the atmosphere," said Rinto. "Anger and grudges are prevalent throughout the local region, and this Purple Rainbow Fluorite is verifying that the dual crystal transmitters are feeding energy into the appropriate quantum reality programs to keep the negativity alive."

"That's what we've been suspecting," said Robert.

Rinto swapped the Purple Rainbow Fluorite for the clear quartz crystal. "Fraxino! Write this data down on paper!" he suddenly told his brother with enthusiasm as he reacted to the sudden coordinate data that popped up on the screen. "Chispo, bring me that piece of orange Calcite from our craft. I'm going to scan the appropriate data into it so I can take it to the cave and use it to grow the intelligence into the crystals."

"Wait up a minute. I'll be right back," Chispo responded. He walked to the craft.

Meanwhile, Fraxino began writing pertinent data on several pages of paper. "Wow, dudes!" he remarked. "This is some *radical* coordinate data!" He continued jotting it down while the others looked on.

Chispo returned with the piece of Calcite in his hand. Rinto began scanning with it.

"So, how will this data help you?" Robert wanted to know.

"This data will assist the crystals we're going to grow," Fraxino replied, "with the task of how to properly direct the shutdown and elimination forces, once we strategically place them in the mountains when we return to Mexico."

"How many of them are you going to grow?" Chris asked.

"We're not sure yet," Rinto replied. "Probably four or five, whatever this data appropriately directs us to do."

"What we're going to do when we return to Mexico is place certain ones at a safe distance," Fraxino informed them, "and place some sort of catalyst crystal right by each of the two dodecahedrons and then leave. We'll probably keep another crystal with us and telepathically send a trigger message to begin the process of shutdown."

"We're not sure yet how it may turn out," Rinto added.

Andrew, Robert, and Chispo had been translating to Rudy what was said throughout. He had never seen anything of the like, and much of what Rinto and Fraxino's crystal base computer was doing seemed like magic to him. Oddly enough, Rudy still had a deep down feeling that he had been here in Zotola before. In a different way, the computer setup and what they did with crystals did not seem entirely foreign to him.

After Fraxino had finished writing the data on paper, Rinto placed the piece of Kanágran on the tray again. "There. That's more like it," he said. "This has more precise and fine-tuned data for our close range requirements. Fraxino, start writing." Meanwhile, Rinto scanned the new data with the same piece of Calcite.

"Guys, no offense, but my brother and I now need to be alone to solve this complicated problem," Rinto told the six others.

"That's right, dudes," Fraxino now told them. "We're going to have to, as you call it on your world, brainstorm. It's probably going to take us three or four days, initially to figure this out and then grow the appropriate crystals, programming the necessary intelligence into them pertinent to the task we aim to have them accomplish in Mexico."

"Chispo, can you keep our Earthly friends company?" Rinto requested. "Maybe you can take them on a tour somewhere. I'd say you could use our craft, but Fraxino and I are going to need it to go back and forth to the mountains."

"You mean you're not going to include us in this?" Chispo jokingly asked. He realized and understood the seriousness of Rinto's request, but he couldn't resist making light of it.

In all seriousness, Rinto replied, "No offense, Chispo, but Fraxino and I will have to use total meditative concentration for the crystal programming procedure. We would have you all come with us, but we can't have any extra interference."

"Oh, I know, man," said Chispo reassuringly. "I was only joking. Sure, man, I'll take them cruising in my Velva Dibe. We'll let you two do the work for a while."

"Thanks, Chispo," said Rinto. At the moment, he was in no position to joke around and be humorous with Chispo. The serious task at hand was beginning to overwhelm Rinto and Fraxino, and they felt the tension and pressure of what they would need to do.

"If you like," Chispo offered, "our friends can stay with me at my place for the next few days."

"No, that's okay, Chispo," Rinto reassured him. "They're welcome to stay here. We're going to be up in the mountains most of the time, anyway. Besides, your parents are usually not at home."

"Yeah, that's true," Chispo admitted.

Rinto was already directing his concentration at the data on the screen.

Chispo thought for a moment. "You know, I just thought of something. I can drive them up north to Caloma and visit some of my relatives in the Vovvitlet Valley. I haven't been there since I was a child."

"That's a good idea," said Rinto. "They'll enjoy that."

"All right, man. See you around dudes," Chispo told Rinto and Fraxino.

With that he left the room accompanied by Rudy, Andrew, Chris, Robert, and Steven. While Rinto and Fraxino spent the next several days concentrating on the tedious task of growing the crystals, the others became Chispo's companions.

"Where is Caloma?" Robert wanted to know.

"That's a region north of Zotola," Chispo answered. "Like Zotola is a region, so is Caloma. The Vovvitlet Valley is in its east-central portion, and it's nestled within the Urlachia Mountains. Actually, it's not too different from your Switzerland on your world."

"Really? That sounds good," Robert responded.

"Let's go," Steven eagerly stated.

"Dudes, it's 1,500 kilometers north of here," Chispo informed them. "If we leave right now, we'll get there by midnight tonight."

"Is it cold up there?" Chris asked.

"Not at this time of year," Chispo answered.

They were now in the room where they had placed their backpacks, and they picked them up.

"See you around, Mr. Zapatero," Chispo called into the back of the house.

"See you later. Take care," they heard Glecko call back.

"Let's go on over to my house and get ready," Chispo announced. They walked with him to his house, crossing under the tall row of bushes separating their backyards.

As they were approaching the house, Rudy said, "¿Este es tu carro, Chispo?" asking Chispo if the car he saw parked by the house was his.

"Sí," answering yes.

"Se ve un buen carro. Que elegante. ¿Vuela también?" said Rudy, complimenting Chispo's car and saying how elegant it appeared, and he asked him if it could also fly.

Chispo explained that Rinto and Fraxino's Velosa cruiser craft was very unique and that his Velva Dibe was more normal, in that it didn't fly. He showed Rudy and the others his car and at the same time, gave the engine fluid levels, the tires, and the entire car a checking over.

"All right, dudes. We're ready to go," Chispo announced with enthusiasm as he closed the hood. "Just throw your backpacks in the trunk. I'll go inside and leave a note for Mom and Dad, saying where I'm going, and then we're cruising." While they loaded their backpacks into the car, Chispo went inside the house. The 2-door car was fairly large, and it sat all six of them with no problem. There were seatbelts for all of them, and they fastened them.

Five minutes later, Chispo was backing them out of the driveway. Once on the road, he took off and accelerated rather swiftly, laying them back in their seats. He enjoyed his Velva Dibe with its powerful and quick Richmond V-8 engine, and he was showing off to them. He quickly went through the gears and had it in fourth gear almost before they realized it.

"Golly, Chispo!" Robert exclaimed. "This car's quick!"

"That's right, man," he verified. "It's like I told you, this car will flat get up and go!"

"Nunca he visto un carro con tanta fuerza," Rudy told Chispo, commenting that he had never seen a car with such power.

"Sí, verdad," Chispo agreed, telling Rudy that was right.

"And you said the police force's Skiivona Zetna is quicker than this?" Steven asked.

"Dude, those cars are like greased lightning!" Chispo replied and laughed.

He drove them to a nearby Exxoll station, and one of the attendants filled the car's tank with hydrogen. With that done and paid for, Chispo drove them out the northeast side of Zantaayer.

For the first 100 kilometers, the two-lane highway followed alongside the coast. Along the way, they made a stop so they could see the beach and take a quick swim. It was Rudy's first time to ever see an ocean at all. He had never been to the Gulf of Mexico nor the Pacific Ocean in Mexico. They enjoyed the swim, rode the waves, and then returned to Chispo's car.

The highway soon turned inland, and for the next fourteen hours, Chispo drove them most of the way to the Vovvitlet Valley in Caloma. He was able to average 100 km/h. Along the way, Chispo played several pop songs and albums, including *The Hydragyros*, in his on-board holodisk player.

Most of the two-lane highways were straight and narrow, but there was one range of mountains they had to cross halfway there, and the curves of the road required slower driving. It was at the crest of these mountains that they left Zotola, entering Caloma.

Now that they were further north, most of the terrain was greener, not so desert-like as it was in Zotola. Some of the land was forested with a mixture of various hardwoods and conifers, and others areas were farmland.

Later in the afternoon, Chispo grew tired, and he let Robert drive for several hours.

Then Rudy said, "¿Me dejas manejar también?" asking Chispo if he would let him drive also.

"¿Sabes como manejar bien?" said Chispo, asking Rudy if he knew pretty well how to drive.

"Sí," he answered, and he explained that he had driven other friends' cars around Bustamante a few times over the past year.

Chispo consented. After Robert had driven for a few hours, he pulled over, and Rudy got in the driver's seat. Rudy proved his truthfulness as he pulled away from a stop, going through the gears as if it was second nature to him. He soon attained a cruising speed of 100 km/h on the straight two-lane highway, and he drove for an hour. The smile on his face showed that he was content. He enjoyed having the chance to drive.

Chispo and Robert had become close friends with Rudy. They had an inner understanding for one another which could best be described as a sense that made them feel like they had known each other since time began. For some reason, Chispo and Robert felt the close friendship more so than the others. For Robert, knowing Spanish made it easier. For Chispo, he would always be grateful to Rudy for his having instantly telepathically given him the Spanish language the first day they had met.

As darkness arrived, they could begin to see some mountains in the distance. Chispo informed them that they were the Urlachia Mountains surrounding the Vovvitlet Valley. They still had two more hours on the road to get there. Rudy pulled over, and Chispo drove the rest of the way.

An hour later, they reached the base of the mountains, and the highway ascended through the forest with many switchbacks and hairpin curves. Chispo whizzed up the mountain seemingly with the greatest of ease, and half an hour later, they reached the crest where he pulled over.

"Take a look straight ahead, dudes," Chispo announced and indicated. The lights of a city were visible way below them in a valley. "That's the city of Zwever situated in the Vovvitlet Valley, and the Vovvitlet River runs through it, flowing towards the northwest."

"It looks like a pretty area," said Andrew.

"It's way on down there," Robert remarked.

"That's right," Chispo agreed. "By the way, there's a trail that runs the ridge of these mountains called the Wyndham Way."

"Really?" Steven responded. "Let's go walking on it before we return to Zantaayer."

"All right, man." Chispo now proceeded again, and the narrow two-lane highway steeply descended into the valley. The whole time, the city lights below them could be seen through the Firs and Spruces. Chispo used lower gears, and half an hour later, they reached the valley, soon entering the city of Zwever.

"Dudes, it's been so long since I've been here," Chispo informed them. "Back when my parents used to be home more often, they brought me here several times when I was a child. I even spent one summer here. Dad's from here, in case you didn't know it. He grew up right over there," and Chispo indicated by pointing to a distant hillside on the southern side of the city.

"Why haven't you been back more recently?" Andrew wanted to know.

"It sort of got away from us," Chispo answered. "Once Dad's parents passed on, Zwever became low on his priority list, and with my parents having become busier with their careers, we just never came back. I remember the last time we came here. Grandma Colancha had just passed away, and we drove up here for her service on a cold, snowy, winter's weekend, just a few days after the day of Cresma. Like I said, I was just a child then.

"After the service," Chispo continued, "my father's family all gathered over at Aunt Esalina's house. While they visited and celebrated their mother's life, I went out and played with my cousins. We had a blast, playing in the snow and sledding down the hillsides behind her house. My aunt lives on the southern edge of the city, and that's where we're going."

By now, Chispo was driving them down the main boulevard approaching the city's central district. He turned right and took a street that took them to the southern district of Zwever, and the street climbed uphill for the last kilometer, arriving at the edge of the city. His aunt Esalina lived at the base of the Urlachia mountain range, and her house had an excellent view overlooking the Vovvitlet Valley with the city of Zwever to the north.

"I called her up from my house right before we left this morning," Chispo told everyone. "So, she's expecting us." He reached her driveway and drove up its steep grade, arriving at the back of her house. It was nearly midnight.

Everyone stepped out of the car, and Chispo went to knock on the door. His cousin answered.

"Cliss?" Chispo asked him, not sure if he was looking at his cousin.

"Chispo, is that you?" he asked him in Artenian.

"It is, man," Chispo answered in Artenian.

"How are you doing, man? What a surprise!" Cliss told him in Artenian.

"I'm doing great. Man, you won't believe what all I've . . ." Chispo's friends were now walking up to the door from the car.

"Oh, right. You've got some friends with you," Cliss interrupted and said to him.

"Right, these are my friends," Chispo informed him. He introduced them and told Cliss they were his companions from planet Earth and that they had decided to make a road trip to the Vovvitlet Valley for several days.

"Is that right?" Cliss responded with surprise. "Far out! Come in. Come on in. Tell your friends to come inside also."

"He says you can come on in. Dice que pases," Chispo told everyone, including Rudy.

"Man, you act like you didn't know I was coming," Chispo now said to his cousin.

"I didn't."

"You mean your mom didn't tell you?" Chispo asked with surprise. "I called her this morning."

"No, not a word," Cliss answered. "I just got in a little while ago, and Mom's not here at the moment." Suddenly he noticed a piece of paper stuck on a counter. "Oh, wait. Here's something." He picked up the piece of paper and read a note from Esalina. "Right, she says she had to go on an errand to the store and says you all would be getting in around midnight . . . right now. Well, good! Make yourselves at home. Mom will be home soon."

They now took seats in the front room.

"Man, I'll never forget that time I last came up here," said Chispo. "We had a blast, playing and sledding in the snow."

"Yes, that was a lot of fun," Cliss agreed. "It was right after the day of Cresma . . . Grandmother's service, wasn't it?"

"That's right."

"And to think we were only children in those days," Cliss remarked. "That was twelve years ago. I'll never forget it."

"Me neither, man."

"It's really great to see you, after all this time," Cliss told Chispo. "You barely caught me. Tomorrow, I'm setting out for eastern Caloma. I'm starting a job there with a research group. My car's already loaded, and I'm driving out in the morning."

"Really? Well, best of luck. I'm glad I got to see you before you leave. By the way, you won't believe some of the research my friends and I have been into. I've got two guru neighbor friends who took a Velosa cruiser craft and grew an array of crystals and programmed them with intelligence. Man, I'm telling you, those two geniuses made that vehicle fly! They've been going to and from Earth, doing research on our ancestral homeland, Atlantis. They took me there last year, and I was an exchange student in a region they call Tennessee."

"You've actually *been* to planet Earth?" Cliss asked, wide-eyed in amazement.

"Oh yeah, man," Chispo confirmed. "It's a wild place down there. Like I said, my friends here are from there. The two guru friends I was telling you about . . . By the way, their names are Rinto and Fraxino. They brought home some Earthlings several weeks ago. I'm telling you, we've had a blast! We went to an ancient galactic dump site and found a crateload of holographic plates. We took them back to their house and analyzed . . ." and Chispo related the whole story over a period of fifteen minutes, telling about the Atascosa, the soul link, the trip to Mexico, the ancient paintings, and the crystal transmitter device. ". . . and we picked up a new friend in Mexico, Rudy, who's here with us. Right now, my guru friends are deep in a project, growing intelligence into some crystals for use in switching off that device in Mexico. We're going back in a few days."

"Wow, Chispo!" Cliss remarked. "You've really had some action packed adventures!"

Chispo's aunt, Esalina, pulled up outside in her car.

"Mom's home," Cliss announced.

A minute later, the door opened, and she stepped inside. She was carrying two sacks of groceries. "Well, hello there! How are you?" she said to Chispo and his friends in Artenian.

"I'm fine, Aunt Esalina. How are you?" Chispo responded in Artenian.

"I'm doing just fine. How great that you've come!" she told him in Artenian. "By the way, son, there are some more sacks of groceries out in the car," she now said to Cliss. He left the house to fetch them.

"It's been a while, hasn't it?" Chispo told her, and they gave each other hugs.

"I know it has," she agreed. "You're all grown up, and you're every bit as handsome as your grandfather Colancha was. Anyway, who are your friends here?"

Chispo introduced them, and they shook hands.

"You barely caught Cliss," she told Chispo. "He leaves tomorrow for eastern Caloma to begin a job with a research group."

"Yes, he was saying," Chispo responded.

"Anyway, make yourselves at home," she offered. "There is plenty of space upstairs for everyone. I'll take you up there in a while. Have you had something to eat?"

"Well, not since this afternoon," Chispo admitted.

"Come on in the kitchen. I'll fix you and your friends something." They followed her in there. Cliss came into the kitchen with more sacks. "On the floor will be fine. Thanks, son."

Chispo visited with his aunt and cousin for some time while they ate a midnight snack. Then everyone got his backpack out of Chispo's car and carried it upstairs. Esalina showed them where they would be sleeping. By now, it was an hour after midnight. Cliss said goodbye to everyone, as he would be leaving first thing in the morning.

It had been a very long day for all of them, coming all the way from Pinos, Zacatecas this morning, spending time at the Zapateros in Zantaayer, and then driving fourteen hours to the Vovvitlet Valley. They slept soundly, needless to say.

Morning arrived mostly sunny. Since they had arrived late last night, they had not been able to see the beauty of Zwever's surrounding mountains. Beautiful they were indeed! Robert and his friends agreed that the place did have some resemblance to Switzerland back on Earth. The mountains towered above the valley on three sides while the northwest side of the Vovvitlet Valley gently descended into the distance. Snow and clouds covered the peaks in places, and it was from these mountains that the Vovvitlet River originated, fed by the high mountain glaciers of their upper slopes.

"Golly! This place is beautiful!" Steven remarked.

"¡Caray! Que bonito," Rudy remarked, saying how pretty the mountain scenery was.

By the time they had waked up, it was mid morning. Esalina called them to come downstairs and have some breakfast. They soon came down and visited with her while they ate. Cliss had already gone earlier this morning. She suggested they have a look around the city and to also take a tour of the mountains. She would have taken them herself, but she had to go to work at the middle of the day and would return by early evening.

That sounded fine with everyone. After breakfast, they piled into Chispo's car, and he took them to Zwever's central district. Since Chispo had spent one summer here as a child, he knew his way around Zwever pretty well.

The climate was indeed cooler here than down south in Zotola. The cool mountain air blew in from the surrounding snow-covered peaks. As they toured different stores, flea markets, and parks, the weather became more cloudy, becoming totally overcast by afternoon. Only the lower slopes of the mountains were now visible.

Rudy, more than anyone, took delight in purchasing some unique souvenirs, including a shirt, a hat, and some native relics. He could now show off to Roel and to his friends. Since Rudy only had Mexican money, he swapped out with Chispo who supplied him with Zotolan zúbolas, which they did honor here in Caloma. Chispo also treated the five of them to lunch.

The day went by before they realized it. They returned to the car where Chispo had parked on the street side, and he started to drive them back to Esalina's house.

"Oh, cool! It's already out and showing," said Chispo as he noticed and passed by a sign posted on the side of the boulevard.

"What's showing?" Robert asked him.

"*The Chill of the Vovvitlet.* It's a movie that's just been released."

"Really?" Robert responded. "That sounds interesting."

"Wanna go see it?" Chispo offered everyone.

"Sure, why not?" Andrew approved.

"I didn't know you had movies here," said Chris.

"Oh yeah, man. We've got movies, just like you guys do." Chispo turned and drove around the block in the process of turning around, and he drove them back to the movie theater.

"How did that get by us?" Steven wanted to know. "We didn't know your world had movies."

"You probably didn't notice the signs, since they're written in Artenian script," Chispo answered.

"Yeah, that would make sense," Steven admitted. "We wouldn't have known what we were looking at."

Chispo pulled into the parking lot and parked, and the six of them walked inside. He paid the way for all of them, and they entered.

For the next three hours they saw the chilling ghostly legends of the upper Vovvitlet River. The movie was based on a true story of an expedition team who went to climb the highest peak of the Urlachia Mountains, Horcones Peak, and they were confronted with ghostly apparitions. There were chilling accounts of talking to spirits of people and also of other worldly beings. Since the expedition team consisted entirely of straightforward non-believers, they were scared by what they experienced. The mountain scenery was beautiful, and there were several scenes of the upper mountain streams that were tributaries to the Vovvitlet River. Although Chispo was the only one who understood the dialogue throughout, the action and scenery made up for it. Nevertheless, he quietly translated to the others from time to time and kept them filled in.

When they exited the movie, it was beginning to get dark. They returned to Chispo's car, and he drove them back to Esalina's house.

"That movie was pretty good," Chris commented.

"Yes, it had a lot of good scenery," said Andrew.

"And it had almost no violence," Steven added.

"It just sent chills down our spines, right?" Chispo commented to them.

"It did that all right," Chris agreed.

"I finally got to see a movie with no preceeding commercials," Robert proudly stated.

"That's right, man," Chispo agreed. "Here, we don't fool around. We get right to the movie with no delaying commercials ahead of it."

In fifteen minutes, they were pulling into the driveway of Esalina's house. She was outside taking down some laundry that had been drying on the line. She greeted them as they were stepping out of the car and asked them how their day went.

"We had a nice time in the central district," Chispo said to her in Artenian. "We went to the market, saw the parks, and we saw a movie on the way home."

"What movie did you see?" she asked.

"*The Chill of the Vovvitlet*," Chispo answered.

"Excellent," she commented. "That is an intriguing movie, isn't it?"

"Yes, it is."

"So, what are your plans tomorrow?" she wanted to know.

"I think I'll take them up into the mountains," Chispo answered.

"That will be nice. They'll enjoy that," she said. "I must warn you to beware of any chilling spirits."

Chispo laughed. "Don't worry. We'll be fine."

They entered the house. While they waited in the adjoining front room, she went into the kitchen and fixed some supper for them.

"You know," Andrew brought up, "I just realized I haven't seen a television anywhere on this world."

"We haven't got any, man," Chispo informed him.

"You all don't have televisions?" Andrew asked with surprise.

"They never caught on, nor did radios," Chispo answered.

"How do you function in a modern society without them?" Steven wanted to know.

"We do fine," Chispo explained. "We have newspapers and, of course, phone service."

"Yes, but still, what if you all had a national emergency or something?" Chris wanted to know.

"Televisions and radios are not as necessary as you might think," Chispo explained. "Most people have phone service, and our government and media already have a step-by-step calling procedure in case there were some emergency. In a matter of twenty minutes, everyone can be phoned and notified. It's pretty efficient."

"Why didn't TV's and radios catch on?" Robert asked.

"They were interfering to some of our people," Chispo replied, "in addition to being disturbing to the whales, dolphins, and other life in our oceans. Some of our native races, like the Atascosa people for example, are very perceptive, and when the governments of our world started to broadcast electromagnetic waves for television and radio, they got so many disturbing complaints that they had to abandon their plans."

"That is strange," Chris remarked.

"What about telephone communication?" Steven asked. "Don't you communicate over long distances by microwave repeater towers?"

"Not on Artenia, man," Chispo replied. "You certainly won't see any of those towers, nor any cell towers, either. They're against government regulations. Our communications company, Astrelcom, uses buried trunk cables and fiberoptic cables. Trunk cables are now giving way to fiberoptic cables, here in the last few years."

"That's interesting," Steven commented. "No electromagnetic waves."

Esalina called them into the kitchen. They entered, and while they ate, she talked to them about life in Zwever and informed Chispo about his cousins and what they were all doing. She hadn't had a chance to tell him last night, since it had been so late.

Here it became dark later in the evening than in Zotola, since they were further north. They soon went upstairs and went to sleep for the night.

The next day, Chispo took them into the mountains. Only a few blocks from Esalina's house, there was a trail that left the edge of the city. Chispo left his car parked at her house for the day, and they walked to the trailhead.

The clouds had cleared away entirely, and they had fantastic, crystal clear views of the surrounding mountains. All of the high snow-covered peaks were clearly visible. The whole valley was visible as well.

They walked the trail as it switchbacked up the forested mountain slope. Most of the trees were Firs and Spruces, but there were some Alders and true Poplars, such as the Aspen. An hour and a half later, they reached the main ridge of the Urlachia Mountains.

Here, they intersected the Wyndham Way. They turned left and now walked along more easily, as this trail was generally level with only a few ups and downs as it followed the main ridge. Most of it was forested, but they did pass through some beautiful alpine meadows where they were afforded spectacular views to the north of the Vovvitlet Valley, the city of Zwever, and of the high mountain peaks. On the other side of the ridge to the south, they could see the plains way below them stretching to the horizon. All of them, especially Rudy, were impressed by the scenery.

Later on, the ridge widened. They were now at another alpine meadow, and this one had a small lake. Chispo told them it was called Clisk Lake. Deer-like animals could be seen grazing, and there were also other animals and birds that inhabited these mountains. They stopped to have lunch by the lakeshore, and they rested for a while.

There was another trail that came up to this lake from the city. Chispo took them back down to Zwever along that trail. It descended rather steeply and followed the course of one of the Vovvitlet River's tributaries. In a little over an hour, they had reached the foot of the mountain and came out onto a street at the very edge of Zwever. Chispo recognized the street, and they followed him the kilometer back to his aunt's house. She was home, greeted them, and let them inside.

It was now mid afternoon. Rudy requested they go back to Zwever's central district to enjoy another evening. Chispo consented, and after they relaxed and also visited with Esalina for a while, he took them in his car.

Rudy bought a couple more souvenirs, and he also bought a useful piece of cookware for his mother. Andrew and Robert bought a few souvenirs as well, since they hadn't bought anything yesterday. Chris and Steven just browsed again. They also ate supper at one of the restaurants within the market setup.

Rudy wasn't sure why, but he still felt a sense of familiarity. The whole city and Vovvitlet Valley seemed vaguely familar to him. Their way of life seemed second nature to him in one sense. Then in another sense, it didn't. He could not successfully pinpoint within himself what the familiarity was. Nevertheless, he was enjoying his new friends on a distant land, literally light years from Mexico.

Later that night, they returned to Esalina's house. Her brother and his family had come over, and they visited with Chispo for the evening.

Afterwards they went upstairs to sleep for the night.

Morning arrived entirely sunny. A few clouds surrounded the snow-covered peaks to the east.

"All right, dudes," Chispo announced, waking everyone up. "Let's make tracks and head back to Zantaayer." Next he told Rudy in Spanish.

"¿Ya tenemos que salir? Me gusta aquí," Rudy responded, asking if they really had to leave and saying that he liked it here.

"Sí," Chispo answered, saying yes.

"Do you think Rinto and Fraxino succeeded?" Robert asked Chispo.

"Man, those two gurus can do anything! We've been out of their hair long enough. It's time for us to go back there and then return with them to Mexico."

They packed up their bedrolls, loaded their backpacks, and took them to Chispo's car. Esalina served them some breakfast. She and Chispo talked with each other in Artenian while they were eating. Then they got up to leave.

"Chispo, it was great to see you," she told him, "and I enjoyed meeting and getting to know your friends." She handed them some sack lunches to take with them.

"Thanks for everything, Aunt Esalina," Chispo told her.

"You're very welcome. My regards to your father and mother. Don't wait so long next time before you come back."

"Don't worry," Chispo reassured her. "I'll be back to visit sooner next time. Give my regards to Cousin Cliss."

"I will tell him. Have a safe trip back home." She hugged him. Then she said goodbye to the others.

They walked to the car, piled in, and Chispo drove them away. Esalina was waving to them.

"You've got a really nice aunt," Robert told Chispo.

"I know, man," Chispo agreed. "She's a really nice lady."

Chispo drove them down the street and intersected the main boulevard nearer the central district. He turned left and drove them out of Zwever the same way they had entered the other night. On the edge of town, he stopped at an Exxoll station and refueled.

Half an hour later, they reached the crest of the Urlachia Mountains, and he pulled over.

"Take one last look, dudes, and we're out of here," Chispo announced. They took his timely suggestion and looked behind them at the Vovvitlet Valley and Zwever below them. Then he proceeded, and as he crossed the crest of the mountains, the view disappeared. They were now making the winding descent through the forest to the plains of Caloma way below them.

They were on the road the whole day. Chispo did the majority of the driving with Robert and Rudy helping at times. They listened to pop music from Chispo's on-board holodisk player.

Al Nitak was just setting in the western sky behind the Ciruclar Mountains when they rolled into Zantaayer. Twenty minutes later, they were pulling into the Colancha's driveway. Chispo parked his car and switched off the engine.

"We're back, dudes," Chispo announced. "Let's see if Glecko and Sosta can tell us what our two guru friends are up to."

"I hope they've completed the growing procedure," said Andrew.

"I do too, man," Chispo agreed.

Neither of Chispo's parents were home. They got out of his car, took their backpacks out of the trunk, and they all walked over to the Zapatero's house, crossing under the row of tall bushes separating the backyards.

Glecko saw them approaching, and he opened the door, greeting them. "Hi, guys. How was your trip?"

"We had a great time, Mr. Zapatero," Chispo answered.

"Did your car make the trip without any trouble?" Glecko asked him.

"It drove like a dream."

"That's great. Listen, Rinto and Fraxino aren't back yet, but they said if you happened to be arriving today to just go ahead and make yourselves at home. They've been terribly busy with considerable complications in feeding the appropriate intelligence into their crystals, but they did say they hope to have them successfully grown by morning. They're staying in the cave tonight while they oversee the final growing process to be sure everything goes properly."

"That's good to hear," said Chispo.

"Come on in. Supper's ready. I was anticipating your coming."

"Thanks. We're hungry, too," Chispo said to him.

They walked into the kitchen. As they were eating, they told Glecko about their latest adventures in Caloma.

"Yes, your father has told me of his homeland, Chispo," said Glecko. "It's a beautiful place, I hear. I've never been there."

"It had been a while since I had been there myself, twelve years," Chispo admitted.

"We went and saw this really neat movie called *The Chill of the Vovvitlet*," Chris told Glecko.

"Really? I've heard about that movie . . . supposed to really put chills down your back. I haven't seen it yet."

"It certainly had our hairs standing on end," Steven told him.

"At the same time, it had some really great mountain scenery," Robert mentioned.

"I'll bet it did," Glecko agreed.

"By the way, where's Sosta?" Chris wanted to know.

"She's here. She's already gone to bed."

They continued talking for a while. Rudy showed Glecko the souvenirs he had bought. Once they finished supper, they spread out their bedrolls on the floor, and they went to sleep. Chispo slept with them at the Zapateros also.

They were awakened in the morning by the sound of Rinto and Fraxino walking in through the back door.

"Oh, cool! You're back, right on time!" said Rinto when he saw them asleep on the floor.

"We've had radical success, dudes!" Fraxino informed them.

"Huh? What's going on?" Robert asked, just waking up.

"Man, where do you get all that energy?" Chispo asked them. "We're just waking up."

"Come on out and see the gems," Rinto invited them.

Over the next ten minutes, they finished waking up and packed their bedrolls. Robert and Chispo were the first ones to go outside and see their setup.

"Oh, cool!" Chispo declared. "Those are far out!"

"Yes, I agree!" said Robert, impressed.

The intelligently grown crystals were sitting in a large box which was open. Each piece was resting on padding with cushioning on all sides. They were a marvel to look at. The center piece was a large mass of numerous translucent hexagonal plates. Within it were several phantom red quartz crystals.

"That large piece is called Kaolinite," Fraxino informed them. "It's our central processor crystal. We programmed it with the necessary intelligence by growing those red phantom image crystals within the hexagons."

"We're going to place that piece on top of the Cypress ridge," said Rinto, "since it's on a direct vertical plane with the two transmitter crystals."

"Kaolinite is generally rare," Fraxino told them, "but we had some starts in our collection, and we grew this piece. This type of mineral is, oddly enough, known for helping people over the high ridges of life and its conflicts. Since the people of Bustamante are having such tension and conflict, we determined that Kaolinite would be most effective in communicating to the ether the need to switch off and then to issue the process of elimination to both of the transmitter crystals. The four red phantom crystals within the Kaolinite carry the base program, and through the assistance of the two pieces of Kanágran on each side of it, they will communicate with the two crystal transmitter dodecahedrons and trick them into switching themselves off."

"It's like a phantom reality shift," Rinto explained. "These red phantom crystals will cause the dodecahedrons to think they were never tampered with and that the 500 years is up."

"That's brilliant," said Robert. "I believe that will work."

"Thanks," said Fraxino. "Also, those two Ruby crystals will telepathically receive the trigger signal we plan to send them from atop the Lion's Head Mountain, and they are excellent gems for releasing the blocking forces caused by the crystal transmitters. Plus, they are good for helping human progress toward enlightenment, as well as the healing forces they contain."

"That's right," Rinto added, "and we've got two more pieces of directional Kanágran that Fraxino and I will use to transmit the trigger signals."

"We also have to place a receiver catalyst crystal on both ledges next to each dodecahedron," Fraxino explained. "Those two pieces of clear quartz prismatic directional receiver crystals will be used for that. They'll each reflect our trigger signal into each of the two dodecahedrons and begin the process while we're at a safe distance atop the Lion's Head."

"Dudes, you two are geniuses, sure enough!" Chispo declared. "How did you think of all that?"

"Just crystallized common sense and concentration," Rinto replied.

The others now came out to look at Rinto and Fraxino's masterpiece work.

"¡Caray! Que curioso," Rudy exclaimed, saying how curious the display appeared.

"Rinto, Fraxino, with you two, nothing surprises me anymore!" Steven declared.

"That's pretty good, indeed," Andrew stated.

Chris looked inside and marveled at the setup.

"Right, let's eat some breakfast," Fraxino told everyone, "and then we'll zip back to Mexico."

They walked back inside the house. Glecko and Sosta were just getting up, and everyone helped himself to cereal and fruit. Glecko read Zantaayer's morning newspaper while they ate.

Afterwards, Glecko and Sosta walked outside and looked at their sons' masterpiece.

"Rinto and Fraxino, you never cease to amaze me," Glecko complimented.

"I never would have thought you two could have made such good use out of all that junk you've dragged home," Sosta declared. Although she didn't totally understand her sons' ways of thinking, she realized the impressiveness of their work.

Chispo, Rudy, Robert, and the others went back inside, brought their backpacks outside, and loaded them into the vehicle-craft.

"Oh, yeah," Robert suddenly recalled. "My rocks and crystals I've collected here."

"Oh, that's right," said Andrew, realizing he'd also forgotten his pieces.

"Robert, don't forget the crystal display cabinets Fraxino gave us," Steven reminded him. "One of them is for Tom."

They went back inside and picked up their pieces they had stored with the Zapateros on one of their bookshelves, returned to the vehicle-craft, and placed them in their backpacks.

Rinto was already in the driver's seat. "Ready to go, everyone?"

"All set," Chispo replied.

"Guys, all the best," Glecko told them. "Come back to see us."

"Thank you for everything," Robert told him and Sosta.

"Take care," Glecko told them.

Rinto backed the vehicle-craft out of the driveway.

"How much fuel do we have?" Chispo asked Rinto.

He looked at the gauge. "Nearly a full tank."

"Good. Let's go."

Rinto drove them to the nearby mountains on the western edge of Zantaayer. For the next half hour, he drove them up the switchbacking gravel road, and when they reached the forested ridge top, he pulled back the lever. They left the ground, gained altitude, and Rinto flew them west of the mountain range. As the craft swiftly accelerated, the forcefield accompanied by a faint green glow overtook them, and they felt themselves dematerializing.

CHAPTER 14

SOLUTION FROM THE MOUNTAINS

Before they totally realized it, they made their appearance, and they were now flying over the desert valley north of the double mesa. Rinto lowered the craft's air speed and brought it in for a landing on the road near the entrance to the canyon. As opposed to the way Fraxino had made his rough landing the first time they came to Mexico, Rinto slowed the craft to almost zero velocity and gently touched down on the rough gravel lane. He now drove them into the canyon.

It was the middle of the afternoon on Monday, July 22, and the weather was hot and sunny as usual. The sky was clear and blue.

When they saw the Ojo del Agua on the left side of the road, Rinto pulled over and parked.

"All right, guys, how do we want to do this?" he asked everyone.

"Let's go on in to Bustamante and leave our backpacks and equipment at Rudy's house," Chispo suggested.

"Do you think it's safe?" Steven asked.

"Oh yeah, man," Fraxino confidently stated. "It's daytime. No one's going to bother us."

"I don't know, dudes," Chispo said with more hesitation. "Let's deliver our equipment and then cruise on up to the mountains before dark."

"Good idea," Robert approved.

Rinto proceeded and drove them the ten kilometers through the canyon to Bustamante. Everything appeared normal enough as they entered town, passing by the molino on the left. He turned right and drove them to Rudy's house where he parked. As they were unloading their backpacks, María came outside to greet them.

"Buenas tardes. Roel llamó y dijo que se fueron a otra estrella," she said, greeting them and telling them that Roel called and told her that they had gone to another star system.

"¿Roel dijo eso?" said Rudy in a surprised manner, asking his mother if Roel really said that.

"Sí," answering yes. She further explained that she was very surprised and that she hadn't realized that some of them were extraterrestrials.

Everyone walked into the house and placed his backpack on the floor in the front room. Nora and Idalia weren't at home at the moment.

"Siéntense, por favor. Tengo que decirles algo," said María, telling them to have a seat and that she had to tell them something.

"¿Qué pasó?" Rudy asked her, wanting to know what happened. "¿Dónde está Roel?" asking where Roel was.

"Está en Zacatecas todavía," saying he was still in Zacatecas. "Roel dijo que no quería seguir con ustedes porque pensaba que eran maricones," María informed

Rudy, saying that Roel said he didn't want to continue with them because he thought they were gay.

"¡Pura mentira! No somos maricones, Mamá," Rudy firmly told her, saying that was a lie and that they certainly were not gay. "No quiso regresar aquí porque tiene miedo de Pegaso," telling her the real reason Roel didn't want to return here was because he was afraid of Pegaso.

"Pues, como quiera, dice todo el pueblo que ustedes son maricones," said María, informing Rudy that no matter what, the whole town was now saying they were gay. "Por eso, Roel no quiere andar con ustedes," saying for that, Roel didn't want to continue accompanying them.

Evidently, María had told Roel over the phone about the most recent rumor that was brewing in Bustamante. Over the past few days since Pegaso and Beto had been released from jail, they had maliciously started a rumor that the seven of them were gay. It was the latest talk of the town that the seven Americans in the "futuristic prototype vehicle" had come to town so that they could call attention to such issues as gay awareness and other related concepts. As a result, the whole town was in turmoil about it.

Again, Rudy insisted that his friends weren't gay.

"Mira, ya no te dejo que andes con ellos," she said, ordering Rudy to no longer accompany them, that she would no longer let him.

"Pero Mamá, ellos son mis amigos, y es mi obligación ser su guía," said Rudy defensively, telling his mother that they were his friends and that it was his obligation to be their guide.

Next, María cleverly designed a question and asked them how they liked her son.

Chispo answered for everyone. "Pues, nos gusta, y le disfrutamos mucho también," saying that Rudy pleased them and that they also enjoyed him very much.

Though Chispo didn't realize it, he had just put his foot in his mouth. Those were just the words María wanted to hear, and she just about threw a fit!

"¿Ves, Rudy? Es cierto. ¡Son maricones!" María fervently said, telling her son it was certain that they were gay.

For a third time, Rudy insisted that his friends weren't gay, but now María stubbornly refused to believe the truth, based on Chispo's innocent statement. She went on to say that they were having a bad impression on him.

"¿Qué hemos hecho mal?" Chispo asked, wanting to know what they had done wrong.

"Es que no se puede decir que un amigo te gusta ni que le disfrutas," Rudy answered, informing Chispo that one cannot say that a friend pleases him nor can he say that he enjoys him.

"Estás jugando. Nadie me había dicho eso," said Chispo, telling Rudy he must be joking and that no one had ever told him not to say that. He then asked Rudy why he hadn't explained that to him when they had their discussion about culture differences right after the fight with Pegaso.

"Se me olvidó. Perdón," said Rudy, admitting he had forgotten and to please forgive him.

"Sí, hombre," saying, Sure, man.

"¡Retírense, por favor!" María angrily said to them, ordering them to leave her house. She went on to tell Rudy to make them leave and for him to stay here. Then she started ranting and raving.

"¡Ya, Mamá, ya!" Rudy shouted, telling her enough already. "No son maricones," saying they weren't gay.

"Te estoy deciendo que ya no vayas con ellos," María said to Rudy, mandating him to no longer accompany them.

"Es mi obligación, Mamá. No les voy a abandonar como Roel lo hizo," he answered, insisting that it was his obligation and that he was not going to abandon them like Roel did.

She ranted and raved some more, made some threats, and was carrying on.

"¡Ya, ya, Mamá!" Rudy shouted again, telling her enough.

He had no choice in this matter, and he decided to disobey her. His friends were important to him, and he was not going to abandon them upon his mother's unreasonable orders.

"Rudy, le voy a decir a tu papá," she told him, threatening to tell his father.

"Vámonos, ya. Voy con ustedes," Rudy said to them, telling them he was coming with them right now. He said for them to recollect their backpacks from the front room and that they were going camping tonight.

Chispo, Andrew, and Robert translated to the others what Rudy said. They collected their backpacks, took them to the vehicle-craft, and climbed in. All of them felt bad feelings of rejection, and they felt somewhat nervous as a result.

Rudy felt bad, having to disobey his mother. It was not a normal practice for him. Even though María had not physically resisted Rudy's leaving with them, she did do as much as to stand outside and make final gestures of threats, all of which Rudy ignored. He simply told her he had a mission to accomplish with them, that it was important, and that they would return soon, possibly tomorrow.

As Rinto drove away, Chispo asked Rudy, "¿Qué pasó con tu mamá?" wanting to know what happened to his mother.

"No sé. Está loca," Rudy answered, saying he didn't know what had gotten into her and that she was crazy. He thought for a moment and then said, "Pues, a lo mejor, el transmisor le afectó," saying that quite possibly the transmitter device affected her.

As Rinto turned left on Calle Mier, they spotted Pegaso and Beto walking toward them from the molino.

"Oh my goodness!" Steven remarked.

"Step on it, Rinto!" Chispo commanded. "It's Pegaso and Beto."

Rinto quickly accelerated. Pegaso and Beto stood in the middle of the street with their arms crossed, thinking surely they had them blocked.

"See if you can block *this* one!" Rinto proudly stated. He pulled back the lever, and the craft briefly left the ground, passing just over their heads. Then Rinto brought the craft back down to the road again. Pegaso and Beto were shocked. As Chispo, Robert, and their friends looked out the back window at them, Pegaso and Beto both put their hands down in a certain way, mocking to them that they were gay.

"Well, María was right about that much," Andrew admitted. "They think we're gay."

"Yes, sure enough," said Robert. "What a shame!"

"That's lame, dudes," Chispo remarked. "By the way, for those of you who didn't understand the discussion with Rudy's mom, she asked us if we liked Rudy. I told her that he pleases us, and that we enjoy him very much. Do you know you can't even say that, here in Mexico?"

"Yeah, that's what I just heard Rudy tell you," Robert acknowledged. "Why can't you say a friend pleases you and that you enjoy him?"

"In Mexican culture," Andrew explained, "the words *gustar* and *disfrutar* in reference to male friends, have developed negative connotations, implying a sexual relationship."

"No way! You've got to be kidding," Steven responded.

"So, *that's* why María asked us that question," Robert realized. "Your answer, Chispo, gave her an excuse to run us off."

Chispo then asked Rudy more about those two words, and Rudy explained the whole thing over a period of several minutes.

"That's lame," Chispo remarked again. "You know, as I think about it, this whole conflict about people being gay is likely a spinoff from one of those quantum energy systems set in motion by some of those devious Atlantean scientists, and it was designed to damage friendships and to prevent others from even starting, all because of homophobia."

"Yeah, really," Chris agreed. "I mean, since when was it ever wrong to say that a friend pleases you and that you enjoy him?"

"I know," Steven agreed. "How absurd!"

"Well, the way I see it, dudes," Chispo told them, "I enjoy having friends. They make life fun and interesting. Everyone has the right to have friends, regardless of some stupid homophobia concept!"

"Right on, Chispo!" Fraxino agreed.

"I agree with you, Chispo" said Robert. "We're all in this to enjoy each other, please each other, and to be friends, and if they can't say it that way here in Mexico, then that's their tough problem!"

"I'll bet those two transmitter devices are the reason this bad concept got started in the first place," Steven speculated. "They probably fed energy into one of the quantum reality programs designed to create various unexpected forms of homophobia."

"That's really a shame!" Rinto remarked. "People really need to be friends with each other and not be hung up on some homophobia concept. Back in Zotola on our world, no one has ever heard of homophobia, let alone not being able to say you enjoy a friend."

"I hear you, man," Chispo agreed.

"Let's get on up to the mountains and get started," Rinto suggested. "The sooner those transmitter crystals are switched off, the better."

By now, they were several kilometers out of town, and they were back on the one-lane gravel road heading into the canyon.

To Rudy, the whole issue about homophobia and what you can and cannot say in reference to it and possible bad implications it might present, was not much of a concern. More and more, he was realizing that his spirit was from Artenia, especially now since he had just been there with his new friends.

Before they reached the Ojo del Agua, Rinto pulled back the lever, and they left the ground. They flew through the canyon and gained altitude as they cruised over to the mountain range on the other side of the double mesa, touching down on the flat-topped second peak.

Fraxino reached back and took one of the pieces of clear quartz prismatic receiver crystal. "All right, who wants to rappel down to the ledge and place this receiver crystal next to the dodecahedron?" he asked them.

"I can do it, man," Chispo volunteered.

"I'll accompany him down there," Robert offered.

"Right, here it is, dude," said Fraxino. He handed the piece to Chispo.

While the rest of them waited in the vehicle-craft, Chispo reached into his backpack and took out his rope. Then he and Robert stepped out of the vehicle-craft and walked over to the edge of the cliff on the southern edge of the flat table of bedrock. Chispo secured the rope to a Cypress shrub nearby, and he started descending to the ledge below him. Robert followed, and they were soon standing by the large, greenish-yellow dodecahedron.

"Wow, man! That really is one impressive piece of crystal," Chispo remarked.

"You got that right," Robert agreed. "It's amazing how it's in such good condition after sitting here for over 12,000 years."

"I know, man, but then the Atlanteans programmed them with the intelligence to periodically refresh themselves and keep their outer appearance looking like new."

"Really? That's amazing!" Robert responded.

"Rinto said he wanted it on the opposite side of the dodecahedron, right?" Chispo checked.

"That's right," Robert answered.

"All right, man. There it is," as Chispo placed the piece of clear quartz prismatic receiver crystal on the western side of it. "Let's go back up there quickly."

Both of them climbed back up to the top of the cliff, Chispo then Robert. As soon as Chispo untied his rope, they returned to the vehicle-craft and climbed in.

"We got it, man. Let's go," Chispo told Rinto.

Immediately, the craft left the ground, and they cruised over to the top of the Cypress ridge, where they touched down.

"I believe we better deposit our central crystal, our piece of Kaolinite, right now," Rinto suggested to his brother.

"Good idea, Rinto," Fraxino said to him.

Both of them unloaded the box containing the Kaolinite along with the two pieces of Kanágran and the two pieces of Ruby. They checked coordinates. Next, they took the Kaolinite out of the box and strategically placed it on a limestone rock which afforded them views on both sides of the ridge. Then they carefully placed the pieces of Kanágran and Ruby on each side, spacing them a meter from the central crystal.

"All right, that's all set," Rinto announced. "We're out of here."

"Dudes, I believe you might better gather those pieces and cover them with a blanket for now," Chispo suggested. "The dodecahedrons might detect our actions and become suspicious."

"Hmm . . ." as Rinto thought about it. "Good thinking, Chispo. I knew you came along on this mission for a good reason. Right, let's do as Chispo says," he now told his brother.

After gathering them and covering them with a blanket, they all climbed back into the craft. Rinto flew them down to the free standing rock wall, touching down on its top.

"All right, who wants to take this piece down there?" Rinto asked everyone as he reached for the other piece of quartz prismatic receiver crystal and showed it to them.

Both Chispo and Robert volunteered again. Chispo made his rope double and secured it to a scrub Oak tree, and they climbed down at the same time. The others stepped out of the craft and watched. Once on the ledge, Chispo placed the piece

of clear quartz prismatic receiver crystal on the eastern side of the dodecahedron, and they immediately climbed back up.

"Okay, dudes, back to the Cypress ridge," Chispo told everyone as he untied his rope.

They got back in the craft, and Rinto flew them up there. Once they touched down, Rinto and Fraxino stepped outside, took the blanket off, and realigned the central crystal and the pieces of Kanágran and Ruby. They rechecked coordinates and then announced that it was all ready.

Once Rinto and his brother climbed back inside the craft, he flew them over to the summit of the Lion's Head Mountain, where they touched down on the flat limestone bedrock and next to one of the Cypress shrubs.

"We'll camp here for the night," Rinto announced.

"I don't know if we told you," Fraxino brought up, "but we need to wait until it gets dark before we trigger the process. Meanwhile, the pieces we set up will self-synchronize and become accustomed to their new surroundings."

It was already early evening, and they decided to take their backpacks out of the vehicle-craft and set up camp for the night. They prepared and ate supper, and they explored the summit, looking over the edges of the cliff and checking out the numerous cracks and crevices in the bedrock.

Darkness arrived, and they could see the lights of Bustamante way below them to the east. The lights of the other towns in the distance could also be seen. The stars were now clearly visible above them, and they really stood out since they were on the second highest peak in the district.

Rinto now took the two extra pieces of Kanágran out of a compartment in the vehicle-craft, and he handed one of them to Fraxino.

"I believe we're ready to begin," Rinto announced to everyone. "Chispo, do you feel like the time is right?"

He paused and appeared to concentrate briefly. "As far as I can tell."

"Right, dudes," Fraxino now said. "Here it goes."

"Okay, on the count of three," Rinto directed, "we'll simultaneously transmit the trigger signals, first to the Ruby crystals on the Cypress ridge and second to the dodecahedrons. I'll do the eastern side, and you do the western side."

"Right on, brother!" Fraxino enthusiastically declared.

They stood beside each other on the top of the cliff at the southern edge of the summit. Each one of them had his right arm outstretched and holding a piece of Kanágran crystal. The others stood further back and quietly waited.

"One . . . two . . . three!" Rinto called out. He and Fraxino concentrated and directed their attention first toward the Cypress ridge and then toward the location of each dodecahedron transmitter crystal. Half a minute passed by. Then they turned around and faced the others.

"Done!" Rinto triumphantly declared.

"That's it?" Robert asked them.

"¿Es todo?" said Rudy, asking the same question.

"They're switched off, dudes," Fraxino confidently informed them.

"Hey! What was that?" Chris suddenly asked everyone. He had seen a quick flash of white light in the location of the free standing rock cliff. A faint audible pow was heard seconds later.

Rinto and Fraxino quickly turned around in alarm and looked. In seconds there was another white flash of light.

"Oh my goodness!" Steven exclaimed.

"Quick, everyone!" Rinto shouted. "Take cover!"

Immediately, all of them ran to the nearest crevice they could find, and they did their best to get between the rocks. Another flash of light was visible from the other mountain range where the other dodecahedron crystal was. Meanwhile, they were still struggling to find available crevices, and some of them ended up piling on top of each other. Chris stumbled and fell.

More flashes occurred, and a few seconds later, surges of white light shot across the region, literally from one mountain to the other, followed by the sounds of explosions in the distance. They also began to hear what sounded like rock slides. Next, the whole sky lit up almost like it was day, and a spectacular display of lightning surges shot east across Bustamante, the final surge occurring fifteen seconds later. It shot out of the canyon north of them and raced across Bustamante in a southeasterly direction. It also passed over Villaldama in the distance and ricocheted off the lower mountain range east of there. One of its reflections returned and shot straight over the summit of the Lion's Head Mountain.

The vehicle-craft deflected part of the beam, and Chris suddenly gave out a scream! He had been stunned by the energy. All was now quiet.

"Chris, what happened to you?" Robert wanted to know as they were all climbing out of the crevices where they had taken cover.

He didn't answer.

"Chris!" Robert shouted as he walked over to him. The others arrived to him as quickly as possible. He was lying there and appeared lifeless.

"Oh, no!" Steven exclaimed. "He looks dead!"

"¡Caramba! Parece está muerto," said Rudy, making a similar comment.

"Chispo, quick!" Rinto commanded. "Run to the craft and get our first aid box. Hurry!"

Chispo did just that. Meanwhile, Rinto turned Chris over so he was lying on his back.

"His life force got knocked away from him," Rinto told everyone as he was standing over Chris.

Ten seconds later, Chispo dashed back over and handed Rinto the box. Immediately, Rinto opened it and without saying a word, placed several crystals on top of him, one on his forehead and the others on his abdomen. He took another one in his hand and waved it over his body from top to bottom. In seconds, Chris regained consciousness. He showed that he was suffering from intense pain, but in just a few seconds, a smile came across his face as the pain quickly faded away.

"He's completely healed and restored to life," Rinto then announced.

"Golly! That's amazing!" Robert declared.

"I didn't know you could do that," Andrew told Rinto.

"It was the only solution to save him," Rinto told everyone. "There was not time to rush him to the nearest hospital. Besides, they don't have a cure for what just happened to Chris. He suffered the equivalent of a severe lightning strike."

"Good gracious!" Robert declared. "It might have gotten the rest of us if we had not taken cover."

"I know," said Steven. "Chris didn't make it to a crevice, did he?"

"No, he didn't," said Rinto. "He must have stumbled and fallen."

"Chris, can you speak?" Chispo asked him.

"Wh . . . What just happened?" Chris asked everyone.

"You were zapped by the final surge of energy," Chispo informed him. "Rinto just restored you to life."

". . . How did he do that?" Chris wanted to know. He now sat up and looked around.

"He used our crystal first aid kit and concentrated energy through them and placed your life force back in you," Chispo answered. "Then he caused you to be healed."

"Where did you learn to cure people like that?" Andrew asked Rinto.

"It's just standard first aid procedure for us," he answered. "Everyone is required to know the art, and it's an ancient skill originating long before the days of Atlantis."

"Well, why don't people on Earth use it?" Robert wanted to know.

"It's been lost through the ages on this world," Rinto answered. "People just forgot how."

"There are a few remote tribes of people here on Earth who still know and use the art," Fraxino informed them.

"You don't think the craft got hurt by that surge of energy, do you?" Chispo asked Rinto and Fraxino.

"I don't think so," Rinto answered. He was still tending to Chris and was placing the crystals back into the first aid box. "Fraxino, go check our controls crystal and crystal array."

He walked over to the vehicle-craft, entered it, and gave it a good checking over. Several minutes later, he emerged. "Everything is fine," he called over to Rinto.

"That's good," said Rinto. He was now getting up from having tended to Chris. "Thank goodness we shielded our craft with crystallized protection."

"Rinto," Chris sincerely told him. "Thank you."

Suddenly, they heard a whirring sound to the west, and as they looked, they saw a pink glow materializing on the summit around fifteen meters away from them. The pink glow faded a few seconds later, revealing Morris.

"Morris! How's it going, dude?" Fraxino called over to him.

Everyone else greeted him.

"What a surprise!" said Steven. "What brings you here?"

"How could I help but *notice* that report of energy release?"

"You *heard* that?" Steven asked in disbelief.

"Heard it? Oh, I think the whole galaxy heard that one!" Morris answered, and he laughed. "I was on Delikadove, the world of the dolphins, and I sensed it within myself, even though it was 35 million years in the future from their viewpoint. Immediately, I told them my instincts were directing me to check on my Earthly friends. It looks like all of you survived it okay. You're very lucky."

"We didn't expect such a spectacular report of energy," Rinto admitted.

"Oh, I know you didn't," Morris agreed. "You don't realize how strongly entrenched those quantum reality programs actually were, nor how many of them were running a full blown course in this region."

"Really?" Robert responded.

"Oh yes," Morris affirmed. "There were a total of fifteen major ones that were having a binding stronghold, but they're gone now. You've done an excellent job. That Kaolinite with the phantom red quartz crystals was ingenious and certainly did the trick. Not only did it cause the two dodecahedrons to switch themselves off when you sent those trigger signals, it also went after the quantum reality programs running their course in the ether, and it literally blew every one of them out of existence, separating their life forces from them. That was impressive, I must admit."

"How did you know what we used?" Fraxino wanted to know.

"I saw the setup in my mind just as quickly as I sensed the report of all that energy," Morris replied.

"Wow! You *knew* that?" Fraxino asked.

"Oh yes," Morris verified. "As I'm sure you already know, those quantum reality programs have their origins from the days of Atlantis. You see, quantum reality programs, also known as quantum energy systems, are kept alive by the people who vibrate to them and react to them. They feed their thoughts into them."

"You mean they can be reformatted?" Andrew asked.

"That's right, and over time they can actually evolve," Morris answered. "I believe you're fully aware of what some of the programs were. One was causing certain people to get angry whenever they were charged money. Another one was designed to cause people to be homophobic, making males afraid to have male friends because that might mean they were gay, which of course, is erroneous and negative thinking. It's a shame, really, how many friendships were prevented and lost through the ages because of that one. Another still, caused certain people to be unreasonably defensive about kind comments made about their family members."

"I hear you, man," Chispo responded. "Pegaso and his sister, Lumita."

"Exactly," Morris responded and continued. "There was a really weird one that was activated whenever a fellow told a male friend he loved him. For the embarrassment they were caused to feel, the result was a sure guarantee of destruction of friendship between the two males."

"Golly! That is weird," Robert agreed.

"Yes, very. I agree," Morris responded and continued. "This one will *really* make you laugh. If two male friends have a falling out, and one writes a letter to the other in efforts to make up or fix the friendship, the recipient receives the letter badly and accuses his former friend of being gay."

"What?!" Rinto asked in disbelief.

"Of being *gay*, I said," Morris reiterated.

Both Rinto and Fraxino started laughing, followed by Robert, Steven and the others, who joined in for a really good laugh . . . except for Chispo, and also Rudy.

Chispo had a straight face, and after the laughter eased, he said, "*That's* why Pegaso and his friend Beto started that rumor that we were gay!"

"Why?" Robert asked, not understanding.

"Because I gave Pegaso that letter from Orolizo right after our fight," Chispo answered.

"Oh . . . and Pegaso must have thought *you* wrote him that letter instead," Andrew mentioned.

"Exactly, man," Chispo confirmed.

"Oh my goodness!" Steven remarked.

"How crazy and absurd for Pegaso to think that!" Robert exclaimed.

"You're not wrong," Morris agreed. "Still more, another system caused people to hold grudges. Another one caused friends to not trust each other. The list goes on. It was all about mood control experiments conducted by devious Atlantean scientists. It made no difference at all to them that their programs endured for over 12,000 years, long after those scientists were dead.

"I think all of you are going to be very pleased when you return to Bustamante," Morris went on. "Now that the quantum reality programs are literally dead and gone, the people are now suddenly freed up from them and are no longer vibrating to them. They are now much more likely to think positive. My advice to all of you is to forgive anyone who wronged you and to enjoy your friends. Chispo, that former friend of yours, Pegaso, will be coming to you to ask forgiveness."

"That's good to hear, Morris, but I don't know," Chispo said hesitatingly.

"I realize you may need to think about it," said Morris, "but like I tell you, the programs are dead and gone. Just look him in the eyes. If you read sincerety, you'll know it within yourself that everything is okay."

"I don't mean to be doubtful, Morris," Chispo told him, "but I'll believe that if Pegaso offers his sister to me so I can take her on a date, if I so wish. I mean, the dude wanted to kill me."

"Right, well that's something for you to explore and find out," said Morris. "I will notify Tom that I came and talked to you all. He will be testing out signals and will pay you a visit in Bustamante tomorrow at noon."

"Wait, he's never been to Bustamante," said Robert. "How's he going to teleport there?"

"I will be coming with him," Morris replied.

"Oh, okay. That will work," said Robert.

"As you are likely aware," Morris added, "the people of this region had a reason for behaving badly since those quantum energy systems were, in a sense, running their course. Still, as a general rule, there is no excuse for bad behavior. People are responsible for their own actions and consequences. So, my advice to all of you is this. Don't be too complacent and think you're free floating. A lot of bad energy has been neutralized here. It's like a clean slate now, and it's possible the people of this region could revive the energy systems and programs by their continued thoughts."

"Do you think that's possible?" Chris asked.

"Yes, I do, but at the same time, since the programs are now dead and gone, the people are no longer vibrating to them. So, I believe we're safe on that one. All of us need to think positive thoughts, as all of us have the potential to create and maintain quantum energy systems."

"That's good to hear," said Robert.

"Right, I must go," Morris announced. "Again, excellent work, fellows. Just remember, peace and friendship will now prevail. All the best." With that said, he transported himself away.

"Oh, yeah," Rinto suddenly recalled. "I meant to thank him for his having informed us of that second transmitter crystal."

"You can tell him tomorrow," said Steven.

"Good. Don't let me forget," Rinto requested.

"Golly! I forgot to ask him why he couldn't come with us to Al Nitak!" Andrew stated.

After they calmed down from all the excitement, they entered their tents and went to sleep for the night.

They woke up shortly after the crack of dawn at around 6:30 AM. It was Tuesday, July 23. They zipped open their tents and climbed outside to another clear day.

Steven was the first one to step outside. "Oh my goodness!" he declared when he looked in the distance to the south.

"What?" Robert wanted to know.

"You're not going to believe this, guys," Steven said to them.

"What . . .what?" Chispo wanted to know.

"The whole free standing rock cliff where the crystal transmitter was, is now blown away."

"It's *what*?!" Rinto now asked, surprised. He emerged from his tent.

Though none of them knew it, similar damage had occurred to the back side of the second peak of the mountain range west of them.

Robert stepped out of the tent, and he looked toward the south. "Well, I will say! You weren't kidding!"

"I know, and now look at the Cypress ridge," as Steven pointed toward it.

On top of the ridge in the distance was a gap of freshly exposed rock, showing signs of having undergone the turmoil of an explosion.

Rinto, who was now outside, looked to the south. "Well, so much for our masterpiece central crystal."

"I wanted to take that back home with us," Fraxino said remorsefully.

"What's more important is that we've just accomplished the mission beyond the ice cave," Chispo pointed out.

"That's true," said Rinto.

They continued talking about it as they packed up their tents. Some of them ate some breakfast, and then they boarded the craft. This time, Fraxino operated the craft, and they flew off the summit of the Lion's Head Mountain.

"Let's go check out what happened," Fraxino suggested to everyone.

They cruised south, and Fraxino kept the craft only meters above the terrain so as not to be easily seen by the people down in Bustamante.

He flew them over to where the free standing rock wall used to be.

"Good gracious!" Andrew exclaimed once they reached the site.

"It really did some damage here," Steven remarked.

The whole wall was gone, and there was a pile of rock and rubble strewn down the side of the mountain. Several pieces of rock and boulders had tumbled all the way into the creek at the bottom of the mountain, upstream from the cono at the end of the road.

Next, they went to the Cypress ridge where they found a sizeable gap in the otherwise flat bedrock of the ridge top. Fraxino brought the craft in for a landing and touched down on the ridge a few meters from the site of the blast. He and Rinto stepped outside and searched for any remains of the Kaolinite, Kanágran, and Ruby, but there was absolutely none of it left. Rock and rubble had fallen down either side of the ridge, as far away as several hundred meters. They could see the paths made by some of the boulders that had tumbled all the way down to the foot of the mountain to the desert valley west of them.

They climbed back into the craft, and Fraxino flew them north along the desert valley side of the mountains, soon reaching the canyon. He came in for a landing on the canyon road, gently touching down. Over the next 20 minutes, he drove them to Bustamante, passing by the Ojo del Agua on the way.

As they entered town, they could already feel a difference for the better. Fraxino drove them first to Rudy's house. It was now 9 AM. Nora and Idalia were there, and they were the first ones to come outside and cheerfully greet them. María was also there, and as they stepped out of the vehicle-craft, she came outside.

"Buenos días. ¿Cómo están?" she said to them, greeting them and asking them how they were.

They replied appropriately.

"Mira, quiero pedirles una disculpa por haber pensado mal de todos ustedes," she said, telling them she wanted to ask forgiveness for having thought badly about them. "Rudy, perdóneme, por favor. Tus amigos son buena gente," asking her son to forgive her and stating that his friends were good people.

"Sí, Mamá. Gracias," Rudy responded, telling his mother yes and thanks. Then they hugged each other.

"Pásen," María offered, telling them to come inside.

With that, all of them took their backpacks out of the vehicle-craft and entered. While they still felt uneasy about her, based on her behavior yesterday, they could now sense that she was genuine in her apology, and they appreciated her for having now told them.

"¿Qué pasó anoche? Hubieron muchas explosiones en las montañas acompañadas por unas luces fuertes," María said to everyone, asking them what happened last night because there were a bunch of explosions in the mountains accompanied by flashes of bright lights.

"Sí, las vimos también," said Rudy, telling his mother they saw them also.

Chispo and Rudy then explained to María the project and said what they had been up to, admitting that they had been looking for two crystal transmitters in the mountains, had located them, and eliminated them. They told her the crystals had been there since the days of Atlantis and that they were placed for the purpose of blocking communication to the Orion Belt. They left out the part about their having caused adverse effects such as tension and conflict in the region.

They heard a knock on the door, and María went to answer it. She was quite surprised to see Pegaso and Beto. "¿Qué quieren?" she said to them, asking them what they wanted.

"Venimos para pedirte una disculpa," said Pegaso, telling her they had come to ask forgiveness.

"Pues, gracias," said María, thanking them.

Beto asked forgiveness in a similar manner, and María went ahead and offered them to come inside. Then they saw Rudy, Chispo, Robert, and their friends.

"Chispo, discúlpeme. Siento verguenza por haberte maltratado," said Pegaso, asking Chispo to forgive him and saying that he felt embarrassed for having badly treated him.

"¿Pues, cómo te voy a perdonar desde tú me quisiste matar?" Chispo responded, asking Pegaso how and reminding him that he wanted to kill him.

Pegaso humbly admitted that he didn't know what had gotten into him, but suddenly last night, he felt like a big force was lifted off of him. He also explained that egotistical pride had gotten in his way and had prevented him from apologizing earlier. Ever since he had seen those bright lights and heard those explosions from the mountains, he had felt humble feelings of sorrow for having been so awful to Chispo the other night. His pride was no longer in the way, and he felt strongly compelled to come and beg forgiveness, now realizing that having friends meant a lot more to him than being too proud to apologize. He reached out to shake hands with Chispo.

Chispo looked him in the eyes, and it was indeed like Morris had said. Pegaso was indeed genuine with his gesture. It was a miracle, and it was like a spell was lifted. No matter what, Chispo had to verify Pegaso's authenticity, and he probed Pegaso by asking him how he felt about his sister Lumita and if he would let her go out on a date with him, if he were to want to.

"Sí, hombre. Claro," Pegaso answered, saying yes, of course he could.

Further, Chispo probed Pegaso by staring him in the face and repeating three times, "Lumita es bonita, y me *gustaría* por una novia, si yo quisiera," saying that Lumita was pretty and would please him for a girlfriend, if he wanted one.

Pegaso reacted with a smile. In fact, he was flattered and thanked Chispo for such kind, positive words.

"Pues, bueno, Pegaso. Te perdono," said Chispo, telling him that was good and that he forgives him. They shook hands in a friendly manner.

Then he and Beto humbly asked all of them to forgive them for the firecracker incident. They all shook hands.

"¿Dónde está Roel?" Pegaso asked them, wanting to know where Roel was.

"Pues, le miraste muy enojado, y le asustaste. Está en Zacatecas por el verano," María answered, telling Pegaso that since he had given Roel a very angry look, he had scared him, and as a result, Roel was in Zacatecas for the summer.

Pegaso and Beto asked María to pass on their apology to Roel, and María said thanks and then suggested that they telephone Roel and tell him themselves. With that, she got a pen and paper off a nearby table and wrote out the phone number for her brother, Antonio, in Pinos. Since her parents had no phone, they would have to call and schedule a time for Roel to be at Antonio's to take their call, perhaps the next Sunday.

Though they weren't aware of it, a true miracle had occurred in Bustamante. The conflicts and issues about people possibly being gay had suddenly vanished. That was no longer a concern of theirs, and the town's people now viewed the Americans in the "futuristic prototype vehicle" as good honest people who had come with the purpose of making friends and keeping them.

Over the next 20 minutes, Pegaso and Beto talked with everyone. Their feelings improved during the conversation, and they asked for another ride around the plaza with them in their vehicle-craft. Chispo consented, and all of them left the house and piled into the vehicle with Rinto driving.

They stopped in front of Alvaro's house, and Chispo sounded the horn. Alvaro stepped outside and greeted them. Rinto opened the door and let him in.

"Hola. ¿Cómo están?" said Alvaro, greeting them and asking them how they were doing.

They replied, and then he apologized to Chispo for having told Pegaso what Chispo had said about Pegaso's sister. Both Alvaro and Pegaso admitted that it was entirely wrong of them what they did, and Pegaso further added that getting angry over a kind comment about his sister was absurd. Chispo thanked Alvaro, and they shook hands. They could now move ahead and be friends. Things were now truly the way they were supposed to be. They past was now just that, the past. All grudges were now gone, no longer being fed by the appropriate past quantum reality programs.

Rinto drove them to the town center, and they circled around the plaza several times while Pegaso and Alvaro whistled and waved to other friends. They were laughing and were having fun. Rudy joined in and waved at other friends in the plaza.

For the next two hours, they cruised the town, visiting several people and places. They stopped by the Cantu's store where they all walked inside to buy snacks and sodas.

"Buenos días, muchachos," Mr. Cantu told them, greeting them.

They greeted Chilo. While they were busy buying snacks, Robert happened to notice the *No fio porque cobrar es un lío* sign sitting on the floor by the trash can.

"Tu señal," Robert said to Chilo, pointing at the sign and bringing Chilo's attention to it.

"Sí, hombre, lo quité anoche. Ya no lo quiero," he replied, saying he took it down last night and that he no longer wanted it.

"Que bueno," said Robert, saying that was good.

Chilo said that once he saw all those beams of light flashing across the sky, along with the sound of explosions from the mountains, he suddenly felt overwhelmed with confidence and trust for his clients. In fact, he commented that the sign was an eyesore and might prevent future clients from giving him their business.

As they left, he wished them a pleasant and safe stay for the remainder of their time in Bustamante. They walked back outside and climbed back in the vehicle-craft.

Robert recalled that he wanted a rocking chair from Paco, and Chispo drove them to the Casso's bakery. All of them stepped out of the vehicle, and while they purchased various types of bread from Paco's father, Robert went into the Casso's backyard and found Paco. He bought one of his rocking chairs.

Juan and Alejandro were also back there working. One was hand planing some wood, and the other one was assembling a chair.

"¿Y Roel, dónde está?" Paco asked with a smile, wanting to know where Roel was.

Robert explained that they had gone to Zacatecas last week and that Roel had stayed there to work for one of his uncles.

Then Paco mentioned the curious series of bright flashes of light that shot across the sky last night, followed by the sound of explosions and rock slides.

Robert acknowledged that he had seen and heard the same thing last night, but he didn't tell him any more details.

Paco walked back to the front, carrying Robert's chair, and he wished him and his friends well.

Rinto and Fraxino suddenly decided to buy a rocking chair, followed by Chispo. Paco was pleased, and he now led them to the backyard to choose from his selection. Robert accompanied them and supplied Rinto and Chispo the money since Zotolan zúbolas wouldn't be recognized in Mexico. Paco accompanied them back to the front and helped them load the chairs into the vehicle-craft.

Chispo casually asked Paco where his sisters were, since he didn't see them out front, running the store. Paco informed him that they had gone with their mother to the church. Once they had seen the lights and heard the explosions last night, they felt strongly compelled to visit the church and ask forgiveness for any past wrongdoings of theirs.

Now with three rocking chairs loaded into the vehicle-craft, it was a tight fit. They had to stand up so they could all fit inside. Rinto now drove, and he took them by Felipe's shop at the Hotel Ancira. Several of them bought some of his local handmade crafts.

Rudy talked with Felipe and said that he was still serving as a guide for his friends and that he was really enjoying it. Felipe said it was no problem. He reassured Rudy that when his friends leave Mexico, he would still have his position waiting for him at the carpentry business. As they left, Felipe wished them well.

By now, it was nearly noon. Rinto drove them back toward Rudy's house. On the way, Pegaso and Alvaro stepped down in front of Alvaro's house. The two of them wished them well. Then Rinto drove them to Rudy's house and parked on the streetside.

María was just finishing preparing lunch, and as they all entered, she served them. Antonio walked in a few minutes later and greeted everyone. Nora and Idalia were away, playing with some neighbors. It felt really good to be among friends and to experience such kind hospitality.

While they were eating, there was a knock on the door.

"I'll bet that's Tom and Morris," said Robert.

Antonio went to answer the door and was quite surprised. There were two men, and one of them was wearing a white Sirian robe. He commented to everyone to come forward. María then came from the kitchen to answer the door. Rudy explained to her who they were, and she asked them to come inside. By now, everyone had come into the front room.

"How are you doing?" Robert said to Tom and Morris.

Tom was carrying a briefcase, and he greeted everyone as he and Morris entered. "The Galactic Federation and I have tested out gravity wave signals this morning, and they arrived perfectly, no longer distorted like they used to be. I must declare, you've done fine work!"

"Thank you, Tom," said Rinto.

"We were glad to help," Fraxino added.

"Morris, here, informed me that he paid you all a visit last night on the mountain top, and he also told me there was quite a spectacular explosion, including flashing lights and beams of energy shooting across the region."

"That's true," Andrew admitted.

"To settle the transaction," Tom requested, "may we take care of that within your craft?"

"Certainly," Rinto answered.

"By the way, Rudy was in on this project too," Morris informed Tom. "May he also come with us?"

"Yes, of course," Tom consented.

They put their unfinished lunches down and went outside with Tom. Robert now told Rudy in Spanish to come with them.

"Ahorita regresamos," Rudy told his parents, saying that they would return in a little while.

Antonio and María said that would be fine. They continued eating lunch in the kitchen.

They left the house and entered the vehicle-craft.

"I don't mean to be too private about this," Tom now told them, "but I didn't want to reveal the contents of this briefcase in front of anyone, except for the ones who were directly involved with this project."

"That's okay," said Chispo.

"That was a very impressive procedure you performed to eliminate the two crystal transmitter devices," Tom praised them. "Rinto and Fraxino, you two did an absolutely marvelous job with the ingenious crystal apparatus you grew to catalyze the process. In this briefcase is $25,000 cash. All of it is in $100 notes." He now opened it, revealing the stacks of money. "It is up to you how you want to divide it among yourselves."

"Thank you very much, Tom," Robert sincerely told him.

"This is great! Thank you," said Andrew.

All of them thanked Tom and showed their appreciation.

"Morris," Rinto told him. "I've been meaning to tell you that I really appreciate your bringing our attention to the fact that there was a second transmitter on the other mountain range."

"Oh, that's all right," Morris responded. "Since the federation was in a hurry, they could not afford the possiblity of it being overlooked. So, that's why I showed up and told you about it."

"I'm glad you did, Morris," said Rinto. "I think you deserve part of this money. How much do you think, guys?"

"What about 15%?" Robert proposed.

"That's fine with me," Steven consented.

"Me too," said Chris.

Everyone agreed that was fair because if Morris had not shown up, they would not have succeeded with eliminating the device.

"Let's see," said Steven as he calculated it in his mind. "Fifteen percent would be $3,750."

Tom counted out 38 $100 notes and handed them to Morris.

"Thank you and the federation very much," Morris cheerfully told them. "$3,700 is good enough for me." He handed a $100 note back to Tom. "Now I can help my parents pay their high phone bill, along with buying some other things I've been wanting."

"Okay, that leaves us $21,300," said Andrew.

"You know," Robert brought up. "I remember that Roel and Rudy told us they're about to lose their home and that it's for sale for only $8,000. I'd like to help them buy their home so they can stay here. They've been our guides here in Mexico and our good friends, and I truly appreciate them."

"Yeah, that's a good idea," Andrew agreed.

"I will say that's truly generous of you," Morris commented.

"Rudy's our true friend," Chispo declared. "I want to help him and his family out of their bind."

As they talked it over, they unanimously decided to buy the house together. They handed Rudy the money, and in addition to that, they gave him $100 extra for the time he had spent being their guide.

Rudy was ecstatic. "¡Gracias!" he shouted, thanking them. He asked everyone to wait for him while he went into the house. He opened the door and jumped out of the vehicle-craft. "Mamá, Papá," he shouted as he raced inside.

In less than a minute, his parents were accompanying him back outside. They were beside themselves and thought they must have been dreaming. They weren't sure what to think.

"Vamos a la tienda de Chilo. Vamos a la tienda de Chilo," Rudy repeatedly urged them, saying for them to go to Chilo Cantu's store and buy the house from him.

Rudy opened the door of the vehicle-craft and literally pulled his parents in. Rinto drove them to the Cantu's store in the plaza where he parked. They stepped outside and walked into the store. Mr. Cantu was in the back. Rudy handed his father the $8,000.

"Venimos para comprar la casa," Antonio said to Chilo, telling him they had come to buy his house. He revealed the $8,000 cash.

A look of amazement crossed Chilo's face. He just about dropped the merchandise he was carrying at the moment. "¡Sobres, hombre!" he exclaimed. "Mina, trae los papeles de la casa," he shouted to his wife in the front of the store, telling her to go fetch the papers to the house.

She walked to the back room behind the store and came forward with them a few minutes later. Chilo phoned a notary public to come and witness the transaction, and once he arrived, they signed the deal. Antonio handed Chilo the money, and they shook hands. Both of them were grinning. With that done, Rinto drove them back to their house and parked.

"Pues, muchas gracias a ustedes," María told them, thanking them for what they had done. Antonio commented likewise. Both of them stepped out of the vehicle-craft and entered their house.

"So, how much does that leave us to divide seven ways?" Andrew asked.

"$13,200," Robert answered.

"And divided by seven, that's around $1,900 for each of us," Rinto told them.

"All right, let's just deal out the $100 notes to ourselves until we've counted through them," Robert suggested.

"Sounds good enough to me," Chris approved.

Tom took the 132 $100 notes in his hand and dealt them out to Andrew, Chris, Robert, Steven, Chispo, Rinto, and Fraxino.

"Man, this is great!" Chispo declared. "The only thing is how are we going to exchange it for Zotolan currency?"

"Don't worry about it," Rinto reassured him. "This will make good spending money on our future trips to Earth."

"Good thinking, dude," Chispo told him. He took out his wallet and slid the money into it.

Everyone else did the same.

"Morris, tell us," Andrew requested. "Why couldn't you come with us to

Zotola?"

"Right, that is something I can now tell you," he began. "As you know, since the Orion Belt was spiritually blocked as far as astral travel and mental telepathy was concerned, my spirit would not have arrived with me. For the way the Atlanteans designed that block, the devious scientists who were left on Earth could not have arrived either. You see, they were, in a way, a different type of lifeform spiritually, as they had themselves spread out across various dimensions. They were stretched across interwoven dimensions to such a degree that they could not be physically separated from their base or anchor to transport to Al Nitak, due to the block in place. In case you're wondering how their good scientists were able to leave, they sent a trigger signal to activate the block after they left Earth.

"For me, since I have various parallel lives and soul links spread out across the galaxy, including different time periods, I knew I would not be able to separate myself from all of that and risk passing myself through a block which, harmless to all of you, would have been extremely dangerous to me. Yes, I might have arrived, but I most likely would have died in the process or might have been missing body parts."

"Golly! That would have been awful," Robert remarked.

"Indeed, it would have been," Morris agreed. "Anyway, that's the reason. Of course, if the Atlanteans had never installed that block, I could have come with you all from the start. While it was somewhat irresponsible for the Atlanteans to abandon Earth's problems at that time, I can understand their reasoning since their homeland of Antarctica got destroyed when it was slid to the South Pole during the crustal displacement.

"Now I can come with you all and see the land of Zotola, Artenia, and the whole Orion Belt for that matter. However, I can only come briefly because I have now gotten myself involved with dolphin projects, and I don't want to be away from them for very long."

"We'll be glad to have you come with us," said Rinto.

"And we'll show you around," Fraxino added.

"Thank you," said Morris. "I'm looking forward to it."

"I must return to Sirius B now," Tom announced. "The federation awaits me as we finally establish the telephone link. We're all very excited about it. Thank you fellows again for a job excellently done."

"You're welcome, Tom," said Robert. "Thank you for the reward."

"Thank you," Rudy told Tom in English.

"You're welcome," said Tom. "Enjoy the rest of your travels. I'll contact you if I have any more projects."

"Tom, wait," Steven suddenly said. "We've got a souvenir from Zotola for you."

"Oh, yeah. That's right," Robert recalled. "The crystal display cabinet for Tom. Wait here. I'll be right back." He stepped out of the vehicle-craft, ran into the house, took the small display cabinet out of his backpack, and returned to Tom with it.

By now, Tom and the others had stepped out of the vehicle-craft. Robert handed it to him.

"A crystal display cabinet!" Tom commented with enthusiasm. "Thank you very much."

"You're welcome," said Robert. "It's from all of us."

"A man was selling them at an Exxoll station in a town south of where we turned you loose in the countryside," Fraxino informed Tom.

"Well, I'm very glad to have it. It will make a nice addition to my collection. Like I said, enjoy the rest of your travels." He walked across the street, entered a small, abandoned adobe house, and where no one saw him, he disappeared, teleporting himself back to Sirius B.

The others walked inside with Rudy. Antonio and María were proudly giving the inside of the house a cleaning, now that they were the owners. Their enthusiasm was renewed. Antonio stepped out of the house, saying he was going to Mr. Orolizo to purchase cement so they could begin repairing cracks in the walls, after which they would repair the run-down toilet and the shower.

"So, what do we want to do next?" Robert asked everyone.

"¿Entonces, que hacemos?" Chispo said to Rudy, asking him the same question.

"¿Vamos por Roel?" said Rudy, requesting that they go and fetch Roel.

"What do you say, Morris?" Chris asked him.

"I'm going to briefly transport myself home and give part of my money to my parents. When I return, let's go visit Zotola."

"You know, there's a really neat Ulexite mine along the coast of southern Zotola," Fraxino told Morris. "That might really interest you."

"That would indeed," Morris agreed. "Listen, I'll return in 20 minutes." He started to walk out the door.

"Hey, Morris. Wait," Robert requested. "I'll come with you. Let's go to my place since your parents never knew the truth about where we've been travelling. I need to take several rocks and crystals and other souvenirs home, anyway."

"Good idea, Robert," said Morris.

"Robert, can you take my stuff with you also?" Andrew requested.

Soon all of them emptied their backpacks, and they handed their extra things to Robert and Morris to take to Robert's place and be stored there until the end of the summer. There were blankets, souvenirs, and of course, the rocks and crystals they had collected.

Robert and Morris loaded their backpack with the items, stepped outside, walked across the street, entered the abandoned adobe house, and transported themselves to Tennessee.

Meanwhile, María stopped her cleaning long enough to take their plates of unfinished lunches out of the refrigerator. She placed them on top of the gas stove eyes to warm them up, and then she brought them to them.

As they were eating, they continued discussing possibilities of what they wanted to do next. Rudy didn't really desire returning to his carpentry job at Felipe's. He much preferred to continue being with his new friends. He again expressed his desire to return to Zacatecas to fetch his brother and then for both of them to accompany them back to Zotola.

Morris and Robert returned and walked back inside. María soon brought them their unfinished lunches.

"Okay, we got that taken care of," said Robert. "I stored the items inside the step office building inside the woods."

"So, what have you all decided?" Morris asked everyone.

"Rudy wants to fetch his brother, Roel, in Zacatecas, and then we'll go back to Zotola," Andrew answered.

"That sounds all right," said Morris. "I believe I can put my dolphin projects on hold for a few days. Right, let's go."

Rudy went and told his mother their plans about fetching Roel and then going back to Zotola with them. She came into the front room, thanked them again for the wonderful surprise of making it possible for them to buy their own home, and she wished them well. Further, she repeated her apology for yesterday. She also assured them that she trusts them and that she was very pleased for her sons to have the opportunity to accompany such considerate and genuinely friendly people.

While they reorganized their items in their backpacks and picked them up to leave, Rudy suddenly remembered the piece of cookware and other souvenirs he had purchased in Zwever. He went to his suitcase, took out the items, and he gave his mother the piece of cookware. She was very pleased to receive it, and she thanked him.

With that done, they walked out the door. María wished them well, saying, "Que les vaya bien." They thanked her for everything and climbed inside the vehicle-craft.

"Oh, yeah. The rocking chairs," said Robert when he saw them in the back of the vehicle-craft. "¿Rudy, está bien si dejo mi mecedora aquí hasta despues?" Robert said to Rudy, asking if it would be all right if he could leave his rocking chair here until later.

"Sí," answering yes.

Robert unloaded it and took it into the house. Rudy went inside with him and showed him where to store it. Then they returned to the vehicle-craft.

Rinto started the engine. He drove them out of town and into the canyon. Rudy was looking forward to returning to Zotola, especially since he felt like it was, in a way, his ancient homeland. Morris was looking forward to finally getting to go there.

As soon as they reached the gravel road entering the canyon, Rinto pulled back the lever, and they left the ground. It was Morris' first time to fly in the craft, and he was most thrilled and impressed.

Rinto flew them by the Cypress ridge so Morris could see what the explosion had done. Then the main Ulexite controls crystal gave the craft a surge of energy, and they swiftly accelerated in a southerly direction toward Zacatecas.

The craft gained altitude as Rinto flew them through the desert valley. When he leveled out the craft at an altitude of 8,000 meters, they had a cruising speed of

1,000 km/h. In short order, they were flying by the western side of Monterrey, and a few minutes later, they saw Saltillo on their right.

"Rinto, I must say this craft of yours and Fraxino's certainly cruises smoothly," said Morris.

"Thank you, Morris," Rinto responded. "We're glad to have you aboard."

"Oh, yeah, Morris," said Steven. "I just remembered you had said something about a link to a parallel universe and Robert being a central . . . and you didn't say any more."

"Yes, that's right," Morris admitted. "Basically what it amounts to is that there are parallel universes, much like alternate realities. I've been exploring along some of those lines over the past few weeks. I actually paid myself a visit, you might say, and my parallel world counterpart informed me that from their perceptive viewpoint, Robert's parallel counterpart is aware of us in terms of an alternate reality. Robert in that reality is so aware of us here that he senses our actions and feelings right across the parallel universe barriers to the point that he is sometimes confused about who his true friends are."

"What's that supposed to mean?" Robert asked Morris.

"It means that here in this reality, all of us are very good friends, but in that parallel world I was telling you about, Robert, you have had considerable trouble making friends because that part of you is believing in the friendships from *this* level of reality. Do you understand that?"

"Not quite," Robert admitted. "What do you mean?"

"To put it another way," Morris explained, "those who are your good friends on this level of reality are not necessarily your friends at all in a parallel world or universe, in particular, the parallel world I was just telling you about. It's been a frustrating experience for your parallel counterpart."

"That's strange," Robert remarked.

"Wait a minute," Chispo suddenly spoke. "That holographic plate on mysterious rejections said something about people getting along great in one level of reality but in other realities, they may not get along at all."

"Exactly," Morris said to Chispo. "In fact, in that parallel world I recently visited, you and Robert were friends for only a short while, just long enough for Robert to realize some astounding coincidences and synchronicities between the two of you."

"Man, we *have* had some coincidences between us, haven't we?" Chispo commented to Robert.

"I know," Robert agreed. "We sure have."

"Morris, why weren't Robert and I long term friends in that parallel world?" Chispo sincerely wanted to know.

"We all choose our roads to follow through the time line, and in that parallel world, your roads didn't match very well. Your ways of life were different. Conflicts got in the way, and yes, Chispo, homophobia was one of them."

"Man, that is weird," Chispo remarked. "I'm not at all homophobic. I despise homophobia!"

"That's right," said Morris. "While that's true here, it's not necessarily true there. You see, your soul is living a life in Zotola in this reality, but in that parallel world, it is living a life on Earth. You are better suited to live in Zotola because your soul is sensitive, and on planet Earth in that parallel reality your soul is experiencing too much stress and tension. Unfortunately, there are many quantum energy systems still running their course in that parallel reality on Earth, and due to the stress and tension, you were susceptible to the one pertaining to homophobia. One of you was afraid the other one was gay. The vibrations between you and Robert became incompatible, and as a result, you did not remain friends. At least you are living the majority of this level of existence in Zotola, and you are experiencing and learning the true values of friendship as a result. It's all in the process of learning."

"Morris, a couple of weeks ago," Chispo informed him, "I explained to your friends that when you have a friend on our world of Artenia, that person is your true friend and for life! He or she will help you when asked, defend you in times of danger, and will confide in you, as well."

"Those are excellent qualities, Chispo," Morris told him. "I might add that parallel world existences are not really for us to worry about. We have our lives here, and our counterparts have their lives there. No matter what, it is an interesting concept to explain mysterious behavior and why people sometimes behave in weird ways.

"As far as Robert being a central . . . and I didn't finish what I was saying the other day, he is like a central pivot, not only for people to come together, but of passing on knowledge and a catalyst for things to come. What I mean by that is, in that parallel universe, he has met various people in his life, and while most of them don't know each other, he knows every one of them and is aware of our existence together here in this reality, which from his perception, is a parallel universe."

"That's an interesting concept," Robert admitted.

"Let me add this," Morris continued. "As I mentioned before, all of us can create and maintain quantum energy systems. In an indirect sense, you are like walking crystals. Each of you can add to the whole scheme of quantum reality programs by thinking positive, and you can make this world a better place. Every person is responsible for his or her own actions and consequences."

They continued talking. In less than an hour, they were approaching Pinos, Zacatecas from the north. Rinto lowered the craft's altitude and also slowed down. In minutes, they touched down on the highway, cruising at 100 km/h. No one had seen them making the landing.

Rinto drove the vehicle-craft into town, turned right at the central plaza, and drove them down the street to the lower end of town. He parked in front of Antonio's house. All of them stepped outside, and Rudy went to the door. Antonio saw them from next door at his motorcycle repair shop, and he walked over to them.

"¿Qué tal, Rudy? ¿Comó estás?" said Antonio as he greeted Rudy and asked him how he was.

"Estoy bien. Andamos buscando a Roel," said Rudy, answering he was fine and that they had come to look for Roel.

"Aquí está," said Antonio, telling Rudy that Roel was here. Next, Antonio whistled. "Roel," he called out toward the back of the house.

Roel happened to be visiting them at the moment, and he came forward and emerged. He was glad to see his friends, and a smile came across his face. As he walked over to them, he greeted them, and he shook hands with them.

"Roel, ya está todo arreglado en Bustamante," Rudy said to Roel, informing him that everything was fixed up in Bustamante.

"¿Cómo?" asking how that could be.

"Ya no hay peligro," Rudy answered, saying there was no longer any danger.

"¿Pero Pegaso y Beto?" said Roel, asking about Pegaso and Beto and what they might do.

Rudy informed Roel that last night, they had eliminated the transmitter crystals and that when they returned to Bustamante this morning, Pegaso and Beto had come over and apologized. Then he told Roel about the spectacular explosions and the beams and surges of light that occurred. He assured Roel that it was safe for him to return to Bustamante.

Roel thought about it momentarily. "Está bien. Pues, aquí me quedo como quiera," saying that was good, but no matter what, he was going to stay in Pinos. Roel further explained that he had made some good friends here, including his cousin Camila. He was already accustomed to being here, and the pay was better than he had been getting from Paco, making chairs in Bustamante.

Roel and Rudy chatted for some fifteen minutes. Rudy told his brother all about his adventures in Zotola and Caloma. He also told him they were going to return to Zotola, and he invited Roel to come with them. Chispo, Robert, and Andrew joined in and mentioned some of their experiences, including seeing a movie called *The Chill of the Vovvitlet*. They laughed at times as they chatted with each other, and they found out what Roel had been doing. While Roel had been enjoying Pinos, he now wished in a way that he had continued to accompany them. He apologized for his angry behavior the other day when he had suddenly decided to stay.

"Gracias, pero como quiera, aquí me quedo," Roel told his brother, thanking him anyway and saying that he was going to stay in Zacatecas.

"Sí, hombre. Bueno, que te vaya bien," said Rudy, telling Roel that was okay and wishing him well.

Roel wished them all well. They climbed back into the vehicle-craft. As Rinto drove them away, Roel stood on the streetside in front of his uncle's house and waved.

He drove them down the highway going south. Once they were several kilometers out of town, Rinto pulled back the lever, and they left the surface of the highway. The craft swiftly accelerated. Rinto slowly turned a curve to the right and took them north.

"Man, we've only looked at a small percentage of those holographic plates,"

Chispo brought up.

"I know," Chris agreed. "I'm anxious to see the rest of them."

"At least you fellows have *seen* them," Morris pointed out. "I'm looking forward to it. How nice that the block is cleared."

"Peace and friendship will now prevail over northern Mexico," Robert stated.

"Right on!" Fraxino agreed.

"We still have over a month of summer vacation left," said Steven.

"Man, let's go see the Placatera Mountains above the town of Efforestow," Chispo suggested.

"Are there any more interesting movies to see?" Chris asked.

"Oh yeah, man," Chispo answered. "There's another one just being released called *Vision from the Ciruclar*, and it's really cool. It's about a native from Zantaayer who . . ."

"Zotola, here we come!" Rinto suddenly shouted.

As they were now cruising well above the central Mexican highlands of Zacatecas, Rinto sent his telepathic command to the controls crystal. The green glow overtook them.

They were off to more adventures in Zotola.

-TO BE CONTINUED-

A QUERY FOR THE READER

If you are someone who astral travels to other star systems and are also very interested in trees and shrubs, knowing and having paid special attention to details, such as specific species types, and also knowing which specific star systems you've travelled to, I would like to talk to you about which trees grow where and how they compare to Earth's trees and shrubs, whether the same or different. This is an ongoing subject of interest I am researching. Please contact me.

Robert S. Sanders, Jr.
Armstrong Valley Publishing Company
P.O. Box 1275
Murfreesboro, TN 37133 USA
office: 1-615-895-5445
Fax: 1-615-893-2688

Appendix: Technical Description of Characters

9 Main Characters:

Chanford, Chris:
  species: human being, Earth type
  height: 5' 10"
  hair: brown, straight, medium length (ears partly covered)
  eyes: brown
  appearance: slender and strong with somewhat rounded face, age 17,

Colancha, Chispo:
  species: human being, Zotolan type, descendant from Atlantis
  height: 6 feet
  hair: dark brown, straight, medium length
  eyes: green-brown (more green than brown)
  appearance: tall and slender, appearing to be in his 20's, somewhat longer face,

Joslin, Robert:
  species: human being, Earth type
  height: 5' 10"
  hair: medium brown, slightly curly, shorter length (ears exposed)
  eyes: green-brown (more green than brown)
  appearance: slender and strong with somewhat long, narrow face, age 18,

Price, Steven:
  species: human being, Earth type
  height: 5' 10"
  hair: light brown, straight, medium length
  eyes: blue
  appearance: slender and strong with somewhat rounded face, age 17,

Tremain, Andrew:
  species: human being, Earth type
  height: 5' 9"
  hair: black, straight, medium length
  eyes: brown
  appearance: slender and strong with somewhat narrow but rounded face, age 17,

Roel:
  species: human being, Earth type, Mexican
  height: 5' 10"
  hair: black, straight, medium length
  eyes: dark brown
  appearance: slender and strong with somewhat rounded face, age 16,

Rudy:
  species: human being, Earth type, Mexican
  height: 5' 9"
  hair: black, straight, shorter length
  eyes: brown
  appearance: slender and strong with somewhat squarish face, age 15,

Zapatero, Fraxino:
  species: human being, Zotolan type, descendant from Atlantis
  height: 6 feet
  hair: reddish-blond, straight, shorter length
  eyes: green brown (more brown than green)
  appearance: slender and strong, appearing to be in his 20's, more of a squarish face,

Zapatero, Rinto:
  species: human being, Zotolan type, descendant from Atlantis
  height: 5' 11"
  hair: dark brown, mostly straight, longer length
  eyes: green-brown
  appearance: tall and slender, appearing to be in his 20's, somewhat rounded face.

Other Characters:

Cliss:
  species: human being, Zotolan type, descendant from Atlantis
  height: 5' 11"
  hair: very light brown, straight, medium length
  eyes: green-brown
  appearance: slender, rounded face, appearing to be in his early 20's,
Crate of holographic plates:
  species: irrelevant
  size: the same as a footlocker
  appearance: crate made of tarnished bronze
  description: crate contains 144 bronze metal tablets with holographic material containing data,
Crystal Base Computer:
  Rinto and Fraxino's computer operates by the use of a Ulexite cube and a crystal array serving as an information processor, instead of operating by programs, disks, and hard drives. It is also interfaced with a monitor and a keyboard as an adaptation to accommodate more Earthly related matters. They use it to read the holographic plates and also to analyze other crystals.
Doulos:
  species: human being, Zotolan type, descendant of Atlantis
  height: 5' 9"
  hair: dark brown, straight, medium length
  eyes: brown
  appearance: slender, strong build, appearing to be in his 30's, rounded face,

England, Morris:
  species: human being, Earth type
  height: 5' 8"
  hair: dark brown, mostly straight, shorter length
  eyes: brown
  appearance: strong and stocky with long, rounded face, age 18,
Egg shaped crystals:
  species: crystal, silicon type,
  origin: artificially grown on Earth over 100,000 years ago
  race or color: Quartz, clear
  length: 10 centimters from end to end
  appearance: egg-shaped, known for containing ghostly image of a tree cone within,
Esalina:
  species: human being, Zotolan type, descendant from Atlantis
  height: 5' 7"
  hair: light brown, straight, longer length
  eyes: brown
  appearance: slender, medium height, appearing to be in her 50's, somewhat long but also rounded face,
Exotic Crystal, (peace keeping crystal of Atlantis)
  species: crystal, silicon type
  origin: artificially grown on Earth over 100,000 years ago, stolen from Atlantis over 15,000 years ago, recovered from Aleyone in the Pleiades, returned to Earth, and left on slopes of Mt. Timpanogos in Utah in previous novel,
  race or color: Green Fluorite and Citrine (orange)
  length (end to end): 25 centimeters
  appearance: egg-shaped, greenish-blue appearing in various shades or bands throughout, contains orange colored pyramid within,

Govianna:
  species: human being, Zotolan type
  race or color: Atascosan, slightly green, native of planet Artenia
  height: 5' 10"
  hair: dark brown, straight, long
  eyes: brown
  appearance: slender, young, rounded face, appearing to be in her late teens,
Johns, William:
  species: human being, Earth type
  height: marginal 6 feet
  hair: black, longish, parted in the middle
  eyes: brown
  appearance: slender and strong with somewhat rounded face,
Lumela:
  species: human being, Zotolan type
  race or color: Atascosan, a beautiful olive green complexion, native of planet Artenia
  height: 5' 6"
  hair: brown, straight, longer length
  eyes: green-brown (more green than brown)
  appearance: exquisitely beautiful and attractive, appearing to be in her late teens,
María:
  species: human being, Earth type, Mexican
  height: 5' 3"
  heir: black, slightly wavy, long length
  eyes: dark brown
  appearance: short, stocky, and strong, rounded face, (Roel and Rudy's mother),
Mountain Scene Crystal:
  species: quartz
  race or color: clear
  length or size: around 10 centimeters across
  appearance: rounded on top with a flat base and containing a ghostly image of a range of mountains within,

Orolizo:
  species: human being, Zotolan type
  race or color: Atascosan, slightly green, native of planet Artenia
  height: 5' 11"
  hair: dark brown, straight, medium length
  eyes: brown
  appearance: slender, medium build, appearing to be in his 20's, rounded, almost squarish face,
Orolizo, Pegaso:
  species: human being, Earth type, Mexican
  height: 5' 11"
  hair: black, curly, very short
  eyes: dark brown
  appearance: tall and stocky, imposing stature, somewhat squarish face, age 18,
Ramiro (the cave guide):
  species: human being, Earth type, Mexican
  height: 5' 10"
  hair: black, straight, medium length
  eyes: dark brown
  appearance: tall and somewhat stocky, appearing to be in his early 20's, rounded face,
Sabastian, Xavier:
  species: human being, Earth type, Mexican
  height: 5' 10"
  hair: black, graying, long length
  eyes: dark brown
  appearance: tall, stocky, very much like a native North American, appearing to be in his 50's,

Sacred Story Stone:
   species: crystal, silicon type
   race or color: Calcite, orange
   origin: Vega, known for relating a sacred
      story
   length or size: 15 centimeters from end
      to end
   appearance: orange rock with holo-
      graphic filmstrip pasted onto it, from
      150,000 to 200,000 years old,
Tom, the galactic salesman:
   species: human being, Sirian type
   height: 6' 4"
   hair: nearly black, mostly straight, longer
      length
   eyes: brown
   appearance: tall and slender, almost boy-
      ish with somewhat longer face; wears
      a white robe,
Victor:
   species: human being, Earth type, Mexi-
      can
   height: 5' 9"
   hair: dark brown, straight, medium
      length
   eyes: brown
   appearance: slender and strong with
      somewhat narrow face, age 14,
Wilson, Paul:
   species: human being, Earth type
   height: 5' 10"
   hair: very light brown, somewhat wavy,
      longer length
   eyes: brown
   appearance: slender and strong with
      somewhat narrow face but higher
      cheekbones, age 17,
Westfield, James:
   species: human being, Earth type
   height: 5' 10"
   hair: brown, straight, medium length
   eyes: brown
   appearance: slender and strong with
      somewhat rounded face, age 17,

Zahiyo:
   species: human being, Zotolan type
   race or color: Atascosan, slightly green,
      native of planet Artenia
   height: 5' 11"
   hair: dark brown, straight, medium
      length
   eyes: brown
   appearance: slender, appearing to be in
      his late teens,
Zapatero, Glecko:
   species: human being, Zotolan type, de-
      scendant from Atlantis
   height: 5' 9"
   hair: mostly gray, straight, medium
      length
   eyes: brown
   appearance: stocky build, appearing to
      be in his 60's, rounded face,
Zapatero, Sosta:
   species: human being, Zotolan type, de-
      scendant from Atlantis
   height: 5' 7"
   hair: brownish-gray, straight, longer
      length
   eyes: brown
   appearance: somewhat tall and mostly
      slender, appearing to be in her 50's,
      somewhat long, narrow face,
Zocanto:
   species: human being, Zotolan type
   race or color: Atascosan, slightly green,
      native of planet Artenia
   height: 6' 0"
   hair: dark brown, straight, medium
      length
   eyes: brown
   appearance: slender, strong build, ap-
      pearing to be in his 40's.

Acknowledgments

It was in January 1995 that I began writing my first novel: Mission of the Galactic Salesman. I remember one day that a friend of mine told me how interesting it would be to write a novel about a human civilization on another star system on the same level of technological advancement as we are here on Earth. He is the real Fraxino of this story. I am grateful to him for giving me the seed from which I wrote this sequel: MISSION BEYOND THE ICE CAVE: Atlantis-Mexico-Zotola.

I began writing this sequel in November 1996 when I wrote the first chapter. In 1997, I wrote up through Chapter 4. From February through May 1998, I wrote this novel to its completion.

I am grateful to have met and known certain people over the past several years from whom I have derived takeoffs for this sequel: especially the real Chispo, Rinto, Fraxino, Pegaso, Roel, Rudy, and Morris. Some of them remain my true friends. For some of them, the ones with whom I have lost my friendship, I have given them better characteristics in this novel than they have in real life. However, for the ones I *really* don't like, I portrayed them with worse characteristics and even had one of them killed off. That particular person is not one of the above listed.

I am grateful to my family for their support as I wrote this novel and to my parents for helping me come up with a title for this sequel, something I had not done until I was more than halfway through writing it.

I appreciate David DuBois for his having done the 14 illustrations and the color front cover of this sequel. I have had the pleasure of becoming friends with him while working on this project.

I thank my cousin Eugene Alexander Powell, a Georgia Tech professor, for explaining to me the physics of how supergiants can exist on the outer fringes of the galaxy and for how the distances between stars can be determined.

I appreciate the two times in 1997 that Jesús Lucio of Bustamante, Nuevo León, took me and some friends to see Chiquihuitillos, the ancient paintings on the mesa sidewalls in a desert valley of northern Mexico.

I give thanks to Marietta and Jim Bishop for bringing to my attention the fact that a section of land near Vicksburg, Mississippi has matching soil to a certain region in China.

I am thankful to Paul Wulfsberg for reading, editing, and reviewing this novel, and I also thank Rudy A. Zapata-Rdz. for proofreading and editing the Spanish throughout this novel. In addition to that, I thank Hilda Gonzalez-Elizondo for her editing and proofreading the Spanish, as well.

I give special thanks to Martin A. Enticknap, author of *EXODUS: the Dolph/in Saga*, published 1999, ISBN 1-928798-35-7. I acknowledge the use of the words and concepts of: *Danetar*, *Delikadove*, and *Dolph*, which came from his novel.

It was in June 1994 that I met Martin when I walked into a remote mountain refuge hut. He related to me some exotic stories and various experiences, some of which I found very interesting. I appreciate the time he has spent talking with me since that fateful day. Over many conversations, he has told me his views on human philosophy, and he was very helpful with reading, reviewing, and giving me suggestions for my sequel, along with ideas and concepts he requested I include in my story.

Among them was his theory that Hieroglyphics originated from computer system icons from an ancient civilization. I expanded on that concept as I included it in my sequel. For what I derived from his seed, I served as independent verification for his theory.

He also brought to my attention the theory of Earth crustal displacement and suggested two books for me to read pertaining to that subject.

There were other concepts he told me: like the Orion Belt being blocked, the theory of quantum energy systems, concepts about crystals, and even giving me a brilliant explanation of why the Morris of my story could not accompany his friends to the Orion Belt.

The above said concepts were like catalysts or seeds which spurred me on to deriving good ideas to include in my sequel. He literally said the right things at the right time. It was he who had initially related to me a story about a galactic salesman offering him a crystal ball in a dream.

I want to acknowledge Graham Hancock and his book: *Fingerprints of the Gods* and what he presented about the Orion star system, the star Al Nitak, and the shafts in the pyramids. His discussions in that book suggested the somewhat obvious idea that the descendants of Atlantis fled to that particular star.

I also want to acknowledge Rand and Rose Flem-Ath and their well documented book: *When the Sky Fell, In Search of Atlantis*. That book discusses the details about the Earth crustal displacement that occurred 12,500 years ago, which sent Atlantis (Antarctica) to its icy doom at the South Pole.

Also, some people may be wondering about the human race being far more ancient and dating back further than most people would think (72 million years in the Orion system). Where did I get that information, if it's even true at all? From an outside source, I didn't. That number or idea of that long ago simply popped in my mind while I was writing chapter 4 of this novel, which was October, 1997. Ideas just come to writers that way sometimes (creativity and imagination).

I am grateful to Patrick E. Parris at Parris Graphics and Printing in Murfreesboro, Tennessee for producing the book cover design and for typesetting the entire text, including the illustrations, by converting my Lotus Ami Pro files to Adobe Page Maker so that they could be readable by the equipment at Lightning Print Inc.

I thank Charlie King and Janet Young at Lightning Print Inc. in LaVergne, Tennessee for the publishing, printing, and distribution of this novel.

I also thank the Kearney family of Murfreesboro, Tennessee for having referred me to Lightning Print Inc. in November, 1998 and also for their advice and consultation.

I am grateful to all of those who have supported me and have bought a copy of this novel for their reading enjoyment. Most of all, I sincerely appreciate all of those who are my true friends and will remain my true friends through life.

A QUERY FOR THE READER
If you are someone who astral travels to other star systems and are also very interested in trees and shrubs, knowing and having paid special attention to details, such as specific species types, and also knowing which specific star systems you've travelled to, I would like to talk to you about which trees grow where and how they compare to Earth's trees and shrubs, whether the same or different. This is an ongoing subject of interest I am researching. Please contact me.

Robert S. Sanders, Jr.
Armstrong Valley Publishing Company
P.O. Box 1275
Murfreesboro, TN 37133 USA
office: 1-615-895-5445
Fax: 1-615-893-2688

Robert S. Sanders, Jr.

Copies of *Mission Beyond the Ice Cave: Atlantis-Mexico-Zotola* are available directly from the author at the above listed Armstrong Valley Publishing Company. Copies of its preceeding novel, *Mission of the Galactic Salesman*, are also available.

ORDER FORM

Please send me:		quantity	amount
Mission of the Galactic Salesman	@$14.95	_____	$_____
Mission Beyond the Ice Cave: Atlantis-Mexico-Zotola	@$15.95	_____	$_____
Tennessee residents add 8.25% sales tax			$_____
Plus shipping and handling for one book (surface rates: $3.00 within USA, $5.00 foreign)			$_____
Plus shipping and handling for each additional book (surface rates: $2.00 within USA, $3.00 foreign)		_____	$_____
Please remit funds in US dollars.		Total enclosed	$_____

Discounts:
10 to 99 books: 10% off
100 or more books: 20% off

Books make great gifts for your friends and relatives.

Send order to:
Name _____
Address _____
City_____State_____Postal Code _____
Phone number (optional _____

www.ingramcontent.com/pod-product-compliance
Lightning Source LLC
Chambersburg PA
CBHW020600260626
47157CB00003B/800